W9-BAT-434

LAST
GIRL
GONE

LAST GIRL GONE

A LAURA CHAMBERS MYSTERY

J. G. HETHERTON

CROOKED
LANE

NEW YORK

Published in the United States by Crooked Lane Books, an imprint of The Quick Brown Fox & Company LLC.

Crooked Lane Books and its logo are trademarks of The Quick Brown Fox & Company LLC.

Library of Congress Catalog-in-Publication data available upon request.

ISBN (hardcover): 978-1-68331-617-6
ISBN (ePub): 978-1-68331-618-3
ISBN (ePDF): 978-1-68331-619-0

Cover design by Melanie Sun
Book design by Jennifer Canzone

Printed in the United States.

www.crookedlanebooks.com

Crooked Lane Books
34 West 27th St., 10th Floor
New York, NY 10001

First Edition: June 2018

10 9 8 7 6 5 4 3 2 1

To my wife, Alice. This book couldn't exist without you, and neither could I.

PROLOGUE

I F THERE WAS an art to running away, Patty Finch didn't know it. Twice before she had tried to escape, and twice before she had been caught and returned. This third try, she promised herself, would be different. This third time would be the charm. After this, her mother would never see her again. She would be gone forever. She would simply disappear.

About that much, at least, Patty Finch was right.

Spectators clogged the path connecting the parking lot and gate. She moved along with them, in no rush, studying the crowd. The biggest category comprised single young men, hats perched on the backs of their heads, sweat staining their underarms and backs. Even close to sunset, the day's heat gnawed at them; every few steps they paused to peel cloth from flesh. Less common were the families, fathers with sons up on their shoulders, harried women pushing their daughters along, trying not to lose them in the growing flow of race fans.

It was a valid concern. Patty had never seen so many people in one place. Certainly, she thought, it was more people than lived in all of Hillsborough combined. Folks had come from nearby towns, drawn by the annual exhibition race on an original dirt NASCAR track, excited to see the speed and hear the roar. And they were just a little bit bloodthirsty, secretly hoping for a crash. In 1986, just two years before, Bobby Allison had set a course record and three men had slid cars into the river trying to catch him. Tonight Bobby was back, the best entertainment in fifty miles.

Patty wove through a group of young men slapping each other's backs and singing a Navy song, headed toward a likely looking family. The father had two young children gripped tightly around the wrists, and behind him the mother was carrying a baby. Bringing up the rear was Dot Kamlut, high-stepping to keep her penny loafers clean and fussing at the bow tied in her hair. She was skinny as a stick with an unfortunately shaped nose and not too many friends because of it.

The ideal candidate.

"Hiya, Dot."

Dot examined her for a second, trying to place her. Patty took no offense at this. The Finches hadn't been in town more than a couple of months, plus Dot was in a different class.

Then she had it. "Maggie Finch?"

"Patty," she corrected.

"Sorry."

Patty fell into step next to her and glanced up ahead. Neither Mr. nor Mrs. Kamlut seemed to have noticed.

"You like Mrs. Hall's class?" Dot asked, still tugging at the bow strangling her hair.

Patty shrugged. "It's all right, I guess."

In front of them, the crowd split itself between corrugated metal walls. Dot's father started down the middle of the three chutes, approaching the ticket taker and handing him a thin stack of paper. The ticket taker spoke, and Mr. Kamlut turned and looked back.

Patty pinned her eyes to the dirt and tried to appear insignificant, just another child in the crowd.

Mr. Kamlut gestured backward toward his family, the ticket taker nodded, and then they were moving forward again. Patty slipped an arm around Dot's elbow, put on her friendliest face, and said, "Gee, aren't you excited to see the races?"

Dot, it turned out, was very excited to see the races, particularly the handsome and daring drivers. She blathered on as they slipped through the gate behind Dot's mother.

No one stopped them.

Patty breathed a sigh of relief. Twenty yards past the entrance she cut Dot off. "Gotta go find my mother. See ya, Dot."

Dot gave her a hangdog look, her prospects for friendship once again slim. "Sure, if you say so."

Patty almost felt bad for her.

"But let's keep talking later," she said, and Dot perked back up and gave her a smile. Patty turned and disappeared into the crowd, feeling pretty good about herself. After all, what harm could the promise do? She wouldn't have to break it exactly. No, she'd be gone long before it could become an issue.

The path ended at the top of the stands, big poured-concrete steps set into the hillside. Below them curved the first turn. The track was packed brown dirt and it had a slight inward tilt, the result of bulldozers building up a berm around the outside. Behind turns two and three the Eno River glinted in the fading light. The whole track was fitted into a bend in the river, the area naturally flat as a result.

Patty counted the rubberneckers filling the stands. The number grew and grew, the size of the crowd delighting her. What an immense mass of people to never see again. Her heart fluttered. She knew—felt it in her bones—that where her other schemes had failed, this one would succeed.

Practice, after all, makes perfect.

*　*　*

The first time she ran away, her mistake had been inviting Janet Fontain. Janet was afraid of her own shadow. Patty knew that—hell, everybody knew that—but it had been a calculated risk. Janet's parents were rich enough to own a five-bedroom house on Queen Street. They had a woman who lived in the old converted woodshed and washed and cleaned for them. They had a basement the size of a swimming pool and a larder that took up nearly half that space. Janet would have been a joke out there on the road, nothing but dead weight, but Patty aimed to get at least a few cans of peaches out of her traveling companion before ultimately ditching her.

It hadn't worked out that way. Janet lost her nerve, told at the first opportunity, and a policeman in a shiny black-and-white Ford interrupted Patty's march to the interstate. He turned her around, walked her home, and delivered her right back to her mother.

Mildred Finch answered the door with tears in her eyes, hugged the policeman, thanked him again and again, and made him promise to come over one night for a home-cooked meal. He doffed his hat, said he'd make it if he could.

Then he was gone, and her mother stopped pretending.

"You little monster," had been the first words out of her mouth, followed by a swift backhand that knocked Patty down to the rough floorboards.

"Mama, don't."

"No back talk. That's no way for a little girl to behave, is it?"

Patty shook her head, pain shooting up her neck.

Mildred Finch made a fist, knelt, then buried it in Patty's stomach. Mildred liked to hit. She was good at it and she liked it, and in her experience, such a combination was one of life's rare treasures.

"No what?"

"No, ma'am," Patty said, air slipping out fast between her gapped teeth like a snake's hiss, the starburst of pain in her gut making it difficult to breathe.

"That's better, little one," Mildred said, and launched into her usual lecture about the evils of the world. As always, the chief danger listed was Patty's father. They had been running away from him for two years, hiding themselves in various small towns dotted across the North Carolina countryside. Even at ten years old Patty had a sense of the strange resonance between their original escape and her own current desire to vanish. Her mother had run away and deemed it justice; Patty ran away and her mother labeled it a betrayal.

Mildred worked herself up into the usual frenzy, pacing back and forth, gesticulating wildly with her hands. Patty twitched each time one of the hands came near her.

"He was no-good trash, Patty. He pushed that rotten pecker

into anyone who would take it. And who would take it? Who would let a man like that slide his slimy little worm into them?"

Patty knew the answer to this and gave the response her mother expected to hear.

"Whores, ma'am."

"That's right, little girl. If you want to get by in this world, if you want to see it true, that's all you really need to know. Men are bastards, and any woman who would let them have their way, who would open her legs, is a whore. Isn't that right."

It wasn't a question.

She nodded and tuned out as her mother charged ahead. It was a speech Patty had heard a thousand times before. Even then she was scheming her next attempt.

The second time she ran away, a month after the first, no one knew her plan. The lesson of the first try had been very clear: tell no one, and no one can tell on you. She kept to the alley behind the main street, Churton, and worked her way down to the intersection of Churton and King. A right on King would lead past the two- and three-story brick buildings downtown and then up into the rich neighborhoods filled with big houses. Straight ahead the road carried over a bridge spanning the Eno River and then dropped into the river's floodplain, running a mile and a half past antique stores and fast food restaurants. It ended at the interstate.

Patty headed straight and made her way across the bridge. Fifty yards past it, parked in a turnout, was the black-and-white Ford.

Not again.

A policeman, the same one as before, climbed out and walked over to her. He took off his hat before taking a knee. His hair shone blond in the sunlight and it was thin enough that she could see his scalp.

"Patty Finch?" he asked. This meeting had been no accident.

"Yes." The air slipped out between her teeth the same as when she'd been punched.

"The station got a call from your mama. I guess she saw you tying up that rucksack"—he pointed to her bag—"and put two and two together."

Patty said nothing, just kicked at the dirt with the toe of her shoe.

"You know," he said, "packing like that makes it pretty clear what you're doing, don't you think?"

He was right, of course. All the pieces came together then, and she knew exactly what had happened. Her mother had seen the missing clothes, or caught a glimpse of her stuffing them under her bed, and had divined everything about her plan. How could she have been so obvious? So foolish? She waited meekly for the policeman to smack her and call her stupid.

But he didn't do that.

"Maybe we could take a little ride in my car and talk about why you're running away. What do you think?"

Patty wasn't used to being asked what she thought. She looked up from the ground, surprised. With him kneeling, his eyes weren't more than eight or ten inches up and liquid brown. They had crinkle lines at the edges that made him look like he was smiling even when he wasn't.

She nodded and got into the car with him, into the passenger seat and not the back like a criminal. She let him drive her up and down the streets. He did most of the talking. His name was Donald Rodgers. He was originally from Yanceyville, up near the Virginia border. He had been a police officer for about two years. He liked it just fine, thank you. The police car came to a stop. Patty realized they were sitting outside her house. Her shoulders hunched forward and she slumped down into the seat, watching carefully for any sign of movement at the front window.

"Tell me true, Patty—you scared of going back in there?"

Her head spun around and she looked into those big brown eyes and imagined for a second he would be able to save her. She nodded.

"I had a Pa who I couldn't wait to get away from," Don Rodgers said. "Used to beat me something fierce. And when he was too drunk to aim his punches he'd just swing wild with his belt. Like it was a whip."

He paused, and they sat in the silence for a while.

"I'll see what I can do to help," he said after a bit.

She nodded again and climbed out of the car. He drove away from her slowly, and she sensed some reluctance in it. Could reluctance be detected in the way a car drove? She believed it could. She waited for him to turn the corner before going inside to face the music.

* * *

Sitting on the concrete steps above the racetrack, replaying the scene in her mind, she had the overwhelming urge to reach out and slap herself. "He can't help you, girl! He won't do a thing for you," she wanted to shriek. Instead Patty shook the memory away, turned and spit on the ground. It had been stupid to think Deputy Rodgers could do anything at all, but it was no use ruminating on past mistakes. The cars stacked up at the starting line and fired their engines. The throaty roar lifted up through the pine trees and carried away on the wind.

When the race was over, Patty made her way to the parking lot. This was the crux of her plan: to find a woman, an out-of-towner, and convince her she needed a ride to somewhere like Raleigh or Greensboro. Either way she would have a forty-mile head start. That was all she needed.

Yellow sodium lamps stood in a long line down the center of the lot, hissing and painting the passing crowd in sickly shades of yellow. Mosquitoes hovered in black knots near their glow, occasionally breaking off to dive the spectators in crazed kamikaze runs. The people hurried to their cars.

The plan was working poorly. Patty found it difficult to approach the families as they slid past, and the few times she managed to speak up, they brushed her aside like a panhandler begging for change. In minutes half the lot was empty, the aisles clogged with big curved Fords and Chevys angling toward the exit. Headlights slashed tunnels through the mist rolling in off the river.

The lamps sputtered once and then went out. She walked toward the back of the lot and sat down on a stump. Only a few cars were left, and these she suspected might belong to the workers at the track. All of them were sure to be local. The third attempt had failed like all the others.

Stupid, she thought, and punched herself on the thigh.

Directly behind her, an engine turned over once and twin headlights reached out through the fog, landing on the stump like spotlights.

She turned and looked over her shoulder, squinting into the glare. A car door opened. Boots crunched on gravel. "Hey there," a voice called.

Patty raised a hand and tried to shield her eyes. She couldn't see anything more than the shape of wide shoulders and the outline of a hat hovering above them.

"You out here all alone?" It was a man's voice, raspy, like he'd been punched in the throat.

"I'm just waiting," she said, and stopped. All that preparation and the question still caught her off guard. She tried to cobble together her story, tried to think of the best way to play it. Was he local? The voice wasn't familiar.

"Waiting for who, sweetheart?"

She said nothing.

"Waiting for your boyfriend?"

Patty Finch was ten years old. She had never even held a boy's hand.

"I don't have a boyfriend," she volunteered.

"That's too bad," he said. "That's not right."

A click and the car's lights were gone, but her night vision was ruined. She saw nothing but blackness, heard a rustle and the click of a lighter. For a second she could make out a sharp chin and the end of a hooked nose, but the rest of the man's face remained hidden behind his hat as he craned his neck down toward the flame. Then the lighter went out and he was gone again. The red cherry of his cigarette floated in space, rhythmically glowing and fading, pulsing like the tides.

It was Patty who broke the silence. "I gotta get home," she said.

"Thought you were waiting for a ride."

"I gotta get home," she repeated, and took a step backward.

"Hey, don't I know you?"

"No," she said.

"Sure I do." He threw down the smoke and ground it under his heel, and the darkness was complete again. "You're Patty Finch, aren't you?"

She stopped moving and tried to think of a man who knew the Finch family. Couldn't come up with anyone. There was the principal, Mr. Lugal, and Deputy Rodgers who had given her a ride home, but this man wasn't either of them.

Then who? Someone who knew her mother?

It was as if he could read her mind. "Does your mama know you're out here all alone?"

At the mention of her mother, Patty looked down and started toeing the dirt with one shoe.

"Does she?" he asked again. This time there was an edge in his voice.

"No, sir," she said.

"Well, you shouldn't be. It's not safe to be out here alone at night, a little girl like you. There are dangerous men in the world."

Patty had heard this speech before. It was all her mother ever talked about.

"Yessir," she said.

"Now get in the car. I'm taking you home."

She hesitated.

"Patty Finch, you get in this car. You get in this car right now, and maybe I won't tell your mama where I found you."

She looked up, eyes searching the dark space that housed the voice. A bit of hope straightened her shoulders.

"You promise, mister? You promise you won't tell?"

"I won't tell if you won't, Patty."

And then he laughed. The laugh surprised her. It was an octave higher than his voice and it had a musical quality, almost girlish. She liked the sound of it. Hearing his laugh made the decision much easier.

Besides, what other choice did she have?

The car seat was smooth brown leather redolent of whiskey

and smoke and some kind of perfume. She sank deep into it, and still couldn't make out his face in the darkness.

"Do you have to take me home right away?" she asked.

He weighed this, as though considering doing her a favor.

"If you want," he said finally, "I could take you somewhere else."

She nodded happily, and he started the engine.

PART I

SMALL-TOWN BLUES

GIRL'S BODY FOUND, POLICE CONTINUE SEARCH FOR SECOND MISSING CHILD
By Laura Chambers
July 7, 2017

HILLSBOROUGH, N.C. — Tragedy struck early Thursday morning when the body of a young girl was discovered in a soybean field four miles east of Hillsborough, North Carolina. The deceased has been identified as Olive Hanson.

Hanson, age ten, was reported missing the night of July 4, and a police search has been under way since the early morning hours of July 5. That search came to an end at approximately 7:30 a.m. yesterday morning when her body was discovered by a local farmer.

Police have been closemouthed about details of the case, refusing to either confirm or deny that Hanson's death was the result of foul play. In a statement put out Thursday afternoon, the Orange County Sheriff's Office confirmed the victim's identity and described the investigation as ongoing.

A second child, with Hanson at the time of her disappearance, remains missing. Teresa Mitchem, also age ten, was last seen in the company of the victim on the night of July 4. Asked about the status of the search for Mitchem, Sheriff Walter McKinney reiterated the department's policy not to discuss investigations in progress.

According to a missing persons report filed jointly by the Hanson and Mitchem families the morning of July 5, both girls asked permission to visit the other with plans to set off fireworks. The ruse was discovered when Angie Mitchem, the missing girl's mother, arrived unannounced at the Hanson residence looking for her daughter.

Neither family has been willing to comment. "They were good girls, both of them," said a neighbor, Leann Cooks. "Always together. They didn't have a mean bone in their bodies. Who would do this?"

That attitude of disbelief was echoed on the streets of downtown Thursday night. Citizens gathered in front of the Orange County Courthouse and formed an impromptu vigil, burning candles and singing hymns.

Among the mourners was Hillsborough mayor Craig Smythe. "I have been assured by Sheriff McKinney that he and the fine deputies of the OCSO are doing everything in their power to locate Teresa Mitchem and to bring her home safely," he said. "At this point, there's nothing to do but pray."

Anyone with details about the case was asked to call the Orange County Sheriff's Department's at (555) 890–3600.

CHAPTER

1

LAURA REREAD THE article for the third time and grimaced at the last line. Nothing to do but pray—tell that to the Hanson family. She could picture them in a back room of the mortuary, slumped on pieces of cheap office furniture, flipping through a coffin catalog, faces gray as wet cardboard. Would the mayor have the courage—nay, the faith—to look them in the eye and say it again?

She doubted it.

Her eyes drifted until they landed, again, on her name at the top of the article. *Laura Chambers.* She dragged a fingernail over the letters, scoring a thin line across their middle. Something about physical contact made them more real. Though she was ashamed to admit it, Laura never tired of seeing her name in print.

She started reading the article for a fourth time before crumpling the paper into a ball and shoving it in the trash. Her favorite journalism professor, Murray Popovitch, had talked endlessly about the thrill of millions of people seeing those little letters printed at the top of a front-page story. He called it the vanity of the byline. Murray likened it to a siren's call, praising its motive force while warning his students not to crash their ships onto the rocks.

"Seeing your name in print is beautiful and dangerous," he said.

Murray always talked like that, in complete, poetic sentences. The short, goateed little man had entranced her from the very first class. She'd always understood the concept of journalism as a force for good, but Murray was the one who made her believe it.

Laura shook off the memory and made a mental note not to revisit it. It offered nothing but pain. Murray was dead, she was trapped in a Podunk town in North Carolina, and her only consolation was that her mentor had died in time to avoid witnessing her disgrace.

Nervous energy buzzed in her chest. She forced herself to stand and pace the length of her so-called office. It had been a selling point of the job during her phone interview with Bass Herman, editor-in-chief of the *Hillsborough Gazette*.

"You'll love it," he'd said. "It's cozy. Plenty of character."

Only later had she recognized his pitch as copy torn from a real estate advertisement, the kind used to sell thin, ugly houses no one wanted to buy. An honest ad would have read something like "Stinky hotbox, no views, partially air-conditioned, available immediately. Lots of privacy—no one in their right mind would spend time here."

Beautiful it wasn't.

Unpainted cinder block passed for walls. The only window sat eight feet off the ground, a Lucite slit designed to admit the minimum of light. Two doors and the top of a staircase separated the space from the main newsroom, but no one used the staircase. The door at the bottom was exit only, without an exterior handle. It all added up to a concrete closet at the end of forever, a place the other staffers rarely visited and never lingered.

Which made the squeak of her office door all the more surprising. "Morning, Colin," she said, and gave him one of her best smiles, trying to keep the edge of disgust out of her voice.

Colin Smythe was the child of Mayor Craig Smythe but acted like he was the firstborn son of a king. Two months ago, preparing for her first day at the *Gazette*, Laura had read every back issue dating to the first of the year. Smythe, whose articles appeared at least three times a week, had managed to make her blood curdle long before they ever met. His worldview combined the moral compass of Christopher Columbus with the keen human insight of a bowl of clam chowder. Blacks, women, the poor—if they were down, Colin Smythe's philosophy was: put a boot on their throat and keep them that way.

"You look beautiful this morning, Laura." He spoke in a light country accent. He didn't wink, not that it mattered. A wink from Colin would be the definition of redundant. There were ballistic missiles with more subtlety. He wore a shapeless linen blazer over a crew neck T-shirt the color of fresh blood. One hand held a rolled-up copy of the *Gazette*.

She edged back around the corner of her desk and perched on her chair. "I don't think I've ever seen you in my office."

"You never made the front page before. We've got the morning editorial meeting in a few, so I thought we could chat."

"I've had plenty of front-page stories," she said.

He leaned against the wall. "Sure, in Boston, right?" His eyes fastened on hers, waiting for a reaction. Laura ordered herself not to take the bait.

"Yes, in Boston," she said.

"But not here."

"No, not until this morning."

He winced, and Laura almost smiled.

"How's the job treating you. You like it?"

Now he was acting like her boss. She gritted her teeth. "Bass and I meet every week about my progress here."

"What did you say to him in there anyway? How'd you get the big man to bump this story to the front page?"

"I didn't get him to do anything. All I did was write it up and drop it on his desk. What else was he going to put on the front page? Your review of the local theater production of *Fiddler on the Roof*?" Laura shuffled together her papers and butted the edges until they were flush. "It's news, Colin. Not that this town gets much."

He came off the wall and placed two T-bone-sized hands flat on her desk. "Don't start telling me about this town."

"I was born here."

"And abandoned ship the first chance you got. This story is a ticket to the big time."

She narrowed her eyes.

"Don't give me that look, like it's a betrayal to even say it out loud. No one gets on the *Globe*'s front page without climbing across the bodies of a few fallen comrades. I don't know you that well, Laura, but then again, I don't need to. That's just the way of the world."

Laura checked her watch.

"And don't pretend you've got somewhere important to be. I write features"—he jerked a thumb toward his chest—"and you're on cleanup duty."

"My cleaning up not good enough?" she asked.

He smirked. "Not nearly. You'll have to learn to scrub up a bit better if you ever want to find a husband in this town."

"Are you done?"

"Not even close. Missing girl turns up dead—not drowned by accident in the Eno or killed by her drunken daddy, but taken by some stranger and then left in that field for us to find. I've never heard of something like that. It may happen in other parts of the country, but not here. Major papers will want a piece of what's going on here. This story is a ticket out. And I'm taking it."

Laura stood, came around the desk. "Here's a bit of advice: when you talk about a little girl's death, try not to look so damn excited."

He flushed, then raised the hand holding the rolled-up newspaper toward her face. She turned her head, ready for him to hit her. The paper stopped an inch from her face and he smiled at her wince. Fifteen years into adulthood and still the schoolyard bully.

"How'd you get that story anyway?" His voice came out so quiet it was nearly a whisper. "One second someone finds the body, the next you've already gotten the story typed up and turned in. If I didn't know better, I'd say you killed her."

He moved closer until they were nose to nose. She could see the white spittle collected at the corner of his mouth and smell the onions on his breath.

"No, I know what happened," he continued. "Your boyfriend called you, didn't he? Soon as the sheriff looked away, Deputy Stuart dropped a dime and fed you every last thing you needed. Was that how you climbed the ladder in Boston? On your back?"

The raw, unconcealed hatred radiating outward from him

shocked her. She took a big step back, then tried to take another one, but there was nowhere to go. Her back was pressed against the wall.

Laura had been a consumer of therapy since first escaping Hillsborough at the age of eighteen. Situations like this, her first therapist would have said, offer three options: be neutral, escalate, or deescalate. De-escalation was what most people would call taking the high road. Her therapist had encouraged her to take the high road whenever possible, and probably it was the best decision here too. She'd have to work with Smythe for the foreseeable future.

Calm down, she told herself. *Just play nice.*

But she couldn't do it.

It was his face. Cheekbones that could plane oak. Thin bloodless lips pressed together and turned up at the corner in contempt. An Aryan's wet dream.

She despised that face.

Neutrality was the best she could manage. Arms crossed in front of her, she exhaled sharply, flecks of saliva landing on his chin.

He ran a hand down his face and crumpled the paper, then dropped it into the wastepaper basket. "Anyway," he said, his voice back to its normal, unhurried gait, "just wanted to give you a heads-up. As the more experienced staffer, I'm getting Bass to hand the reins over to me. You got a problem with that?"

Laura shrugged. Anything she said would serve only to burn bridges.

His smile beamed so bright you'd have thought she'd just bent over and kissed his toes. "Didn't think so," he said.

One loud squeak of the rusty hinges and he was gone. Laura gave him a minute, then opened the door herself. She crossed the top landing of the steps and emerged in the small hallway at the back of the newsroom, then ducked into the ladies' room.

Old habits die hard. The daily editorial meeting at the *Boston Globe* had been a crowded affair held in a boardroom with the table and chairs removed to make room for all the staffers and assistants. The object of meetings, Laura believed, was to stand out. She hadn't fussed over her appearance since showing up in

Hillsborough two months ago, but Smythe's arrogance had fired something raw and angry in her belly. Now it was time to be ready.

She took a breath and examined herself in the mirror, running a finger through the dark ringlets of hair that fell to her shoulders, unwinding the kinks.

The dress code at the *Gazette* was decidedly more casual than at the *Globe*. She wore dark-purple jeans, Converse All Stars, and a denim jacket over a black T-shirt emblazoned with the white silhouette of Frank Sinatra. Gold hoop earrings, thin enough to be tasteful, stood out against her light olive skin. Somewhere in her family tree there must have been a relative from Italy. An eighth-inch gap showed between her two front teeth, the source of much torment during her middle school years.

These days, she had bigger problems.

The eyes, she told herself, betrayed a wisdom far beyond her twenty-nine years.

The most difficult thing about her encounter with Colin Smythe had been the little voice inside her screaming, "He's right! He knows!" Even as she pretended disgust at his blatant opportunism, she had been planning her next move. Because he *was* right. This story, told correctly, had the potential to lift its author up and carry them away to bigger and better things. There was only one ticket, and it belonged to the person whose name was printed under the headline.

She ran another finger through her hair and made herself a promise.

It would be her name at the top of the page, no matter what.

CHAPTER

2

"Everyone shut up."

Bass Herman waved a hand at the group, gesturing for them to be seated. He had a gut the size of an aircraft carrier and he navigated like one too, pointing his stomach in the direction he wanted to go and dragging the rest of his body along behind it. Usually, people got out of the way.

He wore a British banker's shirt in salmon, the white collar damp with sweat, suspenders, and cheap slip-on loafers. His hair looked like whitewater and his hands were stained yellow by years of nicotine use.

He pointed a discolored finger at Smythe. "What exactly are we planning for Sunday's feature? Not this solstice festival shit again?"

Smythe coughed into his fist. "Well, my series on local celebrations—"

Bass cut him off. "Forget it. The only thing this town hates more than Jews is pagans."

"The solstice isn't pagan per se," Smythe said.

"Who cares? People think it's devil worship. These are good, Christian people, Mr. Smythe. And their preferred brand of Christianity is loud and proud. None of this love-thy-neighbor, no-hate, believe-what-you-want, hippie-dippy bullshit. These people are Old Testament connoisseurs." Bass smacked a yellow hand down onto the table. "They're Baptists, goddamn it."

Laura knew her office was bad, but the conference room would bring a tenured government worker to tears. It had no windows and few lamps. Piles of paper and other trash leaned into every corner. Moldy ceiling tiles threatened to collapse at any moment.

Inexplicably, Bass Herman liked to use the conference room as part of his office.

"Yes, sir," Smythe said. After just two months, even Laura knew enough to sit down and shut up once Bass Herman started yelling.

"He's right, you know," a nasal voice perked up from the back. Laura twisted in her chair, trying to see who had the guts to speak up.

Natalie something-or-other, the mousy administrative assistant, stood behind Smythe, one hand holding a notepad and the other on his shoulder.

Herman pressed several of his chins into his chest and looked down his nose at her. "Excuse me?"

"I was saying—"

Herman cut her off. "You writing articles now?"

"Me?" She clasped her hands in front of her chest, the notebook pressed between them, face open in genuine surprise.

"Maybe you've been scooping the *Gazette* under some nom de plume? Working nights? Weekends?"

"Nom de plume?" she repeated. Even for a North Carolina native, her French accent was terrible.

Smythe reached up and brushed her hand off his shoulder. He spoke between his teeth. "Sit down and stop talking, Natalie. You're making me look like an idiot."

The light in the girl's eyes died. She hung her head and sat back in her seat against the wall, notepad at the ready. Her expression reminded Laura of a dog whose beloved master had just kicked it in the ribs.

"Okay, enough," Herman said. "You have your assignments. No missed deadlines. Miss Chambers, stay back for a moment."

Everyone else stood and filed out. It gave Laura time to plan out exactly what she wanted to say.

"Miss Chambers." He pronounced it the southern way, as though it ended in a Z—*Mizz Chambers.* "Congratulations on your first front-page story for the *Gazette*. When I hired you, it was because I knew you could produce great journalism here."

"Thank you," she said.

"You're welcome. Now that we have the compliments necessary to massage your journalist's ego out of the way, let's move on to the bad news."

Laura already had a pretty good idea of what was coming.

He put his hands in his pockets and closed his eyes. "I'm considering handing the story off to Colin Smythe."

"You're not happy with my coverage." She didn't phrase it as a question.

"Not at all. You seem to have excellent sources. It's clear you're used to a fast-paced, competitive environment. Hillsborough isn't Boston, but it's nice to get a little hustle. Mr. Smythe met with me this morning—"

"He's campaigning for the story?"

"I wouldn't put it quite like that. But he also made some good points."

"Such as?"

"Such as his local contacts. Certainly you have a few yourself. You couldn't have gotten the story so fast without being persuasive."

"So I'll match him contact for contact. Let me write the story, Bass."

Using his first name seemed to startle him. His eyes flicked open. "There's no comparison, Miss Chambers." His drawl landed even harder on the formal *miss*, stretching it out. "You've been here two months. I know, I know—you grew up here. But you also left a long time ago. People have opened up to Colin before. With you, I'm not so sure."

"So you're saying people won't talk to me because I got too big for my britches and left Hillsborough." Her hands clenched into fists. "As though me leaving for something better draws attention to anything here that's worse."

"That sentiment exists in certain circles, yes."

"So let me take a shot at it," Laura said. "If you're not happy, make the switch."

He nodded. "My thoughts exactly. I need something for Sunday's edition."

"That's in two days."

"Which gives you until tomorrow at deadline."

"There's no way I can—"

He raised a hand, cutting her off. "I need something for Sunday's edition. It has to be good, too. No rehashing of old news. This story will probably get picked up in Raleigh, Atlanta, who knows."

Laura took a deep breath. "Okay."

"Good girl. That's why I hired you."

"I know you took a chance with that, Mr. Herman."

He levered himself down into the room's single chair, leaned back, and laced his fingers over his belly. "We've all made mistakes, Miss Chambers."

"Even you?"

He allowed himself a rare smile. "Even me. In my youth."

"During my interview, you asked about what happened in Boston."

He waited expectantly, his face serene.

"And I confirmed it happened just like the *Globe* told you."

"Mmm," Herman said. " 'Parted ways.' That was their euphemism of choice."

"But you never asked me anything else about it."

"Your memory is correct."

"Why not?"

"Well, that's an interesting question. I could tell you I'm not a nosy person by nature, but who could believe that, me being the editor-in-chief of a local rag? All we do is nose our way into other people's business. I guess maybe it's because I know what shame looks like."

"I don't understand."

He pointed out into the newsroom, a space three or four times the size of the conference room with desks pushed together in groups of two. "I see you walking—no, make that skulking—around out there. Head down. Barely meeting anyone's eye. Hell, you never look at me. You seem to think you sold me a bill of goods, young lady. That you tricked me into buying something damaged and got away with it."

She examined a ceiling tile. "Didn't I?"

"Hardly. Put it behind you, Miss Chambers."

"That doesn't answer anything. Why hire me?"

Herman tapped a copy of the day's paper lying on the table. "Pure self-interest. You've got good instincts. Truth is, if you'd never screwed up, we never could have gotten a reporter of your caliber on staff."

"You think I'm worth the risk?"

Bass Herman nodded his all-knowing nod. "Miss Chambers, I consider you a bargain."

"DID YOU FEEL threatened?"

"It was a newspaper, not a knife."

"Still, in the adult world, we rarely expect to be confronted with any type of physical violence. It doesn't take a lethal weapon. If someone shoved you, or spit on you, wouldn't you feel threatened then?"

"If someone spit on me, I'd feel pissed off."

"But you're not pissed off now."

"Like hell I'm not."

They sat across from each other in overstuffed arm chairs, Laura's with a matching ottoman. Opposite her, Dr. Jasmine DeVane sat perched on the edge of her seat, legs crossed, absentmindedly twirling a pen.

During their first session a month ago, Laura had asked the obvious question: "What, no couch?"

Dr. DeVane had shaken her head. "Too much temptation."

Laura assumed she was referring to some dark corner of her patients' minds, a negative, sexual behavior triggered in the presence of a couch, and Dr. DeVane had seen the look on her face. "No, no, it's not what you're thinking—the temptation is all mine. I used to have one, but I ended up taking too many naps."

It was right then, right at the beginning, when she'd noticed just how funny Dr. DeVane could be. She played the part of the professional well, always in low heels, trousers, and earth-tone tops. Her dark hair had a strain of muted red running through it, and she tended to pull it back in a loose chignon. Because of the polished façade, it was easy to overlook her sense of humor. Most therapists took their work, and themselves, very seriously. Laura had patronized a number of them over the years, and she'd laughed in all her combined therapy sessions about as often as while learning about Nazi Germany. But Dr. DeVane had a light touch, even when she was poking a sore spot.

"Do you think he had the will to do you physical harm?"

"I think he wanted to, yes."

"But those aren't the same thing," Dr. DeVane said. "We all want to do harm at one time or another, even if it's just fantasy. For most of us it stops there, our own little theater of the mind playing out revenge on, say, high school bullies or the dry cleaner who ruined our favorite shirt. Fantasies like that are normal, even healthy in small doses."

"He wanted to hurt me," Laura said. "He had the desire."

"How do you know?"

Laura shrugged. "Just a gut feeling. There was something in his eyes."

"Still, that's only half the equation. Plenty of people *want* to do things. An extra ingredient is necessary to separate fantasy from reality: will. People who cross the line into actual, physical violence need that little something extra."

"This was real. He was there, in the room, staring right through me with those dead eyes of his. Isn't that more than fantasy?"

"Of course. That's exactly what I'm saying. Whether you perceived it as a threat or not, the kind of person who could do what he did—it suggests the capacity for more."

"So what now?"

"I can't tell you that, Laura. But I can tell you to be careful around this one."

Sometimes the doctor's gaze could be a little too penetrating. It gave her the willies and a knot in her stomach, the same one she got from dreams about being naked in front of her sixth-grade class. Laura looked away, pretended to glance around the office even though she remembered every inch. It was a block off Churton Street, Hillsborough's main thoroughfare, in a one-time warehouse split into office suites. Gauzy, floor-to-ceiling curtains admitted plenty of soft, natural light. Exposed brick walls, Asian-inspired decor. Oriental rugs adorned the floors and the walls, sucking up even the smallest sounds. There were no echoes. It felt like talking in a box full of cotton balls.

Which was effective, she had to admit. There was security in knowing that no one could hear them, and no sound from the outside world made it in. A room walled off from the world, like a castle with a moat. Safe.

Best of all, the thermostat was set to sixty-eight degrees.

"Can we back up for a second?"

Laura turned her focus back to the doctor. "To where?"

"Well, you finished the story about your *colleague.*" She said the word with a forced professionalism, almost as if she were rolling her eyes, that made Laura like her all the more. "But you glossed over the other thing."

"What other thing?"

"When he said you get ahead on your back."

Laura said nothing.

"You're normally quick to answer," Dr. DeVane observed.

Laura reexamined the drapes.

"And I can't help but notice your sudden silence."

"You're very perceptive," Laura said.

"Professional hazard."

"Are you asking me whether I'm sleeping with the deputy?"

"Not a bad place to start."

"Is it relevant?"

"Considering the comment that is the focal point of our discussion?" Dr. DeVane tapped her pen against her front teeth. "I'd say it's relevant, yes."

"It shouldn't be. I can sleep with whomever I damn well please." Laura took a deep breath. Despite her best efforts, her voice had doubled in volume.

"Laura. Laura." Dr. DeVane made her voice quieter and more soothing in response. "Of course you can. When I say it's relevant, what I mean is that veracity plays a part here. The barbs people throw at us are sharpened by truth. Even when it's something that has no place being barbed in the first place—our beliefs, our appearance, who we sleep with—the ring of truth provides the necessary weight. It's how words can manage to cut us so deeply."

"So what are you saying?"

"That if someone says something offensive, it hurts, but when we think it's true, that's when it rings in our ears. So, three questions. One: are you in a relationship with—?" She trailed off.

"Franklin Stuart," Laura supplied.

Dr. DeVane raised an eyebrow.

"I know, I know. Everyone calls him Frank."

"Okay, Frank. Are you in a relationship?"

"I've been here two months."

"Is that a yes or a no?"

"Neither. It's just too soon to tell. We're seeing each other."

"Two: in your own mind, are you leveraging your relationship with Frank to get ahead?"

Laura crossed her arms and took another deep breath. "He's the one who called me yesterday, told me what was going on. It got me the article."

"And three: do you feel bad about it?"

Laura shook her head. "No."

Dr. DeVane reached out and put a hand on Laura's knee. "You shouldn't. It's our social connections that let us prosper, and the lack of them that makes people wither. Fathers get jobs for sons, old college friends make the right introductions. That's life. There's no shame in taking help from anyone, and your sex life has nothing to do with it."

"So why are we talking about it?"

"Because this kind of thing does matter a great deal to a great many people, but the only thing I'm concerned about is whether it matters to *you*."

"It doesn't."

The doctor threw up her hands in mock surrender. "Which means I don't think we need to explore it any further." She paused. "But how's Frank?"

Laura felt the corner of her mouth tug up, the beginning of a grin. "I thought we were done exploring."

"My extreme perceptiveness is clueing me in to the fact that it's a little strange you haven't mentioned him. I mean, relationships are the sort of thing most people talk about right away."

"I'm not most people."

"No, you definitely are not."

Laura cocked her head, the second corner of her mouth pushing up now too. Another few seconds and it would count as an actual smile.

Dr. DeVane flushed and fidgeted with the bridge of her glasses. "I hope I didn't offend you. I actually meant that in a good way. Most of the people who visit me here in Hillsborough only come for one or two reasons. My sessions with you are, well . . . I look forward to them, Laura. I like you. If it weren't for the fact that you're my patient, you and I might even have been friends. At the very least, why don't you start calling me Jasmine."

"Jasmine," Laura said, trying it out.

"Okay, if not your love life, how about your career. Can we talk about that?"

"Better than talking about my mother, I guess."

Laura had spent the first two sessions talking almost exclusively about her childhood, a topic that never seemed to wear out. Those years were like a fractal: no matter how closely she examined them, it was the same shit over and over again. Allowing herself to embody a cliché—the patient with mommy issues—had been almost as painful as the memories themselves.

"Do a lot of people come in here and talk about their mothers?"

Dr. DeVane nodded. "It's extremely common, yes."

"Why is that?"

"You're doing it again."

"What?"

"Asking questions. About me, about therapy in general. About the modern state of psychological thinking. I'm supposed to be the one asking the questions."

Laura shrugged. "Professional hazard."

Dr. DeVane nodded. "Point taken, and a perfect segue. Can we talk about your career?"

"Sure," Laura said.

"Can we talk about Boston?"

"Nope," Laura said.

"It's obviously weighing on you. The very refusal to talk about it suggests—"

"Not today, okay?"

"You mentioned it in passing during our first session, and only then to explain your move back to Hillsborough. As far as I can see, it upended your life. And we're not going to talk about it?"

"I don't pay you to bitch at me." The words slipped out, and she regretted them almost instantly.

Most people would have flushed at the comment, but the doctor remained perfectly calm. "Actually, you do," she said. "In fact, that might be one of my favorite descriptions of exactly what I do in here—bitch at people. Shine a light on the things they'd rather not see."

They sat together in silence for a while.

Finally, Laura said, "I'm sorry I snapped."

"I know you are."

"But I just don't want to talk about it today."

"Okay, let's make a deal. We skip it for today, and we talk about it next week."

Laura nodded.

"So tell me about this story."

"The dead girl?"

"I have a feeling that's what everyone's going to mean when they say 'the story,' at least for a while."

"Did you read my article?"

"Of course."

The majority of the seven thousand people in Hillsborough must have read that article. Still, hearing it one-on-one gave a her a little thrill.

"Then you know what I know. Between you and me, that's about all the police know too."

"And do you think the editor, Mr.—"

"Herman."

"Do you think Mr. Herman will take the story away from you?"

"He's giving me until the Sunday edition to come up with something; that's effectively until tomorrow night. He wants me to prove myself, otherwise he's going with Smythe."

"And is that a fair offer?"

Laura weighed this question.

"I think he thinks it is. Finding something new in a murder investigation in about thirty hours, when the police have nothing, isn't exactly easy. On the other hand, that's the nature of the job, investigating facts and reporting them. Bass didn't write the rules; he's just playing by them."

"A brutal set of guidelines for a small-town paper," Dr. DeVane said.

"But not a small-town story."

"How do you think losing the story would make you feel?"

This time Laura didn't weigh her answer. "Bad," she said.

Dr. DeVane shot her a grin. "Can you expand on that? Forgive my ignorance of the profession, but isn't it just one story? Won't there be others?"

"Two-part answer." Laura started ticking them off on her fingers. "One, it's the principle of losing the story. I may be biased, but yes, I'm the better reporter."

Dr. DeVane cut in. "Then why would your boss take you off it?"

"He gave a reason that didn't sound like complete bullshit. Colin Smythe has lived here all his life and might have more success getting locals to open up to him, but I'm the better reporter and he knows it. In the end, Bass is just going with what he knows and who he knows. Bass Herman is old-school, from a different era. It's the same everywhere, the good ol' boys' network at play."

"So he lied to you."

"No, he doesn't see it like that. Which makes it worse. There are no villains in the world, just millions of people with a very screwed-up idea of what constitutes the right thing."

Dr. DeVane's brow furrowed. She said nothing.

"And two," Laura extended two fingers, "yes, losing this specific story would hurt more than losing another."

"Is it the girl?"

"I don't know what you mean."

"Just that this story involves a dead girl, another one missing. It's in progress. Most reporting is on things that have already happened. Here, something you discover could be the key to finding Teresa Mitchem."

Laura gave her a thin smile. "It's not that. When I started in Boston, I covered some horrible things. Husbands killing wives, wives killing husbands, strangers killing strangers. Grown men beating children to death. I started out thinking the random killings were the worst. Then at the end of my first month I get assigned . . . I guess you'd call it a human outrage story."

"Human outrage," Dr. DeVane repeated.

"It was a term of art in the *Globe* newsroom. Like human interest, but not so warm and fuzzy. The opposite, in fact. Stories like that are one step above the police blotter. But it sells papers. People love to hate."

"I don't disagree," Dr. DeVane said.

"But it's never Pulitzer material either. I was new, so I get assigned Howard Jenkins. Howard worked on Fleet Street as a partner at a law firm, and at the ripe old age of forty-nine he was diagnosed with cirrhosis of the liver. Terminal without intervention. Mrs. Jenkins—Susan, that was her name—stepped up and a liver donation was scheduled. It all goes great for Howard. He sheds that jaundiced yellow skin and goes back to playing squash and yachting and sleeping with his mistress."

"His mistress?"

"Turns out that the cirrhosis was caused by hepatitis C, which he picked up sometime during his exploits around town."

"And Susan Jenkins found out."

"By that time it was the least of her problems. You see, the operation didn't go so well for Susan. She got a liver infection. They controlled it with antibiotics, but it had already spread and damaged her kidneys. Fast forward to a year later. She weighs ninety pounds and spends eight hours a day plugged into a dialysis machine. She needs a kidney fast. Luckily, her husband of twenty-five years is a perfect match."

Dr. DeVane said nothing.

"The day she asked for his help was the day he filed for divorce," Laura said, her voice flat as Kansas prairie. "Played dirty too; took everything. She was dead in six months."

The doctor crossed her arms, looked at the ground.

"There was a small outcry, of course, but he hadn't done anything illegal. No one could touch him. And I guarantee he didn't think it was wrong."

"How can you know?"

"He'd never agree to an interview, but I caught up with him outside his building once. I didn't identify myself as a reporter, and he thought I'd just recognized him from one of the other newspaper articles. I asked him, 'Did you learn anything from all this?' I was thinking his answer might acknowledge some of the terrible irony and injustice that had befallen his wife. Do you know what he said?"

Dr. DeVane shook her head.

"He said, 'Yeah, I learned something. Always wear a condom.'"

The silence hung between them like a cloud.

Laura took a breath. "My idealism went the way of the dodo sometime that first year. The job isn't to change the world, just report it."

"We're out of time," Dr. DeVane said.

Laura stood and noticed her hands had balled into fists. Each palm featured four white pinpricks surrounded by red where the fingernails had dug into flesh. She opened the door and stepped into the hall.

"Laura," Jasmine DeVane called after her. "What you said, that there are no villains in the world—I don't agree."

"No? Why not?"

"Because someone out there killed that little girl."

4

Her bedroom hadn't changed a lick in eleven years. Same brown carpet, same Rat Pack poster, same Minnie Mouse bedspread, same faint odor of mildew always on the edge of being noticed.

Home.

Laura had been aghast to find it so untouched. On her return, a fine layer of dust coated everything, even the floor. No footprints. No one had so much as opened the door in years. She'd considered throwing it all out, starting over, but she didn't plan to stay long. What was the point of redecorating? So she'd washed and swept, and now two months later she slept every night clutching Minnie Mouse.

Once changed into a pair of old jeans, she slipped back down the hallway, boots in hand. The old farmhouse had foghorns for floor joists. As a teenager Laura had mapped the various squeaks and pops until she could hop between the solid spots like Indiana Jones at the end of *The Last Crusade*.

She paused, listening outside the door of the master bedroom.

Not a peep, which meant her mother was still asleep. At five thirty in the evening.

More grateful than worried, Laura carried on down the stairs and out the front door. Big blue sky arched over her. The fields, summer green, stretched to the horizon.

She slung a bag onto her back seat and took off down the dirt drive. The car, a 1969 Dodge Dart convertible in midnight blue, had a hundred and fifty thousand miles on its third engine and started on the first turn only half the time. The body was eaten through by rust in at least half a dozen spots. But the soft top still worked, and that was the only thing that mattered.

Laura turned onto asphalt and hit the gas, felt the sweat on her brow evaporate as the wind played through her hair. Frank Sinatra singing the saccharine "New York, New York" carried her three miles south down Highway 57. A new song came on just as she hit the turn on to Highway 86 half a mile north of downtown, brushes on a snare opening Bobby Darin's version of "Mack the Knife."

She turned south. Highway 86 became Churton as it passed through downtown. Beyond the brick buildings at the town's center, beautifully maintained Georgians and Colonial Revivals gave way to low-slung ranches and finally to corrugated warehouses along I-85. She got on and then off again a few miles later, turned in to a neighborhood of double-wides, and stopped outside a yellow one with a pink flamingo mailbox and honked twice. A kid with a 35mm camera slung around his neck and a backpack in his hand came running out and hopped over the door without opening it.

"Nice moves, Leon," Laura said, and threw the car into gear.

"Thanks, Miss Chambers."

They turned back onto the interstate, back toward the Chambers farm. She glanced over at him.

Leon Botton wore his darkish hair buzzed short on the sides with the longer top pushed into the center of his head. Clad in a black T-shirt and black jeans, feet stuffed into oversized combat boots, he appeared every inch the rebellious teenager. But that hadn't been Laura's experience. The few times they'd talked he had been soft-spoken and thoughtful.

Laura caught him staring at her as they pulled away. He'd been doing that a lot lately.

"Getting a good look?" she asked.

He snapped his head forward and started fiddling with the tuner, suddenly concerned about her choice in music.

"You know, Leon, if you want to get a girl's attention, just staring and letting your mouth hang open isn't the best way."

His mouth opened and then closed like a guppy on land.

"I'm just teasing. You know that, right?"

"Yes, Miss Chambers."

She hoped he did. At the age of seventeen, Leon was responsible for more than half the photos in the *Gazette*. He was president of the Orange High photography club and covered all the local high school sports the people around here held dear. And he had a crush on her, of course, obvious in all the dopey Romeo looks he'd been shooting her way in the newsroom. She liked Leon—there was no substitute for manners, in her experience—but ultimately he was a reminder of how far she had fallen. She'd once teamed up with a Pulitzer Prize–winning photojournalist; now she had her very own high school student.

"Miss Chambers?"

"Call me Laura."

"Laura." It rolled off his tongue about as smoothly as molasses. She could almost see his heart flutter.

"Yes, Leon."

"It's great we finally get to work together."

"Great. For sure."

"But when I get an assignment, usually Mr. Herman will, uh, tell me a little bit more about it."

"What does he usually tell you?"

"Oh, I guess he tells me where I'm going, what I'm supposed to take pictures of. You know, um, the basics?"

Laura shot him a look.

"Not that it matters," he added quickly. "I'm just curious." He crossed his arms and watched out his side of the Dart as the buildings yielded to fields once again. He was probably trying to look cool, Laura thought—face scrunched up, hair shifting in the wind. Of course he was trying too hard, but it wasn't bad for a seventeen-year-old.

"You weren't expecting my call," Laura said. "Bass not giving you much work?"

"It's July."

She raised an eyebrow.

"It's summer," he explained. "No sports going on. Nothing worth shooting."

"Almost nothing," she said.

*   *   *

They parked, locked the car, then walked across a field and started climbing the far ridgeline. Near the crest, Laura turned and looked back. The sun was about to dip its toe into the horizon. Low, flat clouds reflected oranges and purples so brightly she had to raise a hand and shield her eyes. A hundred feet below them and a mile distant, a small shine indicated the windshield of the Dart parked on a small dirt shoulder.

"We're shooting the sunset?" Leon panted.

Laura shook her head. She'd failed him as a partner, letting him come out here dressed all in black with heavy combat boots. The sweat poured off his forehead in sheets and he wiped it away with the back of his hand.

"Then what?"

"Other way," she said.

Earlier she'd dug out an old topographical map and picked this spot so that the sunset would be behind them. A one-hundred-foot climb had sounded a lot easier in theory.

Leon turned and scrambled the last ten yards up loose gravel and into the wild grass at the crest. Laura climbed up next to him, took one look over the other side, and shoved him down.

"Stay low."

"Miss Chambers—"

"Stay down and follow me." She got on her hands and knees and then crawled through the brush until they reached a tree barely a foot around and ten feet tall. Still, it was the only object of any size up here. Its irregular shape would help break up their silhouette.

"Here," she said, then lowered herself onto her belly and dragged herself forward on her elbows until she reached a small ledge.

Another moment and Leon was beside her.

"Whoa," he said. "Is that—"

"You bet it is."

"Hey, is it, um, legal for us to be up here?"

"We're probably guilty of a little light trespassing."

"No, I mean, is it legal to take pictures of *that*." He nodded down the east side of the ridge.

Below them another soybean field stretched out like a stage. The sun still stood high enough in the sky for its light to cut over the ridge and slice down into the scene below, a cosmic footlight bathing everything in an unearthly copper glow.

The far edge of the field met a dirt road lined with police cruisers, light bars long since turned off. Laura pulled out binoculars, and through them she could make out the crest of the Orange County Sheriff's Office as well as deputies from neighboring Durham and Person counties. Another line of vehicles formed an interior wall, unmarked Dodge Chargers and Chevy Tahoes in dark blues and blacks. Whippy, aftermarket antennas stuck up from their trunks. Down the center of the field, a muddy track recently cut through the soybeans, and at its end stood a cluster of three vans. Then the yellow tape started. It stretched between wooden stakes, marking off a square area about a hundred feet on a side.

Inside the square stood two men in suits. They wore white, hospital-style elastic booties over their shoes.

"Of course it's legal," Laura said. "It's called the First Amendment."

Leon nodded. "The sunset will actually help us."

"Is the light enough?"

"It's perfect." The shutter on his camera started clicking. After a while he said, "Where's the girl?"

"It was over a hundred degrees today. They found her yesterday morning. I bet they moved her within a couple hours."

"Moved her?"

"To the morgue."

"Oh. Right." The shutter kept clicking away.

"What are you getting?"

"Everything, man," he said. His voice sounded dreamy and far away. In a way, she thought, he actually was distant. He was down there walking through the soybeans, his focus refracted through the lens and cast down into the center of the field with all those cops.

"Wide shots?"

"Sure."

"Did you bring a zoom lens like I asked?"

He pulled himself away from the eyepiece and looked at her as if she'd asked him if he'd ever kissed a girl. "Of course. I mean, shooting sports is my thing, you know?"

She patted his shoulder. "Just asking, sweetheart," she said, and he grinned at her. "Get me some shots as close up as possible. Groupings of people, the vans, the tape, individual shots of whoever is down there if you can."

"You got it."

Laura watched through the binoculars as two men in deputy's uniforms wound up the yellow tape and pulled up the stakes.

"They're done," she said to herself.

Leon popped open the back of the camera, changed out the film, then started shooting again without a word. A few minutes later he said, "That's it."

"You got everything?"

"If it was down there, I got a picture of it. Besides, I'm out of film and we're losing the light."

"Let me see that."

Leon looped the strap over his head and handed over the camera. "Like I said, out of film."

"I just want to take a look."

Supporting the heavy zoom lens in one hand, she lowered her eye to the viewfinder. Everything leapt closer by a factor of ten. The quality of Leon's equipment shocked her. The binoculars had made it easier to see, sure, but suddenly it was as if she was standing mere yards away. She could make out clothing, body language, even facial expressions.

Her gaze shifted to the left as one deputy handed his roll of yellow tape to the other and started approaching the men in suits. He had light brown hair worn long and ramrod-straight posture. He made his way across the field, high-stepping over the rows and making it look like a military exercise.

Frank Stuart.

Laura shifted uncomfortably on her elbows, the rocky ground digging into her bones. Spying on a police investigation in progress was all part of the job. But secretly watching someone with whom she had a personal relationship? It felt dirty, like she was a peeping tom.

Frank turned his head and examined the ridgeline, almost as though he could feel her up there, watching him. Laura jerked back and ducked down, then chastised herself for her stupidity. Making out details with the naked eye at that distance was impossible. But the one thing he might be able to detect was movement on a ridgeline, the sun behind them painting her silhouette dark against the colored sky.

After a few seconds she raised her head and peered through the viewfinder again.

Frank had stopped three feet inside the tape and seemed to be calling over to someone. Laura panned right and found herself looking at Sheriff Walter McKinney. A gray wire-brush mustache dominated his face, topping a small mouth locked in a perpetual frown. He shouted something back, pointing at his feet.

Laura realized Frank had made the mistake of not wearing any foot protection.

McKinney turned to the man next to him, said something, and the other man shrugged. McKinney waved Frank over. He walked over slowly, shoulders slumped, a little boy caught with his hand in the cookie jar. After a few minutes of discussion, mostly the sheriff pointing at him and moving his mouth while Frank just listened, he left the way he came, went all the way down the dirt path to the road, then got in his cruiser and drove away. Most of the other cruisers were already gone.

McKinney left next; then the final deputy finished with the tape and the stakes, loaded them into a van, and bumped it down the track and back onto the road. Laura pulled her head up and stared down into the field without the camera. Only the second man in a suit was left, the field big and empty in the dying light and the man alone in the center of it.

She examined him through the zoom lens. He was a stranger

to her. About forty, dark suit, white shirt turned brown around the collar by all the dust clinging to his sweat. The top of his shaved head glistened, and thick black eyebrows gave him a stern expression even at a distance. He crossed his arms and closed his eyes and just stood there. For five minutes he did absolutely nothing that Laura could see. Then he walked to the last remaining Tahoe, started it up, and disappeared down toward the highway.

Laura handed the camera back to Leon along with her keys. "Go back to the car and wait for me."

"What are you doing?" he asked.

"There's more water in the trunk. I'll be there before dark."

* * *

She made her way across the field, stepping over row after row of green. Even past the line of holes where the stakes had been, the verdant lines of life continued.

Laura knelt and touched the dirt.

A girl had died here, her body planted in the soil, a seed that would never flower, and so there was something deeply offensive about ground so rich and lush with life. To the west, the sun slid behind the ridgeline. The universe ticked on like a station master's watch. It had a schedule to keep, and no small thing—not disease nor death nor the suffering of children—would ever give it pause. Laura closed her eyes and crossed her arms as she'd seen the man do. Maybe it had given him answers. Maybe it would cast the whole terrible thing into some new perspective and make it all seem meaningful.

But all she felt was cold.

* * *

Halfway back up the slope, Laura began to feel very foolish indeed. Twilight had passed ten minutes ago, and her only light came from her phone's flashlight. Its beam carried weakly though the descending dark. Her own feet were barely visible.

Another five minutes of climbing and it seemed she'd advanced only another five feet, but suddenly a rocky outcropping loomed above her. She cast the flashlight's beam upward and side to side.

A large shortleaf pine stood to either side. She vaguely remembered the pine and clambering around a bit of rock like this one. But had it been on her right or her left going down?

There had been too many trees, too many bits of rock. She couldn't remember. Besides, everything looked different in the dark.

She chose a direction and picked her way around the edge of the outcropping. A loose gravel trail cut across its face. Following it, she pushed herself close to the wall, trying not to fall, and banged into another jut of stone.

The way in front of her stood blocked. To the left there was nothing but empty air.

The trail had dead-ended.

Laura took a breath. She had chosen the wrong way, simple as that. Turning carefully, she kept the light pointed at her own feet, aware that any trip from this ledge could be fatal.

The beam caught something on the ground.

In the dirt, under a natural rock overhang too shallow to be called a cave, were a collection of small white cylinders. She picked one up and read the small printing down the side: DUNHILL.

Cigarette butts.

She turned and looked outward just as the moon slid out from behind a cloud. The field spread out below her like a pale porcelain miniature. She could make out the rutted track and the rows of crops and the spot where Olive Hanson's body once lay, all of it silent and still.

She looked down at the filter in her hand. The sides crushed. The end stained yellow. It turned inexplicably hot in her hand and she dropped it back to the ground. She held the hand away from her, careful not to let it touch her clothing or her skin. Her only desire in that moment was for a sink with good, hot water and an endless supply of soap.

He had been here. She was sure of it.

Something in the air vibrated, and once detected it couldn't be ignored. He had stood right here, smoking and watching. His skin had touched this same rock. The saliva of a person who killed children had wetted and collapsed the thin cigarette paper. And she'd touched it.

She shuddered, troubled by the intimacy. To be so close—

A thought arced across her frontal lobe like electricity through a closed bus. She froze.

He had been here, had scaled the rocks and lain in wait—of that much she was certain. But what evidence was there that he had climbed back down? Maybe she was all alone on the rock face, her mind playing tricks on her.

Or maybe he had never left.

5

"ORANGE COUNTY SHERIFF'S Office."

The woman who answered sounded bored. Laura even thought she could hear gum cracking.

"Yes, hello. I'm trying to reach Deputy Franklin Stuart."

"Who's calling, please?" she asked, and cracked her gum again.

Just like her mother taught her, Laura thought. She ignored the question. "Is Deputy Stuart on shift?"

"Who's calling?"

There was an edge in her voice now. It should have been easier than this. Usually small-town law enforcement was more trusting. Maybe the OCSO had been getting calls from other journalists, ones with a little more determination than the staffers at the *Gazette*.

Laura decided to play it straight. "It's Laura Chambers."

No response.

"From the *Gazette*."

The receptionist popped her gum right into the mouthpiece, then relaxed again. "Hey, you're the one seeing him, right?"

"Yes."

"It's me, Liz Paulson?" Her voice went up at the end, making it a question. "We went to high school together. I was a few years ahead of you."

Laura could remember two older girls named Liz. One had been a model-skinny brunette who took pleasure in policing other girls' weight, always pinching love handles and counting calories out loud, and the other one had been a real bitch.

"Liz! Wow, it's so good to talk to you. How long has it been?"

"Ever since you took off for college, left us for all those Yankees. I don't know how you put up with those people, Laura. No manners at all." She smacked her gum so hard, people in Durham must have heard it.

"None whatsoever," Laura agreed. "What have you been up to?"

"Oh, I work the switchboard here nights, try to keep up with the boys during the day."

"What are their names again?" As if she'd ever known or cared.

"Bryce is six, Jaxon just turned three."

"They sound lovely, Liz."

"Cute as buttons. Speaking of, how about that Frank Stuart?"

Laura paused. "He's cute all right."

"Oh, I've seen enough of him to know that. By the way, if I know him like I think I do, he's probably at Hopsky's by now, blowing off a little steam. Like I said, y'all are seeing each other?"

"I'm not sure it's anything worth mentioning."

"Come on, it's just us girls. You know, a lot of the ladies around town are wondering just how you hooked him."

"Hooked him." The words felt mealy in her mouth. "What does that mean? Like a fish?"

"Don't be that way, Laura. You know what I'm asking."

"I really don't."

"I mean, how did you get him to go for"—she paused—"for you."

"I guess that means you don't think it was my looks or my winning personality."

"Oh, I didn't mean it like that."

"No? How'd you mean it?"

"Same old Laura. Always so prim and proper—always too good for the rest of us. You never could take a joke."

She took a deep breath. "Liz, I'm actually calling in more of a professional capacity."

"How do you mean?"

"As a reporter."

"For the *Gazette*? You call that professional?"

"Yes," Laura said, "I do."

"Honey, I personally talked to someone at the *New York Times* today. The *Times*. From New York."

"Yeah? They wanted your stunning insights?"

"Don't take it out on me, sweetheart. I didn't make you small time. You did that all on your own."

Laura bit down on her lip. "You mean small time like working for the *Gazette*? Or small time like answering phones?"

"At least I've got a husband. I'm not thirty years old shacked up with my mother, a living reminder of what happens when little fish wander into a big pond."

Laura squeezed her phone so hard she thought it would shatter.

"And by the way," Liz barreled on, "you think I don't know what this is about? You want to know about that poor little missing girl, same as all the others. But you're worse than they are. You call up, mention Frank all casual, pretend to be buddy-buddy with me, and all to profit off the taking of a child. The Bible tells me exactly where people like you will end up, surely it does."

"Finished?" Laura said.

"Not by a sight. Calling up, talking about being Frank's girl, then pumping me for information without mentioning being a reporter? That's probably impersonation. That's a felony."

"Arrest me," Laura said, and hung up.

* * *

She should have known. Hopsky's was just three blocks away, a perennial favorite among local law enforcement. Walking toward the bar, Laura replayed the conversation in her mind. Even more infuriating than Liz's disgusting self-righteousness was the news that the *New York Times* had called. Best case scenario, someone up there had caught wind of the case and decided it had just enough down-south country flavor for a one-time human interest piece. Worst case scenario, the national press would smell the kind of ratings-boosting, circulation-increasing, day-in, day-out edge-of-your-seat drama that only a missing white girl could deliver.

Worst case scenario, they would descend on Hillsborough like a plague of locusts. She was running out of time.

A red neon sign in the window alternately flashing two words, BEER HERE, marked Hopsky's. The door had once been part of a backhoe, a thick piece of metal painted fire-engine red. Beyond the door, the bar ran front to back along the left-hand wall. Cramped booths upholstered in cracked brown leather ran down the right side. In back the space opened up enough to accommodate two pool tables and a bandstand made of old pallets.

The bandstand was empty but the jukebox blared Michael Jackson, his voice riding the fierce, staccato rhythms of "Smooth Criminal." It was ten thirty on a Friday night and the place was shoulder-to-shoulder, standing room only.

Laura pushed through a group of tall men and short women all wearing boots and cowboy hats and ordered a bourbon neat. The bartender didn't bat an eye. That was her drink, and in Boston it had been her one concession to her origins. Up there, a woman ordering bourbon usually raised an eyebrow or two. Down here it just made her one more southern gal looking to get laid and start the weekend off right.

"Someone buying that for you?"

She glanced into the mirror and spoke without turning around.

"Thanks for the offer, but I'm meeting someone."

"Really? Who is he?"

"A cop, actually."

"Law enforcement?" The man gave a long, low whistle. "Must be tough."

"Like you wouldn't believe."

"I better be careful then."

Laura turned around and looked up at him, then reached out and grabbed a bicep, giving it a squeeze. "You might be okay."

"Think so?"

"Probably. Still, this guy I'm seeing? He's a real bruiser. We have to be careful. Maybe we should get out of here."

Frank Stuart pushed a lock of hair off his forehead and gave her his lopsided grin. "Safety first," he said, and followed her out of the bar.

*   *   *

As was her habit, Laura woke before sunrise. Hard blue predawn light filtered between the drapes. She rolled off the bed and pulled open the drawer of the nightstand. Frank liked to smoke when he'd been drinking, and it only took a moment to locate his pack of cigarettes and a lighter and slip them into the pocket of her robe. Frank's breathing stayed slow and even. A cord ran from the back of the alarm clock, behind the headboard, then along the wall until it reached an outlet near the sliding glass door.

On her way through the door, she reached down and pulled the plug out by its roots.

The apartment's balcony overlooked King Street, the one running perpendicular to Churton. It was ten feet wide and three feet deep, with a decorative wrought-iron railing set at waist height. From the ground it was supposed to add a bit of architectural flair, Laura thought, but it fit the drab apartment building about as well as a square peg did a round hole. Frank and his balcony had that in common—style over substance.

Still, there was room enough for two dingy white plastic chairs and an ashtray. It had been years since she'd smoked more than a few times a month, but the old habit still reared its ugly head during times of stress. She smoked one cigarette and waited for the sun to claw its way over the steeple of the First Baptist Church.

"Laura?"

"I'm here," she said, and tossed her cigarette butt down into the street before ducking inside.

Frank pulled himself up to sit against the headboard and rubbed his eyes. "Thought you snuck out on me."

"Just woke up early. I grew up on a farm, remember?"

He held out an arm and she climbed back under the covers, then lit another cigarette and smoked it looking up at the ceiling. She said nothing. Out on the balcony she'd decided that simple silence would be the best approach. A minute passed. She could feel his eyes on the side of her head.

"Something wrong?"

She exhaled sharply.

"Come on, I know when something's bothering you," he said.

"Six weeks of dating and you know me that well. Amazing."

"Did I do something?"

She shook her head.

"Will you at least talk to me?"

"It's got nothing to do with you, Frank."

"Then—"

She raised a hand, cutting him off. "And it's got everything to do with you."

He reached over and lit one himself, balancing the ashtray on his stomach. "You don't usually make a habit of talking in riddles. Am I supposed to know what that means?"

She rolled over and put her free hand on his chest. "I'm sorry. It's the missing girl, the one who wasn't in the field. It's got me a little shook up."

"Oh," he said.

She held her breath. It was the critical moment, the tipping point. Things could go one way, or they could go another. By any rational measure Frank should realize exactly what was happening. A cop and a reporter in bed together, and suddenly the reporter brings up a big case. It didn't take Sherlock Holmes to put things together.

Still, two powerful forces worked in her favor.

One, Frank just didn't have the experience on a big-city police force, or with a big-city paper, to understand just how transactional this kind of relationship could be. He'd yet to be used, to know what it felt like to be hollowed out of information and then tossed away. Without the memory of being burned, at least once, there was nothing stopping him from reaching out for that hot stove.

And two, he had been raised a quintessential southern gentleman. That training had instilled in him a belief that women are delicate flowers, easily scared and always deserving of protection. He would, Laura suspected, see her more as a damsel in distress than a wolf in sheep's clothing.

And he didn't disappoint.

"It's got you scared, huh?" he said, and pulled her close to him. That simple protective instinct never ceased to amaze. Properly accessed, it blotted out all other motives and perspectives. Instant tunnel vision.

Laura locked eyes with him and then looked away, feigning embarrassment. "Just the idea of Teresa Mitchem out there, all alone, it makes my skin crawl. You know what? I take that back. It's the thought that she's *not* alone. That's what scares me."

"There's nothing to be scared of. We're going to get this guy, Laura."

"That's not what I hear."

He pushed back and took her by the shoulders, turned her to face him. "What do you hear?"

"I mean, have you read the paper, Frank? Were you listening to the people in Hopsky's last night? Teresa Mitchem is all anyone is talking about. To be honest, a lot of them were shooting you sideways glances."

He grimaced. "Why?"

"Probably because they were thinking the same thing I was: how come I found you in a bar, and not out looking for that poor girl?"

"I just had a twenty-four-hour shift. I can't take a break?"

Laura ground her cigarette out in the ashtray. "Cops don't take breaks when they're hot on the trail. Everyone knows what it means. It means the Sheriff's Office has nothing worth working overtime on."

He just stared at her, a faraway look in his eyes. She could guess that he was replaying the bar last night, wondering how many evil eyes he'd missed.

"Tell me I'm wrong," she said.

He rolled his eyes.

"Tell me."

"You're wrong, okay? It's been thirty-six hours. We're still processing evidence. Something will turn up."

"But you don't know what, or even if, it will turn up. Meaning it's true, you've got nothing. Oh God, Frank, I wasn't really being serious. Please tell me the police have something, anything to go on. That girl—"

"Is missing, I know. And we're doing everything we can to find her."

"Okay, physical evidence can take time, I get that. But it's a small town, there aren't any strangers here. Olive Hanson must have spent time with someone, and someone else must have seen it. So who is it?"

"She had a few friends at school, but these kids are the same age to within a few years. We're talking ten-year-olds. How is one of them going to kill a girl, let alone wash the body?"

Laura's eyes widened. "She was washed?"

"Shit. I shouldn't have said that."

"Well, you did say it."

"Yeah, I did." He let out a breath. "But you can't print that. Promise me."

She put a hand on his chest, leaned in and gave him a quick kiss. "Hey, it's me we're talking about. I'm not going to print anything we talk about here. This is just pillow talk."

"I still shouldn't be talking about it."

"Well, the cat's already out of the bag. You can't just say something like that and then not give a little more. I was born with more than my fair share of curiosity."

He chewed it over.

"Okay, but it stays between us."

"Of course."

"Yes, she was washed."

"And moved?"

He gave her a look. "Well, he didn't wash her in the middle of a field, did he?"

"Could have brought a bucket and rags. It's not out of the question."

"It wasn't a bucket and rags."

"This is from the official evidence report?"

"No, my own common sense. You wash a body in the middle of a field, it would have just gotten muddy. The soil is soft there, lots of country clay. She would have been red from head to toe.

But it wasn't like that. Someone washed her and dressed her in a white cotton nightshirt, then drove her out into the center of that field and laid her down. Carefully. No stains on the dress other than where the morning dew had soaked through it. And that happened after"—he coughed—"after she was alone again."

"Meaning she was killed somewhere else."

He nodded.

"That night, Fourth of July, no one saw Olive Hanson and Teresa Mitchem together? Or individually?"

"You really have no respect for the lawmen around here, do you?" He pushed himself up on one elbow. "You and everyone else in town apparently thinks we're just sitting around shooting the shit, but believe it or not we are checking that kind of thing out."

"And?"

"Jesus, you never quit. And we haven't found anything. Like you said, it's not a big town. We've talked to everyone who was anywhere nearby. We pressed anyone who we thought looked fishy. There's nothing there."

"Who was fishy?"

"I'm not doing that, Laura. I'm not giving out names so we can turn into Salem. They were just people nearby who couldn't prove they *didn't* do it. But not everyone has an alibi. That's life."

"That's life," she repeated, and decided to take a shot in the dark. "I heard a rumor the FBI is involved."

He sat up on the edge of the bed facing away from her. "Who said that?"

"Like you said, maybe it's better if we don't use names."

"Well, it's not true."

"You going to look at me and say that?"

He started to turn back before he caught himself. "You always knew how to get what you wanted from me."

"What's that supposed to mean?"

"Come on. I know high school wasn't your favorite time in life, but does that mean you've blocked out everything from back then?"

Laura had graduated Orange High a year early as part of the class of '05. Frank had been in the year behind her. She remembered him just as tall as he was today, but without the mass he'd packed on later during his career as a cop. He'd been partial to band T-shirts and bootcut jeans and she only remembered him because they'd both been in the school band, him on saxophone, her on flute, always sitting together in the woodwind section. She'd catch him looking at her and smile.

"What about it?" she asked.

"You don't remember me playing gopher? I'd get your sheet music, carry your instrument."

"Hell, Frank, it was a flute. It only weighed about two pounds."

"Then why were you always telling me to carry it for you?"

She stood up and pinched the two sides of the robe across her chest. "I don't remember that."

"Well, I do. I used to give you something from my lunch almost every day. That was right after your stepdad took off, when your mom wasn't feeding you right. You'd show up with the same wrinkled paper bag every morning, but most days there wouldn't be much in there besides a baloney sandwich. But I'd share. I'd give you something."

"Maybe once or twice," she said. The feeling of hunger came crashing back to her, knives in her stomach, as vivid and painful as it had been a decade ago. But skinny Franklin Stuart saving her each day? She searched her memory, but nothing like that presented itself.

He turned and looked at her, eyebrows up, forehead crinkled. "You really don't remember it, do you?"

She shrugged.

"I don't know why I'm surprised."

"Look, if I was shit to you back then, it was only because I was shit to everyone. I was angry, and a teenager. I'm not the same person now."

"No?" He stood. "Then why does this"—he pointed back and forth between them—"give me that same feeling in my gut?"

"What feeling?"

"Like it's a one-way street. Like I'm being used."

"Frank, I—"

He picked up his watch, looked at it, then picked up the alarm clock and shook it.

"Shit, the damn cord came loose again. I was supposed to start a shift five minutes ago."

"Frank," she repeated.

He raised a hand. "Just forget about it, okay? I've got to grab a shower."

Had she really been so terrible to him ten years ago? As hard as she tried, Laura couldn't conjure more than an occasional disjointed image of him in high school. Whatever had left such a deep impression on him apparently hadn't even scratched her surface. She waited until the water had been running long enough to get hot, then found his jacket in the closet and started going through the pockets.

She found his notebook and smoothed its pages flat among the tangled sheets, making sure the bedside lamp lit them evenly. Her phone's camera wouldn't focus on his handwriting without the right kind of light. She moved to unlock it, but her finger slipped. On her second try the phone flashed once and displayed WRONG PATTERN—ATTEMPT 2 OF 10. She entered the pattern a hundred times a day. It was burned into her muscle memory, and now, when she needed it most, it was gone. She chased it through her mind, and it fled from her, the void it left filled with Frank's face. One second he was smiling like he had all those years ago; the next his eyes were pleading with her to remember.

The shower faucet creaked and the hiss of water turned to a drip.

Without thinking, her thumb traced the pattern and the phone unlocked. She kneeled next to the bed, flipping through the notebook, capturing every last word.

CHAPTER

6

O F THE PAIN of losing a child Laura knew little, but it didn't take an expert to see the torments reflected in Angie Mitchem's eyes. She looked like a picture of a concentration camp survivor from 1945. She looked hollow.

And angry.

"Get off my porch," she said, a half second after opening the door. Laura hadn't spoken a word. "You damn people are vultures, just hovering overhead, waiting to pick the carcass clean. In case you didn't notice, my daughter isn't dead yet. That's the other one."

"Mrs. Mitchem—"

"And I'm sure that sounds cold. Any other situation I'd be grieving with them. But this isn't any other situation, is it? I can't spend any time or thought on a dead girl, not while mine is out there still alive. Won't spend no time with you neither."

She pulled the screen door shut and disappeared back into the house.

Laura had been prepared for anger; she hadn't been prepared for that.

*　*　*

Eight thirty on a Saturday morning and already her office felt like a furnace. Humidity dampened the papers. Even the Lucite slit had fogged over, like the window of a car parked at a lovers' lane. What light managed to filter through painted the concrete room a flat beige.

Laura turned on her computer and got to work, carefully transcribing everything in the images taken while Frank showered. Then she backed the file up in two separate locations before finally printing a single copy. She pushed it onto the center of her desk and read it over and over again.

Reading between the lines, it was possible to trace the path of the investigation.

* * *

The essence of the notes revealed that, despite his best efforts, Frank had been relegated to the fringes of the case. Sheriff McKinney had refused his request to take the lead, saying he would take it himself. The rest of it was more quick jottings than any kind of organized investigation. Two pages were just a list, a series of road intersections, and she interpreted these to be assignments. In the hours after the discovery of Olive Hanson's body, he'd been posted to a series of roadblocks, mostly around the edges of town.

Then came pages of interview notes. At some point McKinney had declared the roadblocks obsolete. Presumably it had been hours between the placement of the body and deputies starting to check vehicles entering and leaving Hillsborough. McKinney had decided that the perpetrator had either already left town or, if he was a resident, already blended back into the surroundings.

Frank was reassigned to interviewing potential witnesses. Emphasis on potential. One person after another reported nothing more than their movements and those of their compatriots around the time the girls went missing. Mostly he had been working the neighborhood where both girls lived, finding groups that had been outside shooting off fireworks and then pressing them hard for anything they might remember.

In a small way, it had paid off. He'd found one family, the Clonfers, whose daughter Sophie had spoken with Olive Hanson on her way down the street. Sophie Clonfer was in the same grade as Olive and said they had talked briefly about a math assignment due the next day. Sophie reported asking Olive where she was going, and said she hadn't given an answer.

Frank had taken this as a clue about where to start in Teresa Mitchem's neighborhood about a mile away. He'd spoken with every family with a son or daughter in the same grade, then to anyone with a child in the grade above or the grade below. He came up with nothing. Finally he started conducting house-to-house interviews, just talking to anyone who would answer the door. That's when he located another potential witness.

Jasper Collins and his brother Wilbur were both in their thirties, unmarried, working part-time at a garage on the west side of town. Both were alcoholics with beer bellies that made them walk as though pushing a wheelbarrow. They'd been on the back porch of the house they rented together, drunk, on the night of the fourth.

Jasper, answering his door early Friday morning, had reported seeing the "little Mitchem bitch" wandering down the alley that night. Wilbur, who had to be rolled off the couch and force-fed coffee, claimed he had no memory of any such thing. Frank had recorded some of the exchange verbatim.

"You were drunk."

"Not as drunk as you, Jasper."

"No, but I hold it better. That girl waved right at you. You waved back."

"Go fuck yourself."

At that point it devolved into name calling, then a fistfight. Both brothers were considered suspects at first, notwithstanding the fact that Jasper had brought up seeing Teresa Mitchem of his own volition. Frank cuffed them on the pretense of disorderly conduct and then transported them to the Sheriff's Office. McKinney stuck them in interrogation rooms and sweated them for over eight hours.

They knew nothing.

Officially they were cleared via alibi. During the hours of late Wednesday night and early Thursday morning, the brothers had been at a poker game with four other men. Neither had left the room for longer than it took to take a piss.

Unofficially, McKinney and his deputies found them to be massively, legendarily stupid. Both had criminal records, but only for driving under the influence in one case and assault in the other. Frank had also noted that Wilbur had an IQ of only seventy-five, and he'd wet himself during the interrogation. The sophistication of the current crime was deemed far outside the reach of the Collins brothers. They were cut loose, and the OCSO was back to square one.

Frank, for his part, had developed a pet theory. He had presented it to McKinney two separate times, and twice the big man had shot him down. He'd started checking it out once his shifts ended.

The girls had both lied to their parents. Teresa Mitchem had told her mother she was going to the Hanson house, and Olive Hanson had told her father she would be with the Mitchems. Obviously neither had been telling the truth. But where exactly were two ten-year-olds planning to go after dark?

The question clearly bothered Frank, and he'd developed his theory in response. The girls had worked together to deceive their parents, so he assumed they had planned to meet up. Plotting the Mitchem and Hanson homes on a map, he had added points marking the Clonfer home and the rental belonging to the Collins brothers. He drew two lines to represent the approximate route and direction taken by each girl.

Neither one was heading for the other's house. Instead, the lines converged in a wooded area on the banks of the Eno River just north of the old racetrack. The track hadn't seen a race in decades. It had a few historical plaques commemorating the 1949 inaugural NASCAR season, but otherwise it was little more than a mile-long dirt oval set into a bend in the river. Mostly it was used by joggers and dog-walkers during the day, and at night by teenagers looking for a secluded spot to drink or make out or skinny-dip.

Why would they have been going there?

As far as Laura could tell, Frank couldn't prove they ever had been. He had discovered no witness that could place them, no physical evidence in the woods that could tie them to that location. They had evaporated like mist.

The second time he'd presented the theory to McKinney, it had bought him an ass-chewing and a reassignment to guarding the crime scene. But he'd visited the woods twice more in the past few days, still looking for any trace of the girls.

On the last page of the notebook he'd written a single word in capital letters, TIMINSKI, and circled it twice.

*   *   *

Laura finished reading and folded the sheet in half. Sweat had formed on her brow and now trickled down across her cheekbones. She ignored it, too taken with the ins and outs of Olive Hanson's death and Teresa Mitchem's disappearance. Even though neither girl was anywhere in those pages, the notes managed to evoke the hole where once they had been. She could suddenly see the shape of that hole, could feel the presence of the girls in a way she couldn't before. They were real to her now.

It was time to play a hunch.

A quick search of the phone book gave her the number of the closest FBI field office in Raleigh. She dialed the number and tried to sound detached.

"Raleigh office," a man answered.

"Agent Timinski, please."

The man on the other end clicked at a keyboard. "Can I ask who's calling?"

"His tailor. I have a suit ready for him."

"Um, hold on." More clicking. "I can leave him a message if you like."

"I can call back. Will he be around this afternoon?"

"No, I'm afraid he won't be in the office at all this week."

"I see. Well, just give him the message."

She hung up before he could ask for a name or number. He hadn't sounded very interested in the call. Probably he would write something on a scrap of paper and drop it on Timinski's desk.

Out of the office all week—it couldn't be a coincidence.

Her phone rang, and she jumped a foot. For a second she thought it was the FBI calling her back, but the light indicating an internal call blinked away on the phone's top.

"Chambers."

"Are you free?" Bass Herman's baritone echoed through the earpiece.

"I'll be right over."

The temperature was a few degrees cooler on the newsroom floor. Laura made her way through the desks and the conference room, into the cubby that sat behind it.

Herman's office was a testament to dedicated clutter. Back issues of the *Gazette* and every other local and major daily stood stacked to the ceiling. The couch along one wall seemed designated for internal memos and communications. The desk, a varnished piece of walnut the size of a church door, was remarkably clear, sporting only a phone, a desk lamp, and an ink blotter with a manila envelope centered on it.

Even from across the desk, Laura could see her name scribbled on the outside. Bass caught her looking at it and she raised an eyebrow.

"Leon's shots from last night," he said by way of explanation.

Laura fitted herself into the one small guest chair not buried in papers. "Any good?"

"Here, see for yourself." He flicked the envelope into her lap.

She slid the glossy eight-by-tens onto the desk and organized them into a grid, then whistled under her breath. Crisp, clear shots of everything. McKinney, the man in the suit, Frank Stuart. The crime scene vans, the cruisers in the background, all of it surrounded by that beautiful yellow crime scene tape. The shots had a stillness and a kinetic drama all at once. McKinney in particular had a desperate look in some of them, as though he was about to fall to his knees and pray. Something about the failing light had given the scene the look of a stage play, and the obvious tension between the players hinted that someone was about to fall through a trapdoor.

Laura realized she'd been holding her breath and said, "Leon's got real talent."

Bass chuckled. "You can say that again. He's wasted photographing football games, though he frames the action just as succinctly."

Laura tore her gaze away and looked up at him. "So is this meeting to congratulate me?"

"More of a progress report."

She gestured toward the pictures. "These pretty much say it all."

"The photos are great. Leon knocked it out of the park. I was wondering more about the words I might be printing next to them."

Laura ran down everything Frank had told her in bed this morning, although she neglected to mention the setting. She also left out everything gleaned from the notebook. There would be no explanation for that kind of depth of knowledge about an ongoing investigation. He would be able to guess what she had done. While her editor at the *Globe* had always championed a get-ahead-at-any-cost attitude, she suspected Bass would find theft to be an ethical violation worthy of a good old-fashioned firing.

No, she'd have to sit on that info until she had a way to introduce it without incriminating herself.

"So the police have nothing," Bass said when she'd finished.

"Right."

"And what do you have?"

"Well, I've got the inside scoop on the police."

"Meaning, by the transitive property, that you also have nothing."

"I can only report facts, Bass, and I can only report those as they're discovered. Are you expecting me to find something the police didn't?"

"Of course not. But there are other ways to approach this story, other angles we can cover."

"Such as?"

"What about the family?"

"I told you, Angie Mitchem practically spit in my face. And you know what? I wouldn't have taken it personally if she had. Her little girl is missing and talking to the press is just about the last thing on her mind."

"And the Hansons?"

"From what I've heard they're barely leaving the house—they're not even answering the door. Maybe they'll want to tell their story in a few days, but no one can get to them right now."

Bass leaned back in his chair and steepled his fingers. "That's not exactly true."

"No, believe me, I asked around."

"Maybe you didn't ask the right people. Or the right questions."

"Again, there just isn't—"

Bass held up a hand. "Smythe got the interview."

Laura groaned. "You've got to be kidding me. How?"

"Same way you win at boxing. Footwork."

"Meaning he hounded them into submission."

"Meaning he kept at it until he earned their trust," Bass countered. "I'm sure it wasn't easy, not with the state that family's in."

"Some people would call that state vulnerable."

Smythe himself would probably have described them as ripe for the plucking. Laura had to keep that thought to herself; Smythe was very careful never to show that side of himself in front of the editor-in-chief.

Bass waved a hand. "Whatever. They gave the interview of their own free will. He didn't hold a gun to their head."

Laura looked at him.

"I know, I know. Not the best figure of speech, given the circumstances."

"You said I had until the Sunday edition. I still have"—she checked her watch—"almost nine hours until deadline."

He shrugged. "That was yesterday. Today we've got this. The pictures are great, though. They'll compliment the interview nicely."

"So that's it." She sat back. "Smythe gets the story."

"I warned you it might happen. I know he doesn't have your experience, but he's a local. People trust their own, people around here especially. This interview with the family just proves it."

"You promised me until deadline," she said. "You gave your word on that."

He leaned across the desk. "Laura, you've got nothing that would make any kind of story. Period. Even if you cobble together a few more quotes from police sources, it's still not going to knock the grieving mother off the front page. Tell me true—if you were in my position, what story would you choose?"

"If it bleeds, it leads," Laura said.

Bass frowned. "You know I don't subscribe to that kind of reductive thinking. It puts both ourselves and the reading public into a box where neither of us belong. Stories—the good ones at least—aren't that simple. You know that."

"And what's the public to gain from a mother's tears?" she shot back. "It's not a story at all, Bass. It's tabloid gossip designed to sell papers, nothing more."

"I'm sorry you feel that way, Laura."

She stood. "You promised me until deadline."

"I did indeed." He patted the ink blotter in front of him. "Deadline, then."

She turned and opened the door.

"Laura," he called after her. "Don't let this story get the best of you. Not like in Boston."

She left and didn't look back.

7

HILLSBOROUGH, POPULATION 6,568, had exactly three types of accommodations for out-of-town guests. A few chain hotels loitered near the interstate, while the local bed-and-breakfast operated out of a mid-eighteenth-century Georgian Colonial that offered a thin glimpse into the town's sometimes savage pre-revolutionary history of riots and rebellion, period character captured by rooms with heartwood floors and four-poster beds.

At the west edge of town sat the motel owned by Elias Quant, a U-shaped edifice of concrete block painted teal. It didn't have a name, just a neon sign that read MOTEL. And, under that, COLOR TV.

It didn't take a genius to figure out where a government employee would stay.

Laura parked the Dart in the lot and went into the office in the center of the U. Elias Quant, nearing eighty years old, was hard of hearing. She had to shout to him for more than ten minutes, but eventually he got the picture. For ten dollars, he was more than happy to let her just sit in her car outside.

"Are you sure no room?" he said one last time. He had round wire-frame glasses and a Dutch accent, both of which she suspected he'd brought over from the old country.

"No thank you, Mr. Quant," she shouted. "If I get cramped, I'll just come in here and talk to you."

"Or if you get lonely," he said, smoothing the front of his vest, and winked.

She rolled her eyes, but smiled in spite of herself. "Or if I get lonely."

Out in the lot, it wasn't the small space or the lack of company that bothered her. It was the heat. As the hour hand crept past ten, the mercury slid past ninety. Even with all the windows down, the hot sun and the black asphalt proved a relentless combination. Which is how she ended up crouched in the shade next to the ice machine when the black Tahoe pulled into a space in front of the rooms.

The driver was the man from the field with the shaved head and the dark eyebrows. He was wearing a clean white shirt under the same wrinkled blue suit, and he didn't look surprised when she came out from behind the ice machine.

"Agent Timinski?"

"Yes, ma'am."

He said it wearily and with an edge, as though he had no time for fools like her, but public relations training burned into him over the years prevented anything less than a polite response.

"Agent Timinski, my name is Laura Chambers. I'm a reporter for the *Gazette*."

His grimace melted away. She'd been expecting resistance to the press, but when she identified herself, the disinterest gave way to a look that was more complex. She didn't quite have a name for it.

"I don't talk to reporters I don't know."

"So get to know me."

"Miss Chambers, I'm afraid the FBI doesn't communicate with the press except in certain special circumstances. And in those cases, contact is always initiated by the government."

She gave him her most innocent, wide-eyed smile. "Oh, I didn't want to *communicate* with you, Agent Timinski. Just buy you a cup of coffee."

That earned her a grin. "You know where we can get a good one?"

"The best."

He nodded. "Now how could the Bureau turn down valuable intelligence like that?"

* * *

The Blue Ribbon Diner was a short car ride away. Timinski drove. Five minutes later they were ensconced in a back booth with seats more electrical tape than vinyl and being served by a career waitress. She wore reading glasses on a chain around her neck and sensible flats under bulging ankles. Her uniform looked like it hadn't been cleaned since the Bush administration, and the coffee was terrible.

Timinski took his first sip and winced. "Liar."

Laura shrugged. "Okay, the best within a mile. That's the bad news—this is as good as the coffee gets on this side of town."

"Then what's the good news?"

"You were lucky enough to snag some pleasant company."

He took another sip, added more cream, more sugar, sipped again. "Uh-huh."

"I know you're working on the Mitchem case. I have a vital clue that I'd like to pass on."

"You just get right to it, don't you? What, no small talk first?"

"Well, if you want to talk about the weather, we can. Hot out there, huh?"

He raised a hand. "No, it's fine by me if we cut to the chase. Tell me what you've got."

She shook her head. "I'd like to ask you a few questions first."

The waitress reappeared, and Timinski, acting as though he'd had a sudden brainstorm, asked her to take away the coffee and bring lemonade instead. "Hot out there," he said, and she nodded at him like he was an idiot before shuffling away.

He repeated her. "Some questions."

"Yes."

"The FBI doesn't answer questions from reporters. We do, however, accept crime tips."

"Look, usually when I'm working with—"

He held up a hand, cutting her off. "By all means, tell me about some of your other experiences liaising with the FBI. How did your relationship with those agents work?"

She paused. "Well, I've never worked with the FBI per se."

"Well, one of your colleagues then. How did it work for them?"

"Okay, fine. I've never worked directly with the FBI. And I've never worked with anyone who's worked directly with the FBI."

"And you know why that is?"

She shook her head.

"Policy. Policy dictates that press requests be run up the flag-pole to Washington. And the boys in Washington usually don't spend much time considering whether to work with the *Hillsborough Gazette*. Or the *Washington Post*, for that matter. Not officially anyway."

"Agent Timinski—"

"Let's start right there. I'll call you Laura, and you can call me Tim. Everybody does." He took another sip of coffee. "You ever report a homicide before, Laura?"

"Of course. I know the *Gazette* isn't the most prestigious paper, but I cut my teeth at some major dailies. The crime beat has some dedicated guys. They usually stay at it for years."

He nodded his approval. "Been my experience as well."

"But I assisted a few of them," she continued. "There's too much going on in a big city for one person to cover it all. The beat reporter would read the blotter in the morning and then divvy up the juiciest pieces. I got my fair share of homicides. Even got a few bylines myself there at the end."

"Tell me about the end."

"Just got tired of the big city, I guess."

"That's a dodge and you know it."

"Is this an interview?"

He kept the expression on his face unreadable.

She sighed. "Fine. I was born and raised here in Hillsborough. Left for school in Chicago, worked in New York for a few years, then Boston for five or six."

"Then you decided to come back."

"Yes."

"Happy to be home?"

"As much as anyone ever is."

"And you came back because, and let me get this straight"—he ran his finger down a page of imaginary notes—"because you're homesick?"

Laura's lips were a thin, white line. She nodded.

Timinski shook his head and made a *tsk-tsk* sound as though reprimanding a child. "It's the same as with the cup of coffee."

She furrowed her brow. "What?"

"Same as with the coffee, Laura. You're lying again. I can see it in your face."

She could feel her face reddening but tried to meet his gaze. His eyes were chips of dirty winter ice, pale blue shot through with gray, unwavering and unblinking. He stared at her openly until she looked away.

"How long you say you've been back in town?" he asked finally.

"Eight or ten weeks."

"So pretend you're me, good old Tim of the FBI. The special agent in charge of the Raleigh office sends you down here to shore things up. This is a new phenomenon, after all, these disappearing girls. It's deserving of scrutiny. What's the first thing you would do?"

"For a new crime, I'd look at new people."

He leaned back and nodded appreciatively, impressed. "That's exactly right. This man didn't just up and start grabbing children one day. That sort of disease festers in the mind for a long, long time. No one, and I mean no one, has the willpower to keep it all bottled up."

"Maybe it's his first time," she said. "Everyone has to start somewhere."

"No."

"Just no?"

"No," he said again. "Too organized. Too cold. No one hits a home run their first time at the plate."

"*I'm* new in town."

"Not quite how I meant it."

She smiled. "So you don't think I did it."

The smile wasn't returned. "For a variety of reasons, no. But we catalogued you in our initial pass along with all the other new people."

It was a strange moment to realize she'd been examined as a possible suspect, even in the broadest possible sense. Something about being lumped together with the killer created a mixture of outrage and disgust.

"One of the first things we did was run a check on every person who moved to town in the last year," Tim continued. "Our background is very thorough, so while I don't know exactly why the *Globe* dismissed you, I know you were considered a rising star, and that you were fired quite suddenly. Other than that, the paper is being very tight-lipped."

"I don't think it's relevant."

"It's relevant to me. Tell me what happened."

"I'd rather not, Agent Timinski."

He slurped some lemonade. "Tim, please."

"I can't do that, Tim."

"Then I don't see that there's any chance we can work together."

"If I tell you, I'm not sure you'll want to keep talking with me."

"Here's the way I see it. If you don't level with me right now, I'm leaving. You'll never speak with me again, and that is a promise. Right now you're an unknown quantity, and I don't associate with unknown quantities. Given those circumstances, Laura, what exactly do you have to lose?"

Silence hung between them. It lasted only a few seconds, but in Laura's mind it seemed to stretch on for an eternity. Timinski's gaze froze her in place, eyes the color of melting snow that never seemed to blink.

"All right," she said finally. "Is this another test? Like you already know what happened, and you want to see if I give it to you square?"

"No test necessary," he said. "That part of the conversation is already over. You lied to me twice. Makes you a type."

"A type—you mean a liar?"

"Yes, Laura. You're a liar."

It was so brazen, the words delivered so flatly, she wasn't sure how to feel. Either way, it wasn't as though she could deny it.

Laura took a deep breath. "I was trying to write a story about abuse in the Catholic church, and I was having a hell of a time getting people to agree to be interviewed. In the poor, white, religious parts of Boston, that's still not polite to talk about. People were split three ways. A small percentage thought it was blasphemy to slander the church under any circumstances, and another small percentage was devout while being genuinely concerned."

"And the third group?"

"The ones who couldn't be bothered. Christians immune to the suffering of others. Jesus would have hated a hypocrite, don't you think?"

"No argument here."

"Anyway, ideology makes people compete to see who can shout the loudest. Lots of tempers, scathing editorials from all sides."

"And lots of papers sold."

"Anything that scares people sells papers."

He frowned. "You okay working to exploit people's fears?"

"No, but it's not like I have control over the paper."

"But you're part of it. Don't you bear some responsibility?"

"How responsible are you for Hoover keeping blackmail files on members of the U.S. government?"

His frown deepened. "Point taken. Keep talking."

"Working the story, I did a lot of interviews, and I found a young man who'd personally been abused by a member of the church. He had an excellent memory, and he had corroborating evidence. Documents. Letters. Not only that, he'd spent enough time with this man to learn a lot of other dirty secrets. He told me about a warehouse—the church called it a youth refuge—where other boys were kept. It was an ongoing situation, so the *Globe* tipped the police and they raided the place. He was telling the truth."

"Sounds like a slam dunk."

"This story was scathing, Tim. It had everything. It would sell a lot of papers, sure, but it would have righted a wrong in the process. And this priest he accused, Hamilton Odell, this guy had risen through the ranks in the years since to become second in command of the Boston Archdiocese. It was my first front-page story."

Timinski rocked forward in his seat. "And?"

"My source recanted a few days later. He'd been very careful not to allow copies of anything. He wouldn't even allow me to record interviews. He was scared of what would happen when the story came out, and it turned out he had good reason to be. These were powerful men, with a powerful hold on him. They threatened his eternal soul, and they offered him a truly outrageous sum of money as well."

"Son of a bitch. He got away with it."

Laura shrugged. "Knowing what I know now? It's not as surprising as it sounds. My source was a true believer; that's how Odell got control of him in the first place. And he'd been poor all his life. Nobody throws away a winning lottery ticket. We had to print a retraction."

He shook his head in disbelief. "It's just wrong."

"I thought so too. So when I ran into Cardinal Odell on the street a week later, things didn't go great."

"No?"

"Not really. I hit him," Laura said.

Tim snorted.

"You've got to understand, I really connected with this kid. The interviews must have run a hundred hours. And then this piece of shit tells the kid that he's the one going to hell."

"So it was a crime of passion."

"BPD didn't charge me, but he sued me and the paper. He would have won too, but he offered the *Globe* a bargain. He didn't want money."

"Just your head on a platter," Tim said.

She shrugged. "Can you blame them? I punched the subject of an investigative report. People have been fired for less. There's right and there's wrong, and then there's playing the game. I should have played it safe and just forgotten about the whole thing."

"That's the lesson you took away from it all?"

"Absolutely."

"Okay," he said, and stood up from the booth. "We're done here."

He left five dollars on the table and walked out.

* * *

He didn't speak a word on the ride back, didn't open his mouth for the first five minutes parked in the motel lot, engine idling, air-conditioning set to arctic freeze.

Laura broke first. "So that was a deal breaker."

He didn't look at her, just stared at the motel office though mirrored sunglasses. "You've got a temper," he said, "and that's given me pause. Plus, it sounds like getting fired really screwed up your moral compass."

She snorted. "Like cops have a monopoly on morality."

He slipped off the shades and fixed her with those near-colorless eyes. "Of course not. In fact, there's more psychos in the bunch than average. Something about the power and the guns attracts 'em. But this kind of work attracts all types. Some people see the injustice in the world and it just bothers them, like an itch they can't scratch. So they become cops and scratch away at things."

"Boy, Tim, that's a real down-home, country way of saying you're the arbiter of right and wrong, that you get to decide what part of the world needs fixing."

"I do indeed," he said. "I didn't ask to be this way. Blame my mama. She did a damn fine job of raising me, and deciding what's right and what's wrong has never been my problem." He tapped his chest. "I already know. I've known since I was a boy."

Laura stared at him. There was something incredibly old-fashioned about Timinski's worldview, like he'd stepped out of one of her father's westerns. And if he was a cowboy, maybe he knew how to barter.

She said it quietly. "I know something about the case. Maybe I can help you find him."

"Let me guess, you want something in return."

"Yes." She forced the word out. It made her skin feel oily.

Timinski didn't look surprised. "Okay, then. Let's have it."

"I help you, you help me. We trade."

"You could just tell me what you know and hope it helps," he said.

She kept her mouth shut, and finally he nodded. "We trade, but I get to assign the value of this so-called vital clue."

She had nothing but his word, but then again, what else could she hope to get? Her back was against the wall and this was the only play. It was time to take a chance. She walked him through her exploration of the crime scene, climbing the ridge in darkness, finding the recessed ledge.

At the end he said, "That's good. You can take me there."

"Now?"

He looked up at the sun. "In a few hours. I have things to do, and in the meantime maybe some of this heat will burn off."

It would only get hotter throughout the day, the humidity closing in like a wet blanket, but she didn't correct him.

"This can work for both of us," he said, "but I need us to see eye to eye."

"I won't be a mouthpiece, just printing whatever you tell me to print. I need enough agency to present the story as I see it."

"I don't expect to line edit what you write, but I do call the shots. If I ask you to include a specific detail in a story, I need you to do that. If I tell you something's off the record, or ask you to hold back key facts of the investigation, I expect you to honor those requests. And if you burn me on this, well, I don't think your career can take two black eyes." He paused. "Do you?"

He shut off the engine and climbed out, headed toward his motel room. Laura followed him out onto the scorching blacktop and caught up with him in the shade under the strip of roof covering the doors.

"Why work with me at all?" she asked.

"Until we know who he is, the press might be the only way to reach him, and if we can reach him, we can flush him into the open." He wiped his brow with the back of one hand. "And because I know you, Laura. I am you. Recognize my accent?"

She shook her head.

"Tennessee, born and bred. Hill people stock. I remember being desperate to get out of there. Joining the FBI—that was the dream, and it almost didn't happen. I made a mistake. A big one. Pulled my service weapon when I shouldn't have, pulled the trigger when I shouldn't have. Very lucky no one got hurt. It could have ended my career, but someone higher up took pity on me and smoothed it over."

Laura said nothing.

"And I asked him that same question," Timinski continued. "'Why me? Why bet on someone who just exposed themselves as incapable?' You know what he said? He said, 'Tim, the dog that lost the fox is twice as eager to please.' He was sure as hell right about that."

"I'm not a dog," Laura said.

"You're missing the complexity of it. It just occurs to me that you might be the type of person who understands the value of a second chance, and who will be careful not to waste it. I could reach out to the *News & Observer* in Raleigh, or to some other reporter at the *Gazette*."

"But you won't."

"No. I suspect you'll work twice as hard as anyone else."

8

IF SOME MAD scientist had stapled together three normal-sized people, the end result would have been close to Diane Chambers. Curls upon curls of hair blown out daily, costume jewelry dripping down her chins, muumuus sewn to look like shapeless prom dresses. Diane weighed more than three hundred pounds and spoke with a Texas twang despite never having traveled more than a hundred miles from Hillsborough.

Laura came in though the kitchen door. Her mother spent twelve hours a day sleeping and the other twelve fastened to a Barcalounger in the living room. The kitchen served only as staging area for old pizza boxes and slimy dishes. Today, though, the one oversized kitchen chair was occupied.

"Oh no!" Diane clapped her hands together, flabby arms trembling in their own personal earthquake. "Have you been fired again?"

"I make my own hours, Diane."

"Don't call me that!" Her voice combined the worst parts of a wet cough and a leaf blower, a rumbling phlegmy shriek that set Laura's teeth on edge.

"That's your name, isn't it?"

"Call me Momma."

"I think I stopped calling you Momma in the second grade."

"You did, you did," Diane nodded, her chins bouncing. "Such

a thankless child. Always with that sour look on your face. Bring me a glass of water, would you, dear? You owe me that much."

Laura sifted through the dusty glasses in the cabinet, located the cleanest, filled it with tap water, and set it on the table. The old farmhouse lacked any kind of air-conditioning. The kitchen didn't even have a fan. Her mother looked like she was about to melt away into a pool of blubber. Diane slurped the water down in three quick gulps and ran a hand over her bloated lips.

"Why can't you be a good girl like this all the time? I swear, the good Lord put you on this earth to test me."

"It shouldn't be a surprise that raising a child is what follows having a child. You chose to have me."

"Not alone!" Diane pressed a hand over her undoubtedly over-sized heart. "Your father abandoned me."

"By dying. I'm sure he did it just for spite."

Her mother frowned. "I wouldn't be shocked."

Laura remembered her father's funeral. Eight years old and devastated to learn firsthand that a person can simply cease to be. Those were long, empty days in the house without him. She could remember rarely speaking for the first few months.

Her mother, on the other hand, had devoured the attention, consuming hugs and condolence cards as heartily as the casseroles and pies delivered to their door. She wore black for nearly a year, summoned crocodile tears often in public, and complained end-lessly about her dead husband at home. It galled her that he'd had the audacity to die. She hated him for it.

Laura found her mother's behavior disgusting, which in turn made her feel like a hypocrite. She hated her father too. After all, he had left her alone with Diane.

"Probably he saw what a little bitch you were turning into and took the easy way out," Diane said.

Despite herself, Laura felt dampness at the corners of her eyes. She was twenty-nine years old, but her mother could still make her cry.

"Oh, now you're gonna blubber? Don't blame me, girl. I'm just truth-telling. The man was a coward, too yellow to raise a child. A child is a responsibility, Laura. Not like you'd know yourself."

Long experience had taught her to say nothing, to ignore the barbs and just leave.

"But at least you'll never have to know the pain I know," her mother continued. "The pain of having your own child embarrass you."

Laura couldn't believe it. Through middle and high school, her mother had stopped leaving the house entirely. She still had a circle of ladies she called on the phone, fishing for gossip, but none of them visited her and she never ventured out. Laura had made excuses for her all those years, never bringing friends to the house, ashamed to let them see the woman who'd raised her. The words were out of her mouth before she could stop them.

"*Me* embarrass *you*? How?"

"For God's sake, Laura, you made such a stink about leaving Hillsborough, all high and mighty. I could have lived with that. Plenty of people in this town need to be taken down a peg or two. But to come back here with your tail between your legs?" Her mother drained the last bit of water, then spit it back into the glass. "It would have been better if you'd died."

"Maybe it would have been," Laura muttered.

"I see, now you're going to play the martyr, right on schedule. Don't think I forgot your tricks, girl."

Laura shook her head. "I only tried to do the right thing."

"Must not have tried very hard. We're the town punch line because of you. I can hear it in people's voices on the phone. They're all laughing at us behind our back."

"Laughing at you, maybe."

"Oh, Laura. It's as though you forgot all the lessons I tried to teach you. You were supposed to do great things. I didn't raise no ordinary girl, but that's what you are now—plain. Homely. Just another dull piece of ass for the boys to play with."

"Momma—"

"No, don't call me that. I'm not sure I still want a daughter."

Laura turned to go.

"That's right, leave. Just leave me here all alone. All you'll do is prove my point, that you're a good-for-nothing. That you're a stain this family can't wash out. I wish you'd just disappear."

Laura left. In her room she took deep breaths until she was sure the tears wouldn't come. Then she put on her boots, filled a bag with clothes and other essentials, and left through the front door. From the front yard she could still hear the raving, cries like knives cutting through the air. As she walked away, the invective turned to indistinct shouting and guttural moans. She couldn't make out a single word her mother said.

Which was exactly how she liked it.

9

"HOLD UP A second," Timinski said, and stopped climbing. He perched on a rocky outcropping and ran a handkerchief across the top of his head, wicking away the sweat. It didn't seem to do him much good. Three in the afternoon and the humidity was in full bloom. The sun hung in the sky like a white-hot coal, and the ridgeline didn't offer much cover.

Laura looked up and tried to gauge the distance. "It's not much farther now. Just another hundred yards or so." Under her breath, she added, "I hope."

It was the daylight disorienting her. Everything looked different in the absence of shadows. Last night all she could see existed in the narrow tunnel of her flashlight. Now there were more landmarks than she could count, most of them unfamiliar.

"Reminds me of taking the FBI physical."

"Getting down was the tricky part. It was dark."

"You scared to be back up here?"

She shook her head.

"Don't fib. Why are you still trying to be a reporter?"

He held out his hand and she took it, pulling him to his feet.

"We're not as similar as you seem to think we are, Tim."

"No? Every man's an island, like that?"

"I just mean we don't know each other well enough for you to say we're the same."

"Talk about a double-edged sword. If that's true, maybe we're exactly the same and you don't know me well enough to realize it. By the way, one of us reads people for a living."

"I thought law enforcement was about, you know, collecting evidence. Fingerprints and fibers, witness statements, confessions. All that."

"Sure, of course. But the purpose of collecting all that is so it can be presented in court, so some DA can get a conviction."

"And that's not important?"

"More than important. It's what makes the whole thing a worthwhile endeavor. It's the cheese at the end of the maze. But that's just the beginning and the end."

Laura didn't understand that. She said so.

"The beginning and the end." He kept climbing. "You start with a crime scene, you collect evidence. You end with a suspect, collect evidence again. Match the two up, you see? But the middle—boy, that's the tricky part. Hell of a job finding one person hiding among all the other people in the world."

"You mean they don't usually drop their driver's license next to the body?"

He laughed, a hard, short bark. "Not in my experience. The middle of a case is all instinct. Following your gut. Reading people. With enough practice, you start to get a feel for how each type of crime flows."

"Flows," she repeated.

"Water takes the path of least resistance; people are no different." He stopped and scanned the ground ahead. "Which way?"

In front of them stood a stand of scrubby pines she didn't recognize. Laura put a hand on Timinski's shoulder and moved past him, climbed up into the pines, and spotted the rocky outcropping level with their position.

She pointed. "Right there."

Timinski followed as she crabbed across the face of the ridge, twice almost slipping and falling due to the loose, rocky surface. The cave, as she'd come to think of it, was quite a bit more disappointing in the daylight. Last night the walls had extended back several yards and she had been unable to rule out the possibility of some tunnel burrowing deeper into the earth. Now it stood revealed, little more than a three-foot depression set under a slight overhang. Still, the leafy brush in front of it made it an ideal hiding place.

Timinski scrambled up next to her and turned around. "Will you look at that—perfect vantage of the dump site."

"Is that what you call it?"

"Sorry. Inelegant phrasing, I know, but that's what we call it. She wasn't killed there; someone placed her out in that field."

"I heard," Laura said. She followed his gaze out into the soybeans. The muddy track still ended in the middle, and from there she could trace her way to the exact spot Olive Hanson's body had been placed.

She shivered in the heat.

"You've got another law enforcement contact."

The statement caught her off guard, and she almost confirmed it.

He squatted down and examined the slab of rock under their feet. "So where are they?"

Laura turned three hundred and sixty degrees, searching the ground. No cigarette butts. Then she saw one caught in a crack.

"There."

He pulled it out with a pair of tweezers and dropped it into a plastic bag. They looked at it together.

"That's the same one, I'm sure of it."

"How many did you say were up here?"

"More than five, fewer than ten. I didn't count. Maybe the wind took the rest."

He nodded, then made a cursory search of the ground on either side of the rocks. Nothing to see.

"Maybe," he said. "But really the only direction the wind can come from is directly in front of us, which would just blow them up against the wall. I suppose the wind could cut along the ridgeline, but the direction still isn't right. They should be here."

"Meaning what?"

He said nothing.

"You mean someone picked them up. But why the one left in the crack?"

"They missed it. It happens."

"But it only took us a few seconds to spot it."

"Sure, in the daylight. If they were here at sunset, and gone today, maybe they were collected during the night."

Laura's weight shifted under her, as though the ground were suddenly on a ship's deck lurching side to side. She leaned back against the rock and closed her eyes.

"That would mean we were up here together."

"Not necessarily. It could have been after you left."

Laura thought back to her trudge to the center of the field, to standing in the green and looking back toward the ridge, to the electric feeling in the air.

"Not after," she said.

Timinski pushed himself up, pressed his back into the depression, and looked down again. "He was here," he said, almost to himself.

Laura shook off her chill, stepped off the rock. "What makes you so sure it's a he?"

"Statistics. Which isn't the same thing as being sure."

"What does that say about men?"

"Nothing good," he said. "This is the hardest part. I may be good at reading people, but sitting across from someone, looking them in the eye, that's a whole different thing than sitting on a ridge, looking at a field."

"So you're saying you haven't solved it yet?"

That earned her a wry smile. "No, not yet. That thing I said before about the flow of a crime? The flow is weakest in ones like this. It's usually not so difficult to connect point A to point B. A wife dies, look to the husband. A husband dies, look to the wife. Find out who loves, who hates, who inherits. Murder isn't complicated. Quite the opposite: it's very, very old, and very, very simple. Most of the time."

"But for a serial killer—"

He cut her off. "One body does not a serial killer make."

"Two girls taken," she countered.

"Even if Teresa Mitchem was dead, it still wouldn't be enough."

"That doesn't sound like you denying this is a serial killer."

Timinski fixed her with that flat blue gaze. "This is one of those times where we need to be explicit. Are we off the record?"

"Any time you say we're off, we're off."

He nodded. "Okay, yes, whether he is a serial killer or not will ultimately depend on the number of victims. I think what you're really asking is, did a stranger do this? Did a man pick these girls out and then take them, for motives that are hard to put succinctly into words? Is that it?"

"That's it."

Timinski shrugged. "My gut says yes. Could have been a relative, a father or an uncle, being inappropriate with one of the girls. Things get out of hand, he kills Olive Hanson. Then he tries to make it look like something else, get us off the scent."

Laura was ashamed to admit she had never considered the killer to be anything but an outsider, a person unknown to his victims. "Is that possible?" she asked.

"Anything is possible at this point. But we've eliminated all the relatives. Some can't account for their time when the girls were taken, and some can't account for when Olive Hanson was placed in that field, but make a Venn diagram of the two groups and there's no overlap."

"Maybe it's more than one person."

"Sure, it could be," he said. "But look where we've wandered off to. Now we've got two relatives working in tandem, two secret predators who've managed to stay hidden all these years. Call it a gut feeling, call it playing the odds, but it doesn't seem likely, does it?"

Laura shook her head.

"And there's something else. I'm going to ask one more time, we're off the record?"

"Of course."

"Olive Hanson wasn't sexually assaulted."

It rocked Laura back a step. Again, new information challenged the very specific picture of the perpetrator she had in her mind. He was a stranger, a person who did what he did out of some sick sexual need. But if he hadn't even touched her . . .

"You're sure?"

"Fairly certain."

"What does fairly certain mean? He did or he didn't."

"He washed the body."

"So you can't tell."

"Laura, the, um, sorts of things you're thinking of—" He coughed into his hand. "It would have left physiological evidence. Tearing and such."

Laura swallowed hard. She could hear it behind her ears.

"But there was nothing like that. The cause of death was strangulation. Other than the marks on her neck, it's like he never touched her."

"That's good," she said softly.

He shook his head. "This sounds horrible, but in terms of finding this prick, no, that's not good. Sexual assault would have narrowed the profile. The chance of finding physical evidence would have increased, and even if we didn't find anything, at least we would have had a clearer idea of the type of person we're hunting. Instead, all we've done is muddy the waters."

"So what does that leave? Tell me about the profile you do have."

"Off the record—"

"Christ, Tim, I want to help you, I really do. But are you planning to give me anything I can print?"

"Bureau would never let me leak the profile from an ongoing investigation."

"Fine, fine. Off the record."

"Off the record, a relative doesn't make any sense. No one is unaccounted for. Besides, other than the obvious, which we've ruled out, what motive does a family member have to kill a ten-year-old? The same goes for strangers."

"So what are you thinking?"

"That he stood here and watched us down there with the body."

She waited.

"That's it," he said. "That's the profile. He washed her, posed her, left her to be found. Then he watched us mill around and look at her."

"So he returned to the scene of the crime. Lots of criminals do that."

"Sure, but this whole setting"—Timinski gestured to the ridge and the field—"it seems designed to facilitate him watching us."

"Could be he wanted to get a look at you. Keep tabs on the enemy."

Timinski stared off into space, tapped one finger against his front tooth. "Maybe."

"Come on, give me something that's fit to print."

"Well, the truth is that the Bureau would never let me reveal *anything* about an active investigation, period."

Laura narrowed her eyes. "You better be going somewhere with this. We had a deal."

"Nope, I'm afraid I can't tell you a thing about this case on the record. Not while it's open."

"Tim—"

"But," he cut her off, "there's really nothing preventing me from telling you about cases that are closed."

"I—what? Why would I care? I didn't climb up here just to talk about old cases."

"What year were you born?"

"It doesn't matter."

"File on you said twenty-nine, so 1988, right?"

"Yes, but—"

"Interesting year, 1988. Interesting all over, but especially here in Hillsborough. I don't suppose you remember much about it."

"No, Tim, I was an infant."

"Didn't read the paper much then?"

Her face started to flush. "I'm being serious. We had a deal, and it was a deal about this investigation, this crime. I don't want to talk about 1988."

He shook his head. "I beg to differ, Laura. I think you're going to want to hear this."

10

*A*N UNNAMED SOURCE *in law enforcement,* or, *A source close to the investigation.*

That's how Tim had asked to be credited, at least publicly. Privately, though, he'd given his blessing to be discreetly named. His credentials plus the three little letters of his agency would open a lot of doors. It would make writing the story easier, and he needed her story to succeed. Perhaps later she could refer to him by name in print, but for now the weight and authority of a simple unnamed cop would have to be enough. Besides, if everything he'd hinted at was true, the source would be the last thing on anyone's mind.

The Orange County Library building had moved to a modish brick-and-glass building while she was away, but the back of the main hall still had a roll of microfilm readers. August 1988 started out the same as January. The first few *Gazette* front pages featured headlines like "Orange High Panthers Thrash Chapel Hill!" and "Heavy Rains Delay Churton Construction." On August 5, things changed. Laura reached out and touched the screen, ran her finger across the picture they'd printed.

The headline read: GILROY GIRL SEARCH CONTINUES.

And the picture was Olive Hanson rendered in black and white.

Laura double-checked the caption, confirming that this was indeed Susan Gilroy. Looking at the photograph was like looking at a ghost. Corn-silk blond hair. A narrow face ending in a weak chin. Sad eyes. A face that had seen violence and come to accept it, one that expected every adult was two seconds away from lashing out with a slap or a kick. The face of a little girl who had decided to pursue a strategy of blending into the background, hoping never to be noticed. A child who excelled at remaining invisible.

Susan Gilroy appeared to have done this so successfully, all the color had drained out of her. She reminded Laura of homeschooled children, the ones who were never allowed out into the sunlight and turned nearly albino as a result.

And the eyes—cold eyes for a nine-year-old. She stared straight out from the grainy photo like she was asking for something. Or waiting for something.

Laura pushed on through headlines screaming about the search, the discovery of the body, the subsequent failed investigation. After two months the coverage started to falter. Articles moved to the second page, then onto the third. Soon it was mentioned only in follow-ups once a week.

Then it happened again. Another nine-year-old, Alina Scopoloto, disappeared on the night of October 31—the irony of it being Halloween was lost on no one—and again the body was returned. The *Gazette* was in war mode now, endless forty-point headlines, constant references to coverage in the *Raleigh News & Observer* and other dailies. The second killing had transformed a simple murder into something newsworthy on a national level.

And even before the Alina Scopoloto feeding frenzy tapered off, another girl went missing. More grisly font splashed across the front page: KID TAKES ANOTHER GIRL.

At first the headline made no sense to her. A closer reading revealed something she'd missed while skimming. Between the second and third missing girl, this killer had been bestowed with that highest of honors: a nickname in the press. He'd joined the likes of the Zodiac, the Night Stalker, the Boston Strangler, the

Midtown Slasher, the Alligator Man, Son of Sam, and Jack the Ripper. This name, though, seemed so innocuous as to be almost farcical.

They were calling him the Kid.

*   *   *

Laura kept reading, utterly transported. She had spent the first eighteen years of her life in Hillsborough. How had she never heard about any of this?

One name kept appearing again and again: Deputy Donald Rodgers of the Orange County Sheriff's Office. He'd been lead investigator on the case and had been much more willing to talk to the reporters back in 1988 than Sheriff McKinney was today. He used the *Gazette* to appeal directly to citizens, asking them to come forward with any information. He even used it to address to the Kid, pleading for the return of the second missing girl, Alina Scopoloto.

The Kid had responded with a corpse.

Laura kept reading long enough to see the headlines shrieking about the third girl, Maria Mendelsohn, age ten. There was a drudgery in reading about death; it made her tired. She rolled back the microfilm and watched them reappear in reverse order, Maria Mendelsohn, the Scopoloto girl, then little Susan Gilroy.

Donald Rodgers had gone on to be sheriff. Laura remembered him from her high school years. He'd personally broken up a drinking party on the Orange High baseball field late one Friday night. Hadn't handed out tickets, just gave everyone a stern talking to. Perhaps stern wasn't a strong enough word. She remembered several of the baseball players with tears in their eyes, crying as Rodgers laid into them.

He'd been kinder to the girls.

A quick search of the phone book revealed that he was still alive and living four or five miles north of downtown, not too far from the Chambers farm. Laura thought about calling, then dismissed the idea. Why give up the element of surprise?

*   *   *

She drove past the driveway twice before locating the address scrawled on a wooden post toppled into the ditch. It wasn't much more than a rutted clay track, and the Dart's muffler scraped the ground more than once on the way up to the sagging farmhouse.

Laura climbed out of the car. The sun hung above the treetops and the shadows lay stretched out like black oil. She took three steps across the front yard and stopped.

A man emerged from a dark corner of the front porch, a shotgun carried loosely across his chest.

"Sign says no trespassing," he called.

"What sign?"

"One next to the damn address."

"The wooden post? It blew down into the ditch. That sign is long gone."

Rodgers had the same cowboy gait she remembered, as if he'd just spent a day on horseback, and the same liquid brown eyes, but his thin blond hair had turned a dirty gray and his face had changed. Time hadn't been kind. Deep crow's feet pitted his orbital sockets, and trenches etched the lines between his nose and the corners of his mouth. He looked sour as he came down the front steps, and it didn't help when he spit into the dirt.

"Well, I'm telling you then: no trespassing."

"Are you Donald Rodgers?"

"Who's asking? I know you from somewhere?"

"My name is Laura Chambers. I'm a reporter for the *Gazette*." He squinted at her. "Naw, that's not it."

"I also went to high school around here. We never met exactly. But I do remember one time on the baseball field—"

"Laura Chambers, of course. Headed north about as soon as you could, legally speaking."

She nodded.

"I remember you. I remember almost everyone I ever talked to."

The shotgun hadn't moved an inch, which Laura took as an encouraging sign. She started walking across the yard.

"What about Susan Gilroy? Do you remember her?"

Rodgers froze up, and he let the shotgun barrel drop down next to his leg. "Now who mentioned that name to you?"

"An FBI agent named Timinski. People call him Tim."

"Nope, don't know him. Like I said, I'd remember."

"He's the FBI agent here because of Olive Hanson and Teresa Mitchem."

"And he sent you to talk to me?"

"In a manner of speaking."

Rodgers nodded to himself. "Figured someone would be along sooner or later. Didn't expect it to be a damn reporter, but if the F-B-I"—he drew out each letter—"sent you, I guess I better play along."

He stood back and let her walk up the stairs in front of him, then stepped past her and pulled open the screen door.

"Mind the dog," he said. "He don't bite."

*   *   *

Cooper pushed his nose into the back of her knee and gave a few long, careful snorts.

"Cooper, get off the lady."

"It's okay," Laura said.

"He just wants to get your scent. Can't help himself, it's his nature."

Cooper huffed her a few more times, then lolled his tongue out and gave the back of her hand a lick. His ears drooped down nearly to the ground and folds of skin covered most of his eyes.

"Bloodhound?" Laura asked.

"Purebred. Used to really be something, but he's almost twelve years old now. Cooper's enjoying retirement."

"And how about his owner?"

That earned her a small smile. "After years of cleaning up other people's messes, I decided to buy this farm and move outside of town and finally get some alone time with my wife. A golden pond kind of thing. Then she up and died, and I ended up with more alone time than I'd bargained for."

"Sorry to hear it," Laura said.

"Aw, hell, it's a ways back now."

"You could move back to town."

"Nope," he shook his head. "Too stubborn."

"At least you can admit it."

"Admit it? I'm proud of it. I wish folks had more steel in 'em. Seems to me that at least half the people today can be swayed by a gentle breeze. Tempt a husband and he cheats on his wife. Pressure a child and he joins a gang. Pay a politician and he'll do whatever the hell you tell him to. Things used to be different."

"Really? The politicians used to be honest?"

Another small smile. "Fair point. Maybe I'm remembering the good old days a little too good."

Laura smiled back. "Maybe."

"And you, Laura. I heard they kicked your ass out of Boston."

She grimaced.

"Too soon?"

She shook her head. "Is there anyone in town who doesn't know about that?"

"Well, I know about it, and some people describe me as a hermit. No, I think it's safe to assume everyone within a hundred miles has heard that particular story."

The thought entered her mind that her mother might, on some deluded level, have been right. It made Laura's head hurt. At moments like this, it wasn't hard to remember why she had left town in the first place.

Rodgers saw the look on her face. "Sorry to bring it up," he said, and she waved him off.

They sat at the dining room table, glasses of water untouched in front of them. The inside of the farmhouse was surprisingly neat and tidy, swept clean of any dust or clutter. Not what she would have expected from a bachelor.

"So let's talk about trust," he said.

"Go on."

"As in, why should I trust you?"

"I guess mentioning the FBI doesn't get a girl far these days."

He held up both hands. "Don't get me wrong, it's impressive. I served as sheriff for eight years, and you've still met more FBI agents than I have. But that's the point, right? I don't know this

Timinski. I've never talked about this case with anyone, and I'd be perfectly happy to leave things as they are. Why should I start digging up the past?"

Laura leaned back, surprised. "So no one else ever came asking questions?"

"After the beginning of 1989? Nope."

"Well, there you go, Don." He frowned at the use of his first name. "I'm the only one who ever bothered to show up."

His eyebrows crept up his forehead. "I'm getting pretty old. Maybe you better lay that one on me again."

Laura unpacked her bag onto the table, laying out folders, papers, notebooks. "It's like this: maybe you retired to try and forget this kind of thing. Maybe even now you're planning to let me down easy. You'll let me talk a while before kicking me out, getting me out of your hair. Then you can go back to doing whatever you do out here all alone. You can go back to ignoring dead little girls and men with strong hands."

He started to open his mouth; Laura raised a hand to stop him from talking.

"Maybe that's the kind of cop you are, the one who decides to cut bait," she continued. "But maybe you're the other kind, the kind who tries to forget but can't, not in good conscience. If your conscience is nagging you, Don, I'm the only cure. I'm the only one who ever gave enough of a shit about those girls to get in my car, drive out to your farm, sit at your table, and ask you about them. So if you've got something to say, it's now or never."

He paused. "Which do you think I am? Which kind?"

She gestured around her, toward the houses and the surrounding fields. "I think you tried to cut bait. Only it didn't work. The fishhook got caught in the back of your hand. It's still there, bothering you. Begging you to itch at it."

"Well, all right. Okay, then." He sucked a tooth and considered her. "Tell me what you already know and I can try to fill in a few blanks."

Laura fanned a series of photocopies out across the tabletop.

"I know about the three girls—Susan Gilroy, Alina Scopoloto, and Maria Mendelsohn. I know they were taken and killed, the bodies left in fields to be discovered later. I know the case bears a number of similarities to Olive Hanson."

"So basically just what you read in the papers," he said.

"Well . . ." She looked down at her shoes.

Rodgers popped up from his seat and started pacing the room. "Christ, that's really all, isn't it? This Timinski character, he sent you in here half-cocked, you know that?"

"I read all the news coverage from back then," Laura protested. "I read everything you ever said when you were sheriff."

"I spent more time keeping things out of the papers than I ever spent putting things into them, girlie. We gave a lot of statements back then, we were a lot freer with information—it was a different time—but I never broadcast any details. If everything you know came from the papers, you don't know squat."

She felt anger bubble up in her chest. "Oh, so you did have a suspect after all?"

He pointed a finger at her. "Don't make light of it. That case," he said, and stopped.

"What?"

The next words out of his mouth were so quiet she could barely hear them. "Do you really think there's a connection between what happened back then and these two little girls?"

Laura took a deep breath. "I think there's a connection, yes. I can't say why Agent Timinski sent me here without more information. Maybe he thinks I can help."

Rodgers studied her another few moments, his face scrunched up in confusion. Suddenly it cleared. He stopped pacing and grinned.

"Aha," he said.

Laura said nothing.

"I get it," he said.

"What's to get?"

"This so-called connection. Timinski said it was fact, eh?"

"Not in so many words, no. He's a source, and he doesn't want all the facts to come straight from the horse's mouth. If he fed me everything it could be traced back to him. Instead, if I do the footwork, go around collecting facts myself, I can cite those other sources and it will put him in the clear."

"Oh, I bet it will."

"He just pointed me in the right direction."

Rodgers grinned again. "Let me guess, he wants to be credited as an unnamed source in law enforcement."

"Well, yes."

"I think I may have invented that one."

She could feel her face turning red. "You can wipe that look off your face."

He pressed a hand to his chest. "What look?"

"The same one as the cat that ate the canary."

"He's using you. Agent Tim whatever-his-name-is, he's going to have you prop up a theory."

Laura didn't know what that meant, and Rodgers saw it in her face.

"Girlie, didn't you learn anything up there in the big city? A place like Boston, I figured you would have been used enough times to get a feel for when someone's blowing smoke up your ass. In fact," he said, considering her again, "I'm sure you did. This agent fella must be a real smooth cookie."

"Okay, I'll bite—what's propping up a theory?"

"It's a little trick in law enforcement. Say there's a direction you want to take an investigation—a suspect you want to sweat, a location you want to stake out—but the evidence doesn't quite justify it. Doesn't really matter, since a gut feeling is the only thing a cop needs." He paused, took a swig of his drink. "The good ones, anyway."

"And you were a good one."

"I'm sure it didn't seem like it, me spending time chasing you kids off that baseball field. Not exactly glamorous."

"You were just doing your job," she said.

"And if that was the totality of my job, making sure kids don't break arbitrary rules, I wouldn't blame you for thinking less of me. But we did have a few actual crimes when I was sheriff, most of them solved by me. It wasn't like working homicide in a major metro area, but I spent my fair share of time out near the limits of human nature. I was pretty proficient out there too. Always had a feeling about the bad ones."

"And this specific bad one?"

"We'll get to it, okay? But he's having you prop him up, Miss Chambers, no doubt in my mind. If you're lead investigator, and you find yourself in the situation I just described, the thing to do is find a nice young reporter and take them under your wing."

Take them under your wing—he said it with about as much sarcasm as possible.

"Feed them a juicy story, anonymously of course, and let them go public with it. The juicier the story, the better it works. The public is outraged, they demand something be done. Soon enough the boys in elected office start shaking in their boots and word comes down from on high—sweat that suspect, Rodgers! And stake out that address!" He grinned again. "And I would always hang my head a little, like I had weekend plans that just got torpedoed, and say, 'Yes, sir. If you insist, sir.'"

Laura's mouth hung open.

He sipped some more water. "Never failed."

"Look, I'm not unfamiliar with the police using the press, and vice versa for that matter, but Timinski seems like a straight shooter."

"Oh, I'm sure he does."

"And besides, we're both on the same side. I want a story that gets this guy caught, Timinski wants him caught, so what if he's using me to put a little pressure on his superiors?"

"Well, what if he's wrong?"

"I don't follow."

"What if he's wrong, and this so-called connection turns out to be complete and utter horseshit, and you print it on the front page with your name right next to it for everyone to see? He's insulated, right? You can't reveal him as a source, and he's sure as hell not going to reveal himself as a source. You'll take the fall alone."

She tapped her pen against the table. Rodgers put on a convincing show. Could Tim really be using her like that? She remembered her sins against Frank and grimaced. No one was immune to the people they trusted.

"Maybe," she said finally.

"Take my word for it, Miss Chambers. This story is a trial balloon—and you're riding in the balloon."

"I'll think about it."

He studied her for a moment, taking the measure of his guest. "Considering what I just told you, that this whole thing might be a wild-goose chase dangerous enough to end your career, do you still want to hear what I have to say?"

She didn't hesitate. "Absolutely."

He smiled for the third time. "Guess that means you're worth talking to. Let's go back to my den."

CHAPTER

11

THE DEN SQUATTED in the house's northeast corner and received little afternoon sun. Heavy blinds cut off what light managed to sneak around from the west. Boxes stacked five high ran along every wall.

"I knew you didn't leave this behind," Laura said.

Rodgers shrugged and pushed himself down into a chair in front of a cluttered credenza. "What gave me away?"

"You mean, besides the kind of pathology that makes a man keep all this paperwork? Call it a gut feeling. Journalists have them too."

He guffawed. "Yeah, usually they have a gut instinct for self-preservation."

Her shoulders slumped. "I can't deny that."

"Oh, hey." He reached out like he wanted to pat her shoulder, then thought better of it and let his arms hang awkwardly at his sides. "I didn't mean you."

"Don't worry about it."

He nodded. "Okay, so the wall behind you next to the door—that's all 1988."

Her eyes widened. "I thought you might have trouble letting go, that you'd hang on to a lot of files. But that's *all* 1988?"

"I only kept the ones I couldn't forget about."

Her eyes moved up and down the rows, surveying the boxes.

"Even if you wanted to forget, looks like there'd be a hell of a lot to unload."

He stood and walked to the boxes, laid a hand on one in the top row. "It was a bad one all around," he said quietly.

"I don't mean to be disrespectful, er—"

"Don's fine."

"—but can you give me a complete summary? I don't want you to think I'm looking for a shortcut here. I'm not opposed to going through every piece of paper in there twice if the story calls for it. But first I need to see if we can find a connection that justifies such an expense of time and effort."

"A summary I can do."

"Maybe start with the nickname."

"Ah," he said. "Weird how those work, isn't it? No one really picks a nickname, not even for a serial killer. It just floats out of the ether, and in just a matter of days we make some kind of collective unconscious decision: this is what we're going to call the son of a bitch."

"It came from the ether?"

He kept talking without looking at her, almost to himself. "Or maybe it's just convenience. Got to call him something, can't just keep calling him the perp or the suspect. No, in a case that goes on long enough, you get kind of familiar with the person you're hunting. You might not know his face, but all the little details start to fit together like bricks in a wall until finally they've built something. Someone. You know him like an old friend. And he needs a name."

"Is that really how you feel about him?"

Her voice snapped him back from whatever daydream he'd descended into. He shook it off and looked at her again.

"Over the years I've felt just about every emotion possible for a case like that. But the name thing? No, forget all that—I was just talking. After we found Susan Gilroy, the first girl in a field, we were all standing there looking down at her body. She was nine years old, but she seemed smaller. After the things he did to her, she seemed very small indeed. She looked like a flower that had wilted and dried, like the slightest wind might blow her away."

He ran a hand down the stubble on his chin.

"It was horrible. Real bad. Worse thing any of us had seen. And I said something like, 'Are we going to catch this guy?' And one of the other guys there, some detective, I can't remember who, he looked down at her and said, 'We've got to. This kid is a real sick puppy.' Or something similar. And that was it, that was all it took. A few cops started calling him the Kid, and some days later we all were. Then it bled over into the papers. The rest history."

"The Kid," she said under her breath.

"Stupid, right?"

"I don't know. It's better than something huge and over top. Better not to make him a bogeyman."

"Could be you're right," he said, and started pulling down white banker's boxes. He arranged them in sequential order across the floor.

He opened one.

"Let's start with the last one," he said. "Let's start with the Christmas Angel."

*　*　*

"Maria Mendelsohn," Laura said, recognizing the moniker from her reading.

"That's right. December twenty-fifth, 1988."

"There's almost no details about her in the papers."

"No, we left them out that time."

She wanted to ask why, but decided to let him tell the story at his own pace.

"That year was unseasonably cold for central North Carolina, and starting late on Christmas Eve, a rare snow fell. It was a good four or five inches, enough to lay a blanket on the world. Enough that when the Mendelsohns got up Christmas morning, they didn't immediately notice what was in their front yard."

He coughed, sipped his water.

"There's an unusual shape under the snow, but it's hard to make out. It's next to a wide log, what was left of a downed tree from a few weeks earlier. Klaus Mendelsohn had been meaning to get to it, but it's at least four feet in diameter. A big job. In fact, he spends the early morning hours dragging brush from the parts he'd already cut near the top, and shoveling his driveway."

"Seems unnecessary," Laura said.

"Around here? The snow probably would have melted inside of forty-eight hours. But Klaus was looking for something to occupy his hands and his mind. It wasn't a normal Christmas morning, you see. Their daughter Maria had been missing for three days."

"Where was she taken from? Was there any—"

Rodgers cut her off. "Just let me get through this, okay? Anyway, since he couldn't sleep, he'd been at it since dawn. At ten thirty, he takes an early lunch break. Goes into the house, eats with his wife. During that lunch, the low winter sun finally climbs up over the eave of the house and shines directly into the front yard. At eleven thirty Mrs. Mendelsohn looks out the front bay window and starts screaming."

Rodgers shook his head.

"Never stopped screaming as far as I know. Old Klaus ended up sending her to an institution. Of course he was never the same either. Hung himself before Christmas next."

Laura leaned forward, queasy and mesmerized all at once.

"The object by the log," she said. The words came out so quiet, she almost couldn't hear herself.

"It was their daughter. What was left of her, anyway. Someone had removed her nose and lips, perimortem, at another location. She was transported, pushed up against the log with her hands bound behind her. Then he cut into her like he was performing seppuku. Her intestines piled in her lap . . ."

He trailed off, gulped water, ran his shirtsleeve across his brow to stem the tide of sweat. It ran unchecked down the sides of his face.

"She was small enough, and the snow was just thick enough, for it to cover up the details. It gave us a few clues, of course. We know it happened before the snow started. All the blood was covered, and there were no footprints other than Klaus's. No, she was perfectly concealed until the snow started to melt away."

Laura tried to make herself focus, started mapping out a time-line in her notebook. "So he kills her, brings her to the house, then—"

"No, no, no," Rodgers rasped. "He mutilated her, but she was still alive. She was alive when he placed her down next to the log. She was alive when he opened her up."

Laura said nothing.

"She could see her own house, do you understand that? Her parents didn't sleep much. Based on statements from Klaus Mendelsohn, he and his wife were in the front room from sunset onwards. In the front room with the big bay window, curtains open, all the lights blazing."

"She could see them," Laura breathed. "He wanted her to see them."

Rodgers squeezed his eyes shut. His nostrils trembled with every breath. "Now you're getting it. All that little girl wanted to do—all any taken child would want—is to make it home. And this . . . person, he waited until she was close enough to see it, hear it. Almost touch it. *Then* he killed her. Only then."

"Jesus."

"And when you think about it, that's only the beginning. The Kid spent the time and energy to bring her back. He risked someone seeing him, being identified, being caught—everything really—just to create that frozen tableau. To what end?"

Laura shrugged. "To give someone nightmares. Who knows what's going through his head?"

"You say that like he's some kind of mystery, but as far as I'm concerned, your gut reaction is just right. He wanted her parents to see his little diorama. That's part of his game. Maybe it's the end goal."

"What about the other two girls?"

Rodgers snorted. "Practically routine compared to the last one. But there were similarities. The modus operandi—manual strangulation, the bodies discovered in fields around the county. The girls were bound with the same twine. It was twisted out of unusual bright colors. All three of them still had a loop on an ankle or a wrist." He sighed. "But we could never find a match. I imagine your FBI fella has drawn the connection to Olive Hanson using some or all of that."

Laura finished jotting in her notebook before looking back up, waiting for him to continue.

Rodgers scratched at his stubble, said nothing.

"Suspects? Other physical evidence? Theories?"

He shook his head slowly. "Never managed to get that far. You can go through every box if you want, read every piece of paper, but that's a pretty complete summary. I told you everything that matters; the rest is just a very large collection of dead ends."

Laura closed the notebook, stood, and surveyed the boxes one last time.

"So what's not in here?"

"Excuse me?"

"I'm not asking for anything official, so before you answer, understand I'm not recording your answer."

He nodded.

"But come on, open up a little. I know there can't be any real evidence, or anything else with proof to back it up, or it would have been important enough to run up the flagpole. I'm asking, what's not in the files? What are your personal opinions on all this? You've got to give me something, Don. Who do you think did it?"

He laughed, a bark cut off so sharply she thought it might mutate into a sob.

"Who did it? Who did it—you're really asking me that?"

She sat down again, leaned across the table, put her hand on his. "I'm not expecting a revelation, but there must be something."

He cracked the knuckles in his right hand, then his left. "My opinion?"

"Anything," she said.

"Okay, we've dispensed with what I know, so here's what I think: it's not an outsider; it's someone who lives right here in Hillsborough."

"Why?"

"Because the most important connection between all three girls, and between this new one, is that he displays them. Most killers, serial or otherwise, do one of two things upon completing a murder. One"—he ticked them off on his fingers—"they leave the body where it falls, recognizing that transporting it opens them up to being seen. Or two, they transport the body intending to hide it. The Kid does neither of those. He moves the body *out into the open*. At great personal risk, he displays them."

"What does that mean?"

"You're a reporter. When you put together a story, you're writing for an audience, aren't you? You write about some fireman saving a puppy, you're trying to inject them with a little hero worship. You write about molestation, you want them to be appalled."

"I don't understand."

"He's writing for an audience too. All of us." Rodgers gestured to the space around them. "And he wants to see the reactions to his work painted on our faces. I imagine it's sweet to him. How could he do that without living here? Without walking among us?"

"I can't print anything without the evidence to back it up."

"Good," he said. "You print that and you'll set off a panic. Besides, I'd deny every word. But you can have my files."

He walked her out to the car and helped her fill the trunk and back seat with boxes. When they were finished, Laura said, "Let me ask you, do you think it's the same killer? Do you think the Kid took Teresa Mitchem?"

Rodgers shrugged. "Neither of us is inside the investigation. But if the FBI sent you to talk to me, there has to be a reason."

"What does your gut tell you?"

He fixed her with a look. "Maybe you didn't notice, but this whole time we've been talking about him? We've been using the present tense."

An icy finger slid up her spine.

"You have a good day now, Miss Chambers, and please don't come back. I've been trying to forget this for almost thirty years. Now I've passed the torch to you. Consider it my final contribution."

"Don't quit just yet," she said.

But he was already up the stairs and back inside.

12

Two miles east, just as the sun touched Highway 70 in her rearview mirror and pumped the sky full of purple, the needle on the Dart's gas gauge dropped into the E. Laura drifted the car down a rutted clay shoulder and into a gas station's cracked parking lot. As the tank was filling up, she walked around the corner of the building and pulled out her phone.

"Hello, Dr. DeVane's office."

It caught her off guard. "Oh, um, is Dr. DeVane available?"

"Speaking."

"Jasmine, it's Laura Chambers. What are you doing in the office on Saturday evening?"

"I could ask you a version of the same question. As in, what are you doing calling the office on a Saturday night?"

"I didn't expect to get you. Figured I'd leave you a voicemail."

She could hear the doctor's sharp intake of breath. "Laura, is this an emergency?"

A light bulb went off in Laura's head. She realized that the context—a therapy patient calling a therapist outside of business hours—implied she was having some kind of breakdown.

"Nothing like that. No, really, I mean it. I'm getting gas out on the highway, I had a free minute, and I wanted to ask you something. I just figured, why not leave a message."

"That's fine," Jasmine said. "Ask away."

"Really, I don't want to keep you on Saturday night."

"Laura."

"Yes."

"I've been here two months longer than you have and I make a living telling people about their problems. Which, by the way, is something I'm not exactly great at turning off outside the office. Do you really think you're keeping me from anything other than a hot bath and a good book?"

Laura thought for a moment. "In that case, can you meet me for a drink?"

There was a long pause on the other end of the line, then, "I don't think that would be appropriate."

"Look, Doc, this isn't about me. I called because I wanted your professional opinion on the story I'm working on."

Another pause. "The missing girl."

"Yes. I've received a great deal of new information—too much, really—and I could use some help sorting the wheat from the chaff. Plus, I'd like your take on the psychological angle of things. If it works for you, maybe we can do an interview on the record."

"I'm still not sure it's the right thing to do."

"Neither is sitting at home on a Saturday night. Come on, don't make me twist your arm. You're the only person I know who can offer an expert opinion on this. You'd be doing me a favor."

"Well," Jasmine said, and coughed. "I suppose it couldn't hurt."

*　*　*

The inside of Hopsky's was the same as the night before except that half the patrons were wearing bowling shirts. Snatches of conversation here and there make it clear there had been a tournament and this was the after party.

The blue shirts all wore smiles and kept slapping each other on the back. They were drinking hard.

The green shirts grimaced at each new cheer and looked fit to start throwing punches. In between edged whispers, they drank even harder.

Laura spotted Jasmine DeVane secreted away in a back booth

wearing a black cocktail dress and pumps. She waved, got a bourbon rocks from the bar, and slid in across from her.

"Thanks for meeting me."

"I still don't quite feel right about it."

"Well, if it makes you feel better, I can buy your drinks. I mean, if you're going to take advantage of a patient, you might as well make out in the process."

Jasmine smiled. "Okay, I get it, I'm beating a dead horse."

"And believe me, I hear where you're coming from," Laura said. "I know a thing or two about the dangers of navigating professional ethics. But hear me out, because I'm not sure this is any kind of violation. I really do want your help on my story."

Jasmine gave her a look that very clearly said, *You're oversimplifying and you know it.* "You're still my patient."

"I could quit."

"And terminate your therapy for the sake of a news story? Now we really are into the realm of the unprofessional."

"So there's no way you can be my doctor and help me on this too?"

Jasmine DeVane slugged the rest of her vodka tonic. "It's more of a gray area."

"I'll take that as, you'll hear me out."

"Just give me a minute." Jasmine started to stand.

Laura snatched up her glass and headed for the bar before she could protest. Once on a stool, she threw back the rest of her bourbon and ordered another one along with a vodka tonic. The bartender made them both quickly and slid them across the wood without a word.

Behind her, she heard the sharp clack of the cue ball breaking and a shout. She turned with the drinks and walked straight into the back of a cue.

The man wielding it had been bent over the table, lining up his shots, and he cursed, then spun around. "Hey, are you blind or just stupid?"

Laura shrugged and stooped her shoulders, a perfect imitation of a dunce. "Oh, I'm just stupid I guess," she said, exaggerating her southern accent. "About as stupid as getting worked up over a simple accident and a barroom pool game."

"Hey," he said, and his forehead crinkled. It seemed as if he was trying to think of something else to say. Instead, he took two quick steps forward and leaned in close, breathing on her. His mouth smelled of garlic and grease.

Laura took a step back so fast she spilled most of the drinks.

"You gonna clean that up?" he asked. He was one of the men in the green bowling shirts. His was open a third of the way down, displaying a rough thatch of hair threaded with a gold chain. The remaining buttons strained against his beer belly and he had a widow's peak so sharp it looked like he might cut himself.

Maybe all that hair had just slid down to his chest.

"What the hell are you smiling at?"

"Nothing," she said.

"Sure, sure." He squinted, looking her up and down. "No need to be a bitch about it, you know? I'm just having a little fun with you."

"Fun's over," Laura said, and turned on her heel. The bartender had seen everything, and two replacement drinks were already waiting for her.

"No charge," he said.

She thanked him and took the drinks, then made her way around the far side of the pool table. All the while she could feel green shirt's eyes burning holes in the back of her head.

"What was that all about?" Jasmine asked once she was settled.

"Just some asshole. I know, I know—I shouldn't have engaged with him. You're not going to shrink me for giving him shit, are you?"

Jasmine shot a long glance in the direction of the pool table, then shook her head. "No, he must have deserved it."

"He's still giving me the evil eye?"

Jasmine gave a small, almost imperceptible nod. "But forget about him. In a few minutes they'll finish their game and be out of our little corner. Why don't you tell me exactly what you had in mind."

Laura walked her through everything she had learned so far,

from the details of Olive Hanson's body to the killings from 1988 to the mountain of files she'd acquired. They ordered more drinks. And when she looked up, green shirt was long gone.

"So you want a consultation," Jasmine said.

"Correct. The evidence linking the three dead girls from 1988 to Hanson and Teresa Mitchem is anecdotal at best."

"The number of similarities seem too great to simply be coincidence."

"That's my instinct as well. But if I publish a story like that, well, reporters aren't supposed to speculate."

"But psychologists can," Jasmine said.

"Bingo. And reporting the conclusions of a psychologist is a lot different than drawing conclusions on my own."

Jasmine sipped her drink and drummed her fingers on the tabletop. "Let's be clear. If you and I talk, really talk, I may draw some early conclusions. That's the nature of conversation: it bounces around. Can we agree we won't print anything I might say while thinking out loud? I'd want time at the end to prepare a final report for you, and you'd only be able to use what's in the report. If it turns out not to be insightful or glamorous, so be it."

"Sounds fair to me," Laura said. "Since we're laying our cards on the table, can I ask you a few questions about your background?"

Jasmine shifted uncomfortably on her bench. "This is why I thought meeting outside of therapy would be a bad idea. Strange as it may seem, the less you know about me personally, the better I can perform as your doctor."

"But you already know so much about me," Laura said.

"Certainly. That's the way it's supposed to be. It creates a power dynamic, and in the hands of a good therapist, that power can be used to positively influence a patient."

Laura shrugged. "We're talking about professional background here, not your fifth-grade crush."

Jasmine threw back her head and laughed louder than she ever had before. Laura made a mental tally of her trips to the bar. Four, maybe five? *She's drunk,* Laura thought, and smiled at the absurdity of it. *My therapist and I are getting drunk together.*

"What is that little half smile about?" Jasmine asked.

"I wasn't smiling," Laura said quickly.

"No, you were smirking."

"I was not smirking!"

"You'd be a terrible poker player, Laura. It's your tell. You keep good eye contact, you nod along with the conversation, but inside your head, you're in your own little world. And I can tell, because you get this smirk on your face." She covered her mouth with her hands suddenly. "That wasn't mean, was it?"

"Actually, it was pretty solid advice."

Jasmine slouched into the booth a little more. "Okay, professional background. I got my degree from University of Chicago, did my residency at UC Medical Center on the south side. I specialized in abnormal psychology."

Laura perked up. "Abnormal psychology, really?"

"Don't get your hopes up. I see that look on your face, like you just hit a gold mine. It's not like that. Schizophrenia and psychopathy are a lot more common than you would think, especially in a big city like Chicago. We had our hands full, day in and day out. I must have treated"—she sipped her drink and glanced up at the ceiling, putting together an estimate—"let's say somewhere in the low thousands."

Laura whistled.

Jasmine waved her off. "It's a mental hospital. Sometimes I'd see ten a day. But did I ever, in all those thousands, talk to an actual serial killer?"

Laura leaned closer, her hands flat on the tabletop.

"Oh, my, look at your face," Jasmine laughed. "Of course not. Not one in all those years. The media loves serial killers. It's no wonder why—look at the two of us gossiping about it. It makes for compelling reading, but as a percentage of the population they barely exist."

Laura sat back. "But we've got one here in Hillsborough."

"Nothing in the statistics prevents incidences of bad luck."

"That's what you think this is, bad luck?"

The very fine edges of the doctor's speech started to slur. "Well," she said, "it's not exactly good luck, is it?"

Laura changed the subject. "How long were you in Chicago?"

"Almost a decade."

"And then you just decided to move here."

Jasmine paused. Her green eyes, usually so sharp, had started to shimmer under the bar lights. "Not just," she sighed. "Everyone has personal problems. You've got Boston, and I've got . . ."

Something about the look on Jasmine's face touched Laura's maternal instinct. She reached out and put a hand on her doctor's.

"What?"

"Chicago," Jasmine said finally. "Let's just say I have Chicago."

"And we can leave it at that."

"I had to get out of there, you know?" Using her thumb, she started massaging the back of Laura's hand. "And this place seemed as good as any."

"Of all the places in the world, why choose North Carolina? Most people around here rank therapy somewhere between Eastern medicine and voodoo."

"I think you just answered your own question." Jasmine pointed at the long line of men and women waiting to get drinks from the bar. "A seven-thousand-person town, and not a single mental health professional until I came along. Do these people look happy to you?"

Laura glanced over in time to see a man rebuffed turn and say something to his friends, who in turn said something nasty to the group of women. In seconds they were shouting at each other.

"No, they do not."

Jasmine nodded. "Stigma or not, I've got a nice little business running. These people are crying out for help. Not in so many words, but they are."

"But that's not specific to this town, is it?"

Jasmine shook her head. "No, you're right. People are crying out for help no matter where you go."

"I'll drink to that," Laura said, and they did. More than once. A half hour later the two of them were well and truly drunk.

Out of the corner of her eye, Laura saw one man break off from the group at the bar. He was wearing a green bowling shirt.

Not the potbellied, hairy-chested man from before, but his slightly better-looking friend, built like a beanpole with a gaunt face. He sauntered up to the table and leaned down over them. His breath reeked of gin.

"You ladies having a nice night?"

Laura and Jasmine just stared at him.

"Look, I wanted to apologize about Luke earlier."

"That's your friend?" Laura said. "The one who looks like Ron Jeremy, only uglier?"

The beanpole laughed. "Hey, that's not too far off. I'm Jay, and he's Luke. Luke just went through a bad breakup, and he's got a lot of anger floating around in here." He tapped his chest.

"That's not healthy. Here," Jasmine pulled a card from her purse and slid it across the table. "Tell him to come see me sometime."

He picked up the card and read it. Smirked. "Therapy? You want him to, what? Talk about his problems?"

"It's a great way to work through those negative emotions," Jasmine said.

"I don't know, I had a better idea. I was more thinking your friend here"—he pointed at Laura—"could fuck his brains out."

Laura froze.

The man leaned closer to Jasmine until his nose was only inches from hers. "And I was thinking in the meantime me and you and that sweet ass of yours could go in the back." He leered, letting his eyes roam up and down her body, challenging her to stop him.

Jasmine, for her part, didn't seem fazed. She put her chin in her hand and looked up at him, wide-eyed and innocent. "Wow, gee—do you suck your mother's dick with that mouth?"

Laura, in the middle of a sip from her drink, snorted, and a trickle of bourbon came out her nose. It burned, and she started a kind of half-laughing, half-coughing fit.

Beanpole jumped back like he'd been stung by a bee. "You can't talk to me like that."

"Oh, so you can talk about my ass like you've known it for years, but I can't talk about your mother's dick?"

He jumped again, and his hands clenched into fists. "If you

were my woman," he hissed, "I'd show you what happens to girls who mouth off."

"If I were your woman," Jasmine said, "I'd probably die of shame."

Beanpole's face turned the color of a ripe plum. He glanced over his shoulder, then jerked his head. Laura followed his gaze and saw Luke in his cheap gold chain walking around the pool table toward them.

"Jasmine," she said, and nodded toward his incoming friend.

Beanpole grabbed Jasmine by the upper arm and yanked her to her feet. "Someone needs to teach you a lesson."

Everything seemed to happen in slow motion. In some recessed part of her brain, Laura noticed that her friend stood just a few inches shorter than the man pulling her. She kicked off her shoes, planted her feet, put both hands on his chest, and gave him a shove.

His mouth opened in surprise and he stumbled backward, neither quick nor sober enough to recover from Jasmine's sudden shift in momentum.

Luke barreled around the corner of the pool table, and, like magic, a pool cue materialized in Jasmine's hand. His eyes snapped open wide and he lunged at her. Jasmine took one step backward and brought the thick end of the cue across at shoulder height in a perfect baseball swing. The cue slipped over Luke's reaching hands and connected with the side of his jaw. There was a wet cracking sound, and then he was on his knees, face in his hands, moaning.

"Come on, before the rest of them realize what happened."

Jasmine grabbed her by the wrist, pulled her to her feet, and started moving toward the door. Outside the night air was cooling rapidly. The sweat on her brow and under her arms began evaporating, a pleasant chill running across her skin. They turned left and walked as quickly as they could without breaking into a run. A few seconds of silence passed between them. Suddenly they were both laughing, leaning on each other for support, barely able to stand from the hilarity of it all. Tears streamed down Laura's face. She thought she had never felt so good.

When the fits of laughter had passed, she said, "How the hell did you manage that?"

Jasmine shrugged. "I've been playing sports since I was a kid, plus a few self-defense classes. I'm in pretty good shape, Laura. Not that I could say the same for them."

"God, the look on his face! Did you see it?"

"Nope, I was too busy running out of there."

"I don't think we can go to Hopsky's anymore," Laura said, and steadied herself on a light post. "I don't think I can drive home, either."

"You mind sleeping on a couch?"

She shook her head.

"Then stay with me," Jasmine said. She led Laura back to her apartment, silent and completely barefoot.

13

ANYONE OVER THE age of twenty who consumes more than four bourbons is asking for a hangover. A clock chimed six in the morning and Laura pressed at her temples. It felt like her head was stuck in a vise.

"Coffee?" Jasmine called from the hall.

She pried her eyes open and saw the doctor fully dressed and looking sharp in a black pencil skirt and a gray top with a scooping neckline. Laura gave a weak thumbs-up and closed her eyes again. "How can you be showered and dressed already?"

"Tolerance, my child."

"Tolerance?"

Jasmine nodded solemnly. "When it comes to boozing, practice makes perfect."

Once Laura had poured two cups of black coffee down her throat, they walked out together to Jasmine's vehicle. To her surprise, it was a mud-stained black truck, the body rusted through in multiple places.

"Not quite your style, is it?"

Jasmine patted the driver's-side mirror. "Oh, I don't know—I think it suits me. My Volvo died just before I left Chicago. Good thing, too, because it never would have made it all the way down here. I flew down planning to buy a used car."

Laura got it now. "But a lot of the used cars around here are actually used trucks."

"Yep. But it's been great. Makes me feel like I fit in."

They drove down onto Churton past Hopsky's, now cold and dead in the light of morning, and around the corner to the Dart. Together they unloaded the boxes from the back seat and the trunk into the bed of the truck.

"Don't worry, I'm on my way into the office right now," Jasmine said. "I'll get them all inside in case it rains or something."

"Thanks. You work on Sundays?"

Jasmine DeVane smiled ruefully. "If only human pain worked nine to five."

*　*　*

The door to Laura's office stood partially ajar, letting some needed air flow in as she worked. Her fingers flew over the keys, synthesizing every bit of information she had gleaned so far. She had missed Bass's deadline, and there was no way anything she wrote could be in this morning's paper, but none of that mattered. The deadline was artificial anyway. No publisher could turn down a story this good, no matter what day he happened to get it.

Someone pushed the door open a little farther.

"Hello?"

"Morning, Laura," Colin Smythe said brightly, and took the one seat in front of her desk.

"Making yourself at home, I see."

He leaned back in the chair and tented his fingers. "I like that—that's a great way to put it. This is *my* home, after all."

"Well, you're welcome to the office if you like it that much. We can always switch. Actually, I think you deserve it."

"I'm not interested in this closet."

"Could have fooled me. You're in here all the damn time."

"Just checking up on you. I wanted to see what you've got, and I'm starting to think you've got nothing. Bass gave me the story, but he also gave you a chance to get it back."

Laura's face fell. She had hoped Bass Herman would give her a fair shot at the story by keeping Smythe in the dark. Instead he had opened her up to sabotage, forced her into the pot with a losing hand.

Smythe saw the look on her face. "Oh, I practically had to beat it out of him," he said. "He likes you, Laura, he really does. But he also knows which way the wind blows."

"Still the mayor's son, is that it?"

He shrugged. "I didn't ask for it."

"No, but nobody makes you play that particular card either. And here you are, using it again."

His face flushed at the implication he was anything less than self-made. "Nepotism or not, it's over. It's Sunday morning, the Sunday paper is out, and your name is nowhere on it."

"Bass ran your interview," she said, almost to herself.

"Of course he did. It's gold. This one issue will outsell some *months* of *Gazette* circulation."

"He didn't give me enough time."

Smythe waved her off. "Always excuses with women, never results. Face it, Laura. You blew it."

Something about watching Jasmine DeVane's cool arrogance in the face of aggression must have rubbed off on her. In a moment's clarity, all her fear and anxiety—about what violence this man could do to her, about what damage she might do to herself by engaging with him—melted away. It left a hole in her chest that filled quickly with disgust at his naked self-interest and a growing sense of her own superiority. She was better than him, more talented, more insightful. She was everything Colin Smythe wanted to be, and more.

He just didn't know it yet.

She walked over and sat on the edge of her desk. He leaned back in the chair and put his feet up, pleased with himself.

"Sure, you got the story," she said. "But that doesn't make you anything more than the low-rent Machiavelli of a small-time newsroom. I've seen guys like you at other papers, just as ambitious, maybe a little smarter. You're bullies, all of you, determined to climb the ladder by pulling everyone else off it, one by one. Because that's the only way you make it up a rung."

He shot up from the chair. "You wouldn't know a good story if it bit you in the ass."

"Coming from you, that means nothing. I've read your stories, Colin. I read everything you wrote for the last six months, and you know what? It's all just filler. Fluff. Sure, maybe I blew my shot. So what? I have something you'll never have: the talent to get shots at stories like this one. And if I keep at it, I'll get another one, and another one. You may have the story, but that's only because you were in the right place at the right time. This is the only shot you'll ever have."

The whites of his eyes seemed to have doubled in size. Anger came off of him in waves.

"So good luck out there," she said. "I think you'll find it's a pretty brutal world if you ever manage to get out of Hillsborough."

His voice came out choked. "You're nothing compared to me."

She flipped her hair, impatient now. Just a few days ago she would have considered this man something like her nemesis. Now she looked across the desk at him—red face, hands trembling—and all she could feel was pity. She felt sorry for him.

"Oh, come on," she said, "This whole thing has nothing to do with the quality of my reporting, or the fact that I left this town as soon as I could. It's because I'm a woman—nothing more, nothing less."

His expression froze, the corner of his mouth curled up in contempt. "You're not built for this work. You don't have the courage for it. Boston proves that much."

"Have you read yourself, Colin? Human interest stories about the biggest pumpkin at the county fair, op eds that somehow manage to take a neutral stance and offer no opinion at all. You've never taken a professional risk in your entire life, and you couldn't report your way out of a paper bag. You don't have the balls for this game."

He visibly shook with rage—tendons in his neck stood out like ropes and he rocked from foot to foot, filled with pressure, about to burst. "What did you say to me?"

"You're a coward," she said simply.

He exploded around the desk, jammed his fist deep into her hair, and got a good handful of it. Then he started twisting. She cried out and he twisted harder, forcing her down to her knees in front of him.

The pain was like a thousand needles injecting her with fire. She feared a chunk of her scalp would tear free. Still, through the pain, she forced herself to look up at him.

His eyes bored into hers; his breathing reached a fever pitch. "This is the only thing a bitch like you is good for," he wheezed.

Laura squeezed her eyes shut.

And heard a rap on the door.

Before either of them could say anything, it started to swing open. Smythe let go of her hair and stormed through the door, pushing past whoever had opened it.

Laura realized a few tears had escaped their ducts. She wiped them away with back of her hand and turned to see who had saved her.

Natalie, the assistant, stared back at her open-mouthed. As Laura watched, Natalie's mouth snapped shut and her lips pressed into a hard white line. Her eyebrows fell, her nose bent into a snarl. She shot Laura a look of pure, unbridled hatred.

"Not enough you had to fuck your way through half of Boston, now you come and try to steal all the good men here too?"

Laura, still on her knees, repeated her in disbelief. "Good men."

Natalie squared her shoulders and turned up her nose. "Colin's not like that, though—he's not going to fall for your tricks."

And with that, she turned on her heel and disappeared.

*　*　*

Laura found the bathroom empty, locked the door, and allowed herself five minutes to calm down. Air heaved in and out of her chest. Her blood churned as if in a blender. During the—she searched for the right word. Incident? Attack?—everything had taken on a surreal sluggishness, like a movie slowed down to half speed. It hadn't seemed real.

Now, alone in the bathroom, she ticked off all the things that had been working against her: the early hour, the nearly empty newsroom, her own secluded office. Worst of all, she had vastly underestimated the depth of Smythe's insecurities.

Shame burned inside her. A bit because it had been foolish to bait him so openly. But mostly because, once he had revealed himself capable of the violence she had always suspected, she had done nothing. No, she had done worse than nothing. She had *allowed* him to make her get down on her knees. Had allowed him to force her to genuflect before the idol of his own self-image. And what kind of fight had she put up?

What would Jasmine DeVane have done?

In a flash, she had an image of her friend dishing out a swift kick to the balls, of Smythe crumpling to the floor like a bag of bones. Despite everything, she smiled. *Some therapist I found*, she thought.

Could she go to Bass Herman, go to the police, report Smythe to anyone who would listen?

She dismissed the idea as soon as it came. Issues like this were "he said, she said," and in this case it would be more complicated still. Laura didn't doubt for a moment that little Natalie would do anything to protect her crush's reputation. It would be two against one, her word against the town's golden boy. She would not be believed, and then she would be made a pariah, what little reputation she had left stripped away in back rooms and bars, golf games and sewing circles, as the town gossips did what they did best.

No. She wouldn't give them the satisfaction.

Carefully, precisely, she put herself back together, and when she looked halfway normal again she threw open the bathroom door, collected the papers from her office, shot across the newsroom, and launched herself through Bass Herman's office door.

He had folded himself into a leather wingback in the corner and was reading Sunday's *Gazette*, cigar burning in the ashtray at his side.

"Afraid the Sunday paper's already been sent to the printers," he said without looking up. "You know, seeing as it's Sunday morning and all."

Laura sat down across from him, reached out, and forced the paper down into his lap.

He gave her an annoyed look. "What do you want? We were clear on the deadline."

"What I've got here"—she tossed the stack of papers into his lap—"trumps any damn deadline."

Bass put down his paper and started in on the first page. It totaled only a touch over a thousand words, and Laura expected him to be done in five minutes. Instead, he put the story down after five seconds, butted the pages back together, and looked at her over the rims of his reading glasses.

He said nothing.

"Come on, Bass, that story is going to sell a lot of papers."

"Do you think that's all I'm in this for, to sell as many papers as possible?"

Laura just shook her head.

"No, I didn't think so. Someone pointed you toward a thirty-year-old story, and now you want to reprint it with some new conclusions. Am I right?"

"Just read the story."

"Look at this damn headline—'The Return of the Kid.' Could you be any more melodramatic?"

"It's just plain dramatic, Bass. I didn't inflate the facts, and I didn't juice them up with purple prose. It's all there in black and white. The connections speak for themselves."

He stood and walked around behind his desk. "Spare me this tabloid tripe. Everyone in this town who was old enough to talk thirty years ago remembers the Kid. Hell, you think people haven't been talking about it ever since the Hanson girl showed up in that field? But that's all it is. Talk. People bring up the Kid every time someone goes missing. It's the local ghost story."

"Just read it, Bass."

With a sigh, he pushed his reading glasses up his nose and started plowing through the sheets of paper. Five minutes later he looked up at her and whistled.

"Your boyfriend is going to get in a lot of trouble for this."

Laura shrugged.

"He's your source for all this, right?"

"No comment."

Bass shook his head. "Don't know what could have gotten into him. I like Frank Stuart, I do—but when we print this, he's going up in flames."

"There's no evidence he told me a single thing," Laura said. "And I notice you said when, not if."

"Forget about proof. You two are an item, and everyone knows it. Two plus two equals four."

"Whatever. When can we print it?"

He scratched his sideburns. "It's good, Laura. The quotes and confirmations from law enforcement make it a lot more than rumor."

He needed a push. Quickly, Laura spelled out the follow-up. The psychology of a killer courtesy of Dr. Jasmine DeVane.

"And she's agreed to do it?" Bass asked.

"We're set to go. I can schedule the interview and then write it up anytime. All I need is your go-ahead."

He paused, thinking. "I don't know. That whole premise is tangential to the story itself."

"Of course it is," she said. "But it's a big story. Huge. It needs to be fleshed out. It needs context."

"Hmm," he said.

"And it will sell papers. Enter the mind of a killer? Find out what makes the Kid tick? It's the sort of voyeurism that will capture the public interest. It's a slam dunk, and you know it."

He nodded slowly. "Okay. It'll be on the front page tomorrow morning."

She walked back to her office half as quickly as she'd left it. Her anger, the hot red coal that had rented space in her chest for the past month, seemed to bleed out onto the floor. All she could feel was the tingle of anticipation running up and down her spine. All she could think about was her name back in print again.

14

WHEN SHE PUSHED the kitchen door open, the phone was already ringing. She shoved the two overstuffed brown paper bags onto the counter and flinched as a gallon of milk ripped through the bottom and hurtled toward the floor. Her mother had been right about the town gossip, and it left her with a need to bury the hatchet. Restocking the kitchen was an act of service, however small, and she hoped it would assuage her guilt.

The gallon of milk hit the linoleum and bounced. It didn't break.

She sighed. One less thing to fight over.

She picked up the phone and said hello, an edge of irritation creeping into her voice.

"It's me."

"I told you never to call me here, Frank. What if my mother answered?"

"So what if she did?"

"I've told you a million times, she would never approve."

"I get it, she doesn't like me."

"It's nothing to do with you. She wouldn't approve of any man calling here, asking after me. In her mind, I'm still fifteen years old. In her mind, I'm a little slut."

"If she already thinks you're a slut, what does it matter? You already hate the old bitch."

Laura said nothing. Frank Stuart did that sometimes—said things calculated to cut. It was one of his least attractive features. He was quick to say them, and just as quick to take them back. She usually deployed a tactical silence, let whatever venom he had spit hang between them until it couldn't be ignored. It forced a moment of self-reflection, and usually it induced an apology.

Just not this time.

"I need to see you," he said.

"If you think acting like an asshole is the way to my heart, you've got—"

"Can we skip the banter and the judgments, just for today? I need to see you."

"Why the rush?"

"Not on the phone. I'm coming over there."

"Wait, wait—whatever rules we have about calling this house, they go double for actually showing up. Do not come over here."

"I need to see you, Laura. I'm coming over. You can leave if you want. Then it'll be just me and dear old mom."

Laura felt panic rise in her chest. The thought of Frank and her mother in the same room, discussing her, was among her worst nightmares. Neither person would ever look at her the same.

"What if I came to you?" she said.

"You've been dodging my calls since that fight Saturday morning. I know you don't want to see me."

She took a deep breath. "Listen, Frank, I haven't been dodging anything. I just haven't been home."

She could practically hear his hackles go up, even through the phone line. "Kick me while I'm down, why don't you?"

"Look, that came out wrong. I wasn't with anyone else. It was just to get away from her. Tell me where you are and I'll come to you."

He paused. "Fine, I'll be at home for the next hour. If I don't see you before then, I'm getting in my car and heading out to the Chambers farm."

Laura cringed at the thought. "No need for that. I'll be there," she said, and hung up.

Diane Chambers lumbered around the corner from the hall

and lowered herself into the oversized kitchen chair. Laura didn't bother looking at her. "How long have you been listening in?"

"Listening in? Me? I was in the hall and just happened to over-hear you talking with that man everyone says you're fucking."

Laura squeezed her eyes shut. "Can you even hear yourself? Is this how a mother talks to her daughter?"

"When the daughter's in need of a good smack upside the head for being a little whore, that's *exactly* how a mother talks. What kind of mother would I be if I let this kind of behavior go unchecked?"

"So it's for my own good? Bullshit."

Her mother put a hand to her chest, offended at the implica-tion her motives could be anything less than righteous. "Of course! I do it out of love, my dear. Out of pure, unadulterated love."

Laura felt like she wanted to throw up.

"The big city tainted you," Diane said.

She looked away again, refusing to look her mother in the eye.

"But I can help you wash off the stench. Help you find a good man, start a nice family. I have experience in all that, you know."

"Frank *is* a good man. I don't—"

"I don't doubt he is, my dear, but you'll never win him over like that. Men require a soft touch. They like a woman who agrees with him, who doesn't rock the boat or get fresh. They want obedience."

Laura leaned over the sink and looked out the window, agog at her mother's bizarre change of gears. "First you call me a whore for seeing a man, then you want to give me advice on how to hang on to him? Don't you see a contradiction there?"

Her mother's brow crinkled in genuine confusion. "You're already screwing him, aren't you? Marrying him is just about the only way to turn it respectable. You better dig your claws deep into this one, Laura. The way people talk about you, no other man is going to want you. No one will touch you with a ten-foot pole."

How could she be sweating and yet feel so cold? An intense freeze grew out of her stomach, spreading up across her chest and down through her legs. Her knees wobbled. The walls seemed a foot closer than they had before.

"I have to get out of here," she said to herself.

"What? Speak up!"

"I have to go," she said, and snatched the car keys off the counter on her way out the door.

* * *

Frank jerked the door of his apartment open as though he'd been expecting someone to break it down. His uniform was half missing: he still had on the pants and the gun belt, but behind him was his uniform shirt strewn across the floor, badge and all. She could see one shoe sitting on the coffee table.

"It's you," he said, and backed away into the apartment.

"Uh, sure is," she said. His eyes seemed vacant. "Remember, you ordered me to come see you? Or else?" She deepened her voice for the last two words, trying for comedic effect.

"Right," he said, and slid down onto the couch.

"Frank, are you okay?"

He looked up, his eyes snapping into focus for the first time, the pupils tearing into her. "I'm a pretty fucking far distance from okay."

"Yeah, you look terrible."

He shook his head. "I'm gonna look a lot worse unless you do something."

She sat on the couch next to him. "Tell me what's going on. I'll help you if I can."

"Don't pretend like you don't know."

She threw up her hands. "Obviously you think I know what's going on here. Look at me—I don't have the slightest fucking idea." She mirrored his language back at him. "So just forget about the dramatics and tell me."

He took her face in his hands.

She tried to pull back, but he squeezed his hands together tight.

"You didn't write an article for the *Gazette*? 'The Return of the Kid'?"

Shit.

Somehow he had seen it already. The only explanation was

that Bass Herman had reached out to Sheriff McKinney for comment, which in turn had started this ball of shit rolling downhill.
She hadn't intended for him to find out this way.

"Let go of me," she said.

He didn't move, then looked down at his hands as though seeing them for the first time. He jerked them back down into his lap.
"Sorry," he said, his voice shaking.

"I did write an article for the *Gazette*. That's my job."

"Well, it's got stuff we talked about in it, Laura. Stuff about
the investigation."

"Did they let you read it?"

He nodded.

"So you know there are plenty of things in that story we didn't
talk about, things you never breathed a word of. You're not the
source, Frank."

His eyes squished shut so hard it looked like he might hurt
himself. "But they think I'm the source, Laura. They think it's me."

"So tell them you're not."

He laughed, a sharp bark. "Everyone knows we're sleeping
together. Exactly how much do you think my denial is worth?"

"You're an honest guy. Everyone trusts you."

"You're damn right. But in my line of work you learn that people
tell lies, that nine times out of ten a situation is exactly what it
looks like, and this looks bad, Laura."

She shrugged. "I don't know what to tell you. McKinney knows
you, your fellow deputies know you. After all those years, if they
turn on you—I don't know, it's an injustice. But that's between
you and them. It's got nothing to do with me."

He shot to his feet. "It's got everything to do with you!" he
roared, and for a second she thought he would hit her. Instead he
just loomed over her, breathing hard, his chest rising and falling,
hands balled into fists.

"I'm sorry," she said quietly, "but it doesn't."

"You wrote the story, and it's going to end my career. You don't
see any cause and effect there?"

"I was just doing my job. I wouldn't go back and change it
even if I could."

"Come with me." He held out a hand.

"You're not even dressed."

He started pulling on his shoes. "Come with me," he repeated.

"Where?"

"To the station. Tell McKinney I'm not the source. You can still clear all this up."

"No."

He stopped moving, fingers on the laces. "Why won't you help me?"

"I will not answer any questions about a source. That means I will never confirm a source, and I'll never deny one either."

"If you care even a little for me—help me."

She shook her head.

The house phone rang. Frank snatched it up, muttered into the receiver, then tossed it to her.

"It's for you," he said.

Laura wrinkled her nose in confusion.

"Go ahead, take it," he snarled, "I'm sure it's real important. In fact, just lock the door on your way out." He darted into the hall and slammed the door behind him.

Laura lifted the receiver to her ear.

"Hello?"

"I've been following you," the caller said.

It was a man's voice, a rich baritone. There was a hint of an accent, but Laura couldn't place it. It had a lilt, a slight extension of the vowel sounds that made it sound almost Caribbean.

"Excuse me?"

"I know it's you, Laura. I'd recognize your voice anywhere."

He paused, and she listened to the thick, measured breathing on the other end of the line.

"I only wish we could speak in person."

"How are we speaking at all? How—"

"Did I know to find you there at Deputy Stuart's home?" He cut her off, chuckling. "As I said, I've been following you. I was referring to your career the first time I said it—I do believe I've read everything you've ever written—but it's just as true if you want to be literal-minded."

Laura said nothing.

"I've been tracing your progress, what little of it you've made. Trailing behind you as you skitter from place to place."

"This is one of those 'get out of town while you still can' calls, isn't it?"

"Not at all." The voice sounded almost offended. "I'd hate to see you leave. We haven't yet had the chance to meet."

"You're right. Maybe we should get introductions out of the way. You know my name, but I didn't catch yours."

The caller said nothing. She could hear that he was still there, breathing into the receiver. The sound of his breath traveled down the line and funneled into her ear, transformed by the trip. It had a slight electronic tinge, a robot bellows hissing at her.

"Your name?" she said again.

"You know my name."

"That's not how phone calls work. People usually introduce themselves."

"Of course, and I'm not usually so rude. But our present circumstances demand certain precautions. I want to meet you, Laura, really I do. But not until the time is right."

"Okay," she said, dropping onto the couch, phone in her lap, "you don't want to meet me, you don't want to tell me your name. Tell me this, why shouldn't I just hang up?"

"You could do that. You could end the call, but it won't break the connection."

"What does that mean?"

Another pause, more heavy breathing. Then he said, "That's a lovely blouse you're wearing, so white and sheer. When you stand by the window, I can almost see the sunlight peeking through."

Laura shot up from the couch as though hit with an electric shock, jogged to the window, looked down at the street.

No one there. A passing car never paused. The building opposite featured an array of windows. Most of them were covered by blinds. The uncovered ones opened into a vast interior darkness. She scanned them one by one, searching for signs of movement.

Nothing.

She lifted the phone back to her ear. "You can see me?"

"I'm watching you," he said, and there was a kind of glee in his voice, a childlike excitement. "I'm watching you right now."

Laura frowned. "No need to be so creepy."

"Ah, you think I'm playing a game."

"What else would you call it?"

He paused, thoughtful. "More like a work of art."

"Excuse me?"

"This is truly wonderful. I never get to share this side of things with anyone." He stretched the last word into two. "I'm so glad I chose you."

"Chose me."

"You're quite right—we chose each other, didn't we?"

The street below was nothing but stillness. Even the cars had stopped driving past.

"Look, I don't have time to talk to nut jobs, whether they're following me or not. I'm hanging up."

"No," he said, "you're not."

"And why is that?"

"Because you know who I am."

She cradled the receiver between her head and shoulder, rubbing her hands together trying to get the circulation moving. Her fingertips had suddenly gone numb.

"I don't."

"We almost met, you and I."

"Almost only counts in horseshoes and hand grenades."

He chuckled again. "And a sense of humor too! What a catch. I though you looked beautiful in the starlight. That flashlight ruined your night vision and you nearly ran into me. You looked me right in the eye. Nose to nose, feet away. I thought it was all over right then and there. I thought I'd have to squeeze the life out of you. But you had this superbly blank look on your face, and instantly and with perfect clarity, I understood that I was invisible." He giggled. "After that, the hardest part was trying not to laugh."

"What are you talking about?" she asked.

"Friday night, up on the ridge," he said simply. "You found my little hiding spot."

Time seemed to stand still; everything dropped away. Through it all she could hear just two things: the increasing rhythm of her heart and the caller's perfectly even breathing.

"Cat got your tongue?"

She said nothing.

"I could have gotten your tongue, you know. Could have pried it out of your mouth like a hook from a fish's cheek."

"Why didn't you?" Laura said, finding her voice again.

"Because that would have been the end of us. Instead of the beginning."

"Us," she repeated.

"Did you get my message?"

"Yes, I get the message, you can hurt me if you want."

"Oh, that's a given. Small town, open fields—where can you run? But I meant my actual message. Has it arrived yet?"

She shook her head.

"Ah," he said.

He really can see me, she thought.

"Well, my courier must be running a little slow today. No matter, I'm sure he'll be along shortly."

"I'm sure," she said, and the words seemed to come from somewhere outside her. His voice suddenly repulsed her. It was a very pleasant voice on its own, but she knew it was manufactured by a tongue, a tongue lodged in a head, a head connected to a body that in turn led to arms, arms that ended in hands, the same hands that had throttled the life out of a ten-year-old girl.

The line between those hands and her own ear burned brightly in her mind. Her stomach knotted. Bile clawed its way into her throat.

"The more of your work I read, Laura, the more I like you. Do you know why I like it so much?"

She shook her head again.

That seemed enough for him. "It's the strain of empathy that runs through all your writing. Even when you cover the worst humanity has to offer, you reach out from a place of understanding. At the end of your articles, I always feel better about myself."

"You'd know about the worst." She spit the words like acid.

"I'm not what you think I am, Laura." The glee was back in his voice. "So many surprises. I can't wait to see your face."

"Why wait?" she said, the words out before she could stop herself.

"And brave," he said, almost to himself. "Just this morning I was rereading a story you did for the *Globe* a few years ago, that terrible business about the warehouse with the boys who were taken."

"Catching up on some of your colleagues?"

"I would never abuse a child, Laura." He said it with absolute moral indignation, the irony lost on him completely. "Even in that museum of horrors, you didn't portray them as monsters. As men with dirty souls, to be sure, but men just the same. I wonder, do you see me that way?"

"I haven't seen you at all."

"You will," he whispered.

"If you think—"

The dial tone cut her off. He was gone. She scanned the street one more time, then replaced the receiver and left the apartment, locking the door on her way out.

15

Someone was watching her.

Down at street level, eyes were all she could feel. Around every corner, behind every curtain, she could feel them watching her as she hurried to the Dart.

"Laura!"

She jumped a foot in the air, whirled around, keys splayed out between her fingers, ready to maim the first person who touched her.

"Laura, you okay?"

The voice was coming from a black Tahoe stopped in the middle of King Street. Timinski stared at her from the driver's seat, his thick eyebrows raised an inch up his forehead.

"Laura?"

She let herself breathe again. "Yes, I'm fine. You just surprised me."

"Got a few minutes?"

"Do I have a choice?"

He gave her the confused look again. "Sure you do. Feel free to take off. Just know you'll be missing out on something."

She shook herself, trying to get rid of the slimy, unclean feeling the phone call had rubbed off on her, and climbed into the passenger seat.

Timinski kept his gaze trained on her the whole time. "You sure you're okay?" he asked once she was settled.

Most of her brain screamed out to tell him exactly what had just happened. Even without real proof, her gut told her the call had been anything but a prank. The mysterious caller had been him, the Kid, the man they were all hunting, and Timinski was the most experienced hunter in a hundred miles.

And he'll get him, a voice whispered, from somewhere deep down inside.

He'll get him, Laura repeated to herself. She had no illusions. This partnership between them was a means to an end. Timinski wanted to catch the Kid. Once he did that, the flow of information would stop, and she would lose her most valuable source.

"I'm good," she said finally. "Just a little preoccupied."

"Well, buckle up."

"My car." She pointed to it.

"Nice ride," he said. "Don't worry, I'll bring you back when we're done."

* * *

She hadn't thought it possible, but the interior of his motel room was even uglier. At least the outside of Elias Quant's place could be dismissed as utilitarian. Inside it seemed to have been decorated by an insane person. The bed was round, occupying the very center of the room; the curtains were made of orange crushed velvet; the shag carpet looked ready to shed at any moment. Pastel colors and different wallpaper patterns battled against each other, her eyes the only casualty.

"It looks like the seventies threw up in here."

He grinned. "Oh, it gets better. The toilet stinks like old septic and the air-conditioning is broken."

"You've got to be kidding me."

He shook his head.

"So let's go back to the diner. I know you federal guys don't get much of a per diem"—she took a step into the room, trying not to touch anything—"but considering the circumstances, I'm buying."

"Afraid we need the privacy. Here, pull up a chair."

The small breakfast table and two wooden chairs looked clean enough. She lowered herself gingerly into the nearest seat.

Timinski sat across from her, producing a file folder and a yellow legal pad from the inside pocket of his briefcase.

"How'd you find me there on the street?"

"Wasn't too hard. Heard your boyfriend got the talking to of his life this morning.

"He's not my boyfriend. I've only been here a couple of months."

"Hell, I heard McKinney took him into his office and practically skinned him alive."

"And you think I'm the reason."

"Oh, I'd bet you are. Didn't take a genius to figure out you'd be the first person he'd call."

Laura said nothing.

"I bet he begged you to tell them it wasn't him. Did you do it?"

She shook her head.

"Naw, I didn't think you would. Still, you're not totally unfeeling, at least not in my experience. Figured I would find you there at his apartment, making your mea culpas. Did you make up?"

She shook her head again.

"You sorry about that?"

"Not sure yet."

"Damn, that's cold."

She looked up from the tabletop. "You call me here to give me relationship advice?"

"Nothing so simple, I'm afraid." He pushed the file folder in front of him, then folded his hands on top of it. "I brought you here because I'm going to need your help on this. All hell is about to break loose."

"Sounds juicy."

He winced. "Don't be flippant. You're more right than you know. This morning, the Orange County Sheriff's Office received a package."

Did you get my message? The mystery man's words pinged off the inside of her skull.

"What kind of package?"

"FedEx," he said.

"Inside?"

He coughed into his hand. "A human ear, the left ear, along with another section of skin presumed to be from the same person. We believe they belong to Teresa Mitchem."

Laura thought of that voice leading inexorably to the hands that had wielded the knife. She started to gag.

"It's okay, let it out if you need to," Timinski said, and reached over to pat her on the back. She could tell he hadn't expected her to be so queasy.

She sucked at the hot air and said, "Maybe it's not her."

"Maybe not."

"You don't sound convinced."

"Well, there's an earring in the ear. Angie Mitchem pierced her girl's ears not a week before she disappeared. Did it with an ice cube and a sterilized sewing needle, then gave her a pair of her own earrings to wear."

Laura gagged again. She had gotten her ears pierced the same way. It had been a friend holding the needle, and they were under the bleachers after school. She would have been a few years older than Teresa. She pictured the little girl bracing for the pain, fighting through it, smiling with tears in her eyes as she looked in the mirror for the first time. The image smiling back at her suddenly so much older-looking. A grown-up at last.

It was a rite of passage around these parts, one she and Teresa shared. That connection, sudden and unexpected, made the girl so much more real. Laura felt she could reach out and touch her.

"Take a breath," Timinski said.

"What's in the file?" she managed.

"Nothing you need to see."

"You brought it out for me, didn't you? So let's play show and tell."

"It's pictures," he said, and let the implication hang between them.

"Show them to me."

"I'm not sure that's a good idea."

"Show them to me." She made herself sit up straight and steeled her face into a mask.

He nodded, then slid out the packet of glossy five-by-sevens.

The first depicted the ear, now laid out on a spotless white countertop, a small ruler next to it for scale. It was small. Even absent context, it was clearly the ear of a child. Dangling from the lobe was a small bead of blue glass.

"It came like this?"

"It was in a smaller box within the box, lined with cotton to soak up the excess blood. We think he didn't want it to leak in transit. Didn't want to ruin the effect."

"Still performing for the crowd," she said, almost to herself.

"Exactly. That is exactly what he's doing. Why else make contact?"

"And?"

He slid the next two photographs out without a word. She understood his silence; nothing could have prepared her for the images.

The first appeared to be a rectangular section of skin. Based on the ruler in the shot, it was about two inches by three. It was covered in a mass of black scribbles, like ink spilled from a pen.

The second photo was the same section of skin. This time four hands clad in rubber gloves were each holding an edge, pulling and expanding the skin into a rectangle almost twice its original size and stretching the black ink in the process.

It wasn't random scribbling.

It was numbers.

She put a hand to her mouth. "My god."

"You aren't the first one to say that."

Row after row of tiny black numbers, etched meticulously into the skin. She reached out and ran her fingertips across them.

8	27	4	4	3	5
4	9	4	4	8	2
3	6	3	7	11	17
3	6	3	3	8	27
3	6	3	7	8	27
8	27	11	51	11	37

"What are they?" she asked, her voice a whisper.

Timinski sighed. "If you're asking what they mean, I have no idea. As for what they are, it's a tattoo."

"As in, a heart with mom's name across it?"

"Pretty much. Simpler. One type of needle, one color of ink. One very steady hand. They're small, as you can see."

"He tattooed her." It didn't make any sense.

"Yes."

The necessary stretching of the skin and the comment Tim had made about the cotton in the box purposed to soak up blood—both came into sharp relief. Her head snapped up to look at him, her eyes wide.

"She's alive. Isn't she?"

Slowly, he nodded. "As of six or eight hours ago, yes. The blood had barely congealed when the package reached us. And this"—he tapped the tattoo photo—"is recent as well. Teresa was alive when he tattooed her, and she was still breathing when he harvested his work." His voice sounded flat, like he was ordering off a menu at a restaurant.

"He cut it off her."

"It's why it had to be stretched so that we could read it."

"Jesus, listen to yourself. Does it even bother you?"

He reached out, tried to put a hand on top of hers, but she recoiled away from him. "Of course it does. But I have to put all that aside, at least for now. At least until we catch him."

"Why are you telling me all this?"

"Because in helping you, I'm also earning your silence."

He reached out and took her hand again. She tried to jerk away but he snagged her by the wrist, then squeezed hard and pulled her close.

"You're hurting me."

"Look at my face, Laura. I don't care if I'm hurting you." He let go of her arm. "I showed you all this so you understand exactly what we're dealing with. This sick fuck is keeping that little girl alive and flaying her bit by bit. I showed you all this so you can remember it. The first time you even consider deviating from the plan, the first time you so much as muse about doing something other than exactly what I tell you, think of these photos, and of

Teresa Mitchem, and hopefully it will convince you to do the god-damned right thing."

"Maybe we'll disagree on the right thing to do."

"This isn't a democracy. You don't get a vote. I need you to write an article for me, so you will. You've been talking to the local psychologist, right?"

"How do you know about that?"

He snorted. "Please. I do this for a living."

Laura didn't see an advantage in denying it. She nodded.

"That's good. Perfect, in fact. You two are going to produce an article for me, pretty much the one I'm sure you're already planning to write, and you're going to add a few things."

"Or what?"

He smacked the tabletop. "The girl's alive, Laura. It's different now. Besides, nothing I'm asking you to print is incorrect."

"What is it then?"

"Inflammatory—that might be the best word."

"You're trying to make him angry."

"I'm trying to communicate with him. Emotionally."

"And you want to use my paper, my byline, to do it."

"That's our only shot. Right now they're working over that entire package and looking for physical evidence, but I don't have high hopes. And believe it or not, he didn't leave a return address. This is it, Laura. This is the only way I have to reach him."

She gritted her teeth some more, blew air out between them.

"Will you help me?" he asked.

She looked down at the tabletop, then back up at him.

"That depends. Can I keep the pictures?"

16

Bass Herman had never paced before, not to her knowledge. But he was doing it now, racing up and down the length of his office like he'd been stung in the ass by a hornet.

"What a response! Do you know what this means for us?"

"More exposure?" Laura said. She didn't bother to look up and kept jotting notes in the margins of a half-written article.

"Of course, more exposure. Hey, up here."

She finished writing and then raised her head.

He had his hands on his hips, feet shoulder-width apart and planted dead center in the room. "Are you listening?"

"Of course," she said.

Which was a lie. It was Monday afternoon, almost twenty-four hours since Timinski had shown her those pieces of Teresa Mitchem. Laura had expected they would keep her up nights, and it turned out she'd been half right. The previous night had been spent tossing and turning and sweating through her sheets. But it wasn't the photos keeping her awake.

It was the phone call.

She couldn't get his voice out of her head. Every time her eyelids had started to flutter, she heard it like a whisper just behind her.

I'm watching you.

She'd jump and turn around and, when she was sure there was no one behind her, start the process all over again. That meant triple-checking the lock on the farmhouse door, nudging all the windows deeper into their sockets, peering behind curtains and under beds. Satisfied there was no intruder, she'd sprawl on top of her covers, hands behind her head, and try to go to sleep.

I'm watching you right now.

At five in the morning she deemed it hopeless, ate an early breakfast, picked up a copy of the *Gazette*, and arrived at the office a full two hours before anyone else.

Now the lack of sleep was catching up with her.

"Are you listening?" Bass asked again.

She jumped at the sound of his voice. "Sorry, just a little tired."

"Well, you worked hard. You earned it. You know how many calls I've gotten this morning? You should see the list. Just the ones with *Times* in the title—*New York Times, LA Times, Times-Picayune, Sun-Times,* it goes on. They're all picking up the story, Laura."

She yawned. "It's a good story."

He sat down behind the desk, looking perplexed. "I thought this was what you wanted, your name on the front page."

"They're all printing it on the front page?"

He scowled. "Don't be glib."

He was right, of course. This was exactly what she had been working for. Since the beginning, something in her gut had alerted her that this was *the* story, the one that could pick her up and fly her to wherever she wanted to go. Not that it had been a difficult distinction to make—stories set in Hillsborough weren't exactly famous for being noteworthy.

As though he could read her mind, Bass Herman echoed the same sentiment.

"You should be thankful."

"To you?"

"Sure as hell *should* be thankful to me," he muttered. "Not that I'm holding my breath. But I didn't mean it like that. A story that can capture national interest doesn't come along every day. You got lucky."

You got lucky.

The same phrase that had been echoing around inside her head since day one, since the very first time she'd heard about

Olive Hanson laying out in that field. Somewhere between her initial excitement and the moment in the motel room last night, holding a picture of a girl's severed ear, her enthusiasm had evaporated. All she had left was a dry mouth with a sour taste in it, one she couldn't get rid of. How long would that last? she wondered.

"Let's talk about the new article," he said.

She'd briefed him on Timinski's plan, careful to avoid naming her secret source, and presented the psychological workup as the natural progression of a story people were hungry to consume. She'd expected him to put up a fight. But Bass, a man she'd heard pontificate on journalistic ethics more times than she could count, had only one thing to say about printing wild speculation under the banner of news.

"We can run it this week—it'll sell a lot of papers."

And now the story had exploded even further, was getting picked up by dailies all over the country. She stared at him, wondering how long it would be until she could actually see the dollar signs in his eyes.

"Dr. DeVane has agreed to put in her two cents. The two of us can work something up that walks a fine line. We can minimize our exposure, keep it circumspect. We'll cover the serial killer thing in general, do a walkthrough of some of the greats, what made them tick, stuff like that."

"Keep talking."

"It's a psychological profile piece. You know, an attempt to answer the question, what kind of person could do this?"

"And what's the answer?"

"Well, I don't exactly know yet. Based on my conversations with Dr. DeVane, it's a simple question with a very complicated answer. Really, there is no answer, which makes it all the more terrible if you ask me."

Bass tapped a fingernail against one of his front teeth. "People don't like complicated."

"No, they generally don't."

"Maybe we can simplify it?" he asked hopefully.

"Human psychology? Like you said, don't hold your breath. But the thing is, Bass, it doesn't matter. It's the question that's on everyone's mind: Who could do this? What kind of person? How did he get like this?"

"And if we want an article, we need an answer."

"Sure, but you're missing the point. The answer doesn't matter. What matters is that people are asking the question. All we have to do is *claim* to have the answer, claim to know the truth, even just a version of it. We print that in big, black letters at the top of the front page and they'll come running. Agree with us, disagree with us, it won't matter—they'll buy all the same. Asking those kinds of questions leaves a kind of hole in the world that people can't explain. They'll fill it any way they can."

"Agree or disagree has nothing to do with it. We're talking about news, after all."

She stood to go. "Sure we are, Bass," she said. "Sure we are."

* * *

The oppressive heat broke late Monday night and by Tuesday morning the mercury had returned to the eighties, but the coolness of Jasmine DeVane's office was as welcome as ever. Laura rested her head against the wall and let the air of the waiting room suck the sweat off her skin.

The inner door opened and Jasmine entered next to a tall, lanky woman with sun-blasted features that marked a lifetime on a farm. Wet tracks streaked through the dust on her cheeks; a damp tissue jutted out of one hand.

"Same time next week, Rhonda?" Jasmine said.

Rhonda nodded and her features crumpled, threatening tears again.

The doctor put a hand on her shoulder. "Just remember, it's okay to be your own person. Talk with your friends, get out of the house."

Rhonda nodded again and pushed out through the door, sniffling.

Jasmine gestured and Laura followed her into the office.

"Difficult patient?"

Jasmine let herself tip into one of the overstuffed armchairs. "Hardly."

"You look tired, though."

"Oh, I am. Tired like a woman working an assembly line. This must be what it feels like to put together lipsticks all day. Slide the lipstick in the tube, screw the top on, repeat. Again and again."

"A machine probably does that."

Jasmine threw her hands up into the air. "If there's any justice in the world."

"So, not a difficult patient."

"When it comes to difficulty, most people linger near the center of the bell curve. It's like I told you, seven thousand people and not a single mental health professional. There's a lot of low-hanging fruit to deal with. But we shouldn't talk about that."

"It's okay to tell me that kind of thing. I won't go spreading it around town."

"I'm not saying you would, but that still doesn't make it appropriate to the doctor–patient relationship."

"What is—getting drunk and starting bar fights?"

She regretted it the minute she said it. The attempt at levity fell flat. A darkness descended over Jasmine's face like a storm cloud.

"That was a mistake."

"I thought we went over this already," Laura said.

In the wake of Timinski's revelations, she'd made a few phone calls to Jasmine shoring up her agreement to do the article.

"We went over it, but it doesn't change anything. I was way out of line to even end up in that situation."

"Look, I'm sorry, okay?"

Jasmine shook her head. "You've got nothing to be sorry for. You're the patient; I'm the doctor. The responsibility to avoid compromising situations is on my end."

They sat in silence for a few minutes.

Finally, Laura said, "It was fun though, right?"

"Most fun I've had in weeks, but that doesn't change a thing."

"Let's stick to business, then. Let's talk about the article."

She frowned. "What have I gotten myself into?"

"Hey, you already agreed to do it, and I already sold it to my boss. If it's my mental well-being you're interested in protecting—"

"I better make sure you keep your job," Jasmine said. "Got it.

And I'm as good as my word, but this is the last time I get mixed up with one of my patients outside this room."

Patient. Laura had to admit the word stung. She didn't have any real friends in Hillsborough, and she'd come to think of Jasmine as more than just her therapist.

Jasmine caught the look on her face. "What?"

"Just thinking about the Kid. Any early conclusions?"

"I read through everything you gave me, drew up some notes. It's nothing revelatory, just the same old song and dance about psychopathy. Deputy Rodgers drew some startling conclusions about the voyeuristic nature of the crimes."

"Sheriff Rodgers," Laura corrected her.

"Deputy Rodgers at the time. He went on to be sheriff? Doesn't surprise me; he had a sharp mind. His conclusion was that the crime itself, the murder of these girls, was secondary. It was just a foundation, a building block in a larger plan."

"Seeing the reactions was more important than the act itself. Do you put any stock in the idea that he's a local? Someone living right here?"

Jasmine nodded. "Very much so. Rodgers didn't have the experience in clinical work to make some of the connections—plus the literature on serial killers was much smaller back then—but his ideas dovetail with what we know now."

She stood, walked to the drapes, and pushed one aside to let in more light.

"Serial killers work in cycles, and those cycles are predictable even if they're changing. These kinds of people have been thinking about their fantasy, whatever it is, for most of their life. It builds up like pressure in a steam pipe. One day, the pipe bursts. They kill someone. Then what happens?"

Laura shook her head. She didn't know.

"They stop for a while, physically at least. The fantasy sustains them again. It's much stronger now, fueled by details of the actual act. Terrible, of course, but this also prevents them from killing for a while."

"I sense a 'but' coming."

"But," Jasmine said, "over time this refractory period seems to last fewer and fewer months. Before long it's down to weeks, then only days."

"How does that relate to the Kid?"

"Well, if Rodgers was right, this man would be nearly unique in his pathology. He'd get his kicks from the interactions with *living* people, and those interactions would far outnumber his murders. Every news article, every discussion with people on the street, every expression of horror—they'd be like manna from heaven. His murders are spectacle, and he gets to move among the audience, invisible."

She took a breath.

"It must be a feeling of great power. Godlike, even."

"Is that how he sees himself? A god?"

She shook her head. "I don't think so."

"Why?"

"Just a feeling. He is highly organized and very careful, but if your end goal is never to be caught, these kinds of crimes are not how you do it."

"He wants to get caught?"

"Not at all. But I suspect he accepts it as an inevitability, the same way you or I accept our mortality. We're just human beings, after all. So is he; he knows that."

The knot in Laura's stomach returned with a vengeance, the pain so sharp it felt like she'd been stabbed. "Can you sit down?"

Jasmine turned to face her. "Are you all right? Your face is quite pale."

"Just sit," she said, and when the doctor was across from her, she took a minute before speaking.

"He called me."

"Who?"

Laura fixed her with a look.

"I don't believe it," Jasmine said.

"Yes, it was him."

"Oh, he showed you some ID?"

"He said enough."

Laura related the details of the phone call, especially the part about the rocky outcropping on the ridge. When she was finished, she said, "How could he have known about that unless he's exactly who he claims to be?"

Jasmine thought a minute, then said, "You told only Agent Timinski about the cigarette butts?"

Laura nodded.

"And who did he tell?"

"No one."

"You're sure?"

"He said he wouldn't."

"You're a newspaper reporter, not his partner. Do I really need to tell you that police officers, even FBI agents, lie routinely during the course of their duties?"

"How would you know?"

Jasmine waved a hand in disgust. "Please. I testified in more than my fair share of trials back in Chicago, usually for the defense. The Chicago Police Department wanted to put every single mentally ill person in jail, and proof of incapacity rarely dissuaded them. Interrogations are state-sanctioned lies designed to elicit a confession. You know this."

Laura nodded. Jasmine wasn't wrong—the police did often lie as part of an investigation. "So what are you suggesting?"

"That you're not exactly popular with local law enforcement right now. Say Timinski told even one other person. The story could spread, could find its way to someone who would use it against you."

"You really think that's what happened?" Laura asked.

"No, I'm not making a judgment call. You told me you had proof, that you're one hundred percent certain this call was from the Kid. I'm just pointing out that the proof is a little shaky."

"Okay," Laura said slowly. "But based on the details, was it him? What's your gut tell you?"

Jasmine looked at the ceiling for a few seconds, then back down. "Maybe."

"Come on. That's it?"

"I'm sorry, Laura, but a secondhand conversation isn't an ideal tool for analysis. I might as well be playing telephone with the guy. The situation doesn't exactly lend itself to strong conclusions."

Laura dug into her bag, pulled out a notebook and pencil, and balanced them on her knee. "Next question," she said.

Jasmine shook her head. "No, this is your session. We need to talk about you. We can start in on the details at the end of the hour, but the rest of this time has to be for you."

"This is for me. This is all I'm thinking about."

"Come on, I know that's not true. I got your message."

Laura cringed. She'd made another call to Jasmine's office Sunday morning after her encounter with Smythe. She'd called filled with fear and rage and a cocktail of other emotions. More than anything, though, she'd wanted to share her resolve. It was Jasmine, after all, who had inspired her.

"I figured you forgot about it."

"Of course not," Jasmine said.

"But you didn't bring it up."

"Not until now, no. Adequate time and privacy are important."

She tapped the side of her head. "I can't do it right now. It's one extra thing to turn over in here, and my mind is full up. There's no more space."

"Laura, it's taking up space whether you want it to or not. Talking about it is the only way to get it out."

"There's nothing to say. He's a prick."

"A dangerous prick. Have you considered going to the police?"

"Yes, I considered it."

Jasmine waited for her to continue and, when she didn't, said, "And decided not to, I take it."

Laura leaned closer and started talking with her hands. "It doesn't work, see? I say he did, he says he didn't, his little girlfriend backs him up, and no one believes me. It's a credibility issue, understand? I have a lot of experience with those."

"That's a risk, to be sure. So is doing nothing."

"I need to do my job."

"You know, I didn't have the best relationship with my mother either, and—"

Laura threw back her head and laughed. "I never figured you for such a Freudian. I mean, I know I talked about my mother when I first came in, but she's not tied into everything."

"No, let me finish. I didn't have the best relationship with my mother, and she didn't have the best relationship with men. To her, men were all the same: simple, boorish creatures, fated for violence. God's ultimate joke was to sculpt that evil into their very natures and then make them stronger than us, faster than us. To my mother, the result was inevitable—we were destined to be under a man's thumb, born to be slaves. She saw my whole life as an opportunity to spit in the face of that plan. I was adopted, and she saw me as her most important project. She colored my views to match hers. For a long time, I thought men were my enemy."

"You don't think so anymore?" Laura asked. "Even after reading those files?"

Jasmine's eyes snapped into focus. "Don't be reductive," she scoffed. "Of course I don't. Men, women, it doesn't matter—human nature is the enemy. The worst humanity has to offer is very bad indeed, but it doesn't seem to discriminate along gender lines."

"I don't see what this has to do with a prick named Colin Smythe."

"You're right, of course. I'm rambling. My point is that for a long time after I got out of my house, I felt like right and wrong were concepts without any inherent value. They had meaning, but there was just no way to put them into action. Basically, I didn't believe people would do anything if I pointed out an injustice. My mother had me convinced of her philosophy, that the world is a scary place and a cry for help serves only to summon the monsters."

Laura said, "But now you're saying a cry for help is the right move."

"It can be. I don't know if they'll put the mayor's son in jail over one report, but until you try, how do you know yours will be the first?"

Laura chewed that over, and Jasmine seemed perfectly content to stare off into space.

After a while, Laura asked, "What happened to your mother?"

"I shouldn't have brought it up."

"Really, I'm interested."

"It's not a good story. No happy ending. When I was eighteen I left, and later on she died. We never reconciled. I went to the funeral, certain I would find something there. Answers, I guess. But life doesn't work like that."

"What made you start questioning her?"

"You mean her views on the less-fair sex?" Jasmine smiled. "I fell in love."

"That can't have been easy."

"In that house? It was a nightmare. We used to send each other letters in code; the school's copy of *Romeo and Juliet* was the key. A little on the nose to be sure, but as a seventeen-year-old it was the most romantic thing I could imagine."

"Coded messages," Laura repeated.

"Yes. What's wrong? You look even paler than before."

Laura rose out of her seat and started for the door. The good doctor shouted something after her, but she couldn't make it out and didn't bother to try. Three or four separate puzzle pieces had just clicked together in her head.

She had an answer.

POLICE RESCUE SIX CHILDREN IN TRAFFICKING RING BUST
By Laura Chambers
January 27, 2015

BOSTON — Police rescued six children and a 29-year-old woman after busting a child trafficking ring based in Boston's Dorchester neighborhood, according to a statement put out yesterday evening by the Massachusetts State Police.

The children, many suffering from malnutrition, remained unidentified Monday. The lone adult discovered with the children, identified as Cheskka Dimaguiba, is a Filipino national. There is no record of her entering the United States.

The possibility of a crime in progress was uncovered by *Globe* staffers conducting an investigative report, and the paper subsequently made a full report to police. Acting on the tip, police raided a warehouse in Dorchester two nights ago. Further investigation revealed a cache of food and clothing and ultimately led police to a room described as a "hidden dungeon."

"Witness statements and other evidence indicate this warehouse was the scene of more than one crime," Justin Spear, communications director for the Boston Police Department, told the *Globe*. "These crimes were not committed by a single individual."

Asked for the identities of the perpetrators, Spear said, "The property owner was identified and apprehended without incident. He in turn gave us the names of three other individuals. Two have been arrested, and we are currently seeking a third. We will not release their names at this time."

The *Globe* has uncovered evidence of an association with the

Archdiocese of Boston. While the Archdiocese is not the de facto owner of the warehouse, documents indicate financing was arranged two years ago by Cardinal Hamilton Odell as part of the church's Youth Refuge program. Furthermore, Cardinal Odell is named personally as a lienholder on the property, indicating a financial relationship.

The Archdiocese describes their financial involvement as little more than a legal technicality. "We have numerous programs focused on community revitalization," said a spokesperson. "Those programs can involve loans made to low-income individuals. The Archdiocese was not aware of any illegal activity."

Cardinal Odell's personal attorney, when reached for comment, said, "We're talking about a man who's spent eight years in Boston working to help its residents, and that includes helping to finance projects in neglected neighborhoods. To me, this is a case of no good deed goes unpunished. I suspect we'll find this is nothing more than another witch hunt by the city of Boston."

The property owner and other suspects are being held without bond. They are due to be arraigned Tuesday.

CHAPTER

17

I N THE END, it was a mistake that broke the code wide open.
Like the discovery of the heating properties of microwaves, or
of the cosmic microwave background radiation, Laura stumbled
onto the answer blindly.

It happened while she was sitting at a scarred table in the basement of the Orange County Library. The library's basement stacks
stretched the length of the building, floor-to-ceiling metal shelves
supporting the concentrated knowledge of history's scientists, art-
ists, and philosophers. No one in Hillsborough seemed particularly interested, though. She hadn't seen another human being for
at least two hours.

No one heard her groan and crumple up her papers after
the first hour. No one heard her slam a fist into the tabletop after the
second.

Windows admitted long bands of sunlight that contracted as
the time moved toward noon, until the fluorescent lights were her
only company, buzzing away as she rubbed the sore spot on her palm
and cursed herself. Could she really have been so wrong? Maybe
the best thing to do would be to revisit the entire project, reexam-
ine her assumptions. Somewhere in there was the answer.

She could feel it.

A five-minute break was in order. She walked up and down

the aisles, working out the stiffness from hunching over too long. Then she walked back to her table with fresh eyes. Papers covered the top, but two in particular stood at the center. First was the photograph of Teresa Mitchem's skin, stretched back to its normal size. The tattoo was clearly visible. The numbers, even tiny, were perfectly legible:

8	27	4	4	3	5
4	9	4	4	8	2
3	6	3	7	11	17
3	6	3	3	8	27
3	6	3	7	8	27
8	27	11	51	11	37

Thirty-six numbers in total, etched into the skin in a grid. Six rows of six numbers, six columns of six numbers. A perfect square. When it was a two-digit number, the Kid had taken care to mold it into its space in the grid. His work was nothing if not symmetrical.

In retrospect, something about her phone call from the man claiming to be the Kid stood out. He'd said he was following her. He'd meant it first as a journalist, that he was reading her stories. Then he'd made it personal. Once she'd known he was out there—watching, waiting—all references to news articles had blown out of her head as if hit by a hurricane.

This morning, during therapy, Jasmine's comment had forced a jagged shard into place. In the moment before fear had taken her over, Laura had assumed he was talking about her articles in the *Gazette*, the coverage of his own crimes.

But he had mentioned another article, a *Globe* article, and it seemed a strange one to bring up considering the conversation.

She picked up a printout of her story from three years ago, now marked up with her notes, and read it one more time. Why this specific article? The Kid had said it was because of her empathetic treatment of a monstrous man. Indeed, Hamilton Odell was a monster, and she'd remembered the article the moment the Kid mentioned it, but there wasn't anything particularly empathetic about the story, just straight-ahead reporting. It didn't make sense.

Then Jasmine's story about her childhood love shook something loose. Forced to communicate in secret, they had relied on the same copy of *Romeo and Juliet* to hide their messages. It was one of the most basic ways to conceal information.

A book code.

Book codes were about as simple as cipher could get: choose an agreed-upon text, say, a specific edition of the Bible, and then send your message by referencing the letters. Send a message like second page, fourth line, eighth letter, and it leads to *H*; fifth page, second line, tenth letter, you get *I*. Together they spell *HI*. Whole messages could be constructed in a similar fashion.

The thing that had grabbed Laura's attention was the numbers. Once a code was agreed upon, most book codes used a numerical abbreviation. *HI* would be rendered something like 2–4–8, 5–2–10, with not a letter to be seen. She ran a finger down the photograph of the tattoo. Could it really be that simple?

The book code had other advantages. Despite its simplicity, it was nearly impossible to crack. There were too many books in the world. Even for a computer, finding the right one would take hundreds of years.

But what if she already knew which book? What if it wasn't a book at all? What if it was a newspaper article?

First she arranged the numbers in order. The organization of the numbers into a grid meant they could be read up and down or side to side. For the sake of moving forward, she assumed they would be read in a normal left-to-right, top-to-bottom fashion. When she finished, she had a long string of them:

8 27 4 4 3 5 4 9 4 4 8 2 3 6 3 7 11 17 3 6 3 3 8 27 3 6 3 7
8 27 8 27 11 51 11 37

Next she tried to match them to the *Globe* story. The difficulty was that she didn't know exactly how they related to each other and to the article. If they were supposed to indicate, say, sentence, word, then letter, she should organize them into groups of three numbers each. She tried it and got utter gibberish, no matter how she sliced it. She thought maybe it was an anagram and tried reorganizing the letters but couldn't come up with anything.

She went back to the list of numbers and stared at it again. The highest number was fifty-one and the lowest was two, but the distribution was off. The lower numbers were favored by a huge margin. Assuming they indicated sentence and letter, wouldn't there be an easier way to do it?

Laura tried to recreate the same message, gibberish though it was, and found she could locate all the necessary letters much earlier in the article. There was no need to use, say, sentence eleven just to indicate a U and a T.

Just to make it more difficult, maybe?

No, the very creation of a code had a certain logic to it. Even if he was insane, clearly he had the acumen to put something like this together. She would have to assume the code was a product of some kind of logic; otherwise it would be impossible to make any progress at all.

Assuming this is a book code at all, and assuming this is the right text, she thought.

She decided to stick with her interpretation of the list of numbers as ordered pairs and organized them as such.

8–27, 4–4, 3–5, 4–9, 4–4, 8–2, 3–6, 3–7, 11–17, 3–6, 3–3, 8–27, 3–6, 3–7, 8–27, 8–27, 11–51 11–37

Right away she knew she was on to something. There were too many repeats for it to be a coincidence: 8–27 appeared four times, 3–6 appeared three times, while 3–7 and 4–4 both appeared twice.

She was looking at a pattern.

The second thing that jumped out at her was the distribution of the low numbers. If she looked just at the first number in any given pair, the highest they went was eleven. Counting sentences didn't work. What if the first number referenced paragraphs?

The article had only nine. She tried it anyway.

Gibberish again.

"Goddamn it." She rubbed her eyes and started again. This time she would try paragraphs and words. Carefully, she counted down to the eighth paragraph and then across to the twenty-seventh word, THREE.

Almost immediately, she realized her mistake. Her eyes were getting tired; all the parts of the page were starting to blend together. She had counted down from the very top of the page, including the headline, the byline, and the date. She'd ended up on what was really the fifth paragraph, the one that began with the word ASKED.

She sighed and began to start over, then stopped again. Something caught her eye.

It seemed unlikely he had started at the top. But say, just for a second, that he had. Then paragraph eight appeared twice, as 8–27 and 8–2. And 8–27 was the word THREE.

And 8–2?

It only took her a second to count it out. 8–2 led to the word FOR.

She stared at the words for a second, turning the paper back and forth.

THREE and FOR.

Her pulse began to quicken. Again, she didn't believe landing on two numbers, even if one was misspelled, could be a coincidence. Something else stood out: the most common first number was three, and that would indicate the line with the date, January 27, 2015. A quick scan confirmed her suspicions. The date provided two, seven, zero, one, and five, and in the text were the words THREE, FOR, SIX, EIGHT, and the number nine. With a little creative reading, this article made it possible to encode all ten digits.

She started working it out in order: 8–27 would be three, 4–4 would be six. For 3–5, she counted January and then each individual number as its own word: 3–5 was zero, 4–9 meant nine, 4–4 was six again, and 8–2 equaled four.

Cautiously, piece by piece, she put it together. It was all numbers again—numbers translated into numbers. Then she got to the last two pairs, paragraph eleven, words fifty-one and thirty-seven.

She gasped.

Her own handwriting stared back from the paper, dancing in

the light, mocking her, forming her own private message from a monster.

3609641581731533FINDME

FIND ME.

There was no doubt she had cracked the code. She read the two words again and again. Without punctuation, there was no inflection. The phrase seemed to lose all meaning.

FIND ME.

She couldn't tell if he was daring her or begging her.

FIND ME.

But how?

And then she sat back in her chair, wide-eyed. The last piece of the puzzle clicked into place. Find me implied a location, and those numbers . . .

She scribbled them out again.

36.096415, 81.731533.

Her blood ran cold. Coordinates. A location. It wasn't just a tattoo—it was an invitation.

An invitation printed on a young girl's skin.

Doubt gripped her. Could that really be the truth? The message didn't include north, south, east, or west, and she couldn't remember which ones would be near the United States, but it only took her a second to find a website that would match decimal coordinates to locations. She decided to try them all.

It quickly became apparent that the area around thirty-seven degrees south, ninety degrees west was located in the South Pacific, about eight hundred miles off the coast of Chile.

Thirty-seven degrees south, ninety degrees east landed her in the Indian Ocean, more than a thousand miles west of Australia.

Thirty-seven degrees north, ninety degrees east put her in the corner of the Xinjiang Province, northwest China.

The last one was much closer.

The website offered a more detailed map. She zoomed in, then found the latitude line and used her finger to trace a line across the map from left to right. She located the longitude line and slashed her other finger downward, then drew them together at the intersection.

Close-knit topographical curves nestled deep in a sea of green marked the Blue Ridge Mountains, part of the Pisgah National Forest. The spot was in North Carolina, only about a hundred and seventy miles west of Hillsborough, little more than a three-hour drive from the very spot she was standing.

FIND ME.

The words would echo in her dreams. She could feel it.

She tapped the location on the map once more. The message couldn't be clearer: X marks the spot.

18

THE DART'S FLAT blue paint had been sucking up the sun for hours. Even in the relative cool of eighty-something degrees, even with the windows down, the air inside had turned to soup and the cracked leather seats boiled.

None of it reached Laura, who sat in the driver's seat, minute after minute, doing nothing. The keys hung in one hand. She pressed her forehead to the steering wheel and let it burn into her flesh. Hoped it would knock something loose.

Her hands wouldn't stop shaking. Adrenaline, she told herself, and ignored them.

It was everything she wanted. A story that readers wouldn't turn away from, that editors couldn't afford to ignore. Yesterday it had held bushels of mystery and inherent drama, enough of both to make it a hit.

But today? With a message like that tattooed into a chunk of flesh?

It would be a sensation.

She pinched herself, tried to wake up. In her head, she was already writing the book. It would make a hell of a book, a best seller that would give back everything Boston had taken away. Her self-respect, her career, her escape from this godforsaken town— all of it had just been handed back to her on a silver platter.

All she had to do was reach out and take it.

She peeled her forehead off the steering wheel and looked at herself in the mirror, rubbed the angry red mark it had left on her skin, flinched at the sensation of touching her own flesh.

Perimortem.

Everything that had happened to Teresa Mitchem so far had happened while she was still alive. There was no reason to think that had changed. Charging up there with a camera, a notepad, and a pencil might make a great story, but it also might make that little girl dead.

An image crowded into her head. Teresa, ten years old and tied to a table somewhere in the Blue Ridge Mountains, tattooed hour by hour, the relentless buzzing of the gun as he carved into her. Hearing that sound every time he turned it on. The harbinger of pain, the horror of anticipation.

And then to have her skin flayed off? She couldn't imagine it, could not even wrap her head around it. The very thought of . . .

She snapped out of her reverie, crawled out of whatever dark hole she'd fallen into.

Realized she'd been punching the dash over and over.

The knuckles of her right hand were already swollen. Blood ran from an open cut. She reached out and touched the blood. Winced.

"Goddamn it," she said.

And just like that, she made her decision.

*   *   *

The engine turned over once, caught, then sputtered and died. She turned the key again and punched the gas a few times, careful not to flood it.

"Come on."

She turned the key again. A new sound came from the car, a creak of metal grinding. She ignored it and twisted the key harder.

"Come on!" she yelled, and pushed the gas pedal to the floor.

Metal shrieked against metal. The engine coughed one last time and thin black smoke began issuing from under the hood.

*   *   *

Running two blocks soaked her in sweat.

She had a message from the Kid, and a possible location for Teresa Mitchem known to no one else in the world. It seemed unfathomable. If anything happened to Laura, the poor girl would never be found. Desperation flooded through her. She carried a dangerously fragile secret. It needed to spread, to survive. It burned to get out.

Finally, at the corner of Wake and Margaret, she took a breath, pulled out her phone, and called Tim. The line rang four times before his voicemail clicked on. She hung up and dialed again.

"Motel," Elias Quant answered.

"Elias, it's Laura Chambers."

"Motel here," he said again. She could picture him flipping through one of his Dutch magazines, barely able to hear her over the phone.

"I need to get in touch with Agent Timinski. Please connect me with his room."

"Timinski," Quant repeated.

"Yes."

"Which one is he?"

Laura suppressed the urge to bang her phone against a brick wall. "Don't you have a register?"

"Oh, it's around here somewhere," he said in his precise, accented English.

She gritted her teeth. "He's about forty, bushy eyebrows, probably the only current guest who's a goddamned FBI agent. Is it coming back to you?"

"No need to for such language, Miss Chambers."

She said nothing.

"Yes, I do in fact remember him. Room four. I'll connect you now."

The phone rang and rang. Laura let it go on for three or four minutes, hoping Timinski was in the shower or otherwise occupied, that if she let it go on long enough eventually he'd pick it up.

He didn't.

She hung up, dialed again.

"Motel."

"Elias, he didn't answer."

"Now that you mention it, his car is gone. I suspect he may not be in right now."

"Goddamn it!"

"No need for such language, Miss Cha—"

She pressed END and then shoved the phone down into her pocket. The sheriff's station was only another two blocks away.

* * *

McKinney looked younger in person. He was at least fifty—she could remember him campaigning against Don Rodgers during an election back in the day—but up close the steel gray running through his hair served only to contrast against perfectly tanned skin, oily black eyes, and a jawline that would make Superman weep.

"Sheriff McKinney," she said.

He didn't bother to look up but gestured for her to take a seat and kept scratching away at the top of a stack of papers.

She waited, hands folded in her lap, and when two minutes had passed and he hadn't even so much as grunted in her direction, she tried again.

"Sheriff McKinney," she repeated.

"I'll be with you when I'm ready, Miss Chambers." He kept writing.

"Sir, it's quite urgent."

"You know what I'm working on here? No, of course you don't. Let's just say it's official police business. Official police business. You understand what that is? Of course you do. It's not scribbles on a piece of paper. No, here we deal with matters of life and death, Miss Chambers. Life and death. That means it's important."

"Sheriff, I'm sure it's important, but I'm here because—"

"Because the rules of civilized society apparently mean fuck all to you reporters. That's why you're here in my office during the hour I set aside specifically to catch up on this paperwork. You think I like doing paperwork?"

"I—"

"That was not an invitation to speak, Miss Chambers. And it's not like the question needed an answer. Of course I don't like doing paperwork. It's about as fun as licking a porcupine. But it keeps things moving, keeps the wheels turning. It has to be done, for the good of a civil society."

"Sir, please, you need to pay attention—"

He brought one ham-sized fist down onto the desk and rattled every gold trophy on the shelves behind him. "That was not an invitation to speak, Miss Chambers!" he roared at her. "You come into my office, wasting my valuable time. You constantly interrupt me. And now you're telling me how to do my job."

He ticked her offenses off on his fingers, one by one.

"We are not off to a good start, ma'am. No, we are not. That's what you damn reporters just can't seem to understand. Rules exist for a reason. There are no arbitrary rules. We may think them so, but I promise you, every rule ever created by the mind of man or God was in response to some problem, some defect in our very nature. I count myself among the defective, Miss Chambers, and that—that!—is the beginning."

He sat back in his chair and seemed to be waiting for her to speak.

She saw no choice but to indulge him. "The beginning of what?"

"Of understanding what we do here in this building."

"Maybe I could write a feature about you someday."

His nose wrinkled. "If I get my wish, this will be the very last time we ever speak."

"In that case, let's get down to brass tacks. I think I know where Teresa Mitchem is being kept."

McKinney's face went through a remarkable transformation. First his eyes widened in surprise, and his mouth hung open. He started to speak, stopped himself, and the lantern jaw swung shut like a bear trap. The eyes narrowed into thin oblong pools, and she could almost see the calculations running behind his eyes.

"Say that again."

She repeated herself.

McKinney took a breath. "Do you know, ma'am, that making a false police report is a crime in the state of North Carolina?"

"It doesn't matter because this isn't a false report. Listen to me.

Those numbers tattooed on the skin—I figured out what they mean."

He stood abruptly. "I don't know what you're talking about."

"Bullshit. I saw the official pictures."

"If you've seen any official pictures, as you claim, the very act of letting you see them would be illegal. As far as I'm concerned, you've just reported a crime."

She shook her head, dismissing him outright. "Not at all. I'm a journalist. This person was a source. No crime was committed."

"That is my determination to make."

"Well, I'm not giving you a name, so good luck with that."

He rested his huge palms flat on the desk and leaned forward until he towered over her. "I don't know how they do things in Boston"—he spit the last word like a curse—"but down here I tell you how things run. You want to make a First Amendment case about it? Fine. Just remember your place. In here, you and I might as well be all alone together."

His eyes drifted down across her body, then back up to her face. The corner of his mouth turned up into a cruel smile.

She shivered, then tried to put away her disgust.

"Look, I'm sorry if I'm stepping on your toes here, but this is something you need to hear. It's just like you said, a matter of life and death."

He didn't sit down, didn't even move, just kept staring at her. "Okay, tell me how you managed to understand this killer's message when everyone else is so baffled."

"Because he called me."

"And told you what it meant," McKinney said slowly.

"No, he mentioned an article I wrote years ago, and I thought it might be a book code, and I played around with it until I found a good match. The key . . ."

She trailed off. A deep, raspy sound had started somewhere deep in the man's chest. He began shaking. With a start, she realized he was holding in laughter.

Then he couldn't hold it in anymore. A throaty chuckle filled the office. "He called you? He spoke to you in code?" McKinney managed.

"Look, he gave you the code too. Is it really so difficult to believe?"

As quickly as it had started, the laughter stopped. McKinney's face turned back to stone. He sat down and started scratching at his reports again.

"Sheriff."

"I think we're done here," he said.

She couldn't believe it. It was like living a nightmare. To have the knowledge of what might be Teresa Mitchem's exact location, and to be rebuffed by the very man charged with finding her, was nothing less than surreal.

The girl who cried wolf, she thought. Except that she'd never in her life lied to this man. Embarrassed him, maybe, but never lied.

"Is your pride really so important you can't let me help you?" she asked.

He didn't bother looking up. "Help from a woman like you is worthless." He sighed, like he was letting her in on some foregone conclusion. "It'd just be a waste of my time."

"Where's Frank Stuart? I need to speak with him."

"I'm not here to pass messages between lovers. This isn't middle school."

"I need to see Deputy Stuart. Right now."

He glanced up. "Deputy Stuart, who we know is your source, is on suspension. Maybe permanently."

Despite all the promises she had made to herself—promises about all the things she would refuse to do again—she decided to tell him. She'd already thrown away her chance at the story. In for a penny, in for a pound.

"Frank Stuart is not my source," she said. "I'll swear to that on the record."

But Sheriff McKinney just shook his head. "He never should have trusted you."

19

S HE BANGED ON Frank's door. After what felt like an hour but was probably more like three minutes, the door swung open. She barged past him into the living room and started spreading papers out onto the coffee table.

"Laura," he said, his voice a harsh whisper.

She glanced up at him. "You look terrible."

It seemed like he'd lost ten pounds. There were dark hollows under his cheeks, black circles under his eyes. He wore a tank top that had been white once, now yellowed with overuse.

"Well, I feel like shit too," he said.

"What happened?"

"What the fuck do you think happened? They fired me, Laura. With prejudice. I'm done as a cop in Orange County. And what kind of recommendation do you think McKinney will give me?" He ran a hand down his face. "I'm done as a cop period."

"Maybe not in a big city," she said.

"That's your dream, not mine."

"Besides, I heard you're just suspended."

"Administrative bullshit. It takes time to get the paperwork through, but believe me, I'm fired."

She patted the couch cushion. "Sit with me a minute."

All the fight had gone out of him. He folded himself into the space next to her and she could smell his sickly sweet stench, warm booze mixed with body odor.

"I told him you're not the source."

"Who?"

"McKinney."

"You told him," he repeated slowly.

"Yes. I marched into his office, let him fire off a few salvos about my worth, or lack thereof, as a reporter, and about you being my source. And then I corrected him. I told him it wasn't you. I told him I'd go on the record if I had to."

His eyes widened. "And?"

She glanced away. "He didn't believe a word I said."

"But you'll go on the record. If you do that, I don't think he can fire me."

"Maybe so, maybe not. Look, Frank, I want to be straight with you. I didn't visit McKinney to go to bat for you. I went because I know where to find Teresa Mitchem."

He froze.

"Did you hear me?" she asked.

He picked up an open bottle of whiskey and took a swig. "I heard you."

She tried to pry it out of his hands, but he pushed her away and pulled on the bottle again.

"Frank, I need you sober."

"Is this what you told McKinney? That you know where the Mitchem girl is?" He grimaced as he swallowed. "No wonder he didn't take you seriously."

"I know you're hurting. I know what a job can mean to a person. Working the right job, the whole world just makes sense. Without it, everything seems pointless."

He glanced at her out of the corner of his eye, then drank again.

"But you didn't become a cop just to wear a badge and carry a gun, did you?"

"Hell, no."

"Then why?"

He said nothing.

She slipped a picture out of the folder in her hand and held it up for him to see. "This is why."

He stared at it. A girl's ear so small and perfectly formed it looked fake, like it was made of plastic. His face didn't react, but he nodded.

"So let's help her."

Frank considered her for a second, seemed to come to an internal decision, and set his jaw. He nodded again. Even a few days ago he would never have accepted such flimsy evidence, but getting fired had changed him. He was willing to listen, ready to take a risk.

What did he have to lose?

Step by step, she walked him through the process that had led to her conclusions. The phone call. Her therapist's mention of book codes. The critical inductive leap between the Kid's mention of that one specific article and the numbers delivered to the police. Through it all, Frank tried to stop her, tried to ask questions, but she steamrolled right over him. Once she started talking, she couldn't stop. The story poured out, fact after fact, a terrible crescendo of human misery leading inexorably to that green smudge on the map.

When she was finished, he examined the spot pinned down by her index finger, deep in the national forest, then glanced up.

"You're seeing a therapist?"

She gaped at him. "That . . . that's your first question? I'm not crazy, Frank."

He looked up at the ceiling, scratched the underside of his jaw, then looked back at her. "Was it something I did? That made you go?"

"Christ, maybe this was a mistake." She started shuffling the papers back into her bag.

"Laura, I'm not saying you're wrong."

"No?"

"No. You convinced me."

She said nothing.

"I mean it. I'm convinced."

"Okay." She sat back down, relief that someone had finally believed the story flooding through her. "Now what do we do about it?"

He glanced down at the bottle in his hand as though surprised it was there, then set it aside. "McKinney didn't believe you. You still talking to that FBI guy?"

"Who do you mean?"

He just shook his head. "Come on, Laura. I'm not that dumb. No one in the Sheriff's Office is stupid enough to have anything to do with you—me excluded, of course. Who else could have fed you material like that?"

He pointed at the few photos still strewn across the table.

Laura gave a single small nod. If she wanted his help, this was the price of admission.

"Timinski, right?"

Another nod. "He's out at Elias Quant's place. I tried him earlier, but no answer."

"So try him again," he said.

So she did, let his cell ring to voicemail, went through the whole routine with Quant again, but got no response. She called back and got the old man to agree to check the room himself. Ten minutes later her phone rang, and she snatched it up.

"I apologize, Miss Chambers," Quant said. "I knocked for quite some time, and against my better judgment I opened the door. No one in residence."

"Thanks," she said, and ended the call.

Frank rubbed his face in his hands again, checked his watch.

"It's just us," she muttered.

"What's that?"

"I said it's just us. We could sit here waiting for him to come back, but every second we do nothing, Teresa Mitchem will be another second closer to dying."

"If she's still alive," Frank said.

"Don't even say it. She was alive when he cut off her ear."

"Doesn't mean he kept her that way."

"Think about it like this: if she's dead, then we can be careful, take our time, think this thing through. But if she's alive, we have to move." Laura took a breath. "We'd have to do something. Wouldn't we?"

"If she was alive. There's no way to tell."

She stood. "Hope for the best, plan for the worst, right? But let's plan for the best. We need to assume she's alive and act accordingly, so that on the off chance that she is—"

"I can save her," Frank finished.

"We can save her."

He shook his head. "You're a reporter. There's no way I can take you up there with me."

She started shuffling the papers into her bag again. "It's a package deal. If you want to go up there, you're taking me with you."

"Give me the coordinates."

"I put in the work, I figured it out. I've thrown away what could have been the biggest story of my career on the off chance we can save that girl. *We* can save her. You're not leaving me behind."

"Laura."

He grabbed her hand, then started to pry the cell phone from between her fingers. She tried to stop him, tried to hold on to it as tightly as possible. They stood there like opposing sides before the start of a tug of war, just waiting for the whistle. Then he put a flat hand on her chest and pushed. She tumbled backward onto the couch. He stood above her, phone in hand, looking sheepish.

"I'm sorry," he said.

"Don't do this."

"It's for your own good."

"For my good? Listen to yourself—all you want to do is play the hero. If you really cared about that little girl, you'd take any help you could get."

"It's for your own good. You'll thank me later."

She turned away, her face on fire, burning to spit at him or to deliver some cutting remark that would throw his selfishness into perspective. Turning back, she opened her mouth.

But he was already gone. Down on the street, a truck's engine turned over and tires squealed against the road as he took off for the highway.

* * *

A gray wooden shack with a tin roof served as the Orange High photography lab. It was out near the football field. In some prior life it had probably been the equipment shed.

Laura had been interested in journalism even in high school. She knew where it was, only about a mile and a half from Frank Stuart's apartment. School wasn't in session, but she sprinted there anyway.

This was her last chance.

She knocked, and the door opened right away. Leon Botton, wearing the same black T-shirt and black jeans, pushed that long hair out of his eyes and raised his shoulders. He didn't speak, but the message was clear: *What gives?*

"You have a car, Leon?"

"Uh, sure, Miss Chambers."

"Is it that one?"

She pointed back toward the school parking lot, empty save a single vehicle: a beige Ford Taurus, more rust than car.

"Miss Chambers?"

"If I've told you once, I've told you a million times—call me Laura. Is it that one?"

"Uh, yes."

"Okay, that'll have to do. Get your camera, get the keys. We're leaving right now."

20

"THERE'S NO ONE around for miles. If something goes wrong, we're screwed. Are you sure we should do this?"

She looked at Leon and frowned. The last thing she needed was a reluctant partner. All her focus had to be on finding the girl. Coddling a frightened high schooler would be a nightmare, especially out in these remote woods.

But he wasn't wrong.

"Getting cold feet?" she asked.

That one simple question was enough to put a kink in his pride. He drew himself up, as much as was possible while crouched in a laurel thicket, and gave a tight-lipped shake of his head.

"We've come this far," he said.

He whispered it, even though the cabin was at least two hundred yards away.

* * *

We've come this far.

Distance traveled amounted to a hundred and eighty miles. Three hours on the highway, the last thirty minutes on roads progressively more bumpy and remote. Frank had taken her phone, and the coordinates along with them, but there had been nothing to stop her from working them out again.

First she made Leon drive her to the Chambers farm. Her

mother had been asleep in her room, napping the afternoon away. Laura tiptoed down to the basement and found the corner where her father's things were stored. On a high shelf, behind a box of his old ashtrays, she found what she was looking for and pulled it down.

The box was crafted of wood inlaid with gold trim. Inside, a velvet pad held the gun in its center.

She lifted it out.

A Browning Hi-Power.

Before he died, her father had taken her out into the fields a few times and let her plink cans. That's what he called it, anyway, and she had thought it would be like using a BB gun. The first time she pulled the trigger, the gun had jumped back so hard it hit her in the face, splitting open her bottom lip. The sound cracked like a mile-long whip, so loud she couldn't hear afterward. Her father had pressed his grimy shirt cuff against the cut and let the blood thicken, then picked the gun up off the ground and pressed it back into her hands.

Once she could hit her target more than fifty percent of the time, he'd said, "Now you're ready for the shotgun."

And she had learned to shoot that too, to brace herself and prepare for its incredible roar.

She ran her finger down the side of the grip and remembered him doing the same thing while describing the invisible mechanics hidden inside. He'd told her all about it: how it was a knockoff of the Colt 1911 his own father had carried in World War II, how it was a decent copy but still inferior to its inspiration, how a cheap knockoff was all he could afford.

She lifted the heavy velvet lining out and found .40 caliber shells rattling around the box's bottom. One by one, she fed them into the magazine, and when it was loaded, she stuck the gun under her shirt. If her mother was awake upstairs, she didn't want to have to explain anything.

But her mother wasn't awake. Laura had pulled on hiking boots and slipped out the door, into the waiting car. In no time at all, they were gone.

* * *

The Browning hung like a lead weight in her pocket. She tried not to let it bang on the nearby tree as she shifted her weight.

Below them was a large natural bowl carved into the Blue Ridge Mountains. It was too small and shallow to be called a valley, too round to be a canyon. It was almost perfectly circular, with steep walls rising about a hundred feet above the floor and a flat bottom covered in widely spaced pines.

In the center, located directly on top of the message's coordinates, stood a cabin. It looked to be one or two rooms, built of rough unfinished planks and cross-hatched logs. Barely visible behind it was the top of a small outbuilding. A rutted dirt track led in down the shallow side of the bowl, but there were no cars in sight.

"Where's Deputy Stuart? You said he'd be here," Leon said.

"He left thirty minutes before us. Maybe he got lost."

Leon shrugged.

It wasn't impossible. They had never managed to find a spot where the dirt track leading to the cabin connected to any larger road. After driving back and forth a few times, they had simply pulled over and started through the woods on foot, heading toward the coordinates. Eventually they'd hit the edge of the bowl.

"Maybe he's not coming," Leon said.

"I don't think he'd give up that easily."

Leon shrugged again. "You know him a lot better than I do. What about the light, though?"

She looked behind them at the sky. They'd left at about three thirty, and now it was almost half past seven. The sun hovered dangerously close to the horizon.

Leon followed the direction of her gaze. "Could be he realizes how close we are to sunset. Maybe he turned back."

"Maybe," Laura said, and remembered another trick from her time outdoors with her father. She held up her right hand, index and middle fingers extended and pressed together, pointing to her left. It looked like she was making a gun and turning it sideways. Held up to the sky, the arc length of two fingers was about equal to the distance the sun would travel in thirty minutes. She made another gun with her left hand and, starting at the sun, walked her fingers down to the horizon. She counted two thirty-minute spans, plus a little extra. An hour and fifteen minutes.

Down in the bottom of the bowl, though, sunset would come earlier.

"It may only be light down there for another thirty minutes or so."

Opposite them, on the east side, fog started flowing over the rim and pouring down into the bottom. It crept across the floor of the bowl, snaking between the trees, filling it up with a thin mist. The setting sun infused the murk with a faint orange glow, the air smoldering from within.

Beside her, Leon shivered. "You ever see anything like that?"

"Fog in the mountains? Sure."

"No, like that. Fucking orange mist. It looks like goddamn Halloween down there."

It was the first time she'd ever heard him swear, but it sure as hell didn't seem like the right time to dish out a lesson in manners.

"No, I guess not," she conceded.

"And this is where you think a fucking serial killer is hiding?"

"Cold feet?" she asked again, and tried for a grin. As far as coercion went, it sounded weak even to her.

Leon gritted his teeth. "You know what? Yeah, I think my feet are feeling a little frosty."

"We've come this far. We can't turn back now."

"Speak for yourself," he said, and started zipping up his camera bag.

"Leon."

He started buckling straps, getting ready to move.

"Leon, look at me." She reached out and put a hand on his arm.

He froze, and even in the fading light she could see the fine hairs on the back of his arm stand up.

He looked at her.

"Leon, do it for me," she said. "Look, I'm not saying we go down there, okay? Let's just watch and see what we can see. It's probably just a cabin anyway."

He wavered, then shrugged again. "Fine, but there is no way I'm going down that hill."

"Thank you." She took her hand off his arm and went back to watching the cabin. "But at least get some shots while we're up here."

He unzipped his bag and assembled his camera, the same 35mm with attached zoom lens he'd had with him on the ridge near Hillsborough, and started snapping pictures.

"Any good?" she asked after a while.

"Okay, I think. Usually the sunset makes for great light, but with that mist filtering through everything I'm not sure."

"Just do your best."

They waited another ten minutes before the headlights appeared.

*   *   *

Laura noticed them first as a faint glow. There hadn't been time to find a pair of binoculars, so she had a much wider field of view than Leon, who had his eye glued to the viewfinder.

"Hey." She nudged him in the ribs. "Over there."

They both tried to crouch a little lower.

The headlights bounced over the edge of the bowl and down the track, cutting veins through the mist, and stopped fifty yards shy of the cabin.

"Give me that," Laura said, and picked up the camera. She used it as a makeshift telescope trained down toward the lights. "I want to see this car."

But it wasn't a car.

It was a truck.

"Shit," she muttered.

Leon couldn't take the suspense of not knowing. Questions poured out of him rapid-fire.

"Who is it? Is it him? Is it the Kid? What does he look like?"

"It's Frank," she hissed.

He matched her volume and started whispering again. "Deputy Stuart?"

Through the viewfinder, she saw him open his door, then quickly reach up and turn off his dome light. He climbed out and moved around to the hood, leaving the driver's-side door open behind him.

He had pulled an open flannel shirt over his tank top. In his hand she could see something black and boxy.

His gun.

"He's armed," she whispered.

As she said it, he gripped the gun in both hands, pointed it at the ground, and started jogging toward the cabin. He moved lightly from tree to tree, getting closer by the second. At the last tree he broke into a sprint, ran right at the house, and slid to a stop with his back against the planks, his chest heaving up and down.

"What do we do?" Leon asked.

"Nothing," Laura said. She couldn't think of a way to get down off the edge of the bowl. Leon had refused to move, and Frank had no idea she was up here. If she tromped down the side after him, he might well turn and shoot before they could even exchange a word.

She dropped her eye to the camera again.

It was almost like watching a movie. Below them, the tiny version of Frank went into a crouch and crab-walked along the base of the wall. At the window he stopped, raised his head, peered inside. It must not have been interesting because he dropped down and kept moving. In another second he disappeared around the corner.

"I can't see him," she said.

"What do you mean?"

"He's behind the cabin."

They waited. The seconds ticked past.

"Is he still back there?"

"Yes," Laura breathed.

"It's been too long. Maybe we should do something."

"You're not going down there."

"I thought you wanted to go down there," he muttered.

"That was before Frank was running around with a gun."

"We could try to call him." Leon pulled out his phone and unlocked the screen, then shook his head. "No service up here."

Down below, Frank emerged around the far corner and worked his way around to the front. At the cabin door, he reached up and jiggled the knob.

"He's back."

The door swung open.

"It's unlocked," she whispered.

"Let me see."

"Just hold on."

Frank flexed his legs and came to standing, leaned over to peer into the door, then moved inside with the gun extended in front of him.

The darkness inside swallowed him up.

"He's inside."

They waited.

"Oh, god," Leon said.

"He'll be fine."

He grabbed her by the arm.

"What?" she hissed.

"Over there," he said, and the tremble in his voice made her pay attention. She tore her eye off the viewfinder and followed his finger to a spot a hundred feet left of the house.

Nothing there.

"What?" she hissed again.

"Something moved."

"Where?"

"*Right there.*"

She panned the zoom lens left and peered through. Nothing but leaves and pine needles and logs. A perfectly ordinary forest floor.

"You're seeing things. There's nothing—"

Something moved.

As she watched, a section of leaves slid downward, funneling into some kind of hole. The forest floor moved like quicksand, opening like a mouth, the ground itself sinking until it disappeared.

And then it rose out of the hole.

A figure in black, hooded, slim and tall and quick. He appeared from beneath the ground like a devil and bolted toward the cabin. Something strange about his gait. It looked like he was gliding.

"Oh god, oh god, oh god."

Laura wondered who was talking. Realized it was herself.

"What do we do?" Leon said.

Without thinking, she cupped her hands around her mouth and shouted.

"Frank!"

The figure in black snapped its head around, looked right at them, and Laura felt her blood turn to ice.

"Oh Jesus, he sees us," Leon grunted, and buried his face in the ground.

"Frank!" she yelled again.

No movement inside.

The figure turned away from them, charged forward again, faster now, flying toward the cabin.

"Frank!" she screamed.

And then the figure disappeared inside. For a second, nothing happened.

Laura clenched her fists, squeezed her eyes open and shut, tried not to panic.

Then that familiar sound, much sharper at a distance—*CRACK CRACK CRACK*—three gunshots fired in quick succession.

She didn't think, didn't even react. Fear, the same fear she'd struggled all her life to keep locked in a box deep inside her chest, suddenly didn't seem to matter. It crumpled off of her like a tissue paper dress caught in a driving rain.

*   *   *

Laura burst out of the brush at full speed, over the lip—the decision somehow made even though she couldn't remember making it—and then she was flying down the slope, arms pumping, the Browning like a five-pound dumbbell swinging back and forth with dangerous intensity, rocks and logs appearing and then passing under her like water, and then the flat bottom of the bowl rose up to meet her and the surprising flatness, the sudden loss of gravity's assistance, made it feel like running through molasses, and she pumped her arms harder, the lethal weight in her hand making her bicep burn, the cabin growing until she could almost reach out and touch it, and everything else, every fear and whim and care, dropped away until the only sensations left to her were the mist sliding past her skin like oil and the steady burn of cool mountain air on the inside of her lungs.

CRACK.

The sound blistered her eardrums from several directions at once and she realized it was an echo, the curvature of the bowl bouncing reports at her from several directions. The door was close now.

CRACK.

Old wood splintered a hole into the door and something reached out and bit her on the hip. She slid to a stop, raised the Browning into the A-frame stance her father had beat into her, fired twice quickly, the big .40 caliber slugs tearing apple-sized holes in the door, and then she turned sideways and threw herself down behind a pine tree.

The world went very quiet.

And then it started to buzz. She tweaked one ear, trying to fix it, but the gunshots had temporarily ruined her hearing. She became uncomfortably aware that someone could have walked out the cabin door—could be standing behind her right now—and she would never hear a thing.

She twisted at the waist, forced herself to look.

No one there.

She waited like that, tugging an earlobe every few seconds, giving them the time to heal themselves. And they did. Second by second, sound returned. After two minutes she could hear the birds chirping in the trees, undisturbed by the evening's violence.

"He—"

The cry choked off before it had even begun. *Hey? Help?* Either way, she was sure it came from somewhere in front of her.

She came around the side of the tree and jogged the last twenty feet to the cabin's front door, then looked through one of the bullet holes. It was dark inside, the light of the sun nearly gone, but she could make out the major details.

The inside appeared to be split into two small rooms, with the door opening into the hallway that ran front-to-back between them. No sign of Frank. No sign of the hooded figure.

She pushed the door open with the muzzle of the Browning,

slid in between the door and the frame, then ducked into the room on the left. She walked a few feet farther in, surveying the space.

Without warning, the room's door slammed shut behind her, followed by the rapid scrape of wood on wood.

She raised the Browning, pulled the trigger.

And it jammed.

A tired spring in the magazine, maybe, or her own sweat and dirt clogging the mechanism. Or maybe it was the years of disuse. Maybe it was a miracle it had fired at all.

Tears were streaming down her face even though she couldn't remember starting to cry. She was only vaguely aware of them falling onto her hands as she tried to work the gun's action, and when that failed, to pry the breech open with her fingernails. One nail ripped, then another. In a moment of pure frustration, she whipped the five-pound chunk of metal against the door, a final *fuck you* to whoever was out there.

To her surprise, it took out a chunk of wood.

She ran a finger across the hole and felt the damp deep inside. Rotten to the core. The room was empty save a bed frame without a mattress and hanging from one wall some rusted farm implements. She chose a short-handled pickaxe and reached for it, then winced at the pain in her side.

Blood seeped from a wound just above her left hip. She pressed on it, winced again, and tried to forget it was there. The pickaxe came away from the wall and she swung the blunt end against the door, then again, and again. Lumps of wet pine showered her face and chest, her arms shrieked in protest, but she kept up the blows, punching the metal wedge through the barrier with all the strength she could muster. The door groaned once more before giving way.

She was out.

A scream from somewhere at the end of the hall—no, it was too far away. From behind the house. A back door? She reached the end of the hall, her hands searching, finding the knob. She ripped the door open and hurtled out.

A blinding flash rose to greet her followed by a familiar roar, splinters exploded through the air, and she found herself down in the leaves.

Unable to hear.

Unable to see.

* * *

Waking up was like clawing her way out of a hole, and it felt like it took hours. No, it couldn't have taken that long. When she opened her eyes, the smell of gunpowder still hung in the air.

She opened her eyes.

"Frank," she said, and sat up.

All over her body, a million tiny cuts. She ran a hand down one arm and felt miniature toothpicks sticking out of her, hundreds of them. She pulled one out and blood flowed.

"Frank," she said again, and stood.

He wasn't difficult to find. Less than thirty feet away he leaned against a tree, a smile open across his abdomen, eyes dead, the glass doll's eyes of something no longer animate.

"Frank."

She walked to him, every step like torture, wetness flowing down her skin, soaking into her clothes.

Then she saw the mask, a black hood with crude eye holes cut into it. Frank was clutching it in one hand.

He was close.

She took another step.

Stopped.

At her feet lay the remains of the hooded figure. He was just beside the tree, spread-eagle in the grass, shotgun by his side. Even now one hand held to it tightly. One finger still slipped through the trigger guard.

His feet were bare.

And his face was missing. It had been totally and completely annihilated.

She walked between them, turned back, and stared down at the grass, frozen. Stood like that until the pain forced her to her knees. She took Frank's hand and held it, squeezed it, and waited for him to squeeze back.

She waited like that for a long time, room at last inside her to be afraid, nothing left to fill it with but grief.

PART II

NEVER A TRACE OF RED

21

THE DART WAS mostly fixed. She'd killed more than a few
days working on it herself, using the barn as a makeshift
garage, and it was running better than ever. The radio still shorted
out from time to time, and the ignition was sticking again in the
cold weather. The heater didn't work for shit.

So she shivered a little and pulled her coat tight as she braked,
the whistling wind dying down to a hum. The radio had gone out
a few minutes prior, and it crackled back to life as she bounced off
the highway and onto the dirt track the Chambers family called a
driveway.

"—front continues moving in from the northwest. It's a chilly
one and temperatures are going to stay cold the next few days.
Next Monday is Christmas and things may warm up before then.
The real anticipation is centered on the warmer, wetter air moving
in from the southwest. If nothing changes, we may see several
inches of snow this weekend. Other possible—"

Laura clicked off the radio and collected the shopping bags
out of the back seat. She pushed the door open with her hip and
used her foot to shove it closed behind her. She glanced down at
the entryway table at the stack of mail, and that's when she saw the
picture.

She recognized it right away. The picture had run in many
papers, but this version was quite large. Laura was nearly certain

this one had been cut out of the *News & Observer* from July 12, two days after the cabin, when they'd run it on the front page. It had been folded in half once to fit in the plain white envelope still underneath it. The envelope had her name and address printed in neat block letters, and the postmark was from Charlotte.

There was no return address.

She shifted the bags to one arm and snagged the picture between two fingers before pushing through into the kitchen and settling the shopping on the counter. Her mother was in the living room, reclined in her Barcalounger, her stories blaring on the television.

"Mama, this came in the mail?"

Diane grunted.

"It's been opened."

She turned slightly in the chair. "It's my house, isn't it?"

Laura bit her lip, then asked, "Was there anything else in the envelope?"

"I didn't see anything." She shouted it over the hospital scene playing out on *Days of Our Lives.*

"Maybe you could turn it down a bit."

Her mother twisted her bulk, the chair squealing in protest. "Don't you take that tone with me, missy. And wipe that look off your face, like you just been slapped. If seeing that picture again upsets you so, tell your friend not to send clippings."

"It's not from my friend," Laura said.

"Oh no? Who else would it be?"

"Not someone who likes me."

Diane huffed. "Who could? After all that?"

Laura saw her mother with rare clarity in that moment. "You're supposed to," she said. "You're my mother."

"I love you, dear, but I don't have to like you."

"What should I have done? Left that girl to die?"

Diane wrung her hands, looking very much like a bit player on her soap opera. "Oh, Laura, she was already dead."

"We don't know that."

"And Frank died because of your so-called help. That's two dead instead of one. Seems to me the math is real clear."

She turned back to the TV, and Laura let herself back out onto the porch, hands shaking.

The picture's edge sliced into the vulnerable flesh between her forefinger and thumb and she jumped as though bitten. She peeled her eyes away from the opening cut and looked up, out over the large and empty fields. They extended away from the house in every direction. Besides a small stand of river birch shading the area between the house and barn, there wasn't a single tree within three hundred yards of this spot. The fields extended two miles behind her until they ran into another farm of similar size, and the driveway extended almost a mile before connecting with the highway.

One grimy plastic chair lived at the end of the porch. She sat and held up her hand to the light. A red globule of blood hung from fleshy skin, perfectly round, unmoving. Certain people had a total inability to stand the sight of blood, but Laura had acquired a different aversion: the taste. For almost six months she had assiduously avoided even the aroma of blood. She'd spent six months hiding from the crackling fat of rare steaks, six months dodging anyone with a bloody nose, six months flossing regularly and gently, careful of her gums. Anything to avoid tasting it again.

She considered going inside for a bandage, but in that moment she couldn't stand the thought of showing her belly even in such an insignificant way. Disgust at her own weakness welled in the back of her throat. All this time people had been looking at her like she'd collapse at the first sign of difficulty, and even when she was alone a sense of self-doubt and a lingering fragility gnawed at her insides. She'd catch glimpses of her face in the mirror and shudder at the frailty she saw written in her expression. Because she wasn't delicate, not deep down inside. She wasn't a breakable thing, not before and not now, but nothing she'd done in the last six months had proved otherwise to the people around her, or to herself.

Right then, right there on her front porch, she started to get angry.

She studied her hand, and then, before she could talk herself out of it, pressed the drop to her mouth and sucked the cut dry. Her throat started to close up, but she forced herself to breathe through her nose, and then to swallow.

The taste was just as she remembered it—the same as behind the cabin, when it hung so thick in the air she thought she would choke. Wrapping up all the loose ends had happened faster than she ever would have expected. The mysterious, multicolored twine used to bind the victims was tucked away in the other room of the cabin, a large spool of it, apparently handmade. Olive Hanson and the three girls from 1988 had been bound up in identical sky blues and summer greens. There was no question in anyone's mind that the physical evidence was a match.

And they had been able to identify the Kid. His face had been blown off, but his fingerprints were perfectly intact and a match to an old military service record.

Leon Botton was the one who'd sold the picture to the Raleigh *News & Observer*, and it dominated the front page. Over the past six months it had been reprinted in magazines and other major dailies more times than she could count. Laura had never gotten the chance to write the article underneath it. After the cabin, she'd spent twenty-four hours in the hospital with a police guard on her room, and once her fingernails and the cut on her hip had been patched, another eight hours in an interview room before they'd allowed her to leave. News traveled fast, so by then it was already too late. Smythe ended up writing the story, packing it with twists and turns and all the navel-gazing speculation about the nature of the human condition that played so well with the general public. It was his name below all the headlines, so when they called, the job offer was for him. They, in this case, turned out to be the *LA Times*. Two months after it all blew up, Smythe was on a plane headed for California.

Frank Stuart's funeral had been exactly one week after that Monday in the mountains. The whole town turned out. Laura had stood at the very back in dark glasses, trying for anonymity and failing miserably. The energy in the cemetery soured the second she entered. Backs went stiff. The crowd went silent.

Not a single person looked at her; everyone saw her.

Leaving would be a tacit admission of guilt, and she refused to cry in front of the bastards. So she stayed put until the box was in the ground, never letting out so much as a sniffle. Already she could imagine them gathering after he was buried, drinking and trading stories. Eventually the gossip would turn in her direction.

That Chambers is an ice-cold bitch. Got him killed and didn't even shed a tear.

It didn't matter. She wouldn't give them the satisfaction.

Sometime during the minister's remarks, the bandage on her hip soaked through and blood started running down her leg. She kept her hand pressed on the wound and thanked God she was wearing black.

On the porch, cold wind sliced and hummed between the plastic rails of her chair. She pulled the cut out of her mouth and examined it. Her eyes dropped into her lap and found the picture again. She couldn't escape it. It was like a curse. For perhaps the thousandth time, she studied it.

This time it was the composition that struck her most, the way things were organized into a perfect triangle. She occupied the top of the space, Frank was in the middle right, and a pair of legs ending in black boots were perfectly visible sticking into the frame at about middle left. The angle was from down low, the dry leaves and pine needles shrinking back into the shot, providing the needed perspective. It made the viewer feel detached, but also godlike, omniscient. Privy to everything, a fly on the wall, the connoisseur of a voyeuristic dream, but powerless to affect any of the players. The figures in the picture looked close enough to touch, but somehow distant too. Beyond saving.

Leon, Laura later learned, had found his courage up at the top of the bowl. It had taken him a bit longer, but in a way, that only increased her respect. Her reaction had been instinct, nothing more. She hadn't bothered to dwell on her own mortality before climbing over the edge.

Leon had done that and more. He had followed her through the woods and into the cabin armed only with his camera. Despite gunfire, he had gone out the back door, taken a knee, and clicked the shutter.

It was the only picture he took.

She tore herself away from the figures, but her eyes danced

back again. Was this the purpose of sending the pictures? So that she could never look away?

Frank appeared almost dignified. His face cast down, his arms in his lap, like he'd just discovered the damage to his abdomen. On the other side were the remains of the Kid. Laura hovered above them both, motionless.

She was the undeniable center of the image, the source of its inherent drama. Feet shoulder-width apart, shoulders back, head erect, back straight, the picture of perfect posture. Blood streamed off the tips of her fingers—they told her later at the hospital that she'd torn off four of her fingernails—and smeared her cheeks with gruesome blush. Clothes clotted and black at her hip. Hair matted, throat stained a darkening crimson.

Even now Laura couldn't remember exactly what she had been thinking and feeling. Her head was angled down, the eyes cast up under her brow. She looked directly into the camera, pinning the viewer to a wall, her gaze an unearthly mix of solemnity and rage. Behind her, the last rays of sunset shot through the mist, imbuing it with that preternatural orange glow. She seemed a creature, more mythological than human. The vampire queen. The darkling angel. The avatar of death.

It was a one-in-a-million shot, so perfect it looked staged. Only police reports convinced the world of its veracity.

To Laura, the purpose of sending it seemed perfectly clear. The picture was a message, one she was receiving loud and clear. It said: *I haven't forgotten about you.*

She let herself stare at it for another second, then tore it into little pieces and carried them to the garbage can. It was twenty yards away leaned against the side of a shed. She jogged to it, the horizon looming large in the distance, pressing in on her from all three hundred and sixty degrees. That feeling of being watched had returned. A prickly sensation burned on the back of her neck and some ancient reptilian part of her brain roiled with alarm.

She took a deep breath, tried to shake the feeling, told herself it was nothing.

She went back into the house and locked the door behind her.

22

"T HAT'S GOOD, LAURA. Keep going, please."

"There's nothing else to say."

"That's all? The story just ends?"

"It happened quick. Have you ever been in a situation like that? Where time slows down?"

Jasmine DeVane took a minute to consider. "Well, I've been in a few car accidents. I know the feeling you mean, where everything seems to happen in slow motion."

"Exactly."

"But we're not in slow motion now. We're taking it beat by beat. After you found Frank along with—"

"Don't say his name."

"After you found Frank with—"

"I asked you not to say his name." Laura pushed herself up and went to the table by the window. "Please."

"I know it's difficult to talk about."

Laura lifted a glass set out next to a decanter of water. "This clean?"

Jasmine nodded.

She poured herself water, drank it down, poured again, and returned to her seat. "I'm sorry, I should have offered you some."

"You're the patient, I'm the therapist. You're not supposed to get me things. You don't have to feel bad when you don't."

"I don't. Feel bad, that is. It's just a question of manners."

"So, you're behind the cabin."

"Like, for example, basic manners would be that if a patient says she doesn't want to talk about something, maybe you would just let it go."

Jasmine tapped her pen against one tooth. "I see your point."

"You do?"

"Absolutely. I mean, that's life's endeavor in a way, the avoidance of pain. Why hurt when you don't have to?"

"Preach it, sister."

"But there are flaws in that point of view. You're missing some of the nuance of human psychology."

"Educate me, oh wise one."

Jasmine grinned. This teacher–student shtick had been going on between them for a while, but it still made both of them smile. In truth, Laura was fascinated by Jasmine's job and by the entire field of psychology. Only when the conversation shifted to Laura's personal neuroses did things turn icy between them.

Jasmine said, "You joke, but I'm serious. We're talking about instant gratification here, something to which all people—and monkeys and other animals—are prone. You don't talk about this bad thing that happened to you, so you avoid the pain of reliving it. That's good, right?"

"Feels pretty good."

Jasmine shook her head. "Not right at all. You're just passing the buck, handing it to the future version of yourself. It's a lot like procrastination. Every day you put it off until tomorrow. And it never gets done. You never get better. If we can't even mention—"

"Don't say his name," Laura said again. "I just don't like hearing it."

"Okay," Jasmine conceded. "Okay."

"So can we talk about something else?"

"Absolutely not."

"Are you sure? My mother's been a real bitch these past few days."

Jasmine grinned again. "Maybe in a bit."

Laura crossed her arms on her chest. "I just don't understand what talking will accomplish. It won't change anything."

"The therapeutic benefits of talking are myriad."

"There's no point blabbing about it."

Jasmine made a circle with her hand, a gesture inclusive of the couch and the chairs and the bookshelves and the heavy drapes. "There's no point in talking about it? All we do in here is talk about things. I mean, that's a pretty fair definition of therapy, isn't it? Coming to a place to talk about your problems?"

Laura said nothing.

"What's worse," Jasmine continued, "is that you believe in therapy, Laura. I'm not your first therapist, and you were seeing me a long time before—"

She caught herself, didn't say the name.

Laura uncrossed her arms. "Meaning what?"

"Meaning you're rationalizing. You're taking issue with the whole therapeutic process, but really it's a lot simpler than that. You went through a traumatic experience, and now you want to avoid talking about it."

"You'd understand if you'd been there."

Jasmine sighed. "How are you sleeping?"

"Fine," Laura said, and knew the doctor could tell she was lying. The bags under her eyes were impossible to hide.

"A lack of sleep can only exacerbate your other symptoms. How's the paranoia?"

"It's not paranoia."

"Are you still getting the feeling that someone is watching you?"

"It's not just a feeling, Jasmine. You know what I got today? Another one of those damn pictures in the mail. Went out to the grocery store, where no one can look me in the eye, by the way, and came back to that shit."

"Do you think they're related?"

Laura's brow wrinkled. "What and what?"

"The fact that you think no one looks you in the eye at the grocery store, and the picture."

Laura heard a slight inflection on the word *think*. You *think* no one looks you in the eye.

"No one looks me in the eye," she repeated. "I'm not being paranoid."

"We can talk about that too. But I'm saying, let's take it at face value, okay? People in this town are eager to gossip and slow to forget. I get that. So maybe it's all part of the same thing."

"You mean someone is sending the picture again and again as some sort of punishment."

Jasmine shook her head. "That's not the word I'd choose. Punishment is deserved. This is harassment. Intimidation."

"And you think someone in town is doing that to me?"

"It's possible. I also think it's possible that if we could talk to the person doing it, they would describe it as a prank or a joke. Though that's just another creeping rationalization."

Laura turned and looked out the window. "Maybe," she said finally.

"Can I ask you something else?"

"It's therapy, Doc, you don't have to ask me if you can ask me questions."

"Well, let me preface this one. I'm not making a suggestion, or encouraging you. In fact, it would make me sad to see you go. But I'm wondering, why are you still here?"

"I thought we were friends."

Jasmine nodded. "We are. But as your friend, I want what's best for you. And I know you're not blind to all the adversity you face around here. People didn't take Frank Stuart's death very well."

Laura snorted. "That's an understatement."

"You have to understand, in these kinds of situations, people look for someone to blame."

"He went up there on his own."

"I know—you've told me that part of the story a hundred times."

"I didn't make him go."

"Of course not. You can't make anyone do anything. We're responsible for our own decisions."

"And I wouldn't change a thing," Laura said. "If I could go

back, there isn't a single decision I would change. I did the right thing—I tried to contact the police, but no one believed me. Was I supposed to do nothing? Was I supposed to sit by and let that little girl die? She could have been alive in that cabin. She could have been alive and screaming, waiting for someone to help her." The words poured out of her. She couldn't stop them. "She might still be alive. Somewhere."

Jasmine reached out and put a hand on her patient's arm. "You need to cling to that—the fact you wouldn't change a thing. You need to remind yourself of it every day. You didn't make a mistake; Frank Stuart did. Take solace in the belief you made the right choices."

"It doesn't feel like I made the right choices," Laura said.

"Our choices aren't everything. Sometimes things in the world just . . . happen."

"Doesn't feel like anyone else thinks I made the right choices either."

"That's different," Jasmine said. "That's about casting blame. And I know this isn't fair, but they cannot—will not—put the blame on Frank Stuart. No one wants to think ill of the dead."

"So it has to be me."

Jasmine shrugged. "Who else?"

And she was right. It was just that simple: who else? Who had set everything in motion? Besides a high schooler armed only with a camera, who else had walked out of those mountains alive?

"So that's what I mean when I ask why you're still here," Jasmine said. "I don't think you did anything wrong, but most people around here will never agree. Life will be difficult for you. You left once before. Why not again?"

Laura craned her head back to look at the ceiling.

"Laura?"

"I don't know."

"Your mother?"

"So now's a good time to talk about Diane."

Jasmine threw up her hands. "I get it, you don't want to talk about this. But you must. Can we go back to the cabin?"

Laura squeezed her eyes shut, shook her head.

"Does that help?"

"What?"

"Closing your eyes."

"You know it doesn't help. Not at all."

"No," she said. "If closing your eyes helped, you'd be able to sleep."

Laura opened her eyes. "I don't want to talk about the cabin."

"We've been over the story again and again. No one believes you, so you drive up there. The bowl in the woods. Going into the cabin. Opening the back door."

"Yes."

"And then you stop. The story just ends."

"That's what stories do—they end."

"That's not an ending, Laura. Me, and about half the world it seems, read this story in every paper for a month. You find the bodies out back, and then you go back inside."

Laura said nothing.

"To look for Teresa Mitchem."

Laura pulled her knees up to her chest, squeezed them too. Maybe if she squeezed long enough, and hard enough, she'd curl up into a tiny ball and just disappear.

"But you didn't find her," Jasmine finished. "Did you?"

Some hot part of Laura's brain went cold. It had been happening more and more lately, like flipping a safety switch. The horror and fear and anger and shame would swell in her chest and just when there should have been a climax, an explosion, her insides would turn to ice. She felt like a robot, but that didn't bother her. Anything to be free of herself.

When she spoke again, her voice sounded distant and flat.

"I don't want to talk about this anymore, Dr. DeVane."

Jasmine seemed to sense the change in her.

"I know you don't, Laura. I know."

And just as quickly, the rage burned bright again. It had lingered inside her, nourished by the ember of her guilt until it could catch fire once more.

"You know? *You know?*" she yelled.

The nearest small object was her water glass. She hurled it against the brick wall and watched the shards rain down.

Jasmine DeVane was quiet. She was wise enough to let silence do the talking.

"I'm sorry," she said.

"I know."

"I'm really sorry. I just—"

"I know," Jasmine said again.

"I need to go. Can we stop for today?"

"Of course. You're the best gauge of your own mood. If you think it would be better to take a break and continue next time, then that's what we should do."

"Okay," Laura said, and stood. She gathered her bag and her jacket and put a hand on the door handle. Behind her, she heard Jasmine DeVane stand.

"Laura?"

"Tomorrow, okay?"

"Laura, I want you to say his name for me."

"I've got to go."

"Say his name and we'll be done for the day. Say his name and count it a victory. It has no power over you."

Laura turned, and the warm, encouraging look on Jasmine's face melted her defenses. Her therapist was just about her only friend. It was a thought so utterly sad she had to fight off a bout of sudden, manic laughter.

When she spoke, the words came out so quietly, they were almost gone before they arrived. "Eugene Hobbes."

"Again," Jasmine said.

"Eugene Hobbes," she said, then turned and left the building.

MASS-MURDER TRAIL LEADS TO TRAGIC PAST
Colin Smythe, Times Staff Writer
August 4, 2017

HILLSBOROUGH, N.C. — The gruesome trail left across North Carolina by Eugene Francis Hobbes began with a heartbreaking childhood, according to a new journal discovered by his ex-wife.

A month has passed since the disappearance of Teresa Mitchem and the murder of Olive Hanson, and the killings of Susan Gilroy, Alina Scopoloto, and Maria Mendelsohn occurred more than three decades ago. For many close to the case, it remains a harrowing, interminable experience. Their largest questions have always been the chief concerns of any murder investigation: who, and why?

Eugene Francis Hobbes was born in 1948 deep in the Ouachitas, the remote mountains of Arkansas. It was a home birth onto a dirt floor, and he was a large baby. His mother bled to death within a few hours, long before any help could reach them.

His father died in 1953, and Eugene and his brother, Charles, were sent to live with an uncle in east Texas. He joined the army in 1966, and his fingerprints and photograph were taken as a matter of routine. The former would later be used to identify his body; the latter depicts a squint-eyed young man with a crew cut and ghastly acne scarring. He married his first wife in 1975, and they divorced in 1976. In 1979 he married Aubrey Craig, with whom he had one daughter, and they divorced early in 1988.

Between 1988 and 2017, when he was the victim of an apparent suicide, no record of his movements or activities has been found. His motives have remained shrouded in mystery, but a journal discovered by his second wife, a copy of which has been obtained by the *Times*, describes a devastating childhood and offers insight into the making of a monster.

The journal records his earliest memory: shouldering the blame for the death of his mother. At the hands of his father and older brother he was beaten, made to sleep outside, forced to eat raw meat, and required to defecate himself on command. His uncle, with whom he later lived, served three years in a Texas state penitentiary for sexual coercion of a minor. Hobbes relates the abuse he and his brother suffered at his uncle's hands, and how he was subsequently abused by his brother alone.

According to his journal, Eugene Hobbes killed his brother when he was eighteen and Charles was twenty-one. His account has them driving back into Arkansas, up into the Ouachitas. With the help of a bottle of whiskey, a gun, and some strong handcuffs, he apparently subdued his brother, then forced him to dig a hole in the earth before choking him to death.

Police sources have confirmed the discovery of a body, not as yet officially identified, at the location described in the journal.

He remarried in 1979 and moved to Hillsborough, North Carolina, his new wife's hometown. In 1988 she filed for divorce, alleging abuse against their ten-year-old daughter, and obtained custody and a restraining order. Reports from those who knew him at the time portray a man with a strange, antisocial personality unhinged by the destruction of his family, and elements of the timeline seem to support that this was a pivotal moment: not too long after the loss of his daughter, he met little Susan Gilroy.

"They don't have anything to say," said the Gilroy family attorney, Lawrence Phillips. "You can imagine their state of mind."

The families of the other victims did not respond to a request for comment.

23

ORANGE COUNTY SHERIFF was an elected position, and Michael Fuller looked more like a politician than a lawman. His bespoke navy suit sported a subtle pinstripe, and his white dress shirt was of the starched, spread-collar variety. He had a forest-green tie with a ruby stickpin and a baby face split down the middle by a hooked nose of epic proportions. It worked for him though. Without the nose he would have been too perfect. With it, he played a very convincing everyman.

He was up and around the desk before she finished opening the door. He stuck out a hand. "Miss Chambers, Miss Chambers, how are you today?"

"Fine," Laura said, and put her hand in his.

He squeezed and held it, treating his captive to a hundred-watt smile. His teeth were whiter than seemed natural, and he smelled of expensive aftershave.

"So sorry to have kept you waiting."

"Actually, I just got here."

"Hmm? Where are my manners? Please, take a seat." He pulled out a leather club chair for her.

She sat. "You were the district attorney, right?"

He nodded. "Let me assure you, Miss Chambers, that no one in my office—my old office—knew anything about the reports you made to my predecessor, or about the, er, adversarial nature of his response."

"He called me a liar and refused to even see my evidence. I think he was about this close"—she held up her thumb and fore-finger a quarter inch apart—"to just throwing me in a cell."

Fuller tutted disapprovingly. "Terrible. If my office had known, believe me, we would have taken swift, decisive action."

"Pretty easy to say that now."

He spread his arms. "Considering I wasn't contacted at the time, this is the only chance I've had to say anything at all."

"You could have condemned McKinney for his mistake."

"Condemned? He's not on death row, Miss Chambers. One mistake does not a lifetime of public service negate."

"He cost lives. He killed Frank Stuart."

Fuller tutted again, and this time it was aimed at her. "Hardly. We all know who killed Deputy Stuart."

"Actually, that's why I'm—"

Fuller ran right over her with his resonant bass fricatives. "That's not to diminish his mistake, you understand. He should have listened to you. No one is denying that."

"Didn't seem to stop him from winning a state senate seat," Laura said.

"I can understand how that must be perplexing to someone with your experience of the man." He came around the desk and poured two glasses of water from a crystal pitcher and placed one in front of her. "But not everyone saw him that way. This is poli-tics. Any publicity is good publicity."

"Even when a deputy gets killed?"

"All's well that ends well. A savage threat to the public was dispatched."

Laura's nose wrinkled in disgust. "So Frank was what? An acceptable loss?"

Fuller stood again and yanked down on his lapels, straighten-ing his jacket. When he spoke, the note of secrecy was gone from his voice. "Of course not. No officer is expendable. But you and I are talking about an election, which is really just a matter of mathematics. Month after month, McKinney's name was all over the news because of that story." He paused. "What do you think a candidate for state senate normally spends in this part of the state?"

"I don't know."

Fuller stared off into space, adding up the figures. "Couple of hundred thousand, maybe?"

"Like I said, I don't know."

His eyes snapped back in her direction. "Anyway, you can't buy advertising that good. His opponent didn't stand a chance."

Laura wrung her hands. "So basically, I got him elected."

"That's one way to look at it."

"Someone needs to hear what I have to say."

Fuller returned to his chair and sat back, comfortable. "No reason that can't be me. I'm all ears."

"I'm sure you've had a lot of people telling you everything there is to know about the Eugene Hobbes case. Investigators, evidence techs, probably even other reporters."

Fuller raised one eyebrow.

"But among all those experts, I'm a very special and unique case: the only eyewitness. No one else was there."

"The boy, the photographer?"

"He didn't come down to the cabin until after it was all over. I'm your only real eyewitness, and I'm here to clarify my statement. You see, in the context of the coroner's report—"

"The coroner's report. Has that been made public?"

Laura frowned. "I'm using it to help you understand the holes in the official narrative."

"Okay, Miss Chambers, now you've got me interested. I was a lawyer, remember? Digging holes in stories was my stock-in-trade."

"So what do you make of his legs?"

He smiled at her. "You must still have a few sources to know about that."

"The coroner speculated that he hadn't walked in years."

"He shouldn't have done that," Fuller said. "But his legs were quite atrophied, and it is suggestive. Still, he could have been in a wheelchair."

"No." She shook her head. "That's exactly what I'm here to

refute. I made a statement that night, a detective wrote it all down, and I signed it. I think seeing Deputy Stuart hurt like that—"

"You were in shock."

"I wasn't thinking straight. A few days later I actually read the damn thing."

"And it was wrong," Fuller said.

"No, it's technically accurate. But it misses a lot of nuances. Things that didn't seem important at the time become incredibly so in light of the fact Eugene Hobbes didn't have use of his legs."

Fuller frowned. "Go on."

"Well, in my statement it just says I saw him emerge from his hiding place in the leaves and go into the cabin after Stuart. That's correct, but it leaves out *how* he moved."

"And how, may I ask, did he move?"

"Fluid. Light. Like an athlete. He ran to the cabin, but without making any real noise. The man I saw certainly was not in a wheelchair. Let's say, for the sake of argument, that Hobbes could walk. Even then, the man I saw wasn't anywhere near seventy years old."

"How old would you say he was?"

"In his physical prime. Forty or under."

Fuller tapped his pen against his temple. "Interesting."

"It's a hell of a lot more than interesting. How does that square with an old man whose legs don't work?"

"So you're saying there was someone else up there."

Laura watched his face closely. This was the tricky part. "I know how that sounds," she said. "Pretend we're at trial. This is what they call a third-man defense, right?"

"Certainly. The idea that the crime was committed by someone else entirely."

"So maybe we could just, hypothetically, pretend I'm defending Eugene Hobbes, and I could lay out my trial strategy."

He nodded, intrigued.

"I was there. I saw him move. I saw how it could have been done. The first thing you have to understand is the angle. The cabin stood with its front door facing us. Behind it was a shed. From up on high I could just make out the shed's roof; once I got down onto the ground, it was completely concealed behind the cabin. They found electrical tape near Hobbes's body, and in the report they attribute it to the stock of the shotgun, which was wrapped in the same kind of tape. They assume some came loose, clumped together, fell on the ground.

"I have a different idea. I think our third man had Eugene Hobbes as a captive. I think he had him restrained in that shed, the shotgun already loaded and taped into his mouth, so that when the time came . . ."

Laura brought her hands together and then threw them apart, mimicking an explosion.

"He could do it without delay, you see?" she continued. "And the torn bits of electrical tape would have been about all that was left. I mean, the shot tore apart his skull. How much tape would survive under those conditions? Hobbes's hands were restrained, his legs were useless, all he had to do was drag him out of the shed and pull the trigger. You've been up there?"

Fuller nodded.

"Someone shoved that door shut, and I had to fight my way out of the bedroom. Someone shoved a knife into Frank Stuart, got Hobbes out of the shed, killed him, and then pulled his finger through the trigger guard. It's also possible that Frank was already dead by the time I got to the cabin, but even if he wasn't, all that could have been done in ninety seconds, maybe less."

Fuller waited for her to continue, and when he saw she was done, said, "How long were you trapped in the bedroom?"

"About that. Perhaps two minutes. I didn't look at my watch."

"In stressful situations, time seems to stretch. Is it possible what felt like two minutes was really a matter of seconds?"

"No," Laura said. "I had to find the pickaxe and then physically break down the door. It took some time."

Fuller nodded. "I can't say you're wrong, Miss Chambers. I wasn't up there. Things could have happened just the way you say they did."

"You think I'm lying?"

"You misunderstand me. You yourself didn't see what happened behind the cabin, so your version is speculative. I'm saying—yes, I can't prove that it didn't happen just that way. I also can't prove the real killer isn't John Wayne. You see? You're asking me to prove a negative."

"Goddamn it, his legs didn't work. How can you explain it any other way?"

Fuller leaned back in his chair and adjusted the knot in his tie. "I take issue with the idea that you're explaining it any better. You've had the chance to play defense attorney, so now let me play prosecutor. The essence of any third-man defense is the narrative you tell a jury. Someone else committed the crime, and the story you tell has to cover all the normal bases: means, motive, and opportunity. I take it you don't have a potential suspect?"

Laura's face burned. She shook her head.

"Since we don't have an *actual* third man, we can't speak much to means or opportunity. So what about motive? We have Eugene Hobbes's journal. In it, he makes certain confessions, things that only the killer would know. Are you suggesting that he is not the person who killed Susan Gilroy, Alina Scopoloto, and Maria Mendelsohn?"

"No, I'm not denying that. I'm saying he didn't kill Olive Hanson. He didn't take Teresa Mitchem. He lacked the means to commit these new crimes."

"We've discussed that at length, and frankly, you have a point. If this was an actual trial, and I was his defense attorney, that right there might be my strategy. From that alone I could manufacture reasonable doubt."

"But you still don't believe me."

"That's not it at all. You're focusing on flaws in the official narrative while ignoring the flaws in your own. Here's my point: what would be the reason for all this? If someone hates Hobbes, say, because they knew what he had done, why not just expose him?"

Laura said nothing.

"Why kill *as* him, only in service of revealing him? It's needlessly complicated, and it transforms our third man from a whistleblowing hero into a child-murderer. There's nothing to gain from such a turn, and everything to lose."

"I don't have all the answers, Sheriff, but what disturbs me is that I'm the only one looking for them. Maybe the official narrative is more correct than not, but no one is taking the time to actually investigate and find out. Everyone seems content to let sleeping dogs lie. Everyone was so busy getting elected, no one bothered to find out the truth."

Fuller frowned.

"Because what if I'm right? What then?"

The phone on the desk buzzed, and a voice rasped at him through the intercom: "Your three thirty is here."

Fuller pressed a button. "Tell him I'll be finished in just a moment." He looked at Laura and shrugged. "Duty calls."

"That's it?"

"Not at all," he said, getting up and walking toward the door. "I promise to look into it. Anything less would be unethical."

He opened the door, and she walked past him without a word.

"Goodbye, Miss Chambers," he called after her.

She didn't bother to answer. Behind her, she could hear him glad-handing his next constituent. Everything was normal. Business as usual. The horror called Eugene Hobbes was already fading into the past. All's well that ends well—everyone seemed to believe it.

Everyone except Laura Chambers.

24

No shadows fell under the gunmetal-gray sky. A cold wind shook the bare trees, and they swayed to its silent music. Laura wore a sheepskin coat cut to hang almost to her knee, and she pulled it closed near her throat.

"Can you sit?"

He gave a quick sharp bark.

"Sit, Cooper. Sit!"

He sat.

"You sure you have time for this?" Rodgers said.

"Bass Herman lets me come and go as I please. He about had an aneurysm when his photographer sold the only picture of the whole incident to a bigger paper, and Smythe leaving didn't help. Now he wants to forget the whole thing, just like everyone else. I'm getting assignments to write about prospective tax plans, or even worse, the weather. I'm supposed to be an investigative journalist."

"So you come out here and talk to me, because no one else wants to give you the time of day."

"I come, what? Once a week?"

"Twice sometimes."

The field behind the house lay fallow, the rows of dirt extending into the distance. With no obstructions the wind was as brutal as a club. It howled out of the northwest, slapping faces and numbing fingers. Rodgers dug into the bag he carried and came out with a piece of cooked meat. She knew he'd collected it over the past few days, the fatty part of steaks, the scrapings from a roast bone.

Rodgers looked at Cooper. "Stay."

Cooper sat, and Laura held his collar.

Rodgers walked away, zigzagging, making sudden sharp turns. Occasionally, after big movements, he scuffed the dirt with his toe. He ended up about fifty yards away at the stump of a tree that had never been pulled up. Coming back, he was careful to walk precisely the same path, using the scuff marks as a crude map.

"Ready?" he asked Laura.

"Yep."

"Okay then. Seek!"

Laura released the collar, and Cooper was off. He kept his nose pinned to the ground and moved in a circle around them. He'd seen Rodgers walk to the stump, but it didn't seem to matter. He did it the same way every time, driven to complete the pattern, whether by his old training or by something ancient in his cells she didn't know. Halfway around he found the scent of Rodgers's trail but kept moving, completing a full three-hundred-and-sixty-degree pass.

Rodgers narrated. "Got to make sure it's not a false trail."

Cooper swung back to the trail and started following it. The blasts of air from his nose were so intense that they threw up tiny dust clouds. Sometimes he would paw at a place.

"Turns up scent, stuff that might be hidden."

The bloodhound zigged and zagged, moving back and forth, always scanning for other clues. He reached the stump and steak, then threw back his head and bayed at the overcast sky.

"Good boy," Rodgers shouted through cupped hands.

Cooper snatched up the chunk of meat and lumbered over to them.

"He's still got it. I ever tell you about that time he found that boy down by the river?"

"Yep," Laura said.

"How about that, Cooper?" He reached down and scratched him behind one ear. "I ran out of my own stories, now I run outta yours too."

She dug into her coat's other pocket and produced a thick

sheaf of papers held together by an oversized paper clip. "Here, take a look at the coroner's report."

"What coroner's report?"

"The one from the crime scene. From the cabin in the mountains."

He let out a low whistle. "The one on Eugene Hobbes. Where the hell did you get that?"

"Timinski owed me a favor."

"I thought the deal was you getting to write the story. He didn't stop you."

"He didn't exactly help me, either. I called him that day, you know, and he was out chasing some dead end. I think he feels guilty."

Rodgers stomped his feet. "Could be guilt."

"What else?"

"You two seemed to get pretty close."

Laura shrugged. "Who cares if he gives out copies of a little bit of paperwork? It's a closed case. The whole thing will be public record soon enough."

"In my experience, the feds don't like things out in public until they are officially out in public, if you know what I mean. But you asked, and he did it anyway."

"You jealous?"

That earned her another small smile. "Hell, I never had no federal agent do me any favors, not even small ones."

Laura flipped through the pages until she found what she wanted. "Here, read."

"Don't have my glasses."

"Suffer through it then."

Rodgers sighed and used his teeth to pull off one glove so he could turn the pages. He held the paper unnaturally far from his face and started reading. After a few minutes he gave the low whistle again.

"Finished?"

"Yep."

"Thoughts?"

"I think he's better off without a face. Nice to read a story with a happy ending."

"Did you read the part about his legs?"

Rodgers rolled the papers into a tube and tapped it against his leg. "It's tough letting go of something like this. Believe me, I know. You've seen the back rooms in there." He jabbed the tube over his shoulder toward the house. "Boxes everywhere I can fit them, just taking up space. Gathering dust. Look at Cooper out there."

In the distance, the dog sniffed something on the ground, rolled over on his back, jumped to his feet, and kept moving.

"You notice how he moves his nose back and forth like a broom? Side to side, keeping track of the edges. A bad bloodhound doesn't do that, and when they lose the scent, they have to go back and find it. It happens over and over, slowing them down. What happens to footprints when you walk across them enough times?"

She said nothing.

"That's right." His voice had dropped, like he was talking to himself. "They're gone. Destroyed. Nothing left to find but your own breadcrumbs."

He stared out at the dog, hands shoved deep into his pockets.

"You okay?" she asked.

"I've read every box of files in that house a hundred times. I looted them for details until there was nothing left to find. Stare at the same spot long enough and you start to see things. A few days without sleep and you start to wonder if those things are real. A week without sleep, you stop caring. Real and unreal, those are just words. Obsession breaks you eventually."

Laura reached out and took the paper tube from his hand. "How about we make a deal? You let me run it down for you, and then I won't bring it up again."

"Ever?"

"Ever."

"Okay, shoot."

She smoothed the pages on her thigh. "You understand what they're saying in here?"

"I was a cop for almost twenty-five years."

"So then you agree: there's no way he could have walked. He hadn't walked in years."

Rodgers took the report back and ran his finger down it. "Says extreme atrophy, fair confidence that he couldn't walk."

Laura frowned. "What would it take for them to be sure?"

"Maybe if they saw him attempt to walk."

She snorted.

"I'm not joking," he said. "You gotta understand, an autopsy doesn't have all the answers. They usually do a pretty good job on cause of death, but you start asking questions about what a person was like when they were alive, all they can give you is best guess."

"His legs were like twigs. He hadn't used them in years."

"Maybe. But the human body can do amazing things under stress. You always hear those stories about mothers lifting cars off their kids."

"We're not talking about a distressed mother."

"So maybe he did it in a wheelchair."

Laura's mouth hung open.

"It's possible, isn't it?"

Her jaw snapped shut. She gritted her teeth. Between them, she said, "Anything's possible."

"Not anything. But the possible is a large swath of territory. Very large."

"I was out in that field. It was the middle of July, they'd planted soybeans, and the whole thing was covered in rows. Olive Hanson was posed more than two hundred yards from any road. You're saying he managed to get himself out there, and to carry a body along with him, and he did all that in a wheelchair?"

"They make 'em with big off-road tires. They make them electric too. Hell, he might have had an easier time than I would have."

Laura threw up her hands. "There were no tracks!"

"There were no footprints neither," Rodgers said.

"Well, the killer was careful." She pointed to where Cooper had started digging near the base of the stump. "Like you leaving that trail for him to follow. One way in, one way out. He could have just raked them away on his way out."

"Any reason a man with dead legs couldn't have done the same to his wheelchair tracks?"

"I saw someone up there, and they weren't in a damn wheelchair."

Rodgers fumbled inside his jacket pocket and came out with a bottle. The liquid inside was brown and viscous; she could see it sticking to the glass.

"Drink?"

She said nothing.

"Suit yourself." He took a pull, capped it, slid it back into its compartment. "For the sake of argument, let's say you're right. Let's say Hobbes had nothing to do with Olive Hanson. What then?"

"Then I try to prove it."

"But let's get specific. How exactly are you going to do that?"

Laura just pressed her lips together and turned her face into the wind.

"To the rest of the world, the case is closed," he continued. "Where's the evidence to reopen it? Look, I know how difficult Teresa Mitchem was for you. You risked a lot going up there with that kid. To have it come back and bite you—that must be tough."

Laura laughed, a short hard bark. "Yeah, tough."

"You've got to accept it."

"Accept what?"

He pulled out the bottle and drank again, weighing his words. "That she's gone. You missed her."

"There's no body."

He put his hands on her shoulders. His brown irises melted into their pupils, nearly black in the gloom. "There's a lot of acres up there in the national forest, Laura. There's never going to be a body. You have to let it go."

Her phone buzzed in her pocket. On the screen, next to the text icon, appeared the words BASS HERMAN. She pressed her thumb against it, previewing the message. It was short enough that she could read the whole thing.

OFFICE ASAP. EMERGENCY.

Laura tried to remember ever getting a text from Bass, and couldn't. It had never happened before. She looked up at Rodgers and raised an eyebrow.

"Speak of the devil," she said. "Gotta go to work."

25

THE *GAZETTE* DIDN'T have a newsroom anywhere near the size of the *Globe*'s, but there still should have been the low murmur of voices on the phone, and of papers shuffling, and the clack of keyboards. There should have been faces visible above cubicle walls washed out by the ceiling lights' halogen glow. Instead the room was dim, with only every fifth overhead light on, and completely silent. It was empty.

To her left, the door to the men's room opened and Bass tottered out, one hand trailing along the wall next to him. He'd been splashing water on his face. Much of it had gotten on his white collar, soaking it though. He wasn't wearing a tie, or his glasses.

"Bass, where is everyone?"

"Sent them home. We needed some space." His voice quavered, like a low-frequency stutter murmuring in the back of his throat. He took a half step forward, still supporting himself with his arm.

"What's happening?"

"Natalie's in my office. We should speak to her."

"Colin's assistant?"

"She a floater now. She opens the mail." He pulled his hand away from the wall and pointed himself down the row between the cubicles. Some jolt of electricity hit him, straightened his spine, and without warning he broke into a jog, headed for the back offices.

Laura watched him go. The darkness in the corners of the room seemed to close in, and a shudder snaked its way past her heart.

She opens the mail.

Bass looked like he'd seen a ghost, and there was only one ghost Laura could think of. She felt the unmistakable desire to pull a blanket over her head and hunker down, to conceal herself from whatever waited for her in the back office. She recognized the feeling: fear of the thing hiding under the bed.

She walked down the row, checking behind her every other cube.

Bass's office smelled sharply of salt and grease, and in the corner Natalie sat in the guest chair with her knees pulled up to her chin. Where Bass had been dampened by sweat and sink water, Natalie appeared very dry and very cold. Her skin looked like cracked porcelain, with dark smudges around her eyes and furrows beneath them cut through her foundation. She'd been crying, but the tears had long since dried up.

"Natalie."

Her gaze stayed fixed on a blank spot on the wall.

"Natalie." Bass put a hand on her shoulder and gave it a shake. "Tell her what you told me."

Natalie shook her head, turned back to stare at the wall.

"Never mind," Bass said. "It's in the conference room."

He led her inside and hit the light switch. The overheads flickered and hummed, then sprung to life. A brown paper-wrapped package sat on the near edge of the table. Written across the top in neat block letters: LAURA CHAMBERS, C/O BASS HERMAN, and then the address of the *Gazette*.

"There's no postage," Laura said.

"Someone must have dropped it off."

She glanced back at him. "Do I want to know what's inside?"

Mention of the package's contents twisted his face into an expression of seasickness. "I don't know," he said. "But if you do look, wear these."

He pressed something rubbery into her hand.

"And be quick. We waited for you—waited before calling the police. But I need to contact them soon."

Laura opened her hand and found a pair of powderless latex gloves. She took a deep breath before pulling them on, then peeled back the brown paper. Inside was a plain white shoe box. She pulled off the lid. Styrofoam packing peanuts spilled out onto the table, and nestled in the center lay an oddly-sized jewelry box, smaller and thicker than one used to hold a necklace but not nearly small enough for a ring. Steeling herself, she lifted the top.

Perfectly formed and carefully placed, it rested delicately on the box's velveteen display pad, dry and clean, devoid of blood. Whorls of skin spiraled toward a dark hole in the center, a sickening nautilus shell of sinew.

It was another ear.

The fact that it had been sent to both her and Bass, the editor of a newspaper, was not lost on Laura. This was not a private message. An image splashed across her field of vision: Olive Hanson, washed and posed in the center of a field, on display, waiting to be found. The poor girl's end had been only a means to an end, its final goal the elicitation of outrage and fear. Now he was doing it again. He was preening, the ear another corpulent feather in his plumage.

She forced herself to look at it again.

It wasn't just another ear: it was another left ear. Teresa Mitchem's left ear was secure in an evidence locker somewhere, and now another one had arrived. How was that possible?

"God," she whispered. She knew. She knew how it was possible.

From behind her, Bass said, "Turn it over."

She pinched the lobe between two fingers and flipped it. Letters dripped along the outside edge, coiling toward the hole in the center. Another tattoo.

"A name," Bass Herman said.

"Yes," she said. "A new one."

* * *

No one answered the buzzer at Jasmine's office, and she wasn't picking up her phone. Laura drove to her apartment, slipped past someone coming out the front, and started knocking. The rusted black truck was parked out front. She had to be home.

"Who's there?"

"It's Laura, let me in."

"Just give me a moment."

The door opened. Jasmine had on a terrycloth robe with a towel wrapped around her hair. Her cheeks were rosy. "Sorry, I was in the shower."

Laura pushed her way inside and let herself down onto the couch, the same one she'd slept on almost six months ago. "He took another one," she said, and put her head in her hands.

Jasmine didn't ask who, didn't need to be told what had been taken. She saw the look on Laura's face, and that was all the explanation required. Laura told the doctor the story in fits and jumps, taking breaks when she needed, trying not to linger on the gory details. The ending was difficult.

"Another tattoo," she finished. "A name: Samantha Powell."

"Oh, no," Jasmine said, and slumped back into her chair. She pulled the towel off her wet hair, twisting it between her hands.

"You know her," Laura said, suddenly understanding.

"Yes. She's a patient."

"Tell me about her."

Jasmine stood abruptly and pulled the robe tight across her chest. "I can't discuss another patient. I shouldn't even have told you that she's been seeing me."

"Even if it helps to find her? We could—"

She put a hand out in front of her. "Stop. Just stop. You're not a cop, Laura. And if you're really my friend, you'll forget I ever said anything."

"You're right, I'm not a cop. That's what Bass Herman is doing right now, calling the police. You and Bass and Don Rodgers want me to stay far away from this and let the police do their jobs. But there's a problem with that: I've seen how the police do their jobs. Do you know I met with Sheriff Fuller this morning?"

Jasmine shook her head.

"I'll give you one guess how that went."

"But it's different now. It'll all be different now."

"I hope you're right. But my gut tells me he's going to do everything in his power not to resurrect the Hanson and Mitchem cases.

That's two cleared off the books, two in the black. I looked in his eyes: he doesn't want to carry the load."

"So what?"

"He'll call it a copycat. He'll bury it."

Jasmine nodded, went into the kitchen, came back with a glass of water. "What will you do?"

"Maybe go around town, telling everyone 'I told you so.'"

"Don't joke. Not now."

Laura blinked, an idea forming in her mind. "I meant what I said. Fuller is going to insist Hobbes committed those other two murders alone, and Hobbes is already dead. That means the Samantha Powell investigation starts whenever she went missing. No one is going to be looking for the connections. No one is going to be working backwards."

"No one but you," Jasmine said. She sighed. "If you're not careful, you're going to get yourself killed."

*   *   *

"Timinski," a voice said.

It startled her. She'd expected to leave a message. "Tim, it's me."

"Laura." He paused, and she could feel that penetrating stare even over the phone. "You okay?"

She laughed, but it came out strange sounding, almost strangled. "He's taken another one."

"Not every missing girl is connected to Teresa Mitchem."

"When I get their ear in the mail, I'd say it's connected."

He let out a breath.

"Have you been getting my messages?"

"Yes," he said.

"But you've been avoiding them."

"Not at all. You have to understand, I'm busy out here in the district."

"Right, you're in the capital now."

"In the Hoover building," he said, and she could hear the trace of pride in his voice. "It's a big promotion, but they're working me like a dog. I don't have much free time."

"You make it sound like a hobby. Like we're playing Chinese checkers instead of trying to catch a killer."

There was a long pause. "Is it safe to be talking like this?"

"I'm not recording our conversation, if that's what you're asking. I wouldn't do that to you. Besides, I'm the one with the information this time."

"Hold on." She could hear the scrape of a chair, other voices getting louder and then fading away. A door slamming shut. "What do you have?"

She ran down her special delivery with as much detail as possible. "I can't let sleeping dogs lie, Tim. I'm sorry, but I need your help again. Plus, you owe me."

He let out a breath. "I did, Laura. I *did* owe you. But I gave you what you asked for, the entire damn case file. Even though it could have cost me my job."

"And did I write up a story and auction it off to the highest bidder? Did I?" Her voice had risen to a yell.

"No," Timinski said, "you didn't. But the Bureau doesn't plan to make any of that stuff public. The case is closed, and they'd prefer it stay that way."

"Everyone seems to agree on that. Just help me, Tim. Alive or dead, I'm going to find this one. We owe the girl that much."

She waited, listening to the hiss of the open phone line and the pounding of her heart in equal measure.

"All right," he said finally. "I can make you an offer."

"What kind?"

"The crime scene at the cabin is finally being released tomorrow. Everything of forensic value was bagged and tagged a long time ago. I was the lead investigator, so I'm going up there tomorrow morning with a few evidence techs to claim the last few things worth saving. Once everyone else leaves, we could walk through the place."

"Together?"

"Together," he said.

CHAPTER

26

L AURA WOKE WELL before dawn. It wasn't much trouble. She rarely managed to sleep more than a few hours these days.

She dressed warmly, threading on long johns under wool pants, a thick navy turtleneck, and her sheepskin coat. Into a backpack she stuffed a black watch cap, fleece-lined leather work gloves, a blanket, a large bottle of water, trail mix, a compass, a map, a camera with extra rolls of film, a pair of binoculars, a walkie-talkie, and a thermos of hot coffee. She slung it over her shoulder, tiptoed out of the house, and started driving.

*   *   *

Three and a half hours later, with the Dart parked well off the road, she maneuvered herself into the exact spot where she and Leon Botton had hidden six months earlier. Hunkered down, she made a place to sit with her back against the tree. Then she waited.

Dawn was a long time coming. According to the tables, sunrise came a little after seven this time of year. In her calculations, however, she had forgotten about the mountains themselves. It was difficult to say exactly when the sun would claw its way above the far ridgeline. So she waited, teeth chattering, occasionally poking her head up and then staring down into the darkness.

There was nothing to see, which only fired her imagination. Again and again she played the scene out in her head. Frank drives up, she watches him click off his dome light and climb out, closing the door quietly. Should she shout? Should she warn him?

About what?

She'd seen nothing so far, just a creepy, abandoned cabin. No other cars. No other people. And if anything, Frank's greatest tactical advantage had been the element of surprise. Shouting would ruin that. No, she couldn't have told Frank anything he didn't know already.

She nodded to herself. In her mind's eye, the scene faded away. She'd played it out like that a thousand times, and each time she reached the same conclusions: there was nothing she could have done.

But it was no comfort, none at all. Worse, it made her feel helpless, an emotion she detested.

A new picture snapped into focus. Her first instinct was to squeeze her eyes shut. It would do no good. In front of her, in the darkness, she watched the ground open up like a gate to hell and then *he* rose out of it like a demon. Floating across the ground. Death in the shape of a man.

Laura drank some coffee and tried to relax. Her teeth wouldn't stop chattering.

Snap.

Off to the left, something moved. It sounded like it was ambling along the ridgeline, coming right at her.

She fumbled for the Browning in her pocket, realized it wasn't there. It was evidence; the police had never returned it.

The popping and cracking of leaves and branches got steadily louder as the thing approached through the dark.

She shrunk down against the tree, making herself as small as possible. Her teeth were still chattering. She reached up and clamped her own jaw shut, then held it in place.

The snaps picked up pace. Whatever it was, it was running now. It was running right toward the tree.

Her eyes rolled wildly in their sockets, trying to catch even the smallest glimpse of the coming danger, desperate for an ounce of light.

There was nothing but blackness.

Her hands tore through the surrounding dirt, looking for a stick, a rock, anything to defend herself, but she came up empty-handed.

It crashed through the underbrush and stood before her. She could see it now. It was *him*, dressed all in black. More than that: he was made of darkness. His hands were shadows, his face a black hole. He reached for her.

She screamed and—

—snapped upright, the scream dying into a strangled cough. Sunlight streamed through the branches overhead. Birds chirped.

A dream.

She cursed her own weakness. What if he had been up here, waiting for her? The police really had taken the Browning, and so far they'd refused to give it back. And here she was, asleep. Vulnerable. Another part of her was almost impressed. The nature of the dream hinted at her secret fear, but on the other hand, she'd come up to the cabin, at night and alone, and despite everything had somehow drifted off.

What would Dr. DeVane—that's how she thought of her in circumstances like this, not as her friend Jasmine but as Dr. DeVane—think of this? Past all the usual therapeutic bullshit, she was one of the most practical people Laura had ever met.

Laura would say, "What does it mean?"

And Dr. DeVane would fix her with that look of hers and say, "It means you're not getting nearly enough rest."

Laura shook her head and almost smiled. She moved onto her knees and then into a crouch. Slowly, she rose up to the lip of the bowl and peered down through the binoculars.

Everything looked different in the morning.

The position faced east; the sun was directly in her eyes. She blinked furiously and looked again. The scene below was about as nonthreatening as she could ever have imagined. The cabin could have been part of a photo shoot for *Life* Magazine. It sat under the clear blue sky like a sun worshiper on a beach, quiet and relaxed. The pines shone green, and a small stream she hadn't noticed the first time trickled down the bowl to her left and meandered behind the cabin. Even the goddamn birds were chirping.

The other main difference was the two large black vans with

FBI painted on the side in that characteristic yellow. People wearing windbreakers with the same logo on the back milled about. Two of them leaned against one van, sipping coffees and laughing. Another two moved in and out of the cabin, loading small plastic boxes into the back.

It felt almost domestic. They could have been surveyors or utility contractors. Nothing hinted at the nature of their work. They were packaging evidence from acts so inhuman they had captivated a national audience for months, but based on body language they could have been chatting at the water cooler.

She shivered and pulled the blanket closer around her shoulders.

Timinski emerged from the cabin in a white dress shirt with the collar unbuttoned, a heavy-looking plastic container held in front of him. She'd never seen him without a jacket and tie, let alone with his sleeves rolled up over his forearms. Over the next three hours, he and the other agents filled both vans with plastic evidence containers. Finished, they pulled the doors shut and drove down the road to the entrance of the bowl. A temporary metal gate had been erected soon after the cabin's discovery. Using simple hand tools, they disassembled it and loaded the pieces into a small trailer, then backed one van up and attached the trailer to its hitch.

Timinski walked over and said something to the driver of the leading van. The driver produced a clipboard. Timinski signed, and then the vans bumped down the road and disappeared from sight.

Timinski went back to his car and pulled something out from the passenger seat. He spoke into it.

"Shit," Laura said, and scrambled to get her bag open. She dug to the bottom and pulled out the walkie-talkie. It was the exact brand he'd told her to buy. She twisted the volume knob, turning it on, and clicked over to the agreed-upon channel.

"—ome in, over."

She worked the button. "Tim, can you hear me? I'm here."

"Where's here?"

Below, he shielded his eyes and scanned the western edge of the bowl.

"Here." She stood and raised both arms above her head.

The walkie crackled to life. "I see you now. Is that where you were six months ago?"

She nodded, even though he probably couldn't see that. "Yes, exactly here."

"Okay. I'm coming up."

He put his walkie into a pocket and started across the floor of the bowl. By the time he reached the edge of the lip, a slight sheen of sweat clung to stubble on his chin and upper lip. He extended his arm, flashed her a smile. She reached down and took his hand, then pulled him up to the top.

"Good to see you, Laura."

"Good to see you too," she said, and it wasn't just a pleasantry. Timinski had kept her in the loop, and he'd never blamed her for what had happened to Frank Stuart. It was nice to look someone in the eye and see them staring back without that familiar expression, half accusations and half pity.

"You look good," she said, and grinned.

"Bullshit," he said, but he grinned back, his thick eyebrows making it funnier somehow. His eyes sported large dark circles, and he was thinner than she remembered.

"You doing okay?" she asked.

He seemed to know what she meant. "DC isn't exactly the cherry I thought it would be."

"Thought they'd just put you out to pasture."

"You and me both."

A thought occurred to her. "Is it because of me? Of what happened with Hobbes?"

He shrugged. "Even if it was, they'd never say it out loud. I don't know—he's dead, isn't he?"

"And that's enough?"

Timinski shrugged again.

Together, they walked through the entire incident again, recreating Laura's statement in the flesh. From their perch, she pointed out the shed's roof and the spot where the man in black had risen from the ground and moved toward the cabin. They climbed down together. Laura marveled at the terrain she had covered. The pitch was over thirty degrees in places, strewn with rocks and rotten logs. How had she managed to avoid breaking an ankle?

The cabin had a shiny new hasp and padlock. Timinski unlocked it and they walked through the hall, into the first bedroom, then out through the back. Here Laura paused. A slice of air, razor sharp, caught in her throat and for a second she couldn't breathe.

Timinski hung back. He didn't bother telling her to calm down, or that it would all be all right, and for that she liked him even more. He gave her a moment to recover, then walked past her without mentioning the moment of panic.

He pointed to the tree nearest the back door. "It happened here?"

"Yes, he was already leaned up against it by the time I made it out here. He was already—"

"We don't have to get into the gory details." He grimaced. "Sorry, poor choice of words." He walked away without waiting for a response and poked his head into the shed.

"There was a lock on it," Laura called over. "New hasp, new padlock. But they found the padlock sitting inside the door."

"I know. They also didn't find any evidence that there was a person being kept in there."

Laura clasped her hands together. "Define *kept*. I'm not suggesting Hobbes was confined here for any extended period of time, just that the real killer put him in here before Frank or I showed up."

"The real killer." Timinski spoke the words like he had a mouth full of pudding. "Fuller isn't going to like that."

"You talked to him?"

"Not personally, but I made some calls yesterday on my way to the airport. He's boxing us out."

"He doesn't want the FBI's help?"

"He's claiming there's only a thin circumstantial connection between Hobbes and Samantha Powell. The modus operandi is similar, but the story about the ear was in all the papers. Anyone could have joined the party."

"People won't believe it."

He shook his head. "The official position is that Hobbes killed those girls in 1988, and they're not questioning the fact that he killed Olive Hanson and Teresa Mitchem. And Hobbes is dead; that's the one thing everyone knows for sure. How could he have taken Samantha Powell?"

"That's exactly my point!" Laura slapped one hand into her open palm. "He didn't take her, ergo there's someone else. One man, that's all it would take. One man to take Hobbes, to hide him, to kill Frank, to yank Hobbes out and pull the trigger on the shotgun."

"Fuller's circling the wagons. There's no evidence the Powell girl's been taken across state lines, so the FBI can't get involved unless he requests it. Privately in the law enforcement community, he's saying it's not related and stressing the need for discretion. I think he's afraid it might start a panic."

"It damn well should."

"And there's something else. He got your boss to go along with it, and he says Bass agreed not to print anything for the time being."

Laura clenched her hands into fists. "He didn't even need to get a gag order."

"You should cut Bass some slack. He must have been pretty shook up."

She ground her teeth together, nodded once. "It scared him."

"Fuller used that. He's using it on the Powell family, too, telling them that keeping things quiet is the best way to get Samantha back."

She put a hand on his chest and stopped him in his tracks. His flat blue eyes were as unreadable as ever, but he raised one thick eyebrow at her. "Forget the official position," she said. "What do you think?"

He took a step back from her. "I think Sheriff Fuller cares a lot more about appearances than he does clearing cases."

"I take it he doesn't have your vote."

A smile twitched at the corner of his mouth. "No ma'am, he does not."

Laura looked down at the carpet of dead leaves. "I was on the ground right here, blind and deaf from taking a near shotgun blast, and I was right inside that hallway when I heard the shotgun discharge once, which must have been Hobbes getting his head blown off. I open the door and immediately get peppered with buckshot. Luckily someone shortened the barrel of the shotgun, otherwise it would have killed me. So if Hobbes was already dead, who shot at me?"

Timinski shrugged. "You're the only witness. If you want to convince anyone, you're going to need evidence beyond your statement. Accept it."

"That's why we're here, isn't it?"

"I don't know." He chewed his lip. "Techs have been all over this place for months."

"But they weren't looking for a third man."

Timinski kicked at the dead leaves with the tip of his loafer. "No, they weren't," he conceded.

"Do you really think Hobbes climbed that ridgeline above Olive Hanson's body?"

"We never found any proof those cigarette butts belonged to the same person who killed her."

"Except the phone call I got."

"That you got," he said, emphasis on the *you*.

"So what do you think? Come on, be blunt."

He took a deep breath and blew it out, looked up at the tops of the pine trees swaying in a breeze too high to reach them. "No, it doesn't sit right with me."

"Damn straight."

He held up a hand, cutting her off. "Let me finish. What you have to understand is, it *never* sits right. I've worked at least a hundred cases in my time, and here's what I've learned: there are always loose ends. Always. That's just life. Life is messy and imperfect. I used to have a reputation among investigators as a bloodhound. I could sniff out a lie. We'd get called in on a woman killed in a supposed break-in. That kind of thing, you always look to the husband. But how do you separate the killers from the grieving widowers?"

Laura didn't know. She shook her head.

"I used to do it like that." Timinski snapped his fingers. "I'd let the guy tell me his story, and by the time he finished I'd already know. Got quite the reputation," he said again. "Back in '08, in Lexington, we got called in on a kidnapping. Woman married to the golden boy of an old-money clan. It was all bourbon and seersucker suits and half-million-dollar racehorses with that crowd. She was white trash born beautiful, good-looking enough to go big time. Every family member I interviewed, I could see a flash in their eyes when they talked about her. Brows crinkled. Noses turned up. It was contempt. She was beneath them. They believed that in their very bones, in the way only the rich ever can."

"So a husband takes a trophy wife—is that really so suspicious?" Laura asked.

"No, my alarms went off because he was the only one of them who *didn't* come across like he'd treated her as hired help."

Laura frowned. "So, what, he loved his wife? That made him a suspect?"

Timinski fixed her with a look. "You know, sometimes you come across as one of the toughest, most tenacious women I've ever met. In other words, you can be a real pain in the ass when you set your mind to it."

"I'll take that as a compliment."

"But it makes me forget just how naive you can be. Parents make their children. And his parents had had a silver spoon up their collective asses so long, it had probably transmuted into gold. So what, a series of nannies raised him to be a saint?" He shook his head. "Come on."

"You thought he was acting. You didn't believe him."

"No, I did not. Two days after she was kidnapped, we found her shot dead in a motel room along with some stable boy who worked for the family. He'd leaned a hunting rifle against his chest and pulled the trigger with his toe. The story we pieced together was, he'd been obsessed with her from afar. Seemed possible. He'd had a few restraining orders in the past, allegations of stalking. He finally blew his top one day, grabbed her, took her to the motel and killed them both in a fit of love. Or rage. Same thing if you ask me."

An icy wind fired through the trees and caught Laura's hair, tussling it. She stuffed her hands deep into her pockets.

Timinski didn't seem to feel it. He stared off into space, transported. "It couldn't have been the husband, you see. No physical evidence linked him to the crime, he had an airtight alibi for the kidnapping, and there was no motive. They had a prenup, the marriage seemed to be going all right. He wasn't our man; everyone seemed to agree on that."

"But not you."

Timinski smiled bitterly. "No, not me. My fingers started tingling the first time I talked to him. That Cinderella story he told me about meeting her and falling in love—it was just too perfect. And as things progressed, everything was. Perfect, that is. Every question answered, every dangling loose end tied up. The only suspect gift-wrapped in a body bag, conveniently unable to answer any questions."

Laura leaned closer. "What happened?"

"In the end I just lied to him. I told him we found his fingerprint in the motel room, on the wall near the doorknob. It's one thing to make a plan, but it's quite another to stand up to interrogation. I put him in a room and made him tell the story again and again until he couldn't be sure if he'd made a mistake somewhere along the line or not, then hit him with the fingerprint."

"And?"

"And he cracked like an egg. Got life."

She breathed out. "How did you know?"

"When I was young, I couldn't have answered that. I would have said it was just a feeling in my gut, a feeling that was right more often than it was wrong. As I got older, though, I realized it was the stories they would tell. The guilty, I mean. The liars. We all learn as children how to tell stories. We learn from books, from movies, from other people. Narrative aims to answer questions like why and how. But real life isn't a story. In real life, there are always unanswered questions. A story that ties up all the loose ends is just—"

He searched for the word.

"—manufactured. So the fact that Hobbes's legs were atrophied? I don't like it. It doesn't sit right with you, and it doesn't sit right with me either. But I've learned to accept things like that. More than accept them, Laura—I welcome them. They convince me the wool isn't being pulled over my eyes."

27

"Here," Timinski said, and pulled open the door to the second bedroom.

They were back inside the cabin, shielded from the cold wind. Laura unbuttoned her coat and followed him inside. She'd never made it this far during her last visit. The space had clearly been used as a storage room. Cheap metal shelves lined three walls, with rows of them running down the middle. Everything had been covered in a thick layer of dust. The last six months had left footprints and smudges everywhere. Timinski flicked on his flashlight, and the particles in the air sliced across the beam like tiny comets.

It smelled like death.

"You want some Vicks to rub under your nose?"

It was the same stuff they used around a corpse to deaden the smell. Her eyes widened.

"It's not what you think," Timinski said. "They found a dead raccoon over in the corner. The damn things have been living in here."

Laura walked down one aisle between the center row of shelves and the wall. The shelves had boxes on them in places, all marked with evidence stickers. Some of the shelves sagged in the middle even though there was nothing on them.

"They took almost everything," Timinski said, reading her face. "This room was packed to the gills. All the shelf space taken."

"What was in them?"

"These," he said, and pulled a box down onto the floor. It was brown cardboard gone soft with age, and it threatened to crumble at any moment. He pried the top open and gestured.

Laura reached inside and came out with a shoe. It was a loafer, a man's size nine. At some point the tassel had fallen off.

"Is it evidence?"

"Everything's evidence, but this stuff isn't connected with any kind of actual crime. Anything that seemed like it might be useful we packaged up and sent to the lab within the first few weeks."

"So what is this stuff?"

"As far as we can tell, it's just junk. The same sort of thing you or I might collect over the years. Actually, it's particularly boring junk. Who keeps a box of old shoes?"

Laura pictured Hobbes wearing the shoe. She could see it in her mind: the loafer snug around his sockless foot, the sweat seeping out of his pores and soaking into the leather. The shoe suddenly burned hot in her hand. She dropped it back into the box and wiped her palm on the front of her pants.

Timinski said, "I'm loading these up today, taking them back with me. That'll be the end of it."

"And you wanted me to see."

He let out a sigh. "I don't know why I brought you here. Samantha Powell deserves to be home safe in her bed, but I don't think anything here is going to make that happen."

She didn't look at him.

"Here." He shoved the flashlight into her hand. "Take as long as you need. I'll be outside."

She pulled the boxes out randomly, laying them on the floor and peering inside. None was more notable than the next. Old magazines. Costume jewelry. A particularly heavy one yielded rusted tools. More shoes.

The last one she opened was crammed with papers, clearly more than a few decades old. The box smelled like a library book checked out for the first time in ten years and pulled open, spine creaking, giving off that distinct odor of aging paper.

There was nothing else to look at, so she sat on the floor and

pulled the top stack of papers onto her lap. Newspapers dating to
the late 1990s, and pressed into the middle of the stack, something
that made her stomach turn: coloring books and crayons. The paper,
thin to begin with, had started to crumble. She laid the coloring
books out on the floor and used her thumb and forefinger to turn
the pages.

There was nothing to date them. Water had gotten into the box
at some point, and many of the pages were blurred beyond recognition. The one page she could make out featured a large foot in a
strapped sandal, the toenails yellow and curled. The straps wound
their way up the leg, ending midcalf. It was the sort of sandal she
pictured an ancient Greek would wear. Another smaller leg wearing
the same sandal appeared on the other side of the page. Everything
at the top of the page had been melted away by water damage.

She moved through the boxes again, landing on the one filled
with costume jewelry. Something about it was different than the
others. All the other boxes had a distinctly masculine feel to them.
All the objects were the sort of thing a man might accumulate in
his cabin over the years, but a box of jewelry didn't fit the pattern.
She started pulling out pieces: strings of fake pearls, gaudy gem-
stone earrings, brooches set with diamonds the size of almonds. At
the bottom lay a crude wooden box. The latch was rusted shut. She
jammed her thumb into the edge and pressed. The edge was sharper
than she'd thought and it cut into her flesh. She was about to give
up when the latch squeaked and moved to the side. The box opened.

Inside were four gold crosses, small, on thin chains. One
looked like it might be real gold, albeit of inferior quality.

"You almost done in there?" Timinski asked, standing in the
doorway. "It's getting late. I've got a long drive."

"Tim, look at this." She handed him the box and shined the
flashlight inside so he could see.

"Crosses," he said.

"Didn't the description for Susan Gilroy include a small gold
cross?"

He furrowed his brow. "I think so."

"Maybe this is it. No one opened this box, Tim. It was rusted
shut."

"Are you sure it's not just rusty? They may have opened it once already."

She licked her lips, then shook her head. "No, I don't think so."

"And even so, there's nothing about a gold cross in the description of the other two."

"No, but the Scopolotos didn't speak English very well, and the Mendelsohns . . ." She trailed off.

"Were distraught."

"Exactly. I mean, no description is perfect, and a gold cross is a small thing. It could have been left out."

Timinski reached in and drew the crosses out one by one. He examined each, then returned them to the box. "No identifying marks or inscriptions."

"These could be trophies, right? Something he took from the girls."

"They could be anything, but a small gold cross has to be just about the single most common piece of jewelry in North Carolina, don't you think?"

"But it could be," she said.

"It could be," he agreed, and snapped the box shut. "That's why I'm taking them back with me."

"Jesus, Tim. Just promise me you'll take the idea seriously."

"I promise. But I also don't want you to get your hopes up." He rattled the box in his hand. "Besides, there are four of them."

She froze.

Four of them.

He was right. But a wheel started spinning in her mind. All this time she had spent thinking about Hobbes and the man who killed Frank Stuart, she had gotten nowhere. The facts had piled up until they were like a wall in front of her, hiding the truth.

Four of them.

Suddenly, and without warning, she saw a chink in the armor.

"I have to go, Tim."

"Me too, I guess." He reached out, stopped, then finally put a hand on her shoulder. "I wish I could do more to help."

She nodded.

"You can find your way back through the woods?"

"I'm fine," she said.

He frowned. "One day you're gonna say that in a way that makes me believe you."

*   *   *

She walked slowly through the woods, careful not to twist her torso or lift her legs too high, until she got to the car. She opened the trunk and cleared a flat space, then gently tugged the coloring books out from where she'd hidden them, in the back of her pants under her coat. She laid them down and then placed a few heavy books on top, securing them for the drive east back to Hillsborough.

28

S HE WOKE TWO hours before dawn, tossed and turned, and finally gave up. She showered, dressed, brewed coffee, and drank it until the soft buzzing in her head gave way to something resembling quiet.

By eight that morning she was parked outside Olive Hanson's house. *Her former house*, Laura reminded herself. At eight thirty, the sun finally crested the trees and poured weak light down onto the street. At nine, Laura knocked on the front door.

The door swung open. "Who is it?"

Emily Hanson wore a stained pink robe over jeans and a T-shirt. Her colorless hair stood on end on one side of her head and lay flat on the other. She reeked of booze and stale cigarette smoke. The overriding impression was that she had slept in her clothes.

"Mrs. Hanson?"

"I said, who's asking?"

"My name is Laura. I'm a reporter. I'm doing research for a story that involves your daughter."

Emily Hanson plucked a Newport from behind her ear and lit it, all without taking her eyes off Laura. She drew deep and then craned her neck back and blew the smoke straight up. One hand waved back and forth as though she was trying to keep the smell away. The entire house reeked of cigarettes, but that didn't seem to register.

"I was hoping I could ask you a few questions."

"Don't talk to reporters," Emily Hanson said.

"I understand it must be difficult."

"Okay, I'll talk to you a bit," she said, as though changing her mind had been the easiest thing in the world.

Laura's mouth opened in surprise.

"Because you ain't no real reporter," Emily said. "You think I don't recognize you?" She chuckled and then drew on the cigarette hanging in the corner of her mouth. "You the one that got that cop killed. They got you doing weather duty in the *Gazette*."

"I still write news stories, Mrs. Hanson."

"I suppose that's so. But then so can anyone. I can sit in my breakfast nook and scribble away. I can write down all my pussy feelings about how we should pay welfare for people to sit on their asses and all hold hands afterward. Maybe I could write me an editorial about what makes right and what makes wrong, and then tell people who to vote in for judge. I could just take it all down in my Mickey Mouse notebook. Then I'd be writing news stories too, for all the good they'd do."

Laura turned and walked to the rickety-looking porch swing. It groaned, but supported her.

Emily Hanson didn't object, just ground out the Newport with the toe of her slipper and crossed her arms.

"It seems like you know my background, Mrs. Hanson."

"Like I said, killin' that cop. That part doesn't bother me none. Cops never did me any favors." She spit on the porch and it made an oblong wet hole in the dust.

Laura stared at the spot and felt her blood pressure spike. She took a minute, waited until she felt certain her voice would come out even. "Frank Stuart was a lot of things, but he didn't deserve to die."

"Who does, missy?"

"Maybe the man who killed your daughter?"

"He deserved to die by someone's hand, just not his own. One more life where he got to pick and choose the moment it was snuffed out. He was playing God right up until the end, wasn't he, Miss Chambers? You couldn't even take that away from him."

"You believe in God, Mrs. Hanson?"

Emily Hanson spit on the porch again. "Fuck no. Do you?"

"Maybe. I used to."

"Everybody used to. Everybody used to believe in Santa Claus too. The world beats those kind of notions out of you."

"There are good things in the world too."

"Tell that to my daughter."

Laura had nothing to say to that. She studied Emily's face, expecting a tear or a quiver in the lip, but her face was rock solid. The expression reminded her of a pit bull, lip half-curled in a snarl. All anger and not an ounce of grief.

Emily lit another Newport and sat on the rattan chair next to the porch swing. "So why are you here talking to me?"

"Besides Frank Stuart getting killed—"

"I know about your little horror story. The ghost who runs around taking kids."

Laura fixed her with a stare. "It happened."

"Bullshit."

"It happened just like I said." Her voice was louder now.

"You're crazy or a liar. I'm betting on liar. All you people are just in it for the cash and the glory, see who can write the most sensational headline."

It took every ounce of willpower not to throw Samantha Powell in this woman's face. Laura was perfectly willing to use the girl as leverage during an interview. It had been less than forty-eight hours since the ear arrived at the *Gazette*, and she'd yet to speak to Bass Herman, but she would never agree to suppress the truth. Only Bass got to decide what was fit to print, but if telling people about the new missing girl would help shake the trees, she would do it without a second thought.

On the other hand, Emily Hanson might be the worst person in the world to tell.

Laura reached out and took the woman's knee. Her hand was shaking. "Please, I need you to listen to me. Eugene Hobbes didn't kill your daughter. He didn't take Teresa Mitchem either, but I plan to find the man who did. You can help me."

"Don't care," she said.

She said it so quick, so brusque, that for a second it didn't process.

"You don't care," Laura repeated.

"Why should I? Olive's dead. So is Teresa, and you know it. I told that girl not to go wandering off—a million times I told her. What does she do? Wanders off and leaves me holding the bag."

"Holding the bag."

"You deaf? Hell yes, holding the bag. My husband spent a month drunk after we found out and then he took off. God knows where he is now. I suspect he ain't ever coming back. Did you read those damn articles they wrote about me? Making me out to be neglectful and so on? More bullshit. Everyone 'round here lets their kids play outside, go house to house and such. Just bad luck mine happened to be the one snatched up."

"Bad luck."

"Stop acting like that," she said, and slapped Laura's hand off her knee. "'Course it was bad luck. That girl never had trouble making me look bad, but what the hell else would you call it?" She shook her head. "Bad fucking luck."

Laura's skin felt clammy. She pulled her coat closer. "You were right, Mrs. Hanson. It was a mistake to come here." She stood.

"Hey now, not so fast. I'm giving you a hard time, I know, but that don't mean we couldn't work together. I bet you write a real pretty story about her. I bet *Time* would put it on the cover. You get yours and I get mine."

A deep fatigue spread through Laura's core. "Are you asking me for money, Mrs. Hanson?"

"Don't give me that look. I told you, my husband quit on me. Times are tough."

"Times are tough," Laura agreed.

"So we got a deal then. Just need your word you'll make me look good. All them know-it-alls pretending it was my fault she got grabbed up. And that Angie Mitchem, always sitting in church, praying, and everyone treating her like some kind of saint. I want to shake them all and say, hey, her kid's gone too. It's not fair."

"No, it's not. Can I ask you something?"

Emily narrowed her eyes, suspicious. "I suppose."

"Did Olive ever wear a cross? A gold cross around her neck?"

"Lot of girls wear those."

Laura tried not to grit her teeth. "I'm not asking about a lot of girls; I'm asking about your daughter. Did she wear one?"

"Maybe."

"You're not sure?"

"I told you, we're not religious."

"Thank you for your time, Mrs. Hanson."

"So we got a deal? I help you write the story and we split the cash?"

Laura said nothing.

"But no more lies. You got to promise to give me fair treatment."

"If I gave you fair treatment," Laura said, "people would burn you at the stake."

She left Olive Hanson's mother sitting there on the porch, face an ashen snarl, lighting her third cigarette of the day.

*　*　*

Baptists had reigned supreme in Hillsborough's early years, and they'd made good use of their numerous believers by building something that would last, a structure of red brick rising to a peaked roof next to a Romanesque bell tower, its copper roof gone green with age. It stood on the corner of Third and Spring looking a thousand years old. She wondered if that was the point, if the building itself was a message about eternity.

Laura climbed the steps to the front doors, thick wooden slats braced by iron and bolts, and pushed her way into the vestibule. There was no artificial light inside, just a few candles, and she took a few seconds to blink the day away.

Stairways on either side led to the gallery above, originally built for slaves, and another set of doors opened on the aisle running the church's length. She walked up toward the altar, her footsteps echoing off the marble floor. There was more light in the main chamber courtesy of tall stained-glass windows. The walls flickered in blues and yellows and greens, and the marriage of colors filled the nave with an amber glow.

She reached the pulpit. To her left, a woman dressed in black sat in the second row of pews. Her fingers ran up and down the cover of a worn black Bible as she spoke softly under her breath.

"Mrs. Mitchem?"

It came out too loud. Her voice knocked off the walls, the roof, and came back to her a mocking imitation of itself.

Mitchem Mitchem Mitchem.

The woman's head snapped up. She was maybe fifteen years older than Laura, with black hair so thick and long and tangled it must have been impossible to pull a brush through. Her features were full without being plump. There was a certain darkness under her cheekbones, almost like a bruise, hinting at a recent and rapid loss of weight. The cheeks themselves were wet with tears. The eyes were the color of pewter, as though crying had leeched all color out of them.

"Mrs. Mitchem," she said again, careful not to let her voice echo this time.

"Yes."

"May I sit?"

Angie Mitchem perched on the edge of the pew with her knees together. Her fingers never stopped roaming the Bible. She said nothing.

Laura took it as an invitation and sat.

"I know who you are," Angie said. "You came to my house six months ago. I yelled at you."

"Yes."

"I shouldn't have raised my voice."

"No one can blame you," Laura said.

She used the back of her hand to wipe her face. "I understand you're doing your job, but do you really think it's appropriate to approach me here?"

"No ma'am. I can see how it might be construed as disrespectful. This is just the only place I knew to find you."

Angie twisted in place and scanned the rest of the church. Satisfied they were alone, she shrugged. "It's fine, I suppose. But I don't talk to reporters."

Laura tried for levity. She pointed back and forth between them and said, "So what do you call this?"

Angie gave a small smile. "I mean I won't say anything on the record. But I don't mind talking to *you*, Laura." She reached out and put a hand on Laura's knee.

"You know my name."

"I told you, I know who you are."

"Mrs. Mitchem—"

"Call me Angie."

"Angie, I'm real sorry about your daughter."

Angie squeezed her knee. "I know you are."

"I want you to know, I drove up there to the mountains because I didn't know what else to do. I tried to call the man from the FBI, I talked to the sheriff in person. No one believed me."

"To speak and not be heard must be difficult."

"Thank you. I—you're very understanding."

"You risked your own life going up there. I can't see that you gained anything from it, either."

"I risked another person's life, too. He wasn't as lucky."

"He was full grown. He made his own choices."

"Not like Teresa."

Angie made a sound like a sigh, but it came from somewhere deeper than her lungs. "No, not like Teresa."

"I thought I could save her," Laura said, and it came out choked. An invisible hand clamped across her throat. She couldn't talk. She couldn't breathe.

Angie's eyes widened. "Sweetheart, you're crying."

And she was. Her cheeks turned sticky and a sob wracked her chest. "I'm sorry," she managed.

Angie Mitchem didn't hesitate. She opened her arms and embraced her. Into her ear she whispered, "I know."

* * *

"The most awful part is not knowing what happened to her. Night-time is the worst. Eyes open or closed, the darkness is a canvas. My mind goes to work on it in the silence." Angie shuddered. "My imagination can be terrible."

Laura just nodded. Not knowing—she understood that pain. They sat on the church's front steps, letting the cold do its work. It cleared the mind like a slap in the face. They'd been talking for almost an hour.

"Did she ever wear a gold cross?"

"Yes, all the girls here do. It's supposed . . ."

"What?"

"It's supposed to protect them."

Laura reached into her bag and pulled out an envelope. The FedEx package had arrived at the farm around lunch. Timinski had promised to be prompt, and he was as good as his word. From inside the envelope she drew four glossy eight-by-ten photographs, close-ups of each cross found in the cabin.

She held them out to Angie. "Do you think you could take a look at these?"

Angie made no move to reach for them. Something darted behind her eyes. It was the first sign of panic.

"They're just photos, Angie."

"Let me guess. Gold crosses, right?"

"Yes."

"From where?"

"From the cabin in the mountains."

Now the thing moved from behind her eyes and emerged into the open. Her gaze shot left and right, her breathing doubled in pace. She moved to stand, then sat again. "I can't look at those."

"Why not?"

She fixed Laura with a look, as though the question barely deserved an answer. "You know why. What if it's in there?"

"So what if it is? We won't know anything more than we do right now. That he took her."

Angie didn't speak. Her breaths came in long low whooshes through the pert circle of her lips.

Laura pressed her. "Right?"

"Right," Angie said. She took one more deep breath, let it out, and took the pictures. She looked at them carefully, one by one, then shook her head.

"It's not here."

"You're sure?"

"I gave her the cross. It was mine when I was a little girl. Here—" She took Laura's notebook and pen, rested them on her knee, and started drawing. "It was my mother's before that. I used to see it in the mirror around my neck every day, and then again on Teresa." She finished and handed back the notebook.

Laura studied the picture. Angie was a fine artist. With a minimum of strokes she had captured it in detail. It was more ornate than a simple cross. Jesus was present in crude form, and there was a twisting ivy pattern at the top.

"Is it small?"

"Perhaps a bit bigger than is normal for a small girl, and quite tarnished from use. Part of its charm."

Laura nodded. None of the crosses from the photos looked anything like it. She tried to think how to say the next thing. Angie Mitchem was somehow serene in her grief. Laura wondered how deep her convictions went. If she pushed, perhaps this woman would collapse like a house of cards.

"Did you read about him? About Hobbes, I mean."

"Of course. I read everything that relates to Teresa."

"You know about the things in his journal. Not the things he did, but the things that were done to him."

Angie looked off into the distance, gave a curt nod.

"Do you believe they had a hand in his becoming?" Laura asked. "That he was not born but made?"

"I do," she said firmly.

Laura took a deep breath. "If there had been a chance, do you think he could have been unmade?"

Angie turned and stared at her for a beat. Understanding dawned in her eyes. "You're talking about Teresa."

Laura tried to maintain eye contact, failed, and ended up staring at the gray stone steps. "What if she's not the same person. What if she's changed. Do you still want her back?"

"Look at me," Angie said, and she did. Her gaze was clear and unflinching. There was no flimsy house of cards hiding behind those eyes. Just a thousand-year-old church.

"Do you want her back," Laura asked, "even if she's broken?"

Angie set her jaw.

"I want her back," she said, "any way I can get her."

CHAPTER

29

S HE ATE A bowl of cold soup in her room while flipping through
the coloring book. Most of it had crumbled away, but there
were still two pages attached by a single staple. Both were loose
sheets of paper, not part of the coloring book proper. No pictures,
no lines to stay inside, just the raw imagination of a child.

Laura worried for that child.

The first page depicted a long ribbon of blue with a fish poking
its head out. A river. In front of it was an oblong shape done up in
beige. All along its length little pockets of red and yellow and orange
stood out. There wasn't much detail, but Laura took them to be
fires. Down in the corner stood a dark shape. It was indistinct, without clear outlines, but the child had taken great pains to fill in the
space.

Laura ran a finger across the area.

Even after all this time there were gouges in the paper. Someone
had taken a crayon and run it over the area again and again, pressing down as hard as they could. In the center, a single red dot.

The second picture was much worse.

In it, a boy with a frowny face lay on the ground. Unnaturally
large tears leapt out from both eyes and arced toward the ground.
Next to him was what could only be described as a monster, a hid-
eous three-legged, four-armed beast with the head of a dog. Every
hand held a cigarette. Two of the cigarettes were being pressed into

the boy's belly. Above the two of them hung a single bare bulb. Again, darkness was emphasized, the tracks from the black crayon like veins in the paper.

Laura took a breath and flipped back to the first picture, the foot encased in a sandal. There was no proof, of course, that any of this had to do with Hobbes's victims, but something inside her recoiled at the sight of these crude drawings. They had the same flavor of sickness she associated with Hobbes. Could he have passed that sickness on to a child?

Why not?

As his diary made clear, it had been passed on to him like some kind of psychological virus. Sometimes a virus kills its host. Sometimes it leaves them alive but infected. A carrier.

*   *   *

"Obsession is never healthy," Jasmine said.

"And what about the alternative? If I never even try to look for her, by default I spend the rest of my life not knowing."

Jasmine nodded. "That's called acceptance, Laura. And believe it or not, that is a healthy response to certain adversities. We cannot change certain things, and we are not responsible for changing them. All we can do is endure. Like you said, we have to live with it."

She crossed her arms. "It seems like a coward's excuse."

Jasmine took a minute to sip from her water glass. Laura had known her long enough to recognize the look on her face. She was collecting her thoughts.

"In the past," she said finally, "I've had patients diagnosed with a terminal illness. The situation is in some ways similar. They're confronted with not only their own mortality, but also with a profound lack of agency. Often the disease isn't the result of any choice they made or didn't make. It exists as something completely outside their control. If a person like that tried to work toward accepting their fate, would you call it cowardice?"

"Of course not. There's a lot to be said for going out with dignity."

"So they should know when to quit."

"You can stop right there. It's a false analogy. Terminal cancer is one thing; finding Samantha Powell is something else entirely."

"How do you see them as different?"

"Finding Samantha isn't a lost cause."

The doctor drank some more water. "Samantha is a very sweet girl with a very troubled home life. I offered my help to Sheriff Fuller, but he didn't seem interested."

"I'm interested."

"You're not the police."

"But I'm here, and I'm involved whether I like it or not. He sent me an ear, Jasmine. Here, take a look at these." Laura spread the pictures of the crosses out on the low coffee table and explained where she'd gotten them. "What do you think? Some kind of trophy?"

"It's a leap," Jasmine said. "A gold cross necklace must be the most common piece of jewelry besides earrings. Even I wear one." She patted a lump underneath her shirt.

"So you think it's just coincidence."

"No, I think it's more than that. I think it's a product of your need to know."

Laura groaned. "And just like that, back to doctor and patient."

"Listen. Do you know mountain laurel?"

"The plant?"

She nodded. "When I was a girl, we used to spend summers in the mountains. I was an only child, and when my parents were busy I would climb up into high places to be alone. I loved those flowers, the pinks and the whites. To me they were crowns and necklaces and hair clips. Anywhere there was mountain laurel, there was sure to be a wind that would keep me cool after climbing. I thought it was like magic, that the plants themselves summoned the wind. I liked to pretend they summoned it just for me. But of course I had it backwards. The air carries the moisture a plant requires."

"There's a moral in there somewhere, I'm sure."

"I know, I'm being obtuse. Here's my point. You have a gut feeling that these gold crosses are a clue, right?"

"Right."

"Not right. You need to come to terms with the fact that you can't trust your gut feelings. You're in a very vulnerable place, with a deep need for closure. How could your feelings possibly be objective? You *need* to find that these necklaces have meaning, so you decide that they do. Not the other way around."

"You think it's nothing," Laura said.

Jasmine put a hand on her knee, a look of concern on her face. "In the laurels there was always a fresh breeze, because fresh breezes are where laurels grow."

30

COOPER HAD BOUNDED off around the old tree stump, sniffing delicately at the dirt. Once the dog was sufficiently occupied, she told him about the ear. At first he thought it was good news, a sign that Teresa Mitchem was still alive. So she told him it was another left ear, and watched his wishful thinking crease and buckle under the weight of another missing girl.

"Jesus," Rodgers said, and bent over with his hands on his knees, taking quick breaths, his face the color of used-up charcoal.

"Seems Fuller's main concern is avoiding bad press. He's hunkered down for the winter."

Rodgers straightened himself up. "What about your boyfriend, what did he say?

"Who, Timinski?" She tried on a smile, but it dropped away when he didn't respond in kind. "He's off it. OCSO isn't calling in the cavalry, so he's probably not even in the state anymore. But he let me take another look in the cabin."

"You really think anyone would be stupid enough to go back there?"

"No, but I'm working backwards here. If there really is a third man, then this whole thing was designed to bring Hobbes out into the light."

Rodgers rubbed his shoulder. "Easier ways to do that."

"Fuller said the same, but go with me here. Say that's the

case—who would know about Hobbes? Who would want all of us to know about him?"

Rodgers rubbed his chin. "Someone who knew him personally, I suppose."

"Exactly. I mean, a guy like Hobbes, he cuts a swath of destruction through people's lives."

"And generally ends those lives."

"But what if he didn't?" She shoved her hands deeper into her pockets. "Somewhere, sometime, a person tangled with Hobbes but escaped with less than a death sentence. That's the kind of person who might want some measure of revenge."

Rodgers squinted at her. "You think your third man is someone Hobbes abused as a child."

Laura nodded. "And now they're all grown up."

"That's a hell of a broad profile. We don't have the slightest inkling what Hobbes was up to for the last twenty-nine years."

"That's why we need to focus on what we do know. We need to concentrate on the murders from the late '80s."

She produced the manila envelope from inside her jacket and handed it to Rodgers.

He pulled out the photos, examined them, then shrugged. "What am I looking at here?"

"Timinski and I found them in the cabin."

"Gold crosses."

"I was thinking trophies."

He let out a sharp breath. "That's a stretch. Besides, there are four of them."

Laura said nothing.

In a second, he worked it out for himself. "A fourth girl all those years ago?"

"It's not impossible, is it?"

"Let's go inside," she said.

They warmed their hands over the wood-burning stove in the kitchen and Rodgers put the kettle on. When it whistled he poured out two measures of hot water into teacups, then pulled out his bottle of bourbon.

She shook her head once. "Not today."

"Warms the soul," he said, but acquiesced, screwing on the cap and putting the bottle into a cabinet. He handed Laura her tea.

She sipped at it. "Just say I'm right. Who could the fourth victim be?"

"Lot of girls, potentially. Back when it was happening, we would assume the worst every time a girl went missing. Most of them were home safe and sound within a day; that's how missing persons always works. But some weren't."

"They could have been taken by Hobbes."

"Sure, or a hundred other things. We never found them posed in a field. Sometimes people just disappear, and that includes children. It doesn't take a serial killer."

Laura chewed on that, then said, "Let's just keep assuming the theory is true though. One of those girls was actually taken by Hobbes."

"But he didn't pose her in a field," Rodgers said.

"He didn't even kill her. That's the whole idea. Do you have files on the possibles?"

"Of course, I've got copies of everything."

They spent the rest of the day and most of the night reading. At midnight, Don Rodgers stretched and yawned and pushed his chair back from the kitchen table.

"I'm done for the night," he said.

"You sure?"

"When you get older you'll understand. Past a certain age and hour, the mind turns to Swiss cheese. I'll be more use after a good night's rest."

Laura started packing up some of the file folders strewn across the table top. "I can take a hint."

"No, no, stay if you want."

"I'll take off. We can pick it up tomorrow."

He crossed his arms. "How many cups of coffee have you had?"

"Three?"

"In the last hour maybe."

"Okay, call it three plus."

"You drink coffee like a cop. I remember those days, sucking down a metric ton of caffeine and then lying in bed, staring at the ceiling and listening to my heart jitter. Really, you can stay."

"If you're sure."

"I'm sure," he said. "Couch is in the den when you crash. Besides, Cooper can use the company." He hooked his thumb over his shoulder.

On a thick rug in front of the wood-burning stove, Cooper slept on his side, belly toward the heat. Every few seconds he let out a snore.

"Okay, see you in the morning," Laura said.

Once Rodgers had closed the door to his room, she unstacked the file folders, trying to return them to their previous positions. One stack was for unread, and then there were several stacks for already examined. One stack for no, one for the maybes, one for the files she had unresolved questions about. She plucked up another and got back to reading.

An hour and a half later, she found it.

The folder was labeled with a name: FINCH, PATTY. Inside was a copy of the police report, a photo of the girl, and something else. Rodgers had taken from the official file two sheets of construction paper. Both had drawings on them. One of a house, in front of it a boy and a man, hand in hand, smiling. The second one she recognized. It was the same blue ribbon, the same beige oval.

The picture in the Patty Finch file.

The picture from the cabin.

They'd been done by the same person. She could feel it in her bones.

Three quick raps brought Rodgers out of his room, bleary-eyed.

"What the hell, Laura?"

"I found it. Here, look." She laid the file open on the table in front of him.

"So what?" he said, and rubbed at the stubble on his chin, yawning.

"As an ex-cop, you're not going to like this next part."

He frowned. "Go on."

"When I was at the cabin with Timinski, I took something."

He didn't say anything, just glowered at her.

"Wait here a second."

She threw on her coat and bundled out to her car, came back inside with the coloring book clutched to her chest. In the kitchen, Rodgers was fully awake. More than awake. His nostrils flared in anger.

"Christ, Laura, you can't take things from a crime scene! Say it has any value at all. What use will it be in court?"

She pressed the coloring book flat on the table and turned to the page, then lined it up next to the one from the file folder.

Rodgers froze, staring at them.

"They're the same, right?" Laura said, unable to hide the excitement in her voice.

When Rodgers spoke, no excitement colored his inflection. Words came out in a flat monotone. "You found this in the cabin? Hobbes's cabin?"

"Yes. What's wrong?"

His lower lip trembled as he tapped the name on the file folder. "Patty Finch. I know this girl."

"Of course. You've read all these files a hundred times."

He shook his head.

"No, you don't understand. I met her. I found her more than once."

31

"THE FINCHES," RODGERS said, "were new in town. Just the mother and the daughter, Mildred and Patty. The girl was a sweetheart. You saw the picture?"

Laura nodded.

"Doesn't capture her at all. That was the only photo we could get, and she looks happy in it."

"She didn't look happy in real life?"

"In real life she looked like a puppy that'd been kicked too many times. Nice as can be, but she'd cringe every time you lifted your hand."

Laura paused. "What happened to her?"

He stared at her for second. "You live with your mother, don't you? Can't help but notice you never talk about her."

"No, not much," she said, and left it at that.

"Can I assume it's not exactly a loving relationship?"

"You could assume that, yes."

"Same for me. Only I can tell that whatever your mama did to you, it wasn't physical. Otherwise you'd understand exactly what I'm describing. A kid who's been hit so many times, from so many angles, that the possibility of violence starts to live in the back of their mind like a ghost. Never really there, never really gone. Hell, I still can't be around a person carrying a cane without the hair on the back of my neck standing up."

"Your father?"

He gave a curt nod. "The Finch girl was one like me. I knew it the second I saw her. Tried to talk to Mildred, the mom, but she was hard to track down. Never home. Always some excuse."

"Any hint of what might have happened to Patty?"

"This was before she disappeared. It wasn't the first time I'd run into that—a kid with a less-than-stellar home life—and usually the parents were just about what you'd expect. Drunks, antisocial personalities. But Mildred Finch was different."

"Not a drunk," Laura said.

"No way. Very sharp. She had the good-mother act down pat."

"But it was an act."

He thought about that. "Hell, I don't know. I think so. The little girl was being beaten, I'm sure of that much."

"And her mother?"

His eyes narrowed to coin slots. "No kid is that good of an actor, and one of them was putting me on. Who does that leave?"

Laura saw something in his face that made the backs of her hands tingle. Here in his kitchen, she suddenly had the sense of what it must have been like to sit across from him at the interrogation table, and the thought of it made her a little bit scared.

"I'm sorry," he said, sensing her hesitation. "Bad memories. She ran away three times. The first time, she tried to recruit another girl in her class to run away with her. Well, the other girl got scared and told her mama, and her mama called the police. They dispatched me and I found her waiting in the spot they'd arranged, all ready to go. You rarely see that in a ten-year-old, a total readiness to brave the big bad world. No hesitation."

"She made a real impression on you," Laura said.

Rodgers turned his head to hide his face. "She was a good kid. Second time she tried to go on her own, someone spotted her with a bindle, a piece of cloth tied to stick. She probably saw it on TV somewhere. I found her down near the bridge south of downtown."

"And the third time?"

He groaned. "I should have known. It never felt right."

Laura put a hand on top of his. "I'm sure you did what you could."

He drew back from her, used his other hand to rub the spot she'd touched like it had been burned by acid. "Don't do that. Don't pretend you can judge whether my search was adequate. You don't know how hard I looked."

"Okay," Laura said. "How hard did you look?"

He paused, staring at the wall. When he spoke, it was softer than before. "The third time she went to the old speedway."

Laura knew what he meant. On the outskirts of Hillsborough stood a remnant from the early days of stock car racing. It dated from before the sport was televised, before it even had professional drivers. They raced on a dirt track, and years of tires and footsteps had packed the topsoil down good and tight. The track was still there.

"Out by the river," Laura said.

"Out by the river," Rodgers agreed, and tapped a finger on the beige oval from the coloring book.

Laura's hand went to her mouth. "The track."

"Looks like it to me," he said, and went to the cabinet to retrieve his bottle of bourbon. "The third time, Patty Finch went to the track and tried to find someone to give her a ride away from Hillsborough. Once her mother reported her missing, people started coming forward saying they'd seen her."

"Did she get a ride?"

"No one knew. Of course the track hadn't been used by NASCAR in decades, but it hosted an exhibition race—I forget why—and there were people from all over. Always thought one of them gave her a lift, gave her the head start she always wanted. I figured that's why I couldn't find her."

He poured a slug of bourbon into his empty coffee cup and downed it in one swallow.

She gave him a minute, then asked, "You never considered her as a possible victim of the Kid?"

He shook his head. "Not seriously. She wanted to run away so bad, tried so many times, we all just assumed she finally succeeded. Maybe that's just what I wanted to believe." He poured and drank again.

"You said they were new in town."

"They came that winter. Patty registered at the school halfway through the year, I remember that much. By the time summer rolled around, she was gone."

"Where did they come from?"

"It's all in the file."

She paged through his notes, found a notation that read PRE-VIOUS ADDRESS? scrawled across the page. "Here," she said.

"It's coming back. Never could get a straight answer out of Mil-dred Finch. Fact is, I only got to question her twice, maybe three times. She moved again."

Laura sat back. "Her daughter disappeared, and she moved away that quickly?"

Rodgers nodded.

"Seems like a lot of parents might be inclined to stick around, assist in the search. And if they really thought their daughter ran away, they might want to be there in case the child tried to come home."

"You heard my opinion of her," he said. "When I found out she was gone, it wasn't a surprise."

"No forwarding address?"

Rodgers didn't answer, just filled his cup again.

"We need to track her down."

He sighed. "This is a real lead, Laura. You keep tugging at the thread, what are you going to find? I'm worried about you."

"I'm not letting this one get away."

"Let's try talking to Fuller together. I used to be sheriff. He'll listen."

"You can try if you want, but he wants nothing to do with me." She took a breath. "I'm a pariah."

"It's dangerous now. You shouldn't do this alone."

"So help me. Don't quit ten yards from the finish line. You of all people should be ready to back me up."

"The police can do that."

"Christ, take a teaspoon of concrete and harden the fuck up."

He shrugged. "I'm an old man, Laura. I've been looking for Eugene Hobbes for almost thirty years, and now I found him. Haven't I done enough?"

Laura shook her head violently. "Hobbes may be gone, but the other one is still out there. We need to find him. Olive Hanson is dead, but Teresa Mitchem might still be alive. Samantha Powell might still be alive."

"You don't want to end up like me. It's always something. Always one more clue, one more hint. I guess I just can't do it anymore."

She grabbed her coat and slipped her arms inside. "All these years you've been thinking about this case, turning it over in your mind. You know what would cure that? The truth. An answer about what really happened. Maybe saving a little girl's life."

She gestured to the kitchen filled with file boxes in the corner of his shabby house perched among the failing, lonely fields.

"You're right—I don't want to end up like this."

He stared at her for a second. Then his shoulders sagged and he reached for the bottle on the table, poured some into a random glass. When he spoke, his voice was near breaking.

"I just don't have another one in me."

She went to leave.

"Wait. Come back and see me again."

"I'm going to be running this thing down. Maybe in a couple days." She opened the door.

"Two days," he said. "Call at least, so I know you're okay. Promise me."

"I promise," she said.

She turned back, and he did look different. Smaller somehow, as if all along he'd been a set of those Russian nesting dolls and now someone had stripped away the defiant exterior shell, revealing the smaller broken one inside.

CHAPTER

32

"I THINK I'VE got something here, Tim."

"What time is it?"

"After two. Did I wake you?"

"Hold on." A sound like the rustling of sheets.

"Are you alone?"

The shuffling of footsteps, the click of a door latch shooting home. "Sorry, you caught me off guard."

"I shouldn't have called."

"No—it's good to hear your voice."

Quickly, she ran down the story. Stealing the coloring book, matching it to an old Sheriff's Office file, and finding the name associated with that file: a possible fourth victim.

At the end, Timinski said, "You stole evidence?"

"I knew that'd bother you."

"We have to pretend you never told me about this."

"Or you'll cuff me?

"I'm not playing." Steel in his voice. "You just admitted a felony to a federal agent. And don't tell Fuller about this, he'll arrest you just to shut you up. Even if there was another one, where does that leave us?"

"You should take credit for the connection. Maybe get yourself a nice office out it."

"You mean the connection made using stolen evidence? I can't have anything to do with that."

"Not even if we can catch this guy?"

"I'm not going to report you or anything. I just can't help."

"I understand."

"That's probably not what you want to hear, but I've got other things to—"

"Tell it to Angie Mitchem," she said, and hung up the phone.

* * *

She thought of Angie Mitchem, sitting in a worn-smooth pew and clutching her Bible, then glanced down at the images from the coloring book. She'd lined them up on her bed before calling, like soldiers marching across her duvet. Two feet in old-fashioned sandals. One big, one small. Sudden recognition flashed through her mind. There was a story that fit the bill.

David and Goliath.

After a series of gradually narrowing internet searches, she had a spreadsheet with the name and contact information for every publisher that might deal in religious coloring books. To each she sent a brief email explaining the situation and attached an image of the page with the foot in the sandal. It asked that they forward the message along to anyone who purchased such coloring books in bulk. Then she copied the message and sent it along to an ever-widening circle of government agencies, group homes, and churches. She played on their better angels, emphasizing the chance to save a child and imploring them to call if any of their staff recognized the page. It was a long shot, but better ideas were in short supply.

At the bottom of each message, she added her phone number.

* * *

Stranger and stranger—Patty Finch didn't have a birth certificate.

Laura spent the morning and early afternoon on the phone with the state of North Carolina, then with all the surrounding states. Her skills came in handy as she managed to sweet-talk each government office into doing a quick search for her. Each state was adamant that no Patricia Finch had been born in the last hundred years. Other variations of the name were also a bust.

The only thing left to go on was the missing persons report. It listed an address, and at four in the afternoon Laura parked and knocked on the front door. After a few minutes she knocked again just before the door opened.

"So sorry to keep you waiting," the woman said. She sported an elegant housecoat, almost like a kimono, and a shock of white hair as thick as the strand of pearls around her neck. In one hand she clutched an ivory-handled cane. Laura guessed she was at least eighty years old. "Not quite as spry as I used to be."

"Please, no apologies necessary. I was hoping someone could tell me about some tenants who used to live here."

"There are no tenants here, I'm afraid."

"This would have been quite a while ago, back in 1987 and 1988. The Finches."

The old woman nodded once. "Yes, of course. The little girl who disappeared."

Laura was staggered by her luck. "You remember them?"

"Absolutely. I've lived in this house more than forty years. I was their landlord, I suppose."

"May I come in?"

The woman stood aside and swung her cane out of the way.

* * *

The old woman, whose name turned out to be Vivian Koffman, got Laura settled in a chair in the parlor and then tottered off to the kitchen. Five minutes later she returned with tea on a sterling silver tray. She balanced one side of the tray on the top of her cane and scooted along quite efficiently. Before Laura could offer to help, everything was down on the coffee table and Vivian was pouring her a cup of Earl Grey.

"Milk or sugar?"

"No, thank you. You're not from North Carolina," Laura observed.

"No, my husband was. He was a military man, moved around

a lot. We met in Chicago, and after we married he wanted to move back here. He passed a few years ago."

"I'm sorry."

Vivian waved a hand. "No need to be. Now, what's your interest in the Finch girl?"

Laura decided to keep it simple. "I'm working on a story for the *Gazette* about missing children."

"She's still missing then?"

"As far as I know."

Vivian sighed. "I'd always hoped she made it somewhere."

"Somewhere?"

"Oh, I don't know. Somewhere nice, I suppose. Alan was a wonderful husband, and a good father, but he was the one who insisted we move to Hillsborough. I've been here for a long time, and I'm too old to move now, but it was never my first choice. Are you a native? Does that offend you?"

"I moved away for a long time myself."

"But you came back. Why?"

Laura paused. "I guess I had nowhere else to go."

She nodded. "As good a reason as any. It was clear to me that little Patty Finch wanted nothing to do with this town. They were only here a matter of months before she started running away."

"Why did they move here?"

Vivian sipped her tea, then said, "Mildred Finch told me they were in hiding."

Laura sat up straight. "In hiding—what does that mean?"

"She told me they were on the run from her husband. You have to understand, this was 1987. It was a different time. If a woman's husband liked to hit her, sometimes there wasn't much she could do but learn to take a punch."

"And Mildred Finch's husband hit her?"

"She told me horrible stories about him. Just horrible. What I know for sure is that she spun a very compelling yarn."

They looked at each other for a moment.

"I have to say, Vivian, it doesn't sound like you were totally convinced."

"An old house like this has thick walls. People assume privacy," she said. "But in the late 1970s we updated the heating vents. After that, for a number of years until we got it fixed, every word spoken in every room could be heard sitting right where you are now."

Laura leaned forward in her chair.

"Where I used to sit at night," Vivian said.

"And what did you hear?"

"A very nasty woman saying very nasty things. A mother who seemed to enjoy cruelty for cruelty's sake."

"And you never told anyone?"

"I considered it. But as I said, it was a different time. Hitting your child wasn't even really frowned upon, much less illegal. I was seriously considering shaming her in public, but Patty up and disappeared. Soon they were both gone."

Laura said, "And you never spoke of it after that? The police must have asked you questions."

She paused, withdrew a handkerchief from inside the folds of her housecoat, and daubed at her eyes.

"I came home one day and there was a police car parked right out there at the curb. If I'm being honest, my first thought was that Mildred had killed her. But no, she had escaped instead. I was happy for her, you see. I hoped she would get away and somehow make a fresh start."

"So when the police asked you questions—"

"I didn't tell them a damn thing," Vivian said.

Laura tried to think where to go next. She asked, "Mildred moved out after that?"

"Couldn't get out fast enough. Her daughter disappears, and she's in the wind within a week. That should tell you all you need to know."

"Do you know where she went?"

"I do not. I never spoke to her again."

"How about where they came from? Where did they live with Mr. Finch?"

Vivian set her teacup down and steepled her fingers. "Let me see, it was from somewhere farther north, I remember that much. In Virginia. Chesapeake? No, that's not right. Somewhere on the border."

"I don't know Virginia very well," Laura said.

"That's a shame. The old memory isn't what it used to be."

"You seem sharp as a tack."

"Now isn't that sweet of you to say!"

Laura stood. "Thank you for your time, Vivian. It was a pleasure to meet you."

"And you as well, Laura. Tell me, there must be runaways more recent than 1988. How does Patty Finch fit into your story?"

"I can't give you all the details, ma'am."

Vivian smiled knowingly. "I think you're trying to find her."

Laura said nothing.

"Best of luck," she said, and showed her to the door.

Laura got three steps down the walk before the old woman stopped her.

"Mecklenburg!" she said. "They came from Mecklenburg, Virginia. I'm sure of it."

*　*　*

As it turned out, there was no city in Virginia called Mecklenburg.

But it was the name of a county. Another hour on the phone and she had something solid. Mecklenburg County had a 1979 marriage license for a John Lotter and a Mildred Finch. It listed an address. With that in hand, she called the office dealing with the area's property records and flirted with a lonely-sounding man until he agreed to find the information about that particular piece of land and read it to her over the phone. The property was a farm at the southern edge of the county, almost into North Carolina, and sprawled more than five hundred acres.

The current owner was listed as Monica Finch.

*　*　*

She drove north on I-85 for forty miles, then broke off onto US-15 for another thirty-five. A two-lane bridge carried across the half-mile span of the Roanoke River, and she crossed it as the last drops of sun evaporated off the river's surface and watched as the water turned to ink. Ten more minutes and she made Boydton, the county seat. She checked into a motel, took a shower, and forced herself to sleep.

By dawn on Saturday she was winding down country roads, looking for the farm's entrance. The weather was better here, a touch warmer with blue skies. Despite the excellent visibility, she almost missed the turn. A battered red mailbox listed to one side, nearly hidden in three-foot grass. It had FINCH hand-painted on the side in uneven white letters. Laura hit the brakes, and the Dart slid on the gravel, but she made the turn. The driveway was in worse condition than the road, rutted by erosion, and it took ten minutes to reach the end. The trees ended, and the property gave way to cleared fields with a house on a rise in the center. It looked like something out of *Gone with the Wind*, with a huge front porch under a sagging roof supported by white columns.

She parked and knocked.

No answer.

She knocked again and waited.

"Hello?"

Laura jumped. The voice came from behind her. She turned to face its owner and found a woman only a few years older than her.

"Monica Finch?"

"That's right."

She had vibrant red hair and freckles dotted her cheeks. Crow's feet had just started at the edges of her eyes, but they gave her a friendly look, as if she smiled a lot.

From behind her leg, another voice said, "Mommy?"

A little girl stepped out but kept clutching her mother's pant leg. She was Monica in miniature, freckles more prominent, red hair bound up in pigtails.

"Can I help you?" Monica asked.

"I'm a reporter working on a story—"

"Like for the paper?" the little girl interrupted.

The two of them were up on the porch now, and Laura bent down on one knee. "And who's this?"

Her mother smiled. "This is Francine."

Laura extended a hand and Francine shook it, a serious look on her face. "Pleased to meet you," she said.

Laura grinned. "Likewise. Yes, I write the stories that go in the paper."

"How do you know all those things?"

"Well, I don't. But lots of different people know lots of different things, and my job is to ask them questions about it."

Francine nodded, and her nose scrunched up as she processed this revelation about the nature of journalism.

"What a polite little girl," she said to Monica.

"We try our best. Is this about the runoff into Smithfield Creek? We don't actually farm the land anymore, so I'm not sure I have anything to say."

"The runoff," Laura repeated.

Monica said, "But I am against pollution."

"Who isn't?"

"Exactly."

"But I'm not here about the runoff into Smithfield Creek." Monica frowned.

"I'm up here from Hillsborough, North Carolina."

Monica stared at her for another second, recognition dawning on her face. She recoiled away across the porch. In what Laura suspected was an unconscious gesture, one arm grabbed Francine's shoulder and pushed the little girl behind her leg again.

"Mommy?"

"Shh, quiet now, sweetheart." To Laura: "I recognize you. You're the woman who led the police to that serial killer."

33

"**B**UT WHY DO you want to talk to me?"

Laura watched the wheels turn in Monica's head. *Reporter infamous for her connection to serial killer wants an interview, which cannot possibly mean anything good.* The woman took a sudden interest in her surroundings, looking behind her, then scanning the horizon.

"Why do you want to talk to me?" she repeated, a new urgency in her tone.

Laura raised both hands, palms out. "It's nothing like that, nothing dangerous. I'm just doing back story. Can I come inside?"

The sun broke free of the tree line and bathed the porch in golden light. Monica squinted at her. "If it's all the same to you, we can talk right here."

Laura stood and waited. Any person who had raised a child with such excellent manners must have a strong sense of decorum themselves. She thought it would play to her advantage, so she said nothing.

It only took another second for Monica to break. "We can talk out here, but I'll get us some coffee from the kitchen. Cream? Sugar?"

"Black."

"Back in a sec. Have a seat," she said, and pulled Francine along behind her as she vanished through the front door. Francine waved and then disappeared inside before Laura could wave back.

There was an Adirondack chair that proved comfortable, and Laura dug out her pad and pencil and balanced them on its flat arm.

Monica backed through the screen door with a cup of coffee in each hand and gave one to Laura. Behind her, the screen door poked open a few inches.

"You stay inside," she said, and the visible sliver of Francine's face receded from view.

Monica was well-mannered enough to let Laura get in a few sips of coffee before speaking. "This is all very strange."

"I should have called ahead."

Monica ignored that. "What could you possibly want to talk about? How do I fit into a story about a child killer? I really need you to tell me that right now." She nodded back toward the door. "Should I be worried?"

Laura shook her head. "I didn't know you had a daughter. If I had, I definitely would have called. Like I said, this is just back story."

"What kind of back story?"

Laura had spent most of the drive thinking about this moment. For the last six months she had never hesitated to lie in service of the bigger truth. Here, though, things were different. Monica deserved to know. To this woman, sitting in front of her, Patty Finch was blood.

"Before I say anything at all," Laura said, "I need you to understand a few things. My job is just like I explained it to Francine, visiting people and asking questions. Hopefully I end up with something close to the truth. Right now I'm in the middle of that process. I don't know anything for sure."

Monica set her coffee cup down on the low table between them. "Now you're scaring me. Just give me a headline, something I can wrap my head around."

Laura nodded. "Okay, fair enough. Another girl disappeared in Hillsborough, and I think there may be a connection to Mildred Finch and her daughter, Patty."

She watched carefully for Monica's reaction. Would it be fear?

Or despair? Anxiety? She studied her face, attuned to any sign that this woman had knowledge that would help.

Monica cocked her head to one side, eyebrows raised. "Aunt Mildred?"

"She was your aunt, then?"

Laura hadn't been sure about the exact familial relationship, only that an owner of this exact property named Finch could not possibly be a coincidence.

"Yes," Monica said, "my mother's sister."

"Do you know where she is?"

She shook her head. "I haven't seen her since I was a little girl. Younger than Francine."

"And your mother? Would she know how to find her?"

"No, they were never close. When she left, she left for good."

Laura took a breath. This was the moment, the question she'd been waiting to ask, and it surprised her how difficult it was to get the words out. It was fear, she realized. She was afraid of this woman's answer. She was scared of being right.

"What about her daughter, Patty?"

Monica made a face.

"Has anyone in the family had contact with her since 1988?"

"Why 1988?"

Laura pressed her. "Has anyone had contact with her?"

"No, my Aunt Mildred took Patty with her when she left, two years before that. I don't think it was considered strange at the time. Nobody knew we'd never see them again."

"Do you think it's possible another family member might have talked to them? Tracked them down? Even gotten a postcard from them during the last twenty-nine years?"

Monica held up a hand. "I need to stop you right there. I've answered your questions, but I think I need you to answer a few of mine before we go any further."

Laura drained the last of her coffee and set the cup down. "This will sound a little crazy."

Monica crossed her arms over her chest.

"You know the man I—who killed those girls."

"Eugene Hobbes."

"Yes. He also killed three girls in 1988, the first evidence we have of him committing a crime. I think there's a possibility he killed a fourth girl back then."

Monica just stared at her, unmoving, unblinking.

"And I think it's possible that fourth girl was your cousin, Patty."

She summarized the rest, the coloring books, the crosses, the tenuous connections holding everything together. At the end Monica said, "I'm not sure that really proves anything."

"Of course," Laura agreed. "Like I said, I'm in the process of investigating. I may very well be wrong. Partly I hoped you would tell me so, that Patty is alive and well and living in New York or something."

She shook her head. "No, we don't know what happened to them. But—"

"Mommy?" The door poked open again.

"Yes, sweetheart?"

"I'm thirsty."

"Get yourself a glass of water then, like a big girl." When her daughter was gone, she said, "But there's another problem with your story."

"What?"

Monica paused. "In movies, on TV, people tell reporters that things are off the record. Is that a real thing?"

"It's real. It means I can't print anything you say, or attribute it to you."

"But you could take what I say and keep, like, investigating. If you find some other source to confirm what I say, you could write it up."

Laura shrugged. "I suppose. But if you talk to me, it could mean finding out what happened to Patty. Isn't that worth the risk?"

"You might find nothing, and the Finch name could still get dragged through the mud." She paused. "It's not a nice story."

"I wouldn't ask if it wasn't important. But there's another little girl out there, very afraid, and so is her mother."

Monica tapped her fingers against the side of her leg, unsure. But she finally nodded. "They didn't just leave. They ran," she said.

"They ran away from my Uncle John. I know that much because everyone knew it. Aunt Mildred shouted that part from the rooftops, told everyone she could in the week before she disappeared."

"What did she tell them?"

Monica grimaced. "That my Uncle John beat her. She went on and on about it, with very specific details. Things he did with a baseball bat, with a fireplace poker."

"I thought you were just a little girl."

"Oh, I was. But her stories were graphic enough to stick with people, and this is a small town. It came up more than once when I was growing up. Funny thing is, everyone had their own version of what Uncle John did to her. I used to think that was just because of time and retelling, like the telephone game."

"But not anymore?"

Monica shook her head. "Now I think she was lying."

Laura said nothing, just waited for her to collect her thoughts.

"I remember my cousin at least," Monica said. "I lived in town with my mom and dad, and Aunt Mildred and Uncle John lived out here with my grandparents. Memories when you're that young are few and far between, you know?"

Laura nodded.

"But I have this one vivid image. There's a barn behind the house here, and it used to be stocked with hay in the fall. Patty and I would climb into the loft and jump down, again and again. It would kick up loads of dust, and the bits would float in the sunbeams coming in between the slats. Funny how you remember little details like that."

Laura said nothing.

"And that's all I really remember. I was very young."

"That's the whole story?"

She shook her head. "No, I said that's all I remember. The rest of it is secondhand. Promise me again you won't print this anywhere. Promise me you'll just use it to look for them."

"I promise," Laura said, and meant it.

Monica studied her for a second, then nodded. She muttered under her breath, "If my mom was alive, she'd smack me for even thinking about talking to you."

"It's bad," Laura said.

She nodded. "I never knew my father, so my mom and I were always close, but especially so toward the end. I had Francine, then got divorced and moved out here to be with her. So she helped me raise Francine from a baby, you understand? Got to see her grow up. Around when she started walking and talking is when it happened. I found her in her room one afternoon and she was just sobbing. The kind of sobs that run through your body like a shiver and make it so you can't breathe. I never saw her like that before. I ran to her, held her, and in the course of that afternoon she pretty much told me everything."

Laura tried to keep calm. She wanted to grab this woman and shake her, shake the truth right out of her, but it had to come in its own good time.

"It started with my grandfather, I guess," she said, and stopped for a long beat. "He molested her."

"Your mother."

Monica nodded. "And my aunt, both starting when they were young. Very young. That's what set it off. Seeing Francine in this house was like looking back in time, and the past was a very painful thing for my mother. She never got over it. All you need to see is a sixty-year-old woman crying like a baby to understand that. But my aunt . . ." she said.

"Your aunt."

"My aunt was broken by it. She never recovered. My grandfather died when they were in their teens and Aunt Mildred wouldn't believe it. They showed her the body, and she called it 'one of his tricks.' No one could convince her he wasn't out there, just hiding somewhere. Waiting to grab her."

"That must have been crippling," Laura said.

"More than crippling. It made her insane. Her father was an evil man, but she didn't put that label on him alone. It was his very nature that made him into what he was." Her gaze was unfocused, a faraway look in her eyes as she replayed her mother's story. "It was like some kind of twisted syllogism," she said. "My grandfather was a monster, and he was a man, therefore all men are monsters."

"And your Uncle John made her more sure of that."

Monica shook her head. "It got worse and worse as she got older, but even as a young woman all those seeds had been planted. So when it came time to find a husband, she found just about the gentlest, most nonthreatening man in the world. My Uncle John stood about five foot six and had a stutter. He was a pushover. Hell, he was afraid of her."

"So all that talk about him beating her—"

"Was a lie," Monica finished. "He never laid a hand on her. Quite the opposite. He used to show up to church with a black eye. People used to make fun of him for it."

Laura didn't laugh.

"And when she cried abuse, and left, people didn't take it too seriously. She was crazy." Monica took a breath. "It just so happened they never came back."

"That's terrible, Monica."

"Let me finish. Then you'll see Patty can't be the girl you're looking for."

"Isn't it possible they ended up in Hillsborough, and that Patty became one of Hobbes's victims?"

"I bet you're a good reporter," she said.

"Well, thanks."

"I bet you did a records search for Patty Finch."

Laura nodded.

"And what did you find?"

She spread her hands. "Nothing in North Carolina other than a school registration. I couldn't find any paperwork in Virginia. Not even a birth certificate."

"From what I know, a serial killer has a very specific type of victim, is that right?"

Laura frowned.

"And for Hobbes, it was girls. He liked little girls, right?"

Laura tried to cut in. "I don't—"

"And my aunt, she hated men."

"I don't understand," Laura said.

"She hated men. Which is why she refused to even acknowledge she had a son. Aunt Mildred had to have a daughter. It was the only acceptable outcome."

Laura stared at her.

Monica paused a beat, waiting for her to say something, then filled the silence. "There is no birth certificate for a girl named Patty Finch because she doesn't exist."

"Excuse me?" Laura managed.

"Aunt Mildred's child, my cousin—his name was Patrick."

CHAPTER

34

ALONE IN THE car, she caught her breath. There was finally time to think.

Patrick Finch.

The name rolled around inside her head like a tire bouncing down a steep and endless hill. It blared in her ears like overwhelming static, glowed in neon etched on the inside of her skull.

Patrick Finch.

A boy living as a girl. She tried to imagine that. Before puberty it was perfectly possible for a child of one gender to pass as the other. Hell, the girls were even a little bigger around twelve or thirteen. Patrick Finch had only been ten when he disappeared. At that age, so many gender cues hinged on social convention. With long hair and a dress, who would know the difference?

And on top of that, Patrick Finch had apparently been living as Patty for most of his life. She had no trouble believing he would be convincing in the role. After all, he had probably believed it himself. His own mother had conceived the ruse. Who would tell him different?

Monica was so certain that there had been a mistake, that Hobbes would never have been interested in a little boy. Laura refused to speak the terrible thought: if Patrick had fooled everyone into thinking he was a girl, wouldn't he have fooled Hobbes too?

She pictured that day at the racetrack in 1988. Hobbes lures what he thinks is a ten-year-old girl into his car. He takes her wherever he took the others, begins to do what he would do to them. This time is different though. He quickly discovers that this long-haired, dress-wearing creature is male.

And then?

Laura shivered. That was the limit of her imagination. She didn't know what he would do. The surprise must have been almost as great for Hobbes as for Patrick. Would he kill the boy and dispose of the body? Keep him alive?

Nothing good, that was for sure.

Two or three of the different thoughts bouncing around in her head locked together like magnets. A person seemed to have a vendetta against Eugene Hobbes, a man who killed young girls. Until now she had only guesses about the man in black's identity. A father, an uncle, a brother. Someone seeking revenge. The stumbling block had always been this killer's pathology. A simple vendetta didn't explain the murder of Olive Hanson. Who would hate Hobbes but also emulate him? No one fit the bill.

Until now. Now she had the perfect candidate.

What if Hobbes hadn't killed that little boy?

What if Patrick Finch was still alive?

*   *   *

It was almost five by the time she made it back to Hillsborough. The sun would be down in less than half an hour, and the house was creeping into shadow. She parked the Dart and unlocked the front door.

"That you?"

Her mother's voice sounded shriller than usual, but it still came from the living room.

She poked her head in. "Yes, it's me."

Diane Chambers did her best to turn in her recliner. "People been knocking all day looking for you. Where you been, girl?"

"Out. Who's been knocking?"

Her mother snorted. "Nobody for me. Some deputy came by."

Laura paused. "What did they want?"

"I don't appreciate being your errand boy, just waiting around the house to sign for your packages. He brought a box."

"Where is it?"

"You could have at least given me a little warning so I could put my face on. He was a nice-looking young man, and you—"

She grabbed her mother by the arm and squeezed. "Where is it?"

"Laura! No need to—"

She squeezed harder.

Something changed in her mother's eyes. The narrow slits of irritation went wide. Her lip started to tremble. When she spoke, her usual rasp had a quaver.

"Laura, you're hurting me."

She kept squeezing.

"It's in the back room somewhere," her mother said. "He put it back there for me."

Laura found the box and popped off the top. Plastic bags stuffed it. She pulled the first one out, stared, and almost dropped it. It was the shirt she'd been wearing in the mountains the day Frank was killed. Tiny holes salted the chest and left shoulder, peppered with wooden splinters in the aftermath of the shotgun blast. Dirty brown molasses stained the fabric.

Blood.

Her blood or Frank's, she didn't know. Probably it was both. Underneath the shirt, individually bagged, were her pants and underwear and socks. She didn't know why they hadn't burned it all when they were through. At the bottom she found two more items.

Her hiking boots were a little mud-caked but looked otherwise in good condition. She pulled them out. The box was almost empty now. She reached in, felt around, came out with her father's Browning.

It was in a plastic bag with a little tag tied around the trigger guard. She got it unwrapped and tore off the string. Worked the action. The metal didn't slide smooth, but it was nothing a little oil wouldn't fix. She lay it on the ink blotter of her father's desk, sat in his old chair, and pulled open the bottom drawer. Behind old magazines and faded receipts, she touched rags and a bottle of gun oil. The Browning came apart just as she remembered, and it only took a few minutes to lubricate the moving parts and slide them back together again. She ejected the box magazine, and from a pocket of her own bag she recovered the last four rounds from the box in the basement. One by one she slid them home, then put the Browning in the back of the drawer and shoved it closed.

"Who else knocked?" she asked her mother.

"Some little shit playing ding-dong ditch, most likely."

"How do you know it was for me?"

Her mother started to laugh, but it turned into a chest-wracking cough. It took her a second to catch her breath. "Of course it was for you. More people trying to get under your skin."

"So nobody was at the door."

"Not that I could see, but they were all around the house. Rapping on the doors, scratching at the windows. Never said a word."

Goosebumps raised a pattern on her arm. "When was this?"

"Hell," her mother rasped, "I heard it out back just before you pulled up."

Laura kicked off her flats and pulled on the hiking boots, then stuck her hands through the arms of her sheepskin coat.

"You going out?"

"Probably just some asshole, Ma," she said. "Maybe I can catch him." When her mother turned back to the television, she opened the desk drawer and slipped the Browning into her coat pocket. Out on the front porch she looked down the center of the drive-way but couldn't see anything. She made her way off the side of the porch and around the back of the house, careful at the corners, studying her surroundings.

The western horizon bled a dwindling orange, and to the east the sky was shrouded by a wall of dark cloud, the harbinger of a winter storm. Wind licked beneath the eaves and the old farm-house hummed. The rear wall of the house was featureless, so she kept her back to it and directed her attention outward, waiting for something to move. There was nothing to see but the small stand of river birch, devoid of life, and the tree line at the back of the field almost a mile distant.

A sound came from behind her. At first she thought it was the fluttering of birds' wings, but no birds flew this time of the evening, and no birds roosted at the Chambers farmhouse. She turned and saw it.

A picture.

A small metal stake pinned it to the wooden siding, and it trembled in the wind.

Laura took her finger off the butt of the gun and let herself take a breath before ripping it from its pin. The thin paper fluttered in her hand, and her own bloody image flickered into sight and then disappeared, over and over, as though part of a demonic flipbook. It was the same picture that had been mailed to her, cut from the exact same edition of the *News & Observer*. She turned the picture over, and her hand went to her mouth.

Thick black lines blotted out the newsprint on the back, filling up the paper. It was the same neat block lettering from the package sent to the *Gazette*:

DEAR LAURA, I'M SO HAPPY WE GET THE CHANCE TO TALK AGAIN, EVEN LIKE THIS. DURING OUR LAST CONVERSATION YOU ASKED ME IF WE COULD MEET AND I TOLD YOU THE TIME WASN'T RIGHT. I HAVE A SURPRISE FOR YOU: THE TIME IS NOW. HAVE YOU LOOKED UP AT THE SKY? THE FULL MOON IS RISING, FAT AND RED, A BLOOD MOON. THIS NIGHT IS HOLY. THIS IS THE NIGHT FOR SACRED TRANSFORMATIONS. FOLLOW MY INSTRUCTIONS IF YOU WANT TO KNOW WHAT HAPPENED TO TERESA. FOLLOW MY INSTRUCTIONS OR SAMANTHA DIES. IF YOU LIE TO ME I'LL KNOW. I'M WATCHING YOU.

Laura could feel the drone of her heartbeat on her temples and in the ends of her hair as they stood up. She flipped the picture over onto its front, then over again to read the message again.

Instructions. There were no instructions. She had to call Fuller, or

Tim. He'd made direct contact again, and this time the proof was in her hand. She fumbled for her phone, pulled it out of her pocket—

—and it vibrated in her hand. The text icon popped up on the screen next to an unfamiliar number. She touched it.

I'M WATCHING YOU, LAURA. I'M WATCHING YOU RIGHT NOW.

Her knees felt like they might go out from under her. She scanned the horizon, couldn't see anything in the gathering dark. The phone buzzed again.

HOLD THE PHONE UP ABOVE YOUR HEAD.

She didn't move. Could he really see her? The sun had set; the far end of the field was very far away. But high-powered binoculars existed. Telescopes too. Night vision was a thing, she reminded herself. And how else would he have known the exact moment to text her? She felt the phone pulse in her hand.

I'M WAITING.

She extended her arm as high above her head as she could, and looked up at it.

GOOD. THERE IS A ROCK TEN YARDS NORTH. PLACE PHONE IN POCKET. HOLD BOTH HANDS ABOVE YOUR HEAD. WALK TO THE ROCK AND PICK IT UP.

Her first instinct was to run around the corner, into the house. In a matter of seconds a heavy wooden door could be between her and whatever lay hidden in the dark. She tried to turn, but couldn't move. Her legs had turned to stone. All she could picture was a scared little girl already missing an ear if not her soul.

She pushed the phone into her pocket, raised her arms above her head like a robber coming out of a bank, and walked north. The walking bought her time to think. She didn't fully understand his interest in her, but the logic of this small portion of his plan was becoming clear. These movements were designed to prevent her from sending a distress message of any kind. With her hands above her head and the phone in her pocket, he would know if she used it. And then Samantha Powell's blood would be on her hands too.

If she called, the girl would die. And if she didn't call, well, she had a feeling Laura Chambers would just disappear. It was a lose-lose situation, and when it came to a decision, he was counting on her compassion. He was counting on her compliance.

Fuck that, she told herself.

She stopped in front of the rock. It was a broken chunk of concrete with no business in a farm field. It had never been there before. She reached down and tried to pick it up, but it was surprisingly heavy and just rolled over on its side. Underneath, nestled in the earth, was another phone. The screen winked at her, a message appearing.

PICK ME UP. USE THE ROCK TO SMASH YOUR PHONE. I'LL KNOW IF YOU DON'T.

She stole a glance into the distance, saw nothing, then leaned down and pried the new phone out of the ground. Carefully, she pulled hers out of her pocket with two fingers. There wasn't time to talk to anyone, wasn't time to send a text. The only thing that might work was to dial the shortest possible number. As she placed the phone on the ground, when the light from the screen would be facing directly upward, her thumb made a practiced swipe, unlocking it, and then flicked open the keypad and pressed three numbers.

911.

The call started to connect. She wouldn't be able to say anything, but there would be a record of it at least. Someone would know she needed help.

She pretended to struggle with the rock, which didn't require much of a performance, and bought a few seconds. A tinny, almost inaudible voice issued from the phone, sounding as though it were at the end of a long tunnel. "What's your emergency?" Then she was out of time. No point in stalling anymore. She let the rock drop, and heard the crunch of glass and plastic.

The new phone chirped at her.

HIDE THE NOTE UNDER THE ROCK. GO TO YOUR CAR. USE THE EXTRA KEY IN THE GLOVE BOX. DRIVE TO THE SPEEDWAY.

She pinned the newspaper cutting under the chunk of concrete. The phone chirped again.

NO TRICKS, I'LL BE RIGHT BEHIND YOU.

If he knew about the extra key, then he'd been in her car. He'd been watching her more closely than she'd previously imagined, picking apart the details of her life, waiting and planning. A knot of cold fear began to congeal in her gut. But she did have one more trick up her sleeve, and as she turned to go, in one smooth motion, the toe of her boot traced a long, thin oval in the dirt.

*   *   *

The Dart started right up. She flicked on the headlights and turned right onto the highway. Driving with one hand, she examined the phone. It looked like a cheap pay-as-you-go device, not much bigger than two Post-its stuck together. The screen demanded a four-digit passcode, without which there was no way to place a call. If the phone had an emergency calling function, it had been disabled.

The lock screen flashed blue: INCOMING CALL.

She didn't need the code to pick up.

"Laura." He stretched the vowel sounds out, taunting her. "Are you excited, Laura?"

She pressed the phone between her shoulder and ear, focused on keeping the Dart on the road. "That's not the word I would use."

"Turn left here."

She pulled the wheel to the left, checking the rearview mirror, but couldn't see anyone behind her. "You're following me," she said.

"For a long time now," the voice replied in its childish sing-song lilt.

"Want to tell me your name?"

The voice paused. She could hear the wet sound of his breathing. Then: "Soon. Pull into the second parking lot, the service lot. The gate will be open. Park at the back, under the trees. Walk down to the track. I'll be waiting for you, Laura." He giggled. "I can't wait to meet you."

Laura touched the butt of the pistol still stuck in her coat. "Me too," she said.

But the line was already dead.

CHAPTER

35

SNOWFLAKES FELL LIKE daggers through the dark. Heavy with damp, they lanced straight and true out of the blackness above, torpedoing gravel as Laura pulled into the speedway parking lot.

She'd been here as a girl. Even at that point it had been closed for years, but she and her friends would traipse down the footpath to the bend in the Eno. The warm summer memory rubbed sharp against the ice forming on her windshield. The gate to the parking lot had been open, but another metal bar prevented cars from driving the last quarter mile down to the track itself.

There was no choice but to walk.

She wrapped a scarf around her neck and pulled a hat down onto her head. On her hands she wore thin calfskin driving gloves, all she could find on short notice. She checked the load in the Browning, made sure it was secure in her right-hand coat pocket, and climbed out onto the thin layer of snow. The fat flakes spattered on her neck, warmed on her skin, melted, and ran down her spine.

She shivered in the darkness.

The racetrack hadn't had electricity in a long time, and with the cloud cover she could barely see three feet in front of her face. She moved past the metal bar and started walking down the footpath. Pines surrounded it on either side, making the night seem even darker. They had a coating of snow. The whole world was covered in a layer of thick velvet, sucking up the slightest sound before it could be heard.

Laura glimpsed the truth with sudden certainty: if she screamed, no one would hear it.

The path was steep and unfinished, and the last twenty years of disuse hadn't improved things. Erosion had pitted the slope with holes, and more than once she slipped. At the bottom of the hill stood the remains of a ticket booth, the metal turnstile long ago pulled out for scrap. The roof of the hut had collapsed along with two of the walls. The front wall, the one with the little ticket window, still stood.

Was this where Patty Finch had come on her final day in Hillsborough? Had she handed her ticket through the window? Had she touched the wooden shelf underneath?

Laura ran her own gloved hand across the shelf, feeling the calfskin catch on the splinters, and the sensation shot a thrilling tingle through her hand.

Or what about Hobbes? Had he touched this spot?

Just as quickly, she pulled her hand back.

Patty Finch.

Somehow, without thinking about it, she'd gone back to calling the little boy Patty. It was how he had first entered her mind. She pictured her walking into this very place, wearing a dress and patent leather shoes, with long hair twisted into a braid, the image so lifelike that Laura couldn't shake it.

She slipped and went down on one knee, the gravel and the damp biting through her jeans. The air seemed colder. It burned as she pulled it in and out of her lungs. All she could feel in her feet were a thousand tiny needles sliding back and forth under the skin. Shivers wracked her body, and she pulled the sheepskin coat close.

No time for that now.

She forced herself to stand, checked the Browning again, and put one foot in front of another. In two minutes she emerged from the pines next to the ruins of the old stands. All the wooden parts had rotted away, but the stands themselves were large steps of poured concrete. They were undamaged after fifty years and would probably last another hundred and fifty. Along the base ran a small footpath, and beyond that lay the large open swath of ground that had been the track and infield.

She walked out onto the track in front of the stands, her boots crunching now in the snow. Right here—this would have been the starting line, a hundred cars letting their engines rumble and then roaring off toward the first turn.

She spun in a circle, looking forward and back down the length of the track, examining the infield, gazing up into the stands, looking for any sign of life.

Nothing.

No light, no sounds, no footprints. She felt like the last person on earth.

And just then, the snow stopped. She looked up in time to see the dark ragged edge of cloud move out across the horizon, leaving behind only the stars and a thick heavy moon, huge-looking near the horizon, the color of rust and flame. The shade of it shocked her; so did its brightness. The pines cast shadows on the pristine white snow. They looked like a sharp-fingered black hand creeping across the glittering ground, reaching out for her, and when it got hold—

Laura whirled around.

Headlights slashed out toward her, shuddering and waving as the car crossed rough terrain.

Every fiber of her being screamed out: *Run! Hide! Take cover! Get away!* Anything to avoid the man coming toward her. He'd made sure at least one little girl was in the ground. Why would things be any different this time?

Everything at the cabin had happened *to* her, even her own actions. There hadn't been time to think, only to react, and her body had taken care of that. She had made no conscious decision to run down the hill, or to go inside the door, or to walk out the back. When she thought back on it now, it was like being in a fog, and in the fog there had been no such thing as fear or pain or doubt.

This was different.

Now all she had was time. The beams of light tracked toward her at a snail's pace and the urge to flee clawed her insides like a beast. She forced herself to take deep breaths, to stand her ground. She touched the butt of the Browning like it was a talisman and willed herself to be still.

As the vehicle got closer, she could make out details. The headlights were too high for a car. This had to be a truck, which also explained how it could move in such rotten conditions. It had a roll bar on top and mud spatter down the sides. Rust stains pitted what had once been a dark paint color, maybe black.

Flee! the voice said. But it was too late. The headlights finally reached her, nailing her in place. The light hit her eyes and her body tensed. Even her shivering stopped.

A black truck. Mud-stained. Rusted.

An inkling of recognition dawned somewhere in the back of her mind. The truck pulled up next to her, and the window rolled down, and all the fear that had been building up inside her drained out through her toes like someone had pulled the plug in a bathtub.

A black, rusted truck.

Jasmine DeVane's truck.

Jasmine leaned over toward the open passenger-side window. "Need a lift?"

*   *   *

Laura almost couldn't find her voice. "What are you doing out here?" she choked.

"What the hell do you think I'm doing? You called nine one one. The police came and found your phone smashed out back and you gone. Not only that, you were supposed to meet Don Rodgers. You didn't return his calls, no one at the *Gazette* had seen you, so he showed up at your house. And once he heard about the police visit from Diane, he called me." She paused. "Are you okay, Laura? Because the real question is: what are *you* doing out here?"

"How did you know where to find me?"

"I was worried you were feeling overwhelmed, that you smashed your phone out of some frustration with everything that's been going on. After our last conversation"—she shrugged—"it seemed like a good guess where you might go."

Laura tried to think how to explain what was happening. Words swirled in her head, but they refused to come together and make any kind of sense. "He called me," she said finally.

"Who called you? Can we at least talk in the truck?"

"If I leave, he'll kill Samantha Powell."

Jasmine's mouth hung open, then snapped shut like a bear trap. "Get in, we'll talk. I won't drive away unless you say so."

Laura stood there for a second, shivering, trying to remember what it felt like to have sensation in her feet.

"You're shaking like a leaf. Just get in the damn truck," Jasmine said, then rolled up the passenger-side window.

Laura felt the last breath of warm air escape the inside of the cab, gave one last look around the empty track, and climbed into the cab.

"I thought you'd wait out there all night."

Laura didn't say anything. The vents were set to full blast, and she just held her hands up to the stream of hot air.

"He called you again," Jasmine said. It wasn't a question.

"Worse. He was outside my house."

She gasped. "You saw him?"

"Not exactly. But he saw me. He left me a note, made me destroy my phone and drive down here."

"Made you?"

"Or Samantha Powell dies, and Teresa Mitchem stays missing. He told me not to contact anyone. He's expecting me here. Alone. You need to leave."

Jasmine shook her head. "Listen to yourself. Meeting him alone? For the people who care about you, that is wholly unacceptable. You must understand that."

"It's my choice. You can't make me leave."

"Okay, fine—but that's a double-edged sword. I'm staying."

"You can't—"

"I absolutely can. You can't make me leave either."

Laura twisted in her seat to face her. "Please. What if Teresa or Samantha is still alive? What if this is our one chance to find them?"

Jasmine shook her off. "Maybe this is just his plan to snatch you up, to make you disappear."

"I'm willing to take that risk," Laura said.

"I'm not. Look, it's not like the place is surrounded by cops. There's not a helicopter flying through the trees. It's just you and me out here."

She bit her lip. "Might still be enough to scare him off."

"Perhaps, but this is as good as it's going to get. I'm not leaving."

Laura looked out the truck's back window, then turned back to Jasmine. "We need to be ready when he shows up."

"If he shows up."

"He called me, Jasmine. He's real."

"And what did he sound like?"

She closed her eyes and tried to remember. "Soft, low, and kind of rumbly. Maybe he had a trace of an accent, but it was hard to tell. He spoke softly, but it was intense. Does that make sense?"

She opened her eyes.

Jasmine gazed back at her. "Yes, but does it tell you anything about his identity?"

Laura shook her head. "I've been over that a thousand times in my head. He didn't say anything that could lead back to him."

"Interesting."

"How so?"

"Well, why does he take the time to contact you, and to arrange a meeting, if he doesn't want you to know who he is? Those two goals seem opposed."

"Maybe it's somebody I know. Maybe they want to surprise me."

Jasmine gave her a strange look. "Don't drag me down the rabbit hole. I didn't come here to discuss specifics with you. If he's really coming, then sitting out here is genuinely dangerous."

"There's a little girl out there. She could still be alive."

Jasmine reached up and touched the cross she wore. "I pray she is."

"And if your prayer comes true, we're the only ones who can help her. That alone is worth taking the chance."

Jasmine shook her head. "When will it be enough? Your perspective is warped. When they're coerced out into the woods under a blood moon, most people find their limit."

"I—"

A blood moon.

Laura froze. The entire field of snow had turned into a glittering mirror, the moonlight reflecting off the ground and up through the windshield. A dark veil obscured Jasmine's face. The lower half was visible, the jaw, the lips, the teeth. The eyes were shrouded in shadow.

"I shouldn't have come out here," Laura said, almost to herself.

Jasmine's jaw moved. "It's nice to hear you say that out loud. It's good you can admit your mistake."

Laura rubbed her hands once more in front of the vents, then returned them casually to her lap. She willed her right hand to start moving toward her pocket. It stayed put.

The disembodied jaw licked its lips.

Laura's gaze tracked downward. There, hanging just below the collar bone, was the cross. It shimmered in the moonlight, revealing every detail. The emaciated form of Jesus. The spots of tarnish. The loops of ivy winding down across its arms.

"Tonight is the full moon," Laura said. "Tonight is the night for sacred transformations."

Jasmine turned her head, and the crimson lunar glow splashed across her entire face. Clenched jaw. Nostrils flaring. Corded tendons like rope around the neck. The skin seemed drawn and emaciated, the face cast in bone, a skull dipped in blood. The eyes were black liquid pooled in their sockets. She blinked once, and some hidden inner working refracted through their depths: raw, primal, somewhere between rage and ecstasy.

It was the sheen of madness.

Laura plunged her hand into her jacket pocket, fingers scratching, hunting for the Browning's grip.

But she couldn't reach it in time; Jasmine DeVane moved with inhuman speed.

In a heartbeat, she was upon her.

CHAPTER

36

THE BROWNING'S HAMMER caught the pocket's edge. It snagged for only a fraction of a second, but that was enough.

Laura's eyes flicked down, focused on the hunk of metal inexplicably fused to wool. She opened her mouth to yell.

Jasmine launched across the truck and landed on top of her, knocking the air out of her lungs. One hand clamped down, vicelike, across her mouth before she could get a breath, and the other ripped the Browning out of her grasp and tossed it away. She could hear the air whistling in and out of her nose, the sound reminding her of prey on the plains of the Serengeti. The wildebeest or the gazelle with a lion locked on one leg, eyes pinwheeling in terror, air pistoning in and out of their nostrils. Those fights always ended the same way.

And now she was such an animal. Her eyes rolled wildly in their sockets. She whipped her body back and forth, slamming her head into the passenger window.

"Stop struggling," Jasmine murmured in her ear. "I've been preparing for this my whole life. Fighting back won't do any good."

She tried to move, but the seat and the window and the weight of Jasmine's body pressed her into a narrowing triangle.

A hoarse whisper: "You saw me at the cabin."

The man in black, oh god oh god oh god, killer, child-murderer, a visitor from hell sent here to drag her back with him.

True panic set in and she threw her entire body into the struggle, arching her back and screaming into the salty palm pressed into her mouth.

She screamed again, and that's when the knife came out.

One second it wasn't there, and the next it appeared like magic in Jasmine's other hand, a thin curved blade shaped like a comma, razor sharp. The tip flew toward her and stopped, resting at the nape of her neck, grazing her flesh.

Then she truly understood what it felt like to be an animal, to know nothing but the need to survive. Up until that moment her fear had been existential in nature, a fear borne of speculation. She imagined all the things Jasmine would do to her and the possibilities terrified her. Once she saw the knife, though, there was no room left in her brain for imagination. The whole world narrowed down to its wicked silver point. She thought of nothing else. She only watched it, and waited.

"I'll cut you if you make me." A pause filled with a heavy breath. "Don't make me."

Jasmine pulled back until they were nose to nose. Laura stayed perfectly still. Jasmine moved closer. Closer still, never letting the knife waver.

And kissed her. A tongue, simultaneously rough and smooth, probed between her lips.

"Do you like it?" Jasmine said.

The knife point drilled into her throat, and the other hand slipped down the front of her body.

"Do you like me?" she asked, and licked the tip of Laura's nose.

Laura took a deep breath, and spoke. "What should I call you? Patty Finch?"

It was the wrong thing to say. The person she had known as Jasmine DeVane threw back her head and shrieked with laughter.

"Try again," she giggled.

"Patrick Finch, then," she said, the words so quiet they almost dissolved.

Something in Jasmine's face softened. "Poor Patrick. If you know about him, you must know about his mother."

Laura couldn't nod, not with a razor-sharp shard of steel at her neck. She forced herself to speak. "Yes."

The tip of the knife made another pinprick in her throat. "And that's how you put it together? That Patrick became Patty became Jasmine?"

"Yes."

"That is so very disappointing to hear. You were supposed to be such a good little investigator." Jasmine gestured to herself. "You think this is just an act? A costume? I'm not Patrick—I never was."

"You're him."

Jasmine leaned back. Her hand moved in a blur and fished a small black box out of her pocket. She held it up to her face. "I'm not Patrick," she said again, and the words came out in a low rumbly baritone.

"You have to be," Laura heard herself say.

"You have to be," Jasmine repeated, and Laura's words echoed back to her in the killer's voice. Jasmine shoved the box back into her pocket, then reached down and locked a viselike grip around Laura's wrist. "I thought you knew me better than that."

She tried to pull herself free, but Jasmine was stronger than she'd ever imagined.

"There's still time," Jasmine said. She forced Laura's hand between her legs and pressed herself forward. The blade scraped delicately along Laura's temple. Jasmine rolled her hips and closed her legs around Laura's hand. Shaky breaths tingled in her ear. Pressure on the knife forced Laura to turn her head, and Jasmine pressed her lips to Laura's mouth.

"You're female," Laura said.

Jasmine let go of her hand and smiled, and for a second she was her old self again, beautiful and self-aware and not at all violent. "Of course," she said. "Shame on you, Laura, for thinking it had to be a man."

And then her face changed. The smile fell away like a discarded mask. The skin drew tight, the lips wrenched back. Her teeth were fangs in the moonlight.

Laura knew this was not the time to push or to pry. This was the time for self-preservation. The survival instinct roared from the depths of her being, and no one was more surprised than she at what came out of her mouth next.

"Can I ask you a few questions?"

Jasmine paused. "A reporter until the end."

"Is that what this is? The end?"

Jasmine smiled again, all sharp teeth.

Laura shivered. "So what's the harm in a few questions?"

Her therapist seemed to weigh the words. Her hand moved. Laura caught the briefest flash of light on steel before the knife vanished. Jasmine reached up, open handed, and ran a finger through Laura's hair.

"Ask," she said.

Laura took a deep breath. "Who are you?"

"Mildred Finch's daughter, of course. We moved here, my mother and I. It was a terrible time in my life. Horrible mothers— we have that in common."

"Mildred didn't have a daughter."

"No, she had me. She picked me out like one would a pair of shoes to match a dress. She window-shopped girls at group homes until she found the perfect accessory to complement her life. To complete her lie. And she chose me because I was so very desperate for a mommy. I've always worn my heart on my sleeve."

Laura tried to ignore the sensation of Jasmine's leg snuggled up on top of hers. "She adopted you."

"Nothing so legal. They used to line us up in the cold on Saturday mornings like meat hanging on a butcher's hooks, and let prospective parents stare and prod at us. Sometimes another child got lucky. I never did. Then Mildred came two weeks in a row and spoke only to me. The third week she didn't come, and it crushed me, but I recognized her car when it pulled into the back of the lot a few days later. I recognized her face when she waved me over."

"She just took you?"

"A legal adoption was never in the cards for Mildred. But she needed a daughter. She needed someone to be Patty. Patrick outlived his usefulness even before she left Virginia. He's still up there on that farm. She drank too much one time and started kicking me. She liked to hit, only this time she screamed something about how the old Patty was a no-good, evil child, and if I didn't behave, I'd end up just as dead. Told me it was a mercy killing and that she buried him at his favorite hiding spot, some tree near the water." Jasmine paused. "That's how I found out I was a replacement."

"What's your name, then? Your real name?"

Jasmine smirked. "Does it matter? Now that I'm older, I look back and see my mother with new eyes. She was weak and afraid, but she was also a genius."

"A genius," Laura repeated, thinking of what she knew about that torturous, deranged woman.

"Yes, she was *right*, don't you see? The human race is infected, Laura, and she taught that lesson well. Back in 1988, I hated her for it. I was an unappreciative child."

"So you tried to run away."

"Three times. And on the third time, *he* found me."

"Hobbes."

"Who else? He found me and he took me, and in the process he proved to me the truth of things. My mother was quite correct about the devils of our nature. I wasn't the last little girl he stole, but I was the first."

Laura knew Patty Finch had disappeared in July, so indeed, Jasmine had not been the last of them. An image leapt into her mind. The Christmas Angel, Maria Mendelsohn. It had also been a white Christmas when she was killed. The parallel of the two moments separated by twenty-nine years—snow on the ground, bitter air, the acrid taste of pennies in her mouth—resonated so strongly that for a moment Laura felt she would vomit.

"The one he let live," she managed.

"He took us alive, you know. The first thing he made me do was strip, and then he started crying."

Laura furrowed her brow. She'd poured so much time and energy into divining the mind of Eugene Hobbes, but not once had she imagined him shedding tears.

"I reminded him of his daughter, you see. The one that was taken from him. He chose me because I looked like her, and together we started a new family. I was ungrateful at first, but in time he came to enjoy me. He would call me his little secret. Made me dress like her, made me do things. Most of all he liked to make me watch when he worked on the others."

Her voice caught in her throat. "That's horrible."

"*Yes!* Now you're getting it. Just so: a horror show. But it was real, Laura. Real. Do you understand?"

She said nothing.

"Monsters exist," she whispered, "but no one seems to care."

"You killed Olive Hanson."

Jasmine slithered back across the truck's cab. The Browning appeared in her hand. Her face vanished into gloom.

"They cared then, didn't they?" she said.

Laura's jaw worked, but no words came out.

Jasmine continued. "With the last girl, Hobbes made me help. Something broke in me then, something inside me I didn't know existed right up until the moment it shattered. He looked into my eyes and saw it—saw that I was broken. I was of no use anymore. So he sent me off. Just crumpled me up and threw me away. No one even bothered to look."

"Don Rodgers did."

"Don't lie to me. You can't lie to me, not after so many sessions together. Not after you bared your soul."

A small moan escaped between Laura's lips.

"It took him more than two decades to realize I'd been taken. No one looked for me. Someone needed to take action."

"So you killed a little girl," Laura said flatly. "And then Frank Stuart, and then Hobbes."

"I dragged *him* into the light. The rest of them were unfortunate, undeserving, the inevitable consequence of necessity."

"Of your sickness."

"Of my plan. The morning after they found her was beautiful. I walked through the streets and watched people act out grief like wind-up dolls. Human savagery plays nightly on the news and still they were shocked when it happened to them. The first domino had to be real, it had to be personal. A tipping point."

"And Teresa Mitchem? Samantha Powell?"

Jasmine said nothing. She secured her gloves, pulled her hat down over her hair, and reached behind her for the door latch.

When the door was just cracked, she gestured with the barrel of the Browning.

"Get out."

"Jasmine, I—"

"During one of our sessions, you told me no price was too great to pay for the truth. You said you'd die to know what happened to the Mitchem girl. I wonder, do you feel that way still?"

"Please, you don't have to do this."

"Get out of the truck or I'll shoot you."

Laura pulled the door handle and stepped down into the snow. On the other side, Jasmine mirrored her movements, climbing out at the same moment and moving backward around the truck's tailgate.

For a moment, just a moment, she disappeared from view.

Laura ran.

She took five great big strides across the field, careful to lift her feet up and over the snow. She pumped her arms, willing herself to move faster. The air must have been cold moving in and out of her lungs but she couldn't feel it. Blood sluiced through her body's pathways, wild and fierce. She wanted to live.

Five strides.

She made five strides, and then Jasmine tackled her from behind.

They slid through the snow together, Laura's face pressed down into the ground. She could feel the hidden dirt and gravel scraping across her cheek. The blood ran free down her neck. Fevered breath hissed into her ear. Jasmine flipped Laura over like she was a rag doll, then rose over her. They lay in the wide triangle thrown by the truck's headlamps. Jasmine hovered in front of the light. A dark silhouette looming over her. A shade with a gun in its hand.

The gun rose until it was pointing at her, light bouncing off its polished barrel.

"Get up," Jasmine said. "Start walking."

37

S HE STUMBLED UP the diamond-plate steps in the center of the stands. Behind her came a high-pitched tinny scraping and the sharp ping of metal on metal. She stole a glance backward and saw Jasmine oh so casually dragging the gun's barrel down a length of steel handrail like a prison guard running a baton across the cell bars.

At the top, Jasmine shoved her to the left. Ahead lay one of the speedway's only remaining structures: the old concession stand. A new tin roof had been put on sometime in the last thirty years, as though someone had wanted to use it for storage, but it still had two long rusted serving windows facing downhill toward the track, and the side door stood open.

"Inside," Jasmine said.

Laura froze on the doorstep. If she went inside, the chances that she would ever come back out seemed slim. The gun barrel poked painfully into her spine, but still she thought of trying to fight. If she was going to die, let it happen on her own terms. Maybe she could pretend to stumble, then spin around. If she was fast enough to avoid the first bullet, then she might have a chance.

From inside the door came the in-and-out hiss of distressed and rapid breathing.

"Inside," Jasmine said again. "Someone's been waiting for you."

*   *   *

The light of the full moon had been bright, and it took her eyes a moment to adjust. She could make out several metal canisters stacked against the back wall, and next to them, the prone shape of a child.

Laura ran to her, bent down and put a hand on her chest. It moved up and down. She reached up and touched the chin, then gently turned the face toward the light of the door.

It was Samantha Powell. Her eyes were screwed shut like someone trying to ward off a night terror. A large bruise decorated her forehead, and one of her ears had been taped up with bandages. Her chest rose and fell, but the exhalations were far too swift for someone in a state of natural sleep.

She shook her by the shoulder. "Samantha."

No response.

"She can't hear you," Jasmine said. "One of the benefits of my professional license is access to pharmaceuticals. Olive Hanson and Teresa Mitchem received the same treatment, if that makes you feel better."

"You drugged them."

"There was never anything to be derived from their pain." She gestured with the gun. "Sit next to her and put out your hands."

Laura did as she was told.

"Now I'm going to put this gun down here"—she rested it on the cracked concrete floor, on the far side of the girl—"and if you try anything, we'll just see who gets to it first. Don't make me hurt her again."

Laura had seen just how fast Jasmine could move. She produced a dark-colored strip of plastic and looped it around Laura's outstretched hands, mated the ends, and pulled. Laura recognized the distinctive ratcheting sound of a zip tie. Another went around her ankles, and then Jasmine stood. She pocketed the Browning, gathered up the girl, stood again, and carried her outside.

Alone in the crumbling wood room, splinters scraping at her back, Laura tried to think what to do. She had tried to be understanding, but now it was time to try and rattle her cage.

Jasmine came back inside and pulled the door shut behind her, then clicked a padlock onto the hasp. There was no sign of the girl.

"What did you do with her?"

"I wonder if her parents have finally learned to appreciate her," Jasmine said. She was almost invisible in the dark, just a blotch against the light of the door.

"You're just like him, you know. He molded you until it was like looking in a mirror. He was a killer; he begat a killer. You can stop. You have a choice."

The figure shook, and then a sound exploded out from behind it. Thundering. Deafening. Echoing off the walls.

It was laughter.

Jasmine was laughing—no, she was practically convulsing, having a conniption, a bird's warble moving rapidly between deep roar and animal shriek.

And as fast as it began, the laughter vanished.

"Please, Laura. He killed, I kill—so we must be the same? You're such a smart woman; it's not like you to be so reductive. Take a life for pleasure and you're a beast. Take a life in self-defense and you're an honest citizen. Take a life in war, you're a hero. Intent is everything."

"You don't have to do this," she said again, choking on the words.

"I didn't have to do any of it. But someone had to."

"For what?"

Jasmine stepped into the light. "Tell me: do parents around here still let their children roam alone at night?"

Laura balled her hands into fists.

"Of course they don't," Jasmine DeVane said. "They see the world for what it is. What it *truly* is. That's my gift to them all. Perhaps someday there will be a cure for people like Hobbes. People like me." Her voice shuddered. "And in the meantime, they've learned to keep their loved ones close."

Some primal, fearful thing inside Laura wanted to squeeze her eyes shut, but she wouldn't let them close. She wouldn't give her that. She stared upward, defiant, and waited for whatever came next.

"Why else would I have drawn you to the cabin? Because the story needed to be told. It will be passed from generation to generation. A dark fable. A monster story to tell children around the fire. Why else would I have taken another girl and brought you here tonight? Because people need to know the monster still exists, lurking in the darkness, waiting."

Jasmine slid down the wall next to Laura.

"They killed it, and it came back anyway. And us? We're just two more of his victims."

"Victims," Laura said. She didn't understand.

Jasmine pulled out the Browning, used her sleeve to wipe all the surfaces, and tossed it into the corner. The knife got the same treatment. She produced two more zip ties. One she pulled taut around her ankles, the other she tugged onto her wrists. She caught the end between her teeth and yanked it viciously until the thin plastic edge carved into her flesh.

"No matter how hard they look, they'll never find the monster. I'll already be gone."

Laura's head spun with the madness of it. "You didn't have to tell me," she murmured. "You didn't have to kill me."

"I didn't want to," Jasmine said, and a quaver in her voice made it sound like the truth. "But you should have taken my advice and quit. Once you took those pictures from the cabin and connected them to Patty Finch, I didn't have a choice. I couldn't have you putting it all together once I'm gone."

She leaned in and put her head on Laura's shoulder. "But secretly," she whispered, "I was pleased when you didn't listen. I'm so glad I don't have to do this part alone."

She reached over, picked up one of the canisters, and popped the top off with her thumb. Almost instantly the unmistakable odor of nail polish remover filled the room, and Laura realized it was a can of industrial acetone. Jasmine turned it over, letting the clear liquid run out onto the floor, then holding the open mouth over Laura's head. It ran down through her hair like fingers of ice, burning her eyes, dribbling down the outside of her sheepskin jacket. Already she could feel it sucking the heat off her skin as it evaporated into the room.

"They'll never believe it," she managed.

"Why not?" Jasmine opened a second canister and splashed it around the room. "Plenty of people know about your connection to these girls, and I was Samantha Powell's doctor. It won't take them long to find the note under the rock behind your house, and they'll find a nearly identical one on the desk in my office. We were quarry of the same predator, and we suffered the same fate. That's the story they'll put together."

The smell was overpowering, nearly unbearable, but Jasmine seemed unaffected. She broke the seal on the second can and upended it over her own head, its mouth spitting clear fluid into her hair, onto her face, her coat, even her socks were soaked.

She reached into her pocket and came out with a small lighter.

Laura knew from personal experience the properties of acetone. It evaporated faster than alcohol and was more flammable than gasoline. Already the room around them was brimming with its fumes. Jasmine wouldn't need to light the fire. She wouldn't need to touch the flame to anything at all. The moment flint struck steel, at the first hint of a spark, the air itself would ignite. In an instant, a fireball would consume them.

But it would be over just as fast. Laura could remember watching videos of people dipping their hands in acetone, lighting them on fire, and then snuffing them out. The liquid evaporated so quickly that it had a tendency to form a cool barrier near surfaces, above which the vapors burned.

That was it then—her only chance.

Jasmine held the lighter out in front of her. Her eyes glistened, and she opened her mouth, probably to say some final words.

Laura would never know for sure. She lashed out with all her strength, whipping both legs upward into the bottom of Jasmine's wrist. She didn't let go of the lighter, but the tie around Laura's ankles snapped in half.

She rolled once, twice, three times across the concrete floor, then pulled her knees into her chest. She reached over her shoulder, got a grip on her coat's collar, and yanked it up over head before balling herself up, making herself as small as possible inside the thick sheepskin lining.

The lighter clicked.

An intense bloom of heat washed over her, accompanied by a deep percussive report. All the air in the room suddenly went missing, and she gasped and opened her eyes. The ends of her hair were on fire. The coat was in flames. There was no way to remove it, not with her hands tied together.

A glint in the corner caught her eye, and she recognized the knife only a few feet away. Pinning it between the toes of her boots, she bent forward and sawed her wrists back and forth across the blade, begging the plastic to give. Her left shoulder and the center of her back started to sear, but she ignored it, kept moving, kept cutting.

With a crack, the plastic parted. She slipped out of the jacket and kicked it away. The walls were burning, and she could hear the tin roof starting to pop as it reshaped itself in the heat. She turned, and for second she froze.

Jasmine was in the corner of the room, on her knees, her face invisible, a sheet of dripping flame where it used to be. But she was alive. She reached her bound hands out toward Laura, as though begging her to stay. Then came a sound like crumpling paper as the fire ate through the last can of acetone. The entire back wall erupted in a furious blaze.

Laura threw herself against the door, but it didn't move. She shoved her fingers under the articulated metal door closing off one of the serving windows and pulled, screaming. It screeched upward, the wheels turning ponderously in their rusted tracks. It came up ten inches, and stopped. She jerked savagely at it, the metal cutting her palms, the heat growing at her back, but it wouldn't move again. She turned her head and forced it out though the opening, then expelled all the air out of her lungs and pushed, but couldn't get herself through the gap. The pain in her feet was unbearable.

Suddenly Cooper, Rodgers's bloodhound, burst from the tree line, came to heel in front of her, threw back his head, and bayed. Don Rodgers struggled out of the trees and skidded to a stop behind the dog, thick blankets of mist pouring out of his mouth.

"Gotta lift it," she managed to say, and he understood.

He braced himself against the outer wall and got his palms up under the door. "Ready?" he said. "Together. One. Two. Three."

The door groaned once, then shot up another two inches before wedging in place again.

He grabbed her by the elbows and squeezed her out under the door. She hit the ground roughly, but he kept dragging her backward. Glancing down, she noticed her pantlegs were burning. Somehow the pain didn't seem to register in the moment.

"My legs are on fire," she said.

"Shit." He rolled her back and forth through the snow, then pulled off his jacket and beat out the final flames before collapsing in a heap next to her.

Laura forced herself to speak. "Samantha?"

He jerked a thumb over his shoulder. "She's back there, wrapped in a blanket. Couldn't wake her up, but she's alive."

Laura nodded and closed her eyes. She thought she had never been so tired in all her life.

Cooper bounded up and licked her hand. Rodgers tousled his ears. "He found you, followed your scent right up the slope. The police showed up to investigate that call, your mother told me, although it wasn't easy getting it out of her. Cooper led me right to the spot you'd been standing, and I saw your message scratched in the dirt."

"Good boy," she said.

Rodgers looked at the shed, now totally engulfed in flame. "Anyone else in there?"

"No one who could be saved," she said, and let her head fall back against the ground. The last thing she saw before slipping into unconsciousness was the orange and red sparks shooting upward between the pines.

38

HER CALL WAS picked up on the third ring. "Finch residence, Francine speaking."

"Francine, is your mom there?"

She could hear a muffled shout for her mother, and then, "May I ask who's calling, please?"

"It's Laura Chambers, the reporter. I came out there and visited you."

"Yes, I remember. Did you find what you were looking for?"

Laura didn't know how to answer that.

"Hello?"

Do you have a second to talk? Maybe away from Francine."

Another muffled conversation, then the swing and squeak of a screen door. Laura could picture her on the sunny front porch.

"I'm here. Is it about my cousin?"

"I wanted to ask you: did Patrick have a favorite spot to hide? Maybe near a tree, one by the pond?"

A pause. "There's only one way you could know that. You found him. Where is he?"

Laura tried to keep the falter out of her voice. "He never left," she said.

* * *

It was Christmas morning, and the icicles hung in the trees like God's ornaments.

Shacks speckled the ridges and ravines, low-slung homemade constructions with walls of exposed gypsum board and used pallets. The Dart's engine struggled on the upslopes; this part of the Blue Ridge Mountains ran steeper than Laura had expected. Working the manual transmission was a bitch. She wore a heavy parka, a leftover from Boston, on her upper body, but just a loose-fitting skirt on her legs. Thick white gauze wrapped them from the ankles to just above her knees, where her injuries from the fire had crescendoed. Her feet and back had been burned as well, but heavy boots and a thick sheepskin coat had protected her to some degree. Those places on her body would mend completely, the doctors said, but the scars on her legs would never heal. She would carry them for the rest of her life.

The building, when it came into view, stood in shocking contrast to the others in these mountains. Tall ramparts of gray stone. A Tudor-style roof shingled in slate. The gravel drive ended in front of a set of thick wooden doors. Above them, etched into the stone, the words St. Jude School. She had never seen a place quite like it.

Laura took a deep breath, then knocked. The left-hand door opened almost immediately. She'd called ahead. They were expecting her.

"Miss Chambers?"

A thin, beak-nosed woman peered out at her. She wore a dress of gray flannel, black stockings, and simple penny loafers.

"Sister James?"

"Yes, we spoke on the phone. Please come in."

The sister stood aside and Laura moved past her into a large stone-walled foyer. It smelled of incense, and the only light came from a pair of high casement windows facing south.

The door creaked shut behind her. The room darkened.

"Your phone call was very vague," Sister James said. "We endeavor to help wherever we can, but more information may be required."

The sister spoke with a relearned elocution. She had clearly worked hard to transform herself, but every third syllable betrayed a local heritage. She was born and bred in western North Carolina.

"On the phone," Laura said, "you mentioned—"

"Sister Coleman, yes." She cut her off casually, like a teacher overruling a student. Laura supposed she was a teacher. They all were here.

"Can I speak to her?"

"Of course, of course."

They moved through another door and up a set of winding stairs, down a hall, and into a library or a sitting room. It too had casement-style windows and walls covered with books. A row of chairs ran down the middle. In the last chair sat an old woman wearing a nun's habit.

Sister James indicated toward the end of the room, and Laura went and sat in the opposite chair.

"Sister Coleman?"

The old woman, who Laura had thought asleep, opened one eye and peered out from under a thick eyelid. "The one and only."

Laura smiled. Where Sister James was trying to mimic something like received pronunciation, like an actress playing a nun in a movie, Sister Coleman seemed to have discarded such theater long ago. Her voice was pure Brooklyn.

"Well, wadda you want?"

"Sister Coleman, I'm Laura Chambers."

Sister Coleman made the sign of the cross. "Glory be, the one who fought that devil."

"Yes, ma'am."

"The one who called."

"Yes."

"The one who sent us that picture."

From over her shoulder, Sister James said, "We have a computer in the office. It doesn't get much use, and I'm afraid I didn't see your email until a day or two after it came in. But I passed it around after that. Sister Coleman recognized it right away."

"Still have my eyes, you know," Sister Coleman said.

"Thank God for that," Laura said.

"What?" She rapped her cane twice on the polished wood floor. "You'll have to speak up. My ears are a different story."

"You recognized the picture," Laura said, spacing the words out.

"Of course I did. This place is beautiful, isn't it?"

Laura just nodded.

"Was a convent back before we started taking in children, back when people actually became nuns. Even today this property, this building, is just about all of our net worth."

Laura looked at Sister James.

Sister Coleman reached out with the tip of her cane and poked Laura in the shin. "Don't do that. Don't give her that look, like, *is the old woman senile?* I'm not. This"—she tapped her temple—"is like a steel trap. I've got a point, you know. My point is, we never had much. Not much money in raising unwanted children, if you can believe it. So when a company had a misprint and asked us if we wanted that load of coloring books, we said send over the lot." She grinned, half of her teeth missing. "Turned out to be a truck's worth. We used those things for years and years. I may be ninety-one years old, but how could I forget?"

Laura studied her for a second, then asked, "And the name?"

"Yes, yes, I recognized that too. Strange case, that girl. She disappeared. We figured her for a runaway—we get plenty of those up here—but almost two years later a man with a pockmarked face drops her back off along with a very healthy donation. We never saw him again. We recognized the girl, but she'd changed her name. Insisted we call her Patty." She paused. "It didn't go well for her here."

"What happened?"

"Well, she was here for another three, perhaps four years. By that time she was a young woman, and one day she just vanished."

"Ran away again?"

"So we guessed."

"Ever see her after that?"

The old woman closed her eyes, swayed side to side. "Maybe," she muttered. "Maybe."

"Sister Coleman?"

Her eyes snapped open again. "Said I never forget, and that's the truth. But the mind needs more breaks these days. Sometimes I drift off."

"You saw her again."

"Six months ago, a woman showed up here calling herself Jasmine. If it was the same person, probably she didn't think there'd be anyone left to remember. I didn't recognize her at the time, just saw the look in her eyes."

"The look."

"Young thing like you would hardly understand. When you get old, all your life's behind you. All that's left is memories. Spend enough time with memories, good and bad, and it gets so you know the look of someone reliving theirs. That woman from six months ago, she took one look at these old stone walls and got a shimmer in the eyes, like she'd seen a ghost. You might not understand this, but when it comes to memories, some places are more haunted than others."

"I do understand," Laura said.

The old woman studied her face. "I think you do indeed. Anyway, I saw the newspaper article yesterday, you and that business at the racetrack, and they ran the story again this morning. They printed the picture in full color."

"And it's the same person?"

Sister Coleman squinted. "I'd be lying if I said I was a hundred percent sure, but that's where I'd place my bet."

"Why did she come? To relive the past?"

The old nun snorted. "Don't think so."

"Then why?"

Sister Coleman shrugged, as though it were obvious. "To bring us the girl."

*   *   *

By the time Laura's heart had finished fluttering and her hands had stopped shaking, they were down the hall standing in front of another ancient wooden door.

"She's in here," Sister Coleman said. "Physically, she's in good health."

Laura's mouth was parched. Her tongue felt like an overstuffed pillow. "Other than physically?"

Sister Coleman leaned against the wall. "Well, there's no shrinks up here. The nearest regular doctor is almost two hours away. I'm a nurse myself."

"But?"

"She doesn't look at you, doesn't interact with the others, doesn't shed a tear. That's unusual for a new girl. Even stranger: I been with her six months, and she hasn't spoken a word. There's nothing wrong with her tongue or vocal cords—I checked. We called the police, but we get so many strays up here. They don't always pay attention."

Laura nodded. Her hands still trembled, but she pushed the door open anyway. The room was organized as a dormitory, long and narrow, with windows on one side and two rows of single beds. At the end, on the second-to-last bed, a girl sat facing away from the door. Laura hobbled down the aisle, the foam bottoms of her hospital flip-flops chafing on the stone floor, lowered herself onto the last bed, and looked at the girl.

The girl wouldn't meet her gaze. Her head stayed bent in a permanent bow, and a sheet of tangled black hair hid her face. The girl's body was too small. Her knees were knobby. The wristbones threatened to poke through the flesh of her arm.

Laura reached out to touch one.

The girl gave a start, pulled back.

"Mildred doesn't eat much," Sister James said.

Laura raised her eyebrows. "Mildred?"

"That's the name we were given."

"Do you think Mildred and I could have a second alone?"

Sister James tapped her foot for a second, the sound echoing sharply in the empty dormitory, then retreated.

Laura waited for her to get to the other side of the room, then said, "Mildred. Is that your name?"

The girl didn't move. She could have been a statue.

"I didn't think so."

The girl said nothing.

"What about Teresa?"

That got her attention.

She sat up so fast it looked like her head was about to pop off. The long black hair flicked off her face and she stared back at Laura with huge brown eyes.

One ear was missing, a mass of scar tissue in its place.

Her mouth opened, then closed again. She pointed to herself. Laura nodded. "Teresa Mitchem," she said.

And the girl began to cry.

* * *

An explanation to the Holy Mother, followed by an emotional phone call to Angie Mitchem, was enough for the St. Jude School to sign Teresa Mitchem into Laura's care. When the school's headmistress had finished, Sister James took the receiver and passed it along.

Silence. Then, as if from a million miles away: "Is it really her?"

"It's her."

"She's alive?" Angie asked.

"Yes."

"She's alive and well?"

Laura didn't reply. Angie Mitchem began to whimper. The cries burrowed into her ear; she would never get them out.

"Thank you, Laura. Thank you, Jesus."

"I'm bringing her home."

Angie blew her nose. "Are you going to write the story? Somebody's going to write it. I'd like if it was you."

"I'm going now, Angie. We'll leave straightaway."

She placed the receiver in its cradle. It would be a hell of a story. The book advance alone would catapult her wherever she wanted to go. But her dreams, coiled springlike for so long inside her, seemed to have lost their tension. Her hometown was just another brown spot under the same scrubbed blue sky. Was there a place so beautiful it could make her forget?

She doubted it.

Some parts of this story weren't for telling. They were just for her. They would die with her.

* * *

They packed what things she had, stopped by the second-floor library to see Sister Coleman—who kissed the girl once on the forehead but uttered not a word—and then they were off, bouncing over the rutted trail out of the mountains, racing down the freeway, heading east, and still the girl said nothing. After a while Laura flipped on the radio. Teresa turned the dial back and forth. Sometimes she would land on a radio station and stay for a while, listening. Sometimes she would land on static and listen just the same.

They drove with white noise playing for a spell. As the next town approached, "Silent Night" faded in through the hiss. The girl with one ear leaned forward, transfixed, and closed her eyes.

Laura tried not to stare. Frozen, once again a statue, she was a living memorial to all that had happened, a monument both to life's misery and to its hidden corners still replete with hope. She was lightning in a bottle. Laura watched the girl out of the corner of her eye and waited for her to move.

"It's Christmas, you know," she said.

And the girl nodded.

ACKNOWLEDGMENTS

No book is an island. Thanks to Alice, Ellie, and Annie for their love. Thanks to my parents and brother for their endless support. Thanks to Nancy Lamson, Bob Hollister, Alice Lamson, Brooke Lamson, and Tom Pollard, who helped shoulder the burden of all the things that can keep a book from being written. Thanks to Jacqueline Hetherton for her expertise as a reader, and I'm very grateful to Judy Sheridan, who offered insight and encouragement at an important moment. Thanks to my agent, Alice Martell, and to everyone at Crooked Lane Books. I especially want to thank my editor, Jenny Chen, who set this book in motion.